KEEPERS

OF THE

RIVER

A NOVEL

BY

KEITH SCHULZ

ISBN No. 1-57166-230-8

Second printing   2003

Quixote Press
Wever

(800) 571-2665

Cover design by Jen Busard
Jens Graphic Designs
(319)   470-8045

WHAT THEY'RE SAYING ABOUT
KEEPERS OF THE RIVER

"There's a mysterious romance to Mississippi river towns—ask Mark Twain—and Keith Schulz captures the mood and the menace of that romance perfectly in his nicely creepy first horror novel *KEEPERS OF THE RIVER*. This one's indeed a keeper."
—Ed Gorman, noted author and editor of *MYSTERY SCENE*

. . . Keith Schulz has carefully crafted a fine novel of multi-generational terror and he fills you in on the details when the time is right. Schulz puts a large cast of characters from different eras through their paces, including a disillusioned Chicago cop, a steamboat passenger, two young cousins, and aging residents who have kept a dark secret for fifty years. The complex plotting and attention to character and setting are top notch. We can only hope the author is at work on another book. Though *Keepers of the River* did make the preliminary Stoker ballot, it didn't make the final. This is undoubtedly due to its late in the year release . . .
—Garrett Peck, reviewer, *CEMETERY DANCE*

. . . Mystery, science fiction, horror—they're all here in Keith Schulz's novel set in a sleepy Mississippi River town. . . . just as summer camp can be punctuated by eerie stories told around a campfire, so is life in Bruders Landing colored by fear. What's behind the unexplainable mutilations that are butchering both the living and the dead? Schulz crafts a plot that is fascinatingly complex as it moves from one time to another in the town's history. . . . the author shines in his portrayal of two young cousins and their friend.
—Carol Wilcox, editor, *IOWA ALUMNI MAGAZINE*

The quaint little town of Bruders [Landing]—snuggled into the bluffs of the Upper Mississippi . . . harbors a dark secret. From the beautifully groomed pages of this book, to the down and dirty, gritty writing of the author, this book will keep you guessing and on the edge of your seats! Mr. Schulz has created a stunning backdrop, (I am happy to report, free of cliches) with intrigue that will draw you into his dark world and keep you guessing to the very end. I must

warn you, if you are easily spooked (and live to be spooked) then you may want to turn on the lights before you sit down to read . . . you will not want to put this book down! Expect the unexpected, be suspicious of everyone, and be prepared to be surprised when you reach the conclusion. The author's writing is as smooth as silk and will grab the fussiest reader's attention. So . . . snuggle into the couch for a night of entertaining and fascinating reading.
—Joan M. McCarty, senior editor, *ALTERNATE REALITIES*

 . . .it's a great read and one heckuv an imaginative yarn. *KEEPERS OF THE RIVER* will keep you riveted.
—Carolyn Sheridan, writer, *THE DAILY DEMOCRAT*

To my wife, Emily Roane, who moved with me to "Bruders Landing" so this story could be told; to my editor, Sands Hall, who put the story on track; to Bruce and Marilynn Carlson who got the story into print; to the members of a series of writers groups and seminars who listened patiently and commented wisely as the story unfolded; and to my family, friends and colleagues who wondered what could be taking so long.

PROLOGUE

All who go in this strange new land, beware.
For unknown dangers abound.
Woe will befall those who believe no unworldly inhabitants
preceded them,
Nor wait to devour invaders of their lair.

--*Ichabod's Compendium of Troubles in the New World*
A.D. 1642

1846

Raston Bruhl limped down the *Prince Nathan's* Texas deck, taking care not to jostle any of the passengers savoring the warm June sun, when his bad leg caught the foot of a disheveled man sprawled across a deck chair like a puppet without strings.

"So sorry, sir." Raston looked down, afraid the man would wake up yelling. He remembered the face. It was that drummer, Thaddeus somebody, who staggered on board at Bruders Landing. The man merely grunted, exhaling a sour cloud of stale whiskey, and continued snoring.

"Damn this leg," Raston muttered and hobbled on. He maneuvered down the narrow stairway to the main deck, then made his way to the cargo area. There he wedged himself between two bales of cotton. The heat of the June day was oppressive, and he wiped the coating of dirt and sweat from his face with his sleeve.

No breeze reached him where he sat, but it was a place where he could read undisturbed.

Tucking his bad leg into a comfortable position, he opened the book he had pulled from his kit bag: *Ichabod's Compendium of Troubles in the New World,* a compilation of the grave dangers travelers would encounter in America. He had found it in a shop in New Orleans before he signed on the *Prince Nathan* as second mate. What attracted him was a section about Shoquoquon, a valley forged by the Upper Mississippi River that he would see for the first time. He had never been on a voyage above St. Louis and the notion that he would be passing through a site along the Upper Mississippi that was somehow dangerous fascinated him. To add to his anticipation, he had waited to read about Shoquoquon until they were there. Now they were in the heart of it, having left Bruders Landing shortly after dawn, and he had some free time at last.

Brushing away a nettlesome fly, he opened the leather cover and leafed through the pages until he found the section he wanted:

Shoquoquon
Bane of the Upper Mississippi

For centuries the native tribes who inhabit the upper reaches of the Mississippi River Valley brought their dead to Shoquoquon, though it is a place they feared more than any other. In the tribal circles of these Valley Dwellers, Shoquoquon is known as the gathering place of the most powerful and cruel of all evil spirits where no unprepared mortal can venture and return. Legends have been passed through countless generations telling of the death and mutilation of those who stray or are banished into Shoquoquon.

Yet, on its surface, Shoquoquon is beautiful beyond description. At that place along the Mississippi River, towering bluffs of limestone line the western shore like a great wall, their faces craggy with giant gray and brown rocks jutting out boldly between gnarly trees that have taken root in the crevices. In the morning sunlight, the high cliffs appear at their best, the bare stone reflecting warm shades of brown and tan and white, the leaves of the protruding trees and honeysuckle glowing in brilliant hues of green.

Within these bluffs are immense deposits of flint, the stone so coveted by the Valley Dwellers for war and peace—the stone that gave Shoquoquon its name. But to enter Shoquoquon to claim this flint proved deadly to those who attempted, so the flint remains beyond their reach, in the grasp of the evil spirits.

In places within Shoquoquon the river widens to a mile, dividing into sloughs that wind through a field of billowy green islands, the largest of which is called Big Tow.

Big Tow is much larger than other river islands, easily a half mile or more in width and several miles in length. Like most river islands, it is blanketed by a dense growth of hardy trees. Unlike other islands, Big Tow consists of low limestone hills, as if it is an extension of the nearby bluffs. Its interior is pocketed with lakes and ponds refilled by the high water of spring, many of which are connected by a labyrinth of waterways that wend their way through the island. While the river's spring floods are usually of short duration, there is a rare year each century when the snowmelt of an especially severe winter combines with torrential rains in the spring to maintain the water at high levels through the summer and into the fall. Those are killing years for the island, leaving large swaths of dead trees, stripped bare of bark and leaves, standing stark and stiff like a crowd of wizened old men.

To bury their dead, the Valley Dwellers enter Shoquoquon on a night of the full moon when the sky is cloudless. The burial parties consist of those tribal members who have been specially prepared by rituals of torment and fasting. They stay only until sundown of the following day to perform their grisly work then promptly leave.

To properly house the dead, the Valley Dwellers build large earthen mounds at the edge of the bluffs overlooking the river. The mounds are constructed sturdily, a timber frame interlaced with limbs and branches covered with tons of earth. After the bodies are placed inside, the entrance is obliterated with earth to prevent entry. Untold scores of these mounds have been built over the centuries, dotting Shoquoquon's blufftops with miniature hills: the resting places for untold thousands of dead.

While mounds are found at several places along the Upper Mississippi, the explanation most often expressed for the unusually large number in Shoquoquon has to do with Big Tow Island. This island, according to the tribal legends, is the lair of the Old Ones, keepers of the evil spirits in Shoquoquon. Legends say these evil spirits will roam throughout the Valley inflicting unspeakable misery and death on mortals who dwell in the Valley unless the spirits are adequately appeased. And the appeasement required of the Valley Dwellers is to bury their dead in the earth within sight of Big Tow Island.

Today, explorers from Europe rarely believe in the existence of evil spirits yet report a sense of disquiet and foreboding in Shoquoquon whether at night or in the bright light of day. For those anxious to dismiss any notion of the existence of evil, perhaps this disquiet is merely the result of Shoquoquon's function for so many centuries as *a burial ground. But others believe there is truth in the old legends. If that, indeed, is the case, how, one must ask, are the spirits that inhabit the bowels of Shoquoquon and Big Tow Island to be appeased when the dead are no longer delivered to the river bluffs? And when they are not appeased, beware the horrors that will be visited on those who have chosen to enter Shoquoquon.*

Raston shuddered slightly as he shifted his weight to relieve a cramp. Goosebumps had risen on his skin. None of that now, he told himself. Surely there's nothing to this. Just old Indian legends handed down over smoky campfires. But he ought to know the legends surrounding the Mississippi River as well as everything else about it, as long as he didn't put any stock in them. Believing in legends would never do for a riverboat pilot.

After tucking the book in his kit bag, he slung it over his shoulder, rose somewhat stiffly and made for the outer deck. He wanted a good vantage point for a look at the high bluffs and the mounds at their rim. As he passed the open door to the boiler room, a wave of heated air struck him. Surprised by its strength, he looked inside. Immediatly the noise of push rods and pistons assaulted his ears. When his eyes adjusted from the sunlight, he saw both boilers glowing a deep red yet the engineer was on his hands and knees in front of the fire box, throwing in more wood. What in the world is the man doing? As Raston stood riveted by the scene, the starboard boiler gave a deep metallic groan as if in pain.

The sound energized him. He walked swiftly over to the engineer, bent down and shouted into the man's ear: "Hey, Silas, these boilers are overheating."

At the sound of Raston's shout, the engineer straightened up, irritation showing on his soot-covered face. "Just followin' the pilot's orders. He told me to make all the steam I can and that's what he'll get."

"But what if they crack? Don't you think you should damp down those fires and let 'em cool a bit?"

"This ain't none o' your business, Sonny. That'd be goin' against the pilot's orders, and I ain't about to do that."

"Then you need to tell him. If Captain Musser knew how hot these boilers are, he'd slow our speed."

"Not when he's tryin' to make up time like he is, always askin' for more steam. With the temper he's got, I just do what I'm told. Tell you what. You go on up to the pilot house and tell him about them boilers yourself. See if he'll listen to some green kid. Besides, at your age you can prob'ly make it to shore after he tosses your arse over the side." The engineer laughed, then stooped down to pick up more wood.

The starboard boiler groaned once more. Raston blanched. He had seen the results of a boiler explosion before.

* * * * * * * * * * * * *

1948

Herbert Siefken decided he liked the old sheriff as soon as the interview began. Jack Shoof was an affable man, certainly less devious and political than the brass Herbert was used to in the Chicago Police Department, yet the man displayed an intelligence and professionalism that belied his folksy manner. Although a large man, nearly as tall as Herbert, the extra weight the sheriff carried was well-distributed and he still looked fit.

Herbert had prepared for the interview as well as he knew how, spending hours in the Chicago Public Library poring over books about the history of Eagle County, Iowa and maps of the the Upper Mississippi River Valley. Bruders Landing seemed exactly the kind of town he was looking for. But all his preparations did nothing to diminish his concern for the sheriff's reaction when he learned why Herbert wanted to leave Chicago.

At the outset the sheriff did most of the talking, confirming many things Herbert had already learned. But as he tried to explain the need for a deputy with

Herbert's street experience, the sheriff was vague. From what Herbert could see, it didn't appear that Bruders Landing experienced much violence. He listened carefully to the sheriff's words for any hint to the contrary, but he heard none. Could he possibly be holding something back, not wanting to scare him away? Herbert dismissed the notion as his own paranoia. The town was peaceful, pure and simple, a state of affairs he wasn't used to.

As noon approached, the sheriff began to shift his weight frequently in the cracked leather chair he had sunk into. The cigar he was smoking had gone out, and all the fumbling in his desk drawer hadn't produced another. Herbert sensed the interview winding down, and he still hadn't made his confession.

"I'm real pleased with what I've heard so far, Herb. Whad'ya say we take a break for some dinner. I don't know 'bout you, but all this talk's given me an appetite." The sheriff looked like he was about to raise his overstuffed frame out of his chair.

Herbert couldn't put it off any longer. "Dinner sounds good, but there's something I've got to bring up before we go, Sheriff. It's true as I've told you that coming to work in a place like Bruders Landing has a lot to be said for it. But there's something more that makes me want to put Chicago behind me." Herbert cleared his throat and sat straighter in the uncomfortable wood chair. Beads of perspiration gathered on his forehead. "There was a problem back there, a shooting. I made a bad mistake and an innocent person was killed. The fact is that I . . ."

"'Nough said, Herb. I know all about it." The sheriff settled back into the chair again. "I called a lieutenant in your precinct before you came. He told me about the holdup. A terrible thing, but you don't have to retell it here. It's enough that you're willin' to tell me. Those things happen, a real tragedy for everyone, includin' you. The important thing is this lieutenant says you're a fine cop, one of the best." He picked up the unlit cigar butt and put it in the corner of his mouth.

The tightness in Herbert's shoulders eased.

7

"Thanks for that, Sheriff. The whole affair's like a hundred pound weight hanging around my neck. Something I can't seem to shake off."

"You will, in time. A change of scenery will help. But don't kid yourself. Anyplace you go, any town, will have its own set of troubles."

"I understand that all right. But another town'll have different troubles, and that's what I need. Some kind of change. To be honest, after the shooting, especially at night, the Chicago streets have felt, well, downright evil."

The sheriff appeared to stare off into the distance. "I know the feelin'. I've had it here m'self."

"Here? In this town? What in the world could give you that feeling here?" Herbert was afraid he sounded sarcastic.

"Evil's not always where you expect it." The sheriff leaned forward, lowering his voice as if sharing a secret. "It can be in surprising places sometimes. Places you'd never guess in your wildest dreams. Don't think a place can't have its share of evil just because of the way it looks. Sometimes I can sense it around me like a bad smell."

"A good sense for a sheriff to have, I'd say."

"Sometimes yes, but sometimes I'd give it away in a minute if I could." Jack Schoof bit down on his cigar. "But like people, evil comes and goes, you know. It can surprise the hell out of you, and other times it won't show when you most expect it. So you have to keep your feelers out."

Herbert grew uneasy as the sheriff talked. If there was a problem in Bruders Landing, Herbert wanted specifics. "I try to. Too far, I think. I know what gives me the feeling in Chicago. It's in the streets, the feeling I get about people I see there, that everyone has something to hide. But what gives you a sense of evil here?"

The sheriff stiffened in his chair. "Nothin' I can see. Maybe just the place. This town's in Shoquoquon, ya know. There are a lot of old stories about the place. Live here a while and you'll hear 'em. Old Indian legends mostly, about one of the islands north a'here called Big Tow, and the old Indian mounds on top o' the bluffs north o' town. Legends about people dyin' in some bad ways. With all the people those Indians buried up there, it's no wonder. Fact is, people put a lot of stock in those old stories, at least the ones about Big Tow, how there's some old men out there that have a history of doin' bad things to people."

Herbert wrinkled his forehead. "Is there anything to them?"

"I've been to Big Tow a time or two and never seen a thing. But it don't matter. People here are afraid of the place." The sheriff pushed himself up from the chair that had molded to his form. "Enough of that. Let's go get some dinner."

The sheriff had given Herbert a message. Now if he could just figure out what it was.

* * * * * * * * * * * *

1948

Henry Starker pushed through the door with the crowd of other fourth-graders as they escaped the school building for morning recess.

"Hey, Henry, let's go play baseball." His friend Jack Powell had squeezed next to him.

"OK, in a minute. I want to tell Sheila something." Looking out over the schoolyard, he saw his cousin standing by a fence with two other girls.

"Hey, Sheila," he called out, running over to her. "I heard another story about Big Tow Island last night. Want to hear it?"

"I don't want to hear any more of your scary stories about that place." Sheila turned her back and crossed her arms.

"C'mon, it's not like it's *that* close to Grandma and Grandpa's farm. The island's way out in the river . . . ." Henry didn't finish. From the corner of his eye, he saw three boys shoving Jack back and forth between them. As Henry turned to look, the largest of the three kicked Jack's feet out from under him.

"Stop it, Lloyd!" Henry ran toward them, gathering a crowd of small onlookers as he shouted. Jack was lying on his back trying to catch his breath. Henry faced the three snickering boys, fists clenched, eyes glowering.

"Leave him alone. He hasn't done anything to you!"

"Mind your own business." Lloyd Wischmeier spit out the words with a snarl. "Let the little sissy fight his own battles."

"Sure, against three of you."

"You be on his side. Maybe get Sheila, then it'll be even. What d'ya say?" Lloyd put his hands on his hips, thrusting his chest out as a dare. His two accomplices gave a mandatory snicker.

"I say we'd end up in the principal's office."

A small crowd of kids had gathered to watch, staying at a safe distance.

"What are you, a scaredy cat?" Lloyd began strutting back and forth inside the circle of onlookers.

Henry bristled. "You know what the principal does if you're caught fighting. She calls your parents, that's what. You want our parents to come, Lloyd?"

"I don't give a shit. Mine wouldn't do nothin' and Jack's wouldn't even show. They're probably fallin' down drunk someplace."

"You shut up!" Jack yelled, making a move to get off the ground.

Suddenly Sheila emerged from the crowd, her face glowing red. "Why don't you and those other two bullies pick on somebody your own size!"

"You want some, too, Sheila?" Lloyd stepped toward her sneering.

Sheila stood pat. "I'm going to yell for a teacher. Then you'll get it."

"Yeah, you'd do it, too, ya little tattletale. C'mon, you guys, before someone comes. We'll finish this another time." Lloyd glared down at Jack. "We'll be lookin' for ya, sissy."

As the three walked away laughing, Jack got to his feet. "I don't know why he has to pick on me. He's always been like that."

"Lloyd Wischmeier is a big bully, and bullies always pick on people smaller than they are," Sheila said. "And that Larry Fry and Carl Siefert, they just do what he says. Are you hurt any place?"

Jack brushed at the dirt on his pants. "No, but my Ma will give it to me for getting my pants dirty."

The crowd that had gathered hoping for a fight to develop began to drift away.

"I'll tell her it wasn't your fault," Henry offered.

"Great. She'll probably listen to you. And thanks for comin' over like you did. You probably missed your turn at bat or somethin'."

"No, I was talking to Sheila."

"Henry was trying to make me listen to another story about Big Tow Island. He's always trying to give me the creeps."

"I am not. I just thought you'd want to hear about it."

"Well, *I* wanta hear it. It won't give *me* the creeps." Jack said.

Sheila shrugged. "All right, go ahead and tell us."

"OK, then. Seems like a long time ago, maybe fifty years, there were these two murderers who were being taken by boat to Fort Addison to hang. When the boat was passing Big Tow, they beat up the guards and swam to the island."

Jack's eyes opened wider. "Gee, why there? Didn't they know about it?"

"They must not have. Anyway, the guards started a search. Because the island's so big, they tried to get people from around here to help, but no one would go, just like no one goes there now. So they sent for some dogs."

"Bloodhounds, I'll bet." Jack was breathing excitedly.

"Probably, and police dogs. The dogs found the guys' trail right away and started following it. A few times the guards thought they saw figures that could have been the prisoners, but they looked too old and the guards couldn't get close to be sure. After they followed the trail deep into the island, the dogs started whimpering and finally refused to go any further. So the guards tied them up and went on, trying to track the trail themselves without much luck. Just as they were ready to call off the search for the night, this awful screaming started."

"Quit it, Henry," Sheila demanded. "I'll get scared. You're making this up, aren't you?"

"No, this guy swore it's true. Said his Grandpa told him. So the guards lit some lanterns and headed through the trees to where the screaming came from. But when they got close, the screaming stopped." Henry sensed Jack's tension and lowered his voice. "So the guards went on searching, harder than ever. Finally at the bottom of this hill they found a cave, and inside there was a jacket all covered with blood."

"That's it." Sheila turned away abruptly. "I'm not listening to any more of this."

"Aw, c'mon Sheila, just let him finish," Jack pleaded.

"I'm almost at the end. So the guards start looking around but didn't find anything else until one of them saw shoe soles sticking up at the back of the cave like somebody leaned them against the rock. When they brought the lanterns close, they could see the shoes were in front of a hole in the rocks standing in a pool of blood . . . and they still had feet in them." Henry shivered at the effect of his own words.

"What'd they do then?" Jack sounded breathless.

"The guards figured one of the guys must have squirmed into the little hole on his back somehow and cut himself. So they pulled him out."

Sheila put her hands over her ears.

Henry continued unphased: "As they slid the guy out, they see all that's left of him above his shoes is a skeleton."

"Did they find out what happened to him?" Jack asked, rocking from one leg to another.

"Not exactly, but it looked like he'd been eaten, right down to the bone. Pulled into the hole and eaten."

Jack gasped. "What happened to the other guy?"

"They never found him."

"Oh come on," Sheila scoffed. "That's just another one of those Big Tow stories."

But there was no doubt on Jack's face. "Jeez, I can see why nobody wants to go there."

A bell signalling the end of recess rang in the distance, breaking the story's spell. All three raced for the school building.

Chapter One

The Explosion

1846

Raston Bruhl climbed down the stairway from the pilot house and made his way along the main deck toward the boiler room. Things had gone even worse than he had feared. He was sure his chances of becoming a cub to Evan Musser ended as soon as the warning was out of his mouth. It was just as the engineer told him. Musser had demanded all the steam the e;ngineer could give him in order to meet their schedule. And the steamboat's pilot had flown into a rage at Raston's attempt to warn him about the boilers. Not only had Raston sabotaged his best opportunity of ever becoming a cub, Musser was so mad he might have him thrown off the boat as soon as they reach Mistaky. Maybe sooner. Maybe he should save Musser the trouble and just jump over the side. He had no future anyway.

In despair he stopped and seized the side railing tightly in both hands, staring down at the brown water as it foamed into a wake. Somewhere above a crewman announced that they were nearing the infamous Big Tow Island. Suddenly he was startled by a sharp crack like a rifle shot immediately followed by a hiss-like whistle. A slight tremor ran through the boards of the deck.

Raston stiffened. This was the sound he had been told about, the sound he had hoped he would never hear. As he turned toward the pilot house wondering what Evan Musser would do, the *Prince Nathan's* starboard boiler exploded with a thunderous roar. A geyser of smoke and steam burst through the side of the boat, hurtling splinters of wood, glass shards and body parts in shredded clothing into the air. Like shrapnel from an artillery shell, chunks of hot metal screamed in all directions, piercing the stateroom walls and tearing into the bodies of passengers and crew. Super-heated steam scalded skin and lungs. Then the shrieks began.

Blown onto his back by the force of the explosion, Raston slid along the deck until he banged into a storage box headfirst. Immediately something rough and heavy landed on top of him. Stunned, he lay on his back, buried in a tangle of heavy line, listening to an avalanche of debris rain into the water. His eyes burned and he struggled to free his arms. After rubbing his eyes for a moment, he forced them open. Smoke and steam engulfed the ship in a dense fog that smelled of burning wood and hot metal. He began to cough violently, then gagged, feeling as if he would vomit. He could hear the explosion roar on and on as it echoed down the bluffs. Even as the echoes faded, the screaming grew louder.

It took him several minutes to get out from under the tangle of line, splintered boards and broken glass piled on top of him. When at last he could stand, he rushed to the side rail to view the damage, squinting in shock through the smoky haze. A gaping hole had opened in the *Prince Nathan's* side, piercing both decks. Above the second deck, one corner support for the pilot house had been blown away, causing it to list precariously toward the water. The starboard paddle wheel twisted outward at a forty-five degree angle where it hung, turning slowly. People thrashed and struggled in the water, calling to be saved. The surface was littered with endless debris—boards, barrels, crates, bales, trunks, mostly shattered and broken. Cries came from all sides. He saw two people floating motionless, face down near two detached legs and an arm, and began to feel sick again.

His first thought was to help the people in the water before they drowned. He swallowed the bile that had risen in his throat and made for the life rings. However, with his first step he realized the *Prince Nathan was* listing severely to the starboard. His mind raced. They were taking on water but sinking wasn't the greatest danger. The *Prince Nathan* had *two* boilers and only one had exploded. When the river's cold water reached the second, it could explode as well. From the look of the pilot house, there would be no warning for the survivors coming from there.

'Everybody! Off! Get off the boat! Jump! Jump!" Raston yelled in all directions. "It's going to explode!"

His shouts were lost in the screaming. Even passengers close to him didn't seem to hear.

The second explosion tore the *Prince Nathan* in half.

Raston somersaulted down the deck until he hit the railing. He lay still for a moment, stunned, then began moving one limb after another to see if he was intact. His ears rang painfully. As he struggled to rise, he felt the deck tilting upward. The *Prince Nathan's* stern was preparing to slide into the mud at the bottom of the Mississippi and Raston was in danger of being dragged under with the boat's carcass. He knew there were precious few minutes to spare.

He lunged for the rail preparing to jump overboard when his foot caught on some line. A splinter of pain pierced his hand as he tried to break the fall with his arms, then his shoulder hit the lower rail. Despite the pain, he climbed onto the top rail and looked down. Through the cloud of steam and smoke he saw a clear space alongside the ship's hull. Taking a deep breath, he jumped.

The *Prince Nathan* had been docked at Bruders Landing for three days, loading and unloading cargo and straining Evan Musser's patience. As second mate, Raston Bruhl knew Musser's fierce temper would be fueled by the delay and he would be determined to make up the lost time. A morning fog had shrouded the river as the *Prince Nathan* backed from its mooring shortly after dawn. Loaded with all the lumber, salt pork and seed she could hold plus a record forty-seven passengers, the heavily-laden steamboat was slow to get underway. Musser was at the wheel. The *Prince Nathan* was a powerful side-wheeler, her twin boilers and paddle wheels making her the fastest steamboat Raston had ever served on, but Raston had never known the boat to carry so much weight.

Making a full head of steam to push through the river current, dark gray smoke rose from the *Prince Nathan's* twin black smokestacks in tall plumes while her giant paddle wheels churned the muddy Mississippi water into white foam. Raston was sure the big side-wheeler made a grand sight as she steamed north like a ponderous swan thrashing through the brown water of the river.

As the sun burned off the fog, the June day had grown warm. Passengers lined the outer decks on both levels to escape the heat shed by the ship's boilers. They sat reading or sleeping, or stood shoulder to shoulder at the railings enjoying the summer sun that turned the ripples on the water into a thousand sparkling mirrors, and staring at the Indian burial mounds at the crest of the rocky bluffs that seemed to rise straight from the water.

As he ambled stiffly past the passengers on the main deck, Raston deliberated. Should he warn the pilot about the boilers? He knew Musser didn't tolerate anyone questioning his orders. Raston had worked hard for the chance to become a cub, learning to walk erect to disguise his crippled leg. He had shown that he could do the tasks required by the big boats and then some. Still no pilot had shown an interest in him. At twenty-one, Raston knew if he didn't catch on as a cub with a river pilot soon, he never would. He had sought a berth on the *Prince Nathan* because of Musser, whose cub had left him in New Orleans. As the days and weeks of the voyage passed, the pilot began talking to him, giving him special tasks. Musser was pleased with his work, he was sure of it. Was he willing to risk throwing that away?

17

"Raston. Raston Bruhl. Come on up here!" Musser had called from the pilot house, his deep voice rising over the sound of the thrashing paddle wheels. Raston had been startled. Evan Musser had never called him to the pilot house before.

"On my way, Cap'n," Raston shouted.

The pilot house was small—a square room built on beams above the Texas deck with windows on all sides. In front was the large spoked wheel, its smooth wood and decorative brass brightly polished and its handles well worn. On one side were two voice pipes with mouthpieces shaped like funnels that allowed the pilot to communicate with the boiler room if he shouted. In the rear, taking up the length of the back wall, was a tall table littered with maps and charts.

Evan Musser had stood alone at the wheel, his hands firmly grasping its handles, staring out over the broad river ahead. Though the man slouched slightly, he still was taller than Raston by half a head. Musser wore a white shirt, slightly frayed by frequent rough washings. His bushy hair, already gray in his late 30s, bulged out under the band of his cap like sheepskin trim. The air was heavy with the sweet aroma of the tobacco smoldering in his pipe.

"What can I do, sir?" Raston was breathing heavily as he entered.

"Oh, Raston, fine." Musser didn't take his eyes from the river. "Take the helm while I look at the charts and some notes I made 'bout the river on into Mistaky on my last trip. If you want to be a pilot, you better have a taste of it."

His words had so surprised Raston his knees nearly gave way. He had never laid his hands on a wheel when the boat was under steam.

"You'll be all right. I'm staying right here. She's a gentle lass for all 'er size. All you have to do is keep 'er dead center. We got plenty of water and the channel should be clear right into Mistaky. She's steamin' good so we can make up some of the time we lost. C'mon over here now."

"Yes sir." Raston stepped briskly to the wheel and gripped the smooth spokes tightly in his hands.

Moisture gathered in his palms. Afraid even to blink, he peered at the river ahead, intently looking for floating debris or signs of sandbars, anything that might damage the boat or put them aground.

"You're doin' just fine, Raston," Musser said after several minutes. "Ever been this far north on the river before?" Raston turned his head to the rear momentarily and saw the pilot studying a chart spread on the table.

"No sir," Raston answered, clearing his throat to deepen his voice. "Only been as far as St. Louis before this trip."

"Well, it's a mighty interestin' part of the river. Those bluffs over there're fulla flint, but the Indians'd never go get it because of evil spirits they think live there. On top there's their old burial grounds. They put the bodies in big mounds built with timber and dirt. There must be a couple hundred of 'em. Have a look." He handed him a long spyglass.

Raston held it up to his eye. "I see them."

"There's also an island comin' up called Big Tow. The Indians believe evil spirits live there, too. Some white folks say they've seen 'em. Look like old men. Can't say what's true and what's not, but there's been some people disappear on Big Tow, that I know."

"I read about this place," Raston answered proudly. "They call it Shoquoquon. The only time the Indians would ever step foot in it was to bury their dead in those mounds."

"Good, Raston, very good. I like a man who shows an interest in where he is."

Raston glowed with confidence. Everything was working. He truly had a chance of becoming a cub to Musser. Then he remembered the boilers and his spirits plummeted. He had to warn him. There were lives at stake, including their own.

"Sir?"

"What is it, Raston?"

"The boilers, sir."

"What about 'em?"

"Well, it's just that I went by the boiler room and it looks like they're overheating." Raston spoke quickly, twisting his sweaty palms around the spokes.

"Just what the hell took you there? Did anyone ask you to inspect the boilers?" Musser's mercurial temper began to show in his voice.

"No, but I thought you should know so you could tell Silas, uh, the engineer, to damp down the fires." Raston heard a fist slam down on the table.

"Did you talk to him about the fires?"

Raston heard the pilot push back his chair and walk toward him. He stared straight ahead, his knees beginning to weaken.

"Yes . . ."

"Just what did you tell him?".

Raston swallowed hard, wanting to run. "Uh, I said he should damp them down. The boilers are glowing red. I didn't want anything to happen . . ."

"Dammit!" Musser shouted. "*I'll* be the judge of that, Mr. Bruhl! We've got a schedule to make up. If you ever get to be a pilot, which I seriously doubt, you'll learn about schedules. Fortunately, Silas would never listen to some green second mate. Now get down to the boiler room and tell him you're there to haul more wood." A large hand seized Raston's shoulder, pushing him out the pilot house door.

Chapter Two

The Kitten

1908

Emma Florang was a product of Bruders Landing. A town girl. With her sturdy frame, flowing blonde hair which she often wore in pigtails, and ruddy complexion, she looked as if she had stepped out of a Nordic painting. In Emma's third year of high school, she met Lyle Gerdes. He was tall and rangy with brown hair that often looked as if he had forgotten to comb it, and he sported an engaging smile that broke out each time he spoke. He was also the first farm boy Emma had ever been interested in. She was flattered by the attention he paid her, smitten by his slow, deliberate manner and the slight drawl in his voice.

During their time together, Lyle talked so enthusiastically about the family farm that Emma grew anxious to see it and told him so. An invitation to visit wasn't long in coming.

On a mild Saturday in early November, Lyle called for her in a freshly-scrubbed buckboard drawn by a thoroughbred equally well-groomed. The Gerdes farm lay at the north edge of Bruders Landing, less than a half-hour ride in good weather with a fresh horse. Many of the trees lining the road still sported patches of red, yellow and orange leaves that shined brilliantly in the sunlight. Lyle kept the horse at a fast trot, scattering the fallen leaves in their path. Emma found the pace exhilarating, but kept a firm hold on her seat.

"Oh, Lyle," Emma exclaimed as they left the Bruders Landing neighborhoods behind. "I just love this. I hardly ever get to ride in the country, and it's so, well, fresh. The air feels so good on your face, I wish the ride could just go on and on."

Lyle turned to her and grinned. "It could, I guess. We'll be at the farm in a few minutes, but we could just go on by and keep ridin'."

"Oh, no, I was just saying that. I really do want to see your farm."

"You will, pretty soon. It's just on the other side of Walnut Grove Cemetery up the road."

As they approached the cemetery, Emma grew quiet, recalling a cold day in another November when her grandfather was buried. A wild turkey running awkwardly in front of the carriage then becoming airborne brought her back to the present. She giggled. Suddenly everything she saw seemed to be funny. Her laughter was contagious and Lyle was soon infected. They were both laughing to tears when they turned into the tree-shrouded lane that led to the Gerdes farm.

"Is that where you live?" she asked, somewhat in awe.

With the first glimpse of the farmhouse, Emma's lightheartedness started to fade, replaced by a vague unease. The house was unusually tall—three full stories, built of limestone quarried from nearby bluffs. The stones had been so meticulously cut and laid that little mortar was used. Exposed to over fifty harsh Midwestern winters and the blistering sun of the summers, they had uniformly aged to the color of ripened wheat. The windows, trimmed in white with paint that had started to peel, were tall, nearly floor to ceiling on the first and second floors, and arched at the top as if made for a church. The house reminded Emma of the medieval castles in her history books.

"That's it. Lived there all my life like my daddy. Do you like it?"

"Well, yes. I guess so. It's just that it's so, um,

big. I've never seen a house that looks so . . . well, so strong."

"We only live on two of the floors. The third floor's been vacant since Grandma and Grandpa died."

Lyle's father stood on the large, open porch, smoke curling from his pipe. Lyle's mother came out the door wiping her hands on her apron as Lyle and Emma climbed off the buckboard. Lyle, hands in his pockets and feet shuffling, introduced Emma. They shook her hand warmly.

"We're real glad to meet you, dear," Mrs. Gerdes said, " seein' as Lyle has been talkin' about you so much."

"Jeez, Mom, do you . . ."

"Now, hold on there, Mother," Mr. Gerdes chuckled, "we'd best not be embarrassin' him."

"I'm glad Lyle's talked about me," Emma said quickly, sensing his discomfort. "I'd be disappointed if he didn't since he's told me so much about you."

Slowly, the bright red in Lyle's cheeks began to fade.

"I'm makin' some lunch for us, Emma, I hope you'll stay."

"Yes, thank you. My folks don't expect me home until late afternoon."

"Good. That's settled then. Why don't you show Emma around a little, Lyle. I'll ring the dinner bell when lunch is ready."

The farmyard was a collage of buildings accumulated through three generations of the Gerdes family. Lyle led her to the largest structure, a hulking, traditional wood barn that looked ready for another coat of red paint.

"Be careful where you step, Emma. We let the horses and cows go through here, if you know what I mean."

"I know exactly what you mean," Emma answered, looking at the brown piles on the ground around her.

Part of the barn's foundation had been carved into the hillside. The remaining foundation extended out from the hill, built of limestone like the house, but with stones of various sizes which had been skillfully laid in mortar that compensated for the different shapes.

They entered the barn on its lower level. Horse stalls and feed bunks lined the walls on two sides with a passage through the center that dead-ended at the rock wall of the hill. Emma was struck by the strong odor of large farm animals. Mounds of loose hay were scattered on a dirt floor made as hard as cement by the trampling of hooves for half a century. Overhead, the ceiling was a series of planks, warped by time, frigid winters and sweltering summers, nailed on top of the massive timbers that supported the structure.

"Watch your hair," Lyle called out.

She looked up. Hanging from the spaces between the timbers barely over her head were thick spider webs, weighted down by a coating of dust and insect carcasses.

"Here's the way to the hayloft." Lyle pointed to a series of boards on the wall leading to a hole between the timbers overhead. "Do you want to climb, or walk around to the door outside?"

Emma sensed a dare in his voice. Although she was wearing a skirt, there was no way she would let him think she was chicken just because she lived in town.

"I can do it." And she did, keeping pace with Lyle who led the way.

The hayloft was a cavernous room intricately laced overhead with large, square beams that supported a roof shaped like a wood cathedral. A strong aroma of drying hay engulfed her as she climbed through the opening.

"There's so much room in here," Emma exclaimed.

"Got to be. We have to store enough hay to feed the cattle until we get grass again in the spring. Over there're the doors we use to bring it in and at that end's the door we use to pitch it down to the wagon when we feed."

As they left the barn through the large set of double doors, they walked by a silo, standing tall as if at attention, its red paint, like the barn's, faded by the sun.

On the far side of the barn was a chicken coop

built of weathered wood in the shape of a lean-to. Looking through one of its small windows, Emma was mesmerized by the antics of the dozens of chickens she could see inside. When Lyle told her that his mother relied on these chickens not only for eggs but also for their traditional Sunday dinner, she felt her stomach turn.

"Out there's the pasture where we keep the cattle this time of year. Would you like to have a look?" Lyle asked her, pointing to the west.

Before she could answer, a bell began ringing.

"That's Mom callin' us for lunch. We'd best wait to go out there 'til after we eat."

Emma realized she not only liked both the farm and Lyle's parents, but also how connected Lyle and his parents were with their land. If she were to marry him, she would be marrying his family and their farm as well. At first the thought overwhelmed her. Later, as they saw more of each other and their relationship deepened, she began to accept the prospect, even finding it pleasing.

On the night they graduated from high school, he asked her to marry him and she said yes.

The day after they returned from a St. Louis honeymoon was a Monday, and Emma's life on the farm began. At 5:00 in the morning Lyle shook her awake, telling her that breakfast was almost ready. She opened her eyes to the early morning darkness, confused about where she was until she saw Lyle sitting on the side of the bed struggling to pull on overalls. By the time Emma descended to the kitchen, Lyle and his parents were eating the breakfast Mrs. Gerdes made every weekday morning: fried eggs, potatoes, ham and slices of home-baked bread spread with apple butter. No one was talking as she entered the kitchen. They each greeted her, then fell back to eating in silence. Moments later, Mr. Gerdes wiped his plate clean with a crust of bread, stuffed it into his mouth and pushed his chair back from the table, a ritual that signaled breakfast was over.

As they cleared away the breakfast dishes, Mrs. Gerdes made it clear that every Monday was wash day, rain or shine. When she spied Emma glancing doubtfully out the window at the dark, rain-filled clouds, Mrs. Gerdes, in a voice that carried a hint of apprehension, said they would have to hang the clothes in the cellar to dry. Emma had never seen the cellar, and the tone of Mrs. Gerdes' voice puzzled her.

They washed the clothes in tubs brought to the kitchen, rubbing each garment vigorously with bars of soap against the washboards, then wringing the water out by hand, finally piling the clothes into large straw baskets. The muscles in Emma's forearms soon ached, but she wouldn't let herself stop lest Mrs. Gerdes think she was a weakling.

Mrs. Gerdes picked up the first basket, telling Emma to bring the second as soon as it was full. Determined to make a good impression her first wash day, Emma soon had filled the basket as full as she thought she could possibly carry. After struggling to pick it up, she walked to the cellar doorway.

The dim light from the kitchen behind her did little to light the stairs. As she peered out over the clothes basket at the steps, she felt as if she was about to descend into some deep, dark hole in the earth. In a sudden rush of anxiety, she reached for something to hold onto, nearly dropping the basket. Taking a firmer grip on the handles, she told herself to get her imagination under control. As she cautiously descended the narrow stairs, she saw a dim light coming from somewhere below.

When at last she reached the cellar floor, Emma paused to get her bearings. The damp, musty air felt moist on her face, smelling of earth as if the cellar had been freshly dug. The source of the light was an oil lantern off to one side hanging between several clotheslines strung from boards nailed to the floor joists overhead. She could see little beyond the modest circle of light which it cast. Shadows at the circle's edges seemed to dance as the light flickered. Her anxiety started to return. She strained to peer into the darkness beyond the light. She could see no windows, not even the cellar walls. With no sense of the size or shape of the space she was in, she became disoriented, her skin growing wet and clammy.

Suddenly off to her left, at the outer limits of the lantern's light, she saw a figure moving. It appeared to be draped in a large robe, its hands extended toward the ceiling as if worshiping at some unseen altar. Emma grew rigid, unable to move. As fear gripped her, she started to scream but couldn't utter a sound. Her hands lost their grip on the clothes basket and it fell to the dirt floor.

"Emma? Are you all right? Did you fall?" the figure mumbled through a mouth full of clothespins.

Emma leaned over to pick up the basket. "Yes, I'm fine, Mrs. Gerdes. I wasn't sure you were down here," she managed to answer as she tried to mask her embarrassment. "The basket just slipped out of my hands."

"I was worried there for a minute that you fell down those stairs. Come on over here, now." Mrs. Gerdes resumed hanging a sheet, taking a clothespin from her mouth to fasten the end she was holding to the clothesline overhead. "I'm afraid the light's none too good down here, but there's a couple more lanterns we can light there on that shelf. We don't use the cellar for much 'cept dryin' clothes in the winter and on rainy days."

"I've never been down here before," Emma said. As Mrs. Gerdes lit the two lanterns, Emma could see that they were standing at one end of a long room.

"Well, there's not much to see. The fruit cellar's over there. Back there's the furnace. Behind it's the coal bin. The men take care of that, the shoveling and all. Lyle takes turns with his father. There're some stairs that go outside; over there behind the furnace. They use 'em to carry out the ashes."

Through the smoky light Emma could make out the things Mrs. Gerdes pointed to as well as three of the cellar walls. But in the direction of the fourth, the light disappeared into darkness.

"Back there, Mrs. Gerdes, what's back there?"

"Nothing really, except the old cellar, the one under the original house."

"The original house? You mean there was a

house here before this one?"

"That there was. Lyle's great-Grandpa built it in the 1830s. He was one of the first settlers on this side of the Mississippi after the Eagle War. It was pretty small. Only a cabin, really. But it had a cellar, a small one anyway. When Lyle's Grandpa could afford to build this house, he built it right over the old one. They tore it down and used some of the wood for this one. The cellar's all that's left."

"Do you use it for anything?" Emma had the odd feeling there was something about the old cellar that Mrs. Gerdes wasn't telling.

"No, haven't for years," Mrs. Gerdes said quickly. "I don't ever go back there and I don't think you should neither."

Emma had nearly forgotten the old cellar existed, until her kitten ran away. On a cold day in December while working in the barn, she had spied a mother cat and her newborn brood lying in a feed bunk. When she stopped to look, a tiny gray kitten was squirming futilely in its attempt to push through a pile of larger kittens for a place at the mother cat. It took Emma only seconds to decide on a rescue. Tenderly she scooped up the kitten and carried it into the house intending to feed it herself. Try as she might, her attempts to get the kitten to drink warm milk from a saucer were a failure. Frustrated, she dipped her finger into the milk and forced it into the kitten's mouth. The kitten began licking her finger eagerly. For nearly half an hour Emma patiently continued the process until the kitten fell asleep.

Fascinated by the study of Egypt in her last year of high school, Emma named the kitten Pharah, convinced it was the feminine equivalent of Pharaoh. Pharah soon became Emma's devoted companion, regularly padding after her through the house. But Pharah also had an adventurous streak, sometimes disappearing for hours into some nook or cranny of the farmhouse.

On a rainy Monday in March, Pharah followed Emma down to the cellar. It was the first time the kitten had ventured down the steep stairs. Emma was helping

Mrs. Gerdes hang a wet sheet when she saw Pharah dart into the darkness toward the old cellar as if chasing something. Emma called her to come back. When the kitten didn't return, Emma dropped her end of the sheet and ran after her.

"Wait, dear," Mrs. Gerdes warned, almost yelling, "don't go back there. It's too dark. You might trip on something."

"I'm going to get Pharah."

"All right. But wait 'til I fetch a lantern."

Emma stood at the edge of the darkness calling Pharah's name until Mrs. Gerdes came alongside her holding a lantern, its wick burning dimly behind a smoke-coated chimney.

"You stay close to me now, dear. Look where you're walkin', 'cause there's rocks and things on the floor. We haven't done any cleanin' down here in a long time. Don't you worry none, we'll find your kitten."

Mrs. Gerdes cautiously led the way to the old cellar. When she reached the doorway, she thrust the lantern forward as if clearing a path. It cast a weak light around an empty room. Mrs. Gerdes stepped in warily, raising the lantern high over her head. Emma followed close behind, noticing an unusually foul odor. The room seemed colder than the rest of the cellar. Its walls were rough-cut stone and had begun bowing inward. The floor was hard-packed dirt like the rest of the cellar, bare except for several yellowing newspapers scattered about. Pharah was nowhere to be seen.

Emma looked anxiously for a place Pharah could hide. In the east wall directly across from the door, she noticed a small, dark hole about shoulder height. The hole was at the bottom of a section of the wall that looked like part of a larger hole sealed with rock and mortar. A stone the size of the small opening lay on the floor. She walked quickly to the opening.

"Mrs. Gerdes, bring the lantern over here. I think I see where she could have gone."

Mrs. Gerdes took a step toward her, then stopped.

"Pharah might have climbed into this hole. Can you bring the lantern closer so I can look?"

Mrs. Gerdes stood fast, staring at the opening. "Is there something wrong?"

"I don't ever go near that hole. It's deep and it always smells like somethin's dead in there."

"Well, hand me the lantern and *I'll* look."

Emma took the lantern from her hand and went to the opening. The odor she noticed when entering the old cellar grew more sour and putrid. Mrs. Gerdes was right. It was like something dead and rotting. Stepping carefully, she held the lantern up to the opening and peered cautiously inside. She saw what appeared to be a tunnel. The putrid smell from inside was even stronger. She called the kitten's name over and over, hearing her voice disappear into the darkness.

"Pharah must be in here, Mrs. Gerdes. It looks like a tunnel. Do you know where it leads?"

"I have no idea. Lyle's daddy sealed it up years ago. Because of the smell, I guess. That rock must've just fell out.'

Emma stood at the opening in the old cellar wall for over an hour, calling Pharah's name and listening. Twice her hopes were raised by sounds in the distance that might have been the kitten, but they were so faint she was never sure. When the flame in the lantern began to burn low, she reluctantly abandoned her vigil to wait for Lyle's return.

Early that morning Lyle had gone with his father to a neighbor's farm to help repair a cultivator. Emma was helping Mrs. Gerdes fix supper when she heard the sound of the horse and wagon. She immediately put down the bowl she was holding and went outside to meet them.

"Pharah's disappeared in the cellar. You've got to help me find her," Emma pleaded, determined not to cry. "She ran into that old cellar and went into a hole in the wall. I've called her and called her but she won't come out."

Lyle put his arm around her. "OK, Emma, honey. It'll be all right. Now just tell me what happened."

"I just did." Emma shook off his arm. At that point her efforts at control weakened and she began to weep softly.

"Damn, I shoulda been checkin' that wall," Mr. Gerdes exclaimed as he slapped his thigh.

As she wiped her eyes with her apron, Emma saw him exchange a worried glance with Mrs. Gerdes. The two of them walked ahead into the house, engaged in a animated conversation but keeping their voices low.

"Now don't worry, Emma, Pharah will come out of there as soon as she gets hungry," Lyle said, sounding reassuring.

"There's a tunnel back there, you know. Your mom says she doesn't know where it goes. I looked in as far as I could with the lantern but couldn't see anything. Do *you* know where it goes?"

"No, I don't. It's been sealed up since I was a kid. I only saw it once before that. Daddy always told me I'd get the lickin' of my life if I ever went near it. Besides, it always smelled so bad, I never wanted to."

"Your mom said your daddy sealed it up."

Lyle nodded. "It wasn't long after Gram disappeared. I remember some men from town helped. They sealed up the entrance to the old root cellar out by the creek about the same time."

"Your grandma disappeared? The one who your Mom says wasn't quite right? I didn't know she disappeared. I thought she just died of, well, something."

"Yep, she just disappeared. I don't remember her much, 'cept she was real tiny. She stayed in her room mostly. Even ate her meals there. I'd see her once in a while when I was little, wanderin' around the house, kind've like she was lost all the time. Anyway, one day she just disappeared. Everybody looked for her a long time, all the neighbors, but they never found any trace of her."

"How awful," Emma gasped. "Did that have anything to do with your daddy sealing up the hole?"

Lyle acted as if he didn't hear her question.

Mr. Gerdes met them at the bottom of the cellar stairs with a reflecting lantern and led the way into the old room. Lyle took the lantern from him, pointing the beam into the hole.

"I can't see nothin' in there. There's no way to see where it goes." Lyle backed away from the opening. "Besides, it stinks."

"Let's just be quiet a minute and listen," Emma urged. "Maybe we can hear something."

Lyle put his ear next to the hole.

"I don't hear anything," Lyle said after several minutes, straightening up and shaking his head. "Emma, we should put some food here, like bait. When Pharah gets hungry enough, she'll come out to get it. You can be sure of that."

Emma couldn't bear the thought of simply waiting, but Lyle's suggestion made sense. With the thought of the most delectable meal her kitten would want, she went to the kitchen and boiled a piece of beef kidney. When it had cooked enough to give off a strong aroma, she put it on a pie plate which she set in the opening.

The kidney sat untouched through the night and all the next day. Emma went frequently to check, with each trip becoming more fearful that she would never see her kitten again. On the third day, Emma decided to replace the bait. As she walked into the old cellar, a plate of steaming kidney in one hand and a lantern in the other, she heard a soft cry. Holding the lantern out in front of her, she walked quickly across the room to the hole and looked inside. There, chewing hungrily on the old kidney, was Pharah.

Emma could scarcely breathe. She sat the fresh kidney and lantern on the dirt floor beneath the hole and called Pharah's name gently. Slowly she reached into the opening and swept Pharah into her arms, only vaguely aware that the kitten's fur felt crusty and sticky in places. Weeping, Emma held the kitten to her breast. Gradually she noticed a sickening stench. After several minutes she put Pharah down at the fresh kidney to see if she wanted more to eat. Then she picked up the lantern to see what was on her kitten's fur.

What she saw almost caused her to drop the lantern. The fur on Pharah's back and hind quarters was coated with clotted blood. As she stared in alarm, Emma noticed something else—the kitten couldn't rise from her haunches. Holding the lantern closer, Emma saw with horror that Pharah was missing part of both her hind legs.

"Oh my God, what's happened?" Emma's scream tore through the house.

She sat between Lyle and his father on the front seat of the wagon, shivering and holding her mutilated kitten wrapped in a blanket. Smears of blood remained on her neck and hands and the front of her dress. Lyle drove the team as fast as he dared, but it still took nearly an hour to reach the veterinarian's office on the south side of Bruders Landing. It was another hour before Doc Caster returned from helping one of Simka Heinold's cows that had trouble birthing. Sweeping in the front door, Doc Caster glanced at the blood on Emma and the kitten she cradled in her arms. Immediately he motioned them into his examining room.

"Put her down on the table here. You can help by holding her quiet."

Emma nodded. Doc Caster began cleaning the stumps of the kitten's legs with warm soapy water. Lyle and his father stood close, watching intently. As the caked blood was washed off, he gently ruffled the fur on her hind quarters. Emma saw cuts under the fur.

"Not only is your kitten missing the lower part of each of its hind legs, there are some deep bites on its hind quarters. What did this little cat tangle with?" Doc Caster asked while continuing to work on the stumps of its legs.

"We don't know, Doctor," Emma blurted out. "She went into this hole in an old cellar wall three days ago. She was like this when she finally came out."

Doc Caster lifted his head, a startled look on his face. "She went in the hole in your cellar, did she?" He looked sternly at Mr. Gerdes.

"That damn hole was sealed up years ago, Doc," Mr. Gerdes said defensively. "One of the rocks worked itself loose."

Doc Caster jabbed his finger at Mr. Gerdes. "You better get it sealed back up then. Anyway, you can bet this little cat made a big fuss when this happened. Did you hear anything in there?"

"No, I didn't hear anything and I checked at the hole a lot, every couple of hours since she went in," Emma answered.

"She must gotten back in there quite a ways or you sure would've heard something. But you have to tell me something else now. It's time to make a decision. Your cat's alive only because the legs were bitten off right at the joints where the blood supply is limited and it's quicker to clot. Now that the stumps are clean, I can pull the skin over the ends and stitch it. The wounds'll probably heal OK if you keep 'em clean and make her stay quiet for a couple weeks."

He stroked the kitten's back gently. "The question is, do you want me to do that?" He paused momentarily, letting the question sink in. "What we have here is a kitten that will grow into a cat and maybe live a long time, but as a cripple. I've never seen a cat with part of both hind legs missing like this. Maybe it'll be able to do more than I think, but basically you'll have to care for it all its life. So I ask you, should you let it live like that or should we put it to sleep? That's for you to decide."

"Fix her, Doctor," Emma said without hesitating. "Please fix her. I'll take good care of her. I'll give her everything she needs.

"Right, Doc, that's what we'll do, as long as Emma wants her," Lyle answered.

"All right, I'll get on with it. Emma can stay here and you two can just sit in the other room and wait if you want. It'll take me a little while to sew her up and get her bandaged."

Nobody moved.

"Well, then, stay if you like." Doc Caster began gathering instruments and bottles from various drawers and cabinets around the room.

They all looked on quietly as the veterinarian worked. As Emma began feeling more confident about her kitten's survival, a question began to torment her. Finally she could contain it in no longer. "Doctor, what do *you* think might have done this to Pharah?"

There was long pause before he answered. Mr.

Gerdes started shifting his weight from foot to foot, making a shuffling sound.

"Can't be sure, Emma." He said without meeting her eyes.

"Darned if I know either," Lyle offered, shaking his head. "She musta bumped into somethin' real grumpy, like she ran into somethin' sleepin' in there."

Doc Caster slammed his hand on the examination table. Everyone jumped. "You just be sure to get that hole sealed back up, ya hear?"

At breakfast the following morning, Emma listened to Lyle and his father discuss how to seal up the opening in the cellar wall. They agreed the old rocks had to be reinforced, but Lyle wanted to wall-up the doorway, saying they never used that part of the cellar anyway. Mr. Gerdes was reluctant, arguing they needed a way to check on the opening, but Lyle insisted, urged on by Emma and his mother. Finally Mr. Gerdes agreed, but only if they closed the old cellar off with a heavy door instead of a wall.

Later that day Mr. Gerdes drove to town and returned with a stack of square-cut timbers four inches thick from Baumeler's Lumber Yard. He also brought the biggest lock and hinges they had at Meier's Hardware Store. Working steadily in the evenings, Lyle and his father had the door built and installed in two weeks.

"So, Emma, how does she look? We've never built a door like that, never even seen one for that matter. It's strong enough for a bank vault," Lyle said proudly as he and his father showed off their work to Emma and Mrs. Gerdes.

Emma had no doubts about the door's strength. It was built with two layers of the timbers bound together by four rows of iron bands. The lock looked every bit as massive as the timbers. "It sure looks strong, but something might still get out if it's not locked."

"Daddy, why don't we let Emma be in charge of keeping the door locked," Lyle suggested.

"That makes some sense," Mr. Gerdes answered.

"If you know it's locked and hold on to the key, you ought to feel safe enough. What do you say to that, Emma?"

"I guess so. But will I have the only key?"

"Yep, here it is. The only one we got. Now you hide that key real good so none of our grandkids can get in there." He gave Lyle an exaggerated wink.

"That's all well and good, but to tell the truth, I'm still kind of scared down here. I'm not sure I want to come down here by myself." Emma looked toward Mrs. Gerdes. "I don't know how you've been able to do it all these years."

"Maybe it's time I give you something that's made me feel better about it." With a resolute turn of her head, Mrs. Gerdes walked back to the clotheslines and removed an object from the floor joists overhead. When she returned Emma saw that she carried a large revolver, holding it gingerly with the barrel pointed to the floor.

"My father left me this Colt. It gave me comfort to know it was close by when I was down here. I've never had a need to get it down all these years but it felt good knowin' it was there. Now *you* have it, Emma. Maybe it'll give you some comfort, too."

Mrs. Gerdes handed the revolver to Emma before she could object. It was the first time she had ever held a pistol. She was surprised how heavy and cold it felt, and how lethal.

Emma kept both the key and the gun.

Chapter Three

The Farm

1941-1947

Henry Starker was born with a fascination for
the dark. Unlike other children who could become
terror-stricken at bedtime, Henry looked forward to the
moment when his parents would turn off his bedroom
light. To be enveloped by the dark excited him. Henry
was three when he first slipped from under the covers
and crawled through his room, searching in the corners
and under his bed, convinced the darkness held strange
and wonderful things that didn't appear in the daylight.
Soon after turning five, Henry expanded his territory.
He would wait until his parents had gone to bed, then
crawl into the darkest parts of the house, careful not to
make a sound. One night as he got up to relieve
himself, his father was startled to find Henry halfway
inside the linen closet on his hands and knees.

"Henry! What on earth are you doing in there?"
Roy Starker stared down at him, flabbergasted.

Henry backed out of the closet and calmly rose to
his knees. "Exploring, Daddy," he answered quite
matter-of-factly. "I like to explore where it's dark, and

there are a lot more dark places at night."

In spite of being apprehended and made to promise that he would end his nighttime excursions, Henry was determined to continue somehow. In order to keep his promise, he began looking for dark places to explore during the day. This tactic worked well until he was discovered by his mother one afternoon in the far corner of their coal bin, a layer of black dust coating his clothes and every patch of exposed skin.

After she had scrubbed the coal dust off his skin with little of her usual gentleness, Henry's mother held him at arm's length, squeezing his shoulders tightly.

"Henry, now you listen to me! There are going to be some new rules, starting right this minute. Not only are you to stay in your bed after we tuck you in, but you aren't to go outdoors or upstairs or down the cellar unless Daddy or I are with you. Do you understand me?"

"Yes, Mommy, I understand," Henry answered without conviction, feeling frustrated and misunderstood.

"And another thing. These are the rules when you're at Grandma and Grandpa Gerdes's, too."

Henry was devastated. These new rules at home were one thing, but enforcing them at his grandparents' farm was something else entirely. He had become bored with exploring at home and was growing eager to start at the farm.

After years of farm living, Emma Gerdes had grown stout in a way that conveyed strength. Her long hair was now white and she kept it wrapped in a tight roll around the top of her head. There was often a stern look on her face that dissolved into a warm smile whenever she greeted Henry. Lyle Gerdes had aged into a gruff, quiet man, smelling of outdoor sweat and tobacco and, in the evening, a hint of whiskey. He was tall like Henry's father, his weather-worn face lined with wrinkles punctuated by a bushy moustache.

Henry loved his grandparents and always looked forward to visiting their farm, but never so much as recently. Like a moth to fire, he was drawn to the secrets he was sure it held. The farmhouse was where he planned to start.

The lane that led from the road to the farm was lined on both sides by trees, their branches woven together, forming a tunnel-like passageway that Henry found mysterious even in broad daylight. At the end of this passageway, standing majestically on a low hill like an ancient medieval castle, loomed the stone farmhouse. Just the sight of it made Henry's skin tingle. He was certain the old house had secret rooms and passageways his grandparents knew nothing about, places he was determined to discover. And he wasn't about to let his mother's unfair rules stop him. He would simply make his discoveries without anyone finding out.

His road to discovery began on the first floor in his grandfather's den, one of the places off-limits to grandchildren. It was small, paneled floor to ceiling in dark walnut, and filled with the most fascinating things Henry thought he had ever seen in daylight: rods and reels rigged with multicolored lures, a locked case with glass windows that held several rifles and shotguns (as well as his grandfather's store of whiskey), a stuffed fox looking as if it could run off its pedestal any minute, pictures of his grandfather and men he didn't recognize holding strings of fish, several arrowheads and geodes on a shelf, and three waxy fish with open mouths looking like they had been frozen in the air as they leapt for a tasty fly. The den had its own special smell that Henry loved, a blend of gun oil and pipe tobacco.

Often his cousin Sheila McQueen would visit the farm at the same time. She was rather gangly and ordinary looking, but with signs of future attractiveness that escaped Henry entirely. He had once sworn her to secrecy and invited her to explore the den with him, but Sheila soon said it was boring, an attitude which irritated him no end. The fact was that Sheila irritated him much of the time. Since he was a year older than she was, Henry assumed his seniority and gender gave him some power over her, an assumption Sheila instinctively resisted. A sparkle in her eyes was the clue to a spirited and feisty personality. Her independence showed itself in a variety of ways, most often through

stubbornness, frustrating her parents as well as Henry.
Consequently Henry usually chose to ignore her. She
was, after all, only a girl.

Some days Henry found himself staring through
the den windows at the farm fields which stretched as
far as he could see. While he wasn't quite ready to
explore such vast spaces, he had a growing curiosity to
know what was out there. When he could stand the
suspense no longer, he approached his grandfather.

"Grandpa, would you take me for a ride on the
tractor and show me how far the farm goes?"

Lyle Gerdes smiled. "The boundaries? Yeah, I'll
show you, right after lunch. We'll have us a little
adventure."

That afternoon Henry sat on the tractor seat in
front of his grandfather, his hands gripping the
oversized steering wheel pretending to steer the
powerful-sounding machine, yearning to pull the levers
surrounding him.

Driving north, Lyle pointed out where the farm
ended at Herb Bruntmeier's land, then they drove west
until they reached the boundary at the Bohlen place.
Henry stood up repeatedly in front of the tractor seat,
staring intently at the fences.

"Watcha lookin' at, Henry?"

"I want to be sure I remember where those fences
are in case I need to find them."

"Well, they're a lot easier to see this time of year
than later in the summer. There's corn planted on both
sides. Come July that corn'll be taller'n you are. Then
all you'll see'll be an ocean of cornstalks and tassels
wavin' in the wind out here."

Henry was still puzzling on this problem as his
grandfather drove them to the farm's southern
boundary. Here, the fields ended abruptly at Walnut
Grove Cemetery. Henry was entranced by the
landscaped hills dotted with granite stones in all
manner of shapes and sizes. His parents drove by the
cemetery each time they came to the farm, but he had
never seen it like this, so close. Gravestones erupted
everywhere—on the lawn in neat rows, in the shadows of
the large trees, in the deep trough of a rock-lined ravine,

even perched on the side of a hill so steep he imagined the coffins washing out in the rain. He had read where this had happened. During the flood last spring, there was a picture in the *Bruders Landing Gazette* of a boat pulling a line of coffins, hooked together like a train, that had been washed out of the ground from a country cemetery by the Mississippi's current.

Even in the warm sunlight, Henry sensed something mysterious about Walnut Grove Cemetery, the kind of sensation the farmhouse often stirred in him, a sensation that was both exciting and disturbing.

Henry's grandfather saved the most spectacular part of the tour until last. At the farm's eastern edge, the fields ended at a dense woods of giant craggy oaks and maples, even precious walnuts, surrounded by a dense undergrowth of scrub brush and saplings struggling to survive in the shade of their giant cousins. When they reached the trees, his grandfather stopped the tractor and helped him down. Taking Henry by the hand, he picked their way through the underbrush for several yards until they reached a clearing where the trees ended abruptly. As far as Henry could see in both directions were grass-covered mounds, all nearly eight feet high and twenty yards in diameter.

"These're Indian burial mounds, Henry. They're all along the bluffs in these parts. I try to keep the weeds off 'em outa respect."

"Gosh, Grandpa, how many Indians are buried here?"

"On the farm, I don't know. Maybe hundreds. Indians buried their dead along these bluffs for a thousand years, they say. These all look about the same but down in Walnut Grove there's a mound in the shape of a bear. C'mon, now, keep hold of my hand. We'll take a walk through 'em."

Henry walked next to his grandfather as he led them between the mounds, not wanting to be any closer to them than necessary. Suddenly the ground ahead of them disappeared. His grandfather grabbed his hand firmly and brought them to a halt. They were standing at the edge of a high bluff, looking for miles across the Mississippi River and beyond. Henry had to catch his breath. In the distance he could see a cluster of low, green hills rising against the sky beyond the valley's floor. A wind from the south blew over the water with enough strength to raise occasional whitecaps on the river's surface. Henry looked to his left, following the rocky bluff line that first curved inland before bending back toward the river. There the bluff turned to a rich green from a covering of trees in full summer leaf, then fell in a gentle curve to the water. In many places, large rock outcroppings protruded through the bluff's green face. Directly below, so far down he thought it must be at least a mile, was the dark water of the Mississippi surrounding a large island.

"That island there, Henry, that's Big Tow. Some day you're gonna hear stories about it. It's a place you wanta be sure to stay away from."

Henry's skin tingled with excitement. It was a place he definitely had to explore.

Chapter Four

The Drummer

1846

Thaddeus Bump hated the water. He had always hated it, the way it formed dirty puddles and felt slippery on his skin. And the thought of any *large* body of water terrified him. Which was why living in Baltimore made him nervous. It was too close to the Chesapeake Bay.

His employer, the Hentzler Dry Goods Company, in addition to operating a large store in Baltimore, hired salesmen called drummers to sell clothing, cloth and sewing supplies from horse-drawn wagons along routes in Maryland, Virginia, and Kentucky. At eighteen, Thaddeus had started working as one of Hentzler's drummers on a route in eastern Maryland, a territory much closer to the Chesapeake than he wanted. He had worked his route for less than a year when the company's owner, Gus Hentzler, called for volunteers to expand sales into the West. Thaddeus heard the call as his opportunity to leave the Chesapeake far behind.

Thaddeus was congratulated on his pioneer spirit by Gus Hentzler himself. But soon he received the first of two great shocks—his territory would be the Upper Mississippi River Valley. The second was worse—travel in his new territory would not be by wagon but by steamboat, peddling wares from town to town along the Mississippi. Before he could work up enough nerve to resign, Thaddeus found himself with six trunks full of goods and a portable sales booth on a steamboat headed down the Ohio River.

For three excruciating weeks he traveled the Ohio and Mississippi rivers huddled in his cabin. Keeping out of sight of the water helped, but he could feel it below, convinced it would devour him should something happen to the boat.

In November he arrived in St. Louis, astonished to still be alive. All through the winter Thaddeus worked frantically at selling Hentzler dry goods in the city, desperate to prove there was no need to go up river. But competition in the thriving town was brutal and his sales dismal. As spring approached and the ice left the river, he received word from Baltimore to start his trek into the Upper Mississippi. With no other means to support himself, he had no choice but to go.

Even before he stepped foot on the steamboat, his terror returned. When his trembling turned to tremors the night before he was to leave, he drank himself into a stupor. The next morning as he stumbled up the gangway, the agony of his hangover made him forget the water beneath him. Mercifully, he slept through much of the day's trip. Thus began a pattern before each departure.

Bruders Landing was his seventh stop. With the coming of the steamboats, the town had grown rapidly from a camp for settlers moving west into a bustling riverport. Thaddeus was there for six days, longer than he expected. The place was pleasant and sales at first were brisk, but they soon slowed to a trickle. On the seventh day, he had only three paying customers. With little to do, he gazed at the steamboats lined nose-to-nose along the bank. There were seven, the largest of which was the *Prince Nathan*. He quickly made his decision and walked to the foot of its gangway where the pilot was shouting orders to three sweating crew members. Yes, the pilot told him brusquely, they were leaving for Mistaky at first light, and yes, there was room for him and his trunks on deck passage.

Early morning fog shrouded the river as the *Prince Nathan* steamed out of Bruders Landing. Thaddeus had stayed at the Skipper's Skeleton drinking with two other drummers until midnight, then rose at 4:30, thoroughly hung-over as planned. He had watched bleary-eyed as his trunks were loaded onto the boat's main deck. His head throbbing, he intended to sleep through the trip that would take most of the day. On the Texas deck where he found an empty deck chair far enough from the railing that he couldn't see the water, he settled in, setting his leather satchel next to him in the unlikely event he felt like writing his report on sales in Bruders Landing. With the hangover overpowering his anxiety, he fell asleep.

Thaddeus was running out of a boiling surf, trying to escape a school of vicious little fish with needle-sharp teeth biting at his legs, when his nightmare was interrupted by a sound like giant thunder clap. He bolted upright, the memory of the nasty fish evaporating. Smoke and steam enveloped him, obliterating his vision. When he heard people screaming and objects splashing into the water, he began to regain his senses. That wasn't thunder, he concluded. There had been an explosion, somewhere on the other side of the boat. People started rushing by, jostling his chair. Then he heard a call in the distance for everyone to abandon ship. The call was followed by splashes. It dawned on him that people were jumping overboard! His fear of the water was paralyzing. Jump? *He* could never jump. Shaking, he pressed himself deeper into the deck chair.

The next explosion blew out a large section of wall behind him. Still in his deck chair, Thaddeus was blown into the air toward Big Tow Island. For a few brief seconds he felt as if he was riding over the high curve on The Big Thrill, a ferris wheel back in Baltimore. A split second later he realized a harsh end to his ride was coming and gritted his teeth for the inevitable. Fortunately for Thaddeus the deck chair hit the water first, breaking some of his impact. Then he lost consciousness.

When Thaddeus came to, he was lying face up on

what was left of a wall from the boat which had come to rest on shore at the mouth of a small inlet. His first sensation was a gentle rocking motion as the waves licked against the wall, washing over its broken boards and his chest and legs. When he felt the water on his skin, the realization of his circumstances struck like a cannon shot. He sat up in a panic, ripping his shirt on the splintered wood. Ignoring a sharp pain in his neck and leg, he leapt onto dry land. With firm ground under his feet, he leaned against a tree, panting and rubbing a knot that was forming on the back of his head.

Away from the water, Thaddeus became calmer and events began to come back to him. The steamboat's boilers must have exploded, one while he slept and one shortly after the first, catapulting him over the side. Somehow he had survived. Up and down the shore as far as he could see were pieces of debris that must have come from the *Prince Nathan*, but there were no signs of the boat or anyone on it. How long had he been unconscious?

He felt himself slide slowly down the tree trunk he'd been leaning against to the ground. Somehow he had to get back to Bruders Landing. But where was he? Where had the *Prince Nathan* been when she exploded? From the direction of the river's current, he assumed he was on the Illinois shore. But how far out of Bruders Landing had they come? If he walked inland, surely he could find someone, a farmer perhaps, who could help him get back. He checked to be sure he still had his money belt. Already it was afternoon. He needed to get started to avoid spending a night in the woods.

Thaddeus walked south along the shore, looking for a path leading inland through the dense brush and trees. As he walked the soreness in his leg began to subside. After walking several hundred yards and finding no sign of a path, he plunged into the undergrowth, determined to make his way through the thick brush as best he could. The ground beneath his feet was firm, even rocky in places. Occasionally the brush would give way to grass letting him walk faster, but just as quickly the undergrowth would close in again.

Thorns and sharp branches took their toll. His pants and shirt were ripped in a dozen places and scratches on his arms oozed thin lines of blood. Then the ground underfoot softened with small pools of water appearing in his path, their muddy bottoms sucking at his shoes, slowing his pace. The day had become uncomfortably warm and he paused, wiping the sweat from his face with his sleeve. Perhaps he was mistaken and wasn't heading inland as he had thought. It's possible the river curved and that he had made little progress toward Bruders Landing. After all he had fallen asleep as soon as they left port. He decided to continue in the same direction a while longer. Increasingly discouraged as he walked, he was about to retrace his steps when he saw the trees and brush begin to thin in front of him. With the thought that he might be approaching a clearing, maybe a farm, he increased his pace. When he could finally see through the undergrowth, his spirits fell. He was facing a large pond.

The water looked shallow with patches of cattails and lily pads dotting the surface. Tall marsh grasses hugged the shore in front of him. Across the pond rows of dead trees stood side by side at the water's edge like an army of aged soldiers with withered arms raised to the sky in surrender. Although the sun still shone brightly, the scene in front of him had the desolate feel of a place no one had dared visit for a very long time.

A deep-seated curiosity drew him to the barren trees and he began to circle the pond. As he drew close, the trees stretched in front of him as far as he could see. It was a graveyard for once-proud ashes and maples, long since drowned in pools of stagnant water. There were hundreds of them, stripped of their bark and bleached to a dull gray by the sun, some broken by lightning and wind so only their shattered trunks remained upright. At their roots were piles of broken branches rotting in pools of mud and water green with algae; the home of a thousand slithering things Thaddeus didn't dare imagine.

The prospect of wading through those muddy green pools made him break out in a cold sweat. Yet if he didn't, he would have to turn back, which meant he would certainly spend the night in the wild. What sort of creatures prowl here in the dark, he wondered? He decided to continue beyond the pond.

Directly in his path was a long pool of water that looked like split-pea soup and smelled like rotten fish. There was no way to avoid it. For several minutes Thaddeus stood at its edge, mustering his determination. Finally he stepped into the soupy liquid, fighting off the urge to close his eyes. He felt a warm sensation close around his ankles as if they were being swallowed. He froze, staring down at his leg that ended just below the knee. He imagined himself teetering, then falling, unable to rise, smothering in the soupy green water. In a panic he splashed his way through it.

The sunlight came through the barren trees unfiltered. It was like walking out from under a canopy, lifting his spirits. But the pleasant odor of growing vegetation faded, replaced by a smell of rot. Fading as well was the symphony of bird and cricket sounds he had grown used to, leaving an ominous silence. Up close the dead trees looked weathered and craggy, pocked with cavities and hollowed interiors, limbs twisted into tortured shapes as if they had been the victims of a cruel plague. His imagination changed them into fearsome creatures with grotesque faces and misshapen eyes that followed him. He stared down at the mud to reign in his thoughts and made himself walk on.

When he felt that he must have reached the opposite side of the pond, he turned toward it again to make sure of his bearings. At the water's edge the dead trees ended abruptly. Patches of evening mist hovered like specters over the water and the light seemed to dim.

As he started to leave, something unusual caught his eye, something that hadn't been there before. Shrouded in a light fog, it appeared to be a narrow tree trunk standing in the water not more than forty yards from where he stood. It looked taller than any man and pointed at its top like a pencil. Oddly, it seemed to be draped in a robe!

Thaddeus blinked several times to clear his eyes,

then stared harder. Yes, it *was* wearing a robe! But it wasn't a tree trunk. It was a figure, a man with a face, a long face with a narrow white beard. A dark robe hung loosely from its shoulders like a shroud, falling nearly to the water where it stood holding a long staff. On its head was a peaked cap that looked like a witch's hat without a brim. A shadow covered the face, obscuring its features except for two gleaming eyes which seemed to be staring directly at him.

Thaddeus stood and stared, not knowing what else to do. Finally he raised his arm and waved.

The figure remained motionless.

After several seconds, Thaddeus called out: "Hey! Over here! Can you help me?" He paused for a second. "I'm trying to find my way to Bruders Landing."

There was no response.

"I said I'm trying to find a way back to Bruders Landing. Can you help me?"

The figure neither answered nor moved. Thaddeus began to feel apprehensive.

"Hey! You there! Can you hear me?"

When there still was no answer, he grew curious and irritated. Maybe it's some old man who's deaf and dumb, or some kind of statue or scarecrow. He thought about moving closer and looked down at the water's surface, hoping to see through it to a place on the bottom where he could step. As soon as he looked up again, the figure was gone. Thaddeus was dumbfounded. There was nothing in the water where it had been standing a moment earlier, not even a ripple. He looked around the pond quickly. There was no sign of it anywhere. Had he been dreaming, hallucinating? He closed his eyes tightly.

When he opened them, he faced a sight that weakened his knees. In the same spot, standing absolutely still as if frozen in time, were three figures, each practically identical to the one he had seen moments earlier. Dread swept over him. It was darker now. The sun had begun to set and wisps of fog gathered over the water. Suddenly there were five identical figures, closer now, standing side by side like a row of ancient chess pieces.

He stared in disbelief. The figures weren't standing in the water, rather they appeared to be floating above it. He was sure he could see space between the water's surface and their robes! The eyes of each one shined bright red through the mist. A jolt of terror pierced him. He wanted to turn and run back through the trees, but found he was unable to move.

As he stood transfixed by the five figures, he was aware of something forming in his consciousness. Slowly an object took shape in his mind. As it emerged from the shadowy recesses, he recognized a book, open to a page filled with printed words. And somehow he knew what the words said before he read them.

He stood completely still, hearing nothing, as words ran through his head.

It was a long time before the words stopped. When at last they did, Thaddeus felt his body go limp, as if he was melting. When he finally could move again. he turned away from the figures with a jerk and began running, splashing wildly through the water and the mud.

A rescue party found Thaddeus Bump the following day, clothes torn, caked with mud, skin covered with scratches and mosquito bites, lying dazed and exhausted in the sand at the southern tip of Big Tow Island. Barely coherent, he talked of figures who looked as old as the island's dead trees. His rescuers listened wide-eyed and whispered about old Indian legends. They wasted no time in taking Thaddeus off the island.

Chapter Five

The Policeman

1948

His father was killed the day Herbert Siefken celebrated his second anniversary with the Chicago Police Department. Emil Siefken's fire battalion was fighting a raging industrial plant fire on South Halsted. He had just led a hose team onto the plant's roof when an explosion blew it off. They didn't find much of his body. What investigators *did* find were drums of flammable chemicals recently moved into the plant, something the owner failed to mention at the fire scene. They also discovered the plant had been losing a good deal of money. Evidence of arson was strong and it pointed to the plant's owner. When the State's Attorney failed to bring charges, rumors of a cover-up drifted through the Police Department. Herbert was enraged. He refused to sit on the sidelines while his father's killer remained unpunished and pursued every avenue he could think of to force prosecution. His efforts were thwarted at every turn.

Herbert was close to his father, but it hadn't always been that way. Herbert was raised on Chicago's North Side in the German neighborhood his mother called home. Emil Siefken had been a fireman all his working life. From the day Herbert was born, Emil expected his son to follow in his footsteps, as was the neighborhood custom. Herbert was an active and energetic child, usually well-mannered, but with a rebellious nature that surfaced in his teens.

"Herbie, finish washing your hands and get on down here," his mother called up the stairs. "Supper's ready and your Da and me are waiting."

Eating together on evenings Emil Siefken was off-duty was a family tradition that sixteen year-old Herbert found boring and a waste of time.

"Awright, awright," he yelled down testily. "I'll be down in a minute. And my name's Herbert, not Herbie." He stood with his face next to the bathroom mirror, squeezing three new pimples that had erupted next to his nose. Jerking the light cord he opened the bathroom door hard, letting it hit the wall loudly, and headed downstairs.

"Would you mind not bangin' that door," his father said sternly as Herbert came to the table. "And mind your Ma when she calls."

"I did, didn't I? Don't ya see me here?"

"Don't get smart with your Da, young man," his mother said. "He does a lot of dangerous work to make sure there's food on the table."

After Emil Siefken said the blessing in German, Mrs. Siefken passed the steaming dishes of boiled cabbage and potatoes. A strained silence descended as the three of them began eating. Herbert gulped his food as fast as he could. He wanted desperately to leave the table, to go somewhere, anywhere, away from his suffocating family.

"Don't eat so fast," his mother said. "You'll give yourself a stomach ache."

Herbert scowled and shoved another potato into his mouth.

They continued eating quietly for several minutes. Finally Mrs. Siefken, squirming slightly in her chair, spoke: "Isn't it nice Da's home for supper again tonight, Herbie? He was supposed to be on duty but got two hours off to eat with us."

"I guess." Herbert dropped his knife and fork which clattered on the wood table. "But don't call me Herbie anymore. Can't you understand? My name's Herbert." He pushed his chair back from the table scraping the wood floor. "I'm goin' out."

"You shouldn't go out yet, Herbie, uh, Herbert. Your Da came home special to have supper with us tonight."

"Right. He got some time off from that crummy job with the crummy hours that has him hangin' 'round the station house 'most every night playin' cards. And we're s'posed to be thankful for that?. So we had supper. Now I'm goin' out."

"Now hold on here just a minute," Emil Siefken said in a stern voice. "The captain did me a real favor givin' me time off for supper at home. And those crummy hours are what puts a roof over our heads and what keeps this town from burnin' down again. You have to get used to those things if you're gonna join the Department."

"So who says I'm gonna be part of the Department? I been thinkin' 'bout that lately. Maybe I wanta do somethin' else." Herbert shoved his chair back against the table.

"Something else? Why, you can't . . . .why on earth would you want to do something else?"

"Why would I want to be a fireman? Those lousy hours. Workin' crazy times all night. Always havin' to hang around the station. Never knowin' when you're gonna be called out to some fire in the middle of the night. Freezin' your rear end off. Riskin' your neck. Comin' home smellin' like smoke. Why would anyone in their right mind wanta do that?"

"Herbert! Watch your tongue!" his mother cried out.

"Because it's a damn important job, that's why!" Emil Siefken picked his napkin from his lap and threw it on the table. He rose quickly, knocking his chair over backwards, and leaned toward Herbert. "And it's high time you learned to appreciate it!"

"Learned? I learned all I need to know watchin' you. I know what it's about."

"The hell you do!" Emil Siefken slammed his hand on the table, rattling the glasses and utensils.

The sound made Herbert pause, but only for a moment. "I know enough to know I never want to do it. And you can't make me either. I'd rather collect garbage than do what you do."

Herbert surprised himself with the angry words that leapt from his mouth. For a moment he thought his father was going to reach over the table and hit him. Herbert stood his ground, daring him. Finally Emil Siefken set his chair upright and stalked from the room.

In contrast to the tensions at home, Herbert found a degree of success at St. Bonaventure High School. At six feet four and two-hundred ten tightly packed pounds, he made starting linebacker on the football team his junior year, and football was revered at St. Bonaventure. Herbert basked in the glow of popularity during two winning seasons, letting his grades slip lower and lower. When no scholarship offers came at graduation, he found a job in a print shop owned by a friend's father and enrolled part-time in a nearby junior college. For two years he worked and took courses haphazardly, living at home, barely speaking to his father, with no idea where he was headed.

At age twenty, one of his friends told him of his plans to become a policeman, a Chicago cop. Herbert was surprised to find himself envious. On the day after his twenty-first birthday, he applied to the Police Academy, telling no one. Three months after the qualifying exams, Herbert came home as usual from morning classes to change into his work clothes. As he leafed through the morning mail, he found a letter from the Chicago Police Department.

The following morning his father looked up in surprise as Herbert walked into the kitchen. When he was off duty, Emil Siefken was an early riser and he and Herbert rarely crossed paths in the morning, which had suited them both.

"Mornin' Ma. Mornin' Da. Thought I'd get down in time to have some breakfast."

His early arrival was so rare and cheery that his father and mother were both speechless.

"OK, OK, so you're wondering what's going on to get me down here at six in the morning."

"Well, it is a surprise," his mother answered, wiping her hands over and over on her apron. "I'm not used to seeing you for another hour or so. Do you have an early class or something?"

"No, but I do have some news."

His father put down the newspaper he was reading. His mother sat back down and started fidgeting with her hair. "Well, I sure hope it's good," she said.

"It is. I've been accepted at the Police Academy. The class starts in June."

Emil Siefken's eyes widened, then slowly softened and began to glisten. His mouth quivered as he slowly rose from the chair. He stood looking at Herbert, trembling slightly, a tear on his cheek. After a moment he walked over to Herbert and enveloped him in his muscled arms.

Herbert was overcome. He couldn't remember when his father had last hugged him. He began to weep softly. "I'm so sorry, Da."

"Sorry?" Emil Siefken stammered. "Sorry for what? You're doing somethin' almost as good as goin' to the Fire Academy."

"Sorry for, uh, what I said that time at dinner. You know, that I'd rather be a garbage collector."

"Oh my God!" his father said choking, then hugged him again.

Herbert held his father tight. He had missed him more than he realized.

The helplessness Herbert felt after his father's death unleashed pain unlike anything he had ever endured, his suffering magnified by the grief that gripped his mother. Meanwhile the plant's owner received a handsome insurance settlement from a burned-out building he had no plans to rebuild.

Herbert worked out of a South Side precinct where payoffs were readily available. He had brushed off every offer, never wanting to cheat on the law enforcement system he served. But a rage had begun to grow inside him. This system in which he had so much faith had failed him and his family. Each day as he put on the blue uniform, dark feelings rumbled inside him like an approaching thunderstorm. Some days he barely recognized himself, afraid he was about to spin out of control. He knew he needed help, but didn't know where to turn.

It was four weeks after his father's funeral that Herbert found Seamus Flannery waiting in the Station House when he returned at the end of his shift.

"You're Herb Siefken, Emil's boy, right? Remember me, Seamus Flannery?" The big, red-faced police sergeant stepped toward Herbert, his large hand extended. "An old friend of your Da's. We live around the corner from your folks a coupla blocks." There was a wide, infectious grin on his face.

Herbert felt himself smiling back. "Sure, I remember," he fibbed as he shook his hand. "Glad to see you. And to be sure I'm glad to see a friend of my Da's."

"I work in Bunco over in the Twelfth Precinct. I've been meanin' to come see you for weeks. Ever since your Da's funeral."

"I'm glad you did, Seamus, I . . ."

"Ya see, I think I know a little how you must be feelin'. About your Da and how there ain't gonna be any charges brought against that slimy son-of-a-bitch what burned his plant. I've been around a long time. Seen these things before. Thought you might want to talk it over some time. Not that I could help, bein' in Bunco, but I'd be glad to talk."

A recollection of the large Flannery family came to his mind. "Well, I don't . . ."

"Oh, I know. But believe me, I can guess how you're feelin' 'bout the Department and all. Can't say as I blame ya one bit. You've been plenty let down by everybody. But I thought we might talk before ya decide to do somethin' ya might regret. Anyway, me and the missus were thinkin' you might come to supper tomorrow night. We could have us a talk then. Can ya' make it?"

Herbert hesitated, surprised to hear someone

describing so well how he felt. The offer seemed genuine, the tone kindly, not the thing he was used to hearing from veteran cops.

"Well, I'm not on duty . . ."

"It's settled then. We eat at 6:00. Come over at 5:30 and we'll have us a little of the Irish before, if ya like."

Of the seven Flannery children, only Selma was there when Herbert arrived. It was a set-up, Herbert suspected, but when he saw her he didn't mind. She was twenty, no longer the little girl on roller skates he vaguely remembered. Her reddish blonde hair surrounded a warm face dotted by fading freckles. As they were introduced, he caught himself staring at the delightful fullness of her body. And when she spoke, Herbert experienced a yearning that had not been a part of him since his father was killed.

Mrs. Flannery had prepared an Irish meal of banquet proportions, but she needn't have bothered. Herbert barely noticed what he ate or what was said. His attention was entirely on Selma. As the table was cleared, he remembered that he and Seamus had planned to talk but found himself alone with Selma. The Flannerys had quietly disappeared. All through dinner he had found himself tongue-tied whenever he tried to say something to her. With her parents gone, he was afraid he wouldn't be able to speak at all.

"I'm really embarrassed. My folks are so obvious, sometimes!" Selma blurted out suddenly. "It's clear they like you, but it's not fair to you leaving us like this. I don't know what to say. Please, don't feel you have to stay."

Herbert was astounded by her openness and the shy way she expressed her own embarrassment. "Oh, really, I don't mind. Believe me, I don't want to leave. In fact, well . . in fact I like it we're alone. Uh, I mean so we can talk."

"Honest?" she asked, looking straight into his eyes as if she could see directly into his mind. "You're sure you don't mind?"

He felt as if his face was glowing red. "Honest."

"Well, I'm real glad. I don't usually let my parents

choose my friends, but I think I'd like you to be one of them."

"I'd like that, too, now that you've given up those noisy roller skates."

"Who says I have?" she laughed easily.

Alone with Selma, Herbert's shyness faded. They talked about people they both knew in the neighborhood for nearly a half hour before Selma asked about his father. For the first time since his death, Herbert talked about his pain, expressing grief more strongly and openly than he had allowed himself before. Confiding this to her took him by surprise. When tears began forming in his eyes, he was embarrassed, but the look of understanding on her face put him at ease again. He talked about his mother and how concerned he was for her. Then he even talked about the plant owner, how frustrated and disturbed he was when the man wasn't prosecuted. When Herbert looked at his watch, it was almost midnight. They had talked for four hours.

It was surprisingly easy for Herbert to ask if he could see her again. When she agreed, Herbert left the Flannery house on an incredible high, experiencing a lightness to his body he had never felt. Reliving their conversation as he walked home, he realized he had done most of the talking. This had never happened with anyone that he could remember. So he had heard little about Selma and was more eager than ever to see her again. She had a lot of talking to make up for, he told himself.

Within weeks they were constant companions. Selma worked at the kettles in the Campbell Soup factory and changed her shift schedule to match Herbert's. His feelings for her replaced much of the grief and frustration from his father's death which raised feelings of guilt, but he was powerless to stop it. And he wasn't sure he wanted to. The fact was, he finally admitted to himself, that she had put a new meaning in his life and he was in love.

It was a getaway car that killed her. She was walking to the grocery store in the early afternoon, a quick errand for bread and milk before she left for work.

Three men in masks had entered the Bridgeport Avenue Bank and pointed shotguns at the tellers. Two of them vaulted over the railing and scooped money from the cash drawers. As they reached the door to leave, a teller pushed the alarm button. Startled by the loud bell, one of the men turned and emptied his shotgun into the Bank, killing two customers and wounding two tellers. A black Buick was waiting at the curb, the driver gunning its motor. As quickly as the men climbed in, it roared off with a wail of squealing tires, racing toward the intersection that Selma had crossed safely a thousand times in her life.

George Hardy, a retired baker who rarely had a kind word for anyone, witnessed the tragedy as he waited for a bus. A black Buick sped toward the intersection faster than he had ever seen a car go on that street. He watched Selma step nonchalantly from the curb carrying a sack of groceries, looking toward him, away from the speeding car. George thought there was a small smile of recognition. He screamed at her to stop, but she kept walking with a puzzled look on her face until a siren sounded in the distance. Then she turned her head, but the Buick was already there. There was no sound of tires squealing, no sign the car even swerved. It struck her straight on with a sharp, mushy sound, lifting her body high into the air. George watched her arms fly over her head, her legs flailing at odd angles as if she was a mannequin, a stream of groceries trailing from the sack in the air after her. Somersaulting, her body struck the windshield of a parked car. There was a sound of glass breaking, and her body disappeared. Immediately a carton landed on the hood, which suddenly was coated with milk.

In an instant the Buick was gone. Too quick for anyone to get the plate number. George was sure the Buick never slowed, before or after it struck Selma. He ran to the parked car as fast as his old legs would carry him. She was in the front seat, partly draped over the steering wheel, her arms and legs twisted into unnatural positions. Blood was splattered everywhere and had started to pool on the seat where she lay. When the first police car arrived, George Hardy was sitting on the car's running board, crying.

By the time Herbert got to the scene, firemen had removed Selma from the car. Miraculously, she lived for two days. She died without regaining consciousness.

Herbert was enveloped by a relentless, dark, suffocating pall that robbed him of energy and desire, destroying his sleep. He was sure he would never survive another death, and didn't want to.

Even though they hadn't married, the Department gave him extended personal leave for the wake and funeral. Then, after all the activity had ended, Herbert's grief grew deeper, a paralyzing pain worse than when his father died. He found that even leaving his apartment was too hard, too risky, afraid he might see something or a place that would remind him of her. Going out meant bathing and dressing and speaking to people, all of which required more energy than he had. He spent days sitting silently in his only upholstered chair, staring at nothing, sipping from whatever bottle of liquor still had something in it. When night came he moved to his bed, spending the dark hours lying on his back, staring at the ceiling, sleeping in fits, then waking to the crush of remembering what had happened. When the sun rose, he moved back to the chair. The phone rang at least hourly, but he barely noticed, making no move to answer.

For days after the funeral, the only other activity Herbert undertook was to shuffle the ten steps to his bathroom. Occasionally there was a knock on his door, but he never stirred a muscle to respond. The last thing he wanted to do, the last thing he could do, was to see someone, anyone, face-to-face, to summon the energy to talk, to say something that made sense. He was sure he couldn't do it, he couldn't remember how he had *ever* done it.

On the fifth day there was another knock on his door. He was still wearing the clothes he had worn to Selma's funeral. A beard had taken root on his face which glistened with layers of grease and sweat. His hair was oily and swirled in several directions, and he smelled of old butchers' rags and empty whiskey bottles. The trance-like state he managed to achieve hadn't ended his pain, but he wasn't about to risk emerging. He ignored the knocking, but it persisted. After several minutes he heard a voice shouting from the other side of the door, calling his name. The voice was familiar and it began to register somewhere deep in his head. It was his mother. She kept on knocking. He began to think about the sound, what it meant. The thought of opening the door and facing her brought on a panic. He couldn't do it, wouldn't do it. But still she knocked. It began to occur to him that she might never go away. Slowly he became reconciled to the reality that he would have to open the door. It took several more minutes to form a simple plan to leave the chair and walk across the room. Finally he mustered all the strength he could and rose from the chair. He stood unsteadily for a minute getting his balance, then walked to the door in what seemed like slow motion, the effort exhausting. He removed the chain and turned the door knob.

His mother stood in the doorway, crying and bewildered, holding a sack of groceries.

"Oh, Herbert, I'm so sorry."

He stood stiffly and let her hug him. Then she stepped back and looked at him. "Whatever have you been doing to yourself? Have you been in here all this time? When did you eat last?"

When all he could do was stare, she stopped asking questions and steered him back inside.

"I'm going to fix you some breakfast. Then we can talk, but not for long so don't worry. But first I'm going to straighten things up a bit so it's not so depressing in here, and *you* are going to have a bath and change your clothes."

He didn't resist when she pushed him toward the bathroom. The hot shower felt good, better than he expected. Dressed in clean clothes, he emerged to the smell of bacon frying. The small apartment had brightened considerably. His mother had opened the blinds letting in the morning sun and removed the assortment of liquor bottles that had surrounded his chair. She stood over his stove cracking eggs into a skillet. He felt an unfamiliar pang of hunger.

They were quiet while he ate. When he had

polished off his fifth fried egg and a half pound of bacon, she began to talk. "Herbie, I mean Herb. Sorry. Sometimes I forget. You'll have a hard time believing this right now, but you need to try. I know how you feel. Grief is one of the most painful feelings there is, and it comes in a variety of doses. Remember how you felt when your Da died? It was bad, wasn't it? But this is worse, am I right?"

Herbert listened mechanically, making a half-hearted attempt to make sense of her words.

"There's nothing I can say that can make it better. God, I wish there was. It's natural, Herbert. It happens to all of us when we lose someone we love. And it's even worse when the person's so young and the death so senseless, so horrible. But I want you to listen to me now. You *will* get over this. I know that's hard to believe, and you may not even want to be over the pain at this point, but it will pass. It takes time. God knows I still grieve for your Da, but the pain's not so bad all the time anymore. We have to go on living. We owe it to ourselves and the people we love."

Herbert heard, but little registered. Still his mother was right about one thing—he didn't care whether he got over the pain. That wouldn't bring Selma back.

"There's another reason for you to go on as well, Herb. That's to find the people who killed her."

Her words were like a flashbulb going off in his head. Of course. He *had* to make sure the bastards were caught. It was a purpose to live for.

One week to the day after Selma's funeral Herbert returned to duty determined to find out what was happening with the investigation. As soon as roll-call was finished, he called a detective he knew in Homicide at the precinct where she had been killed. The Robbery Detail was handling it, and the person in charge was a detective named Phil O'Malley. Herbert was concerned. As a death in the commission of a felony, it was murder, a matter for Homicide not Robbery. And he had heard about the Robbery Detail in that Precinct, that most of the detectives lived well beyond their means.

He didn't reach O'Malley until the next day. As

soon as he identified himself, the voice on the phone grew chilly—no, they didn't have any suspects. What's more they didn't have any leads, but assured Herbert they were working on it. Something would surely turn up. O'Malley would call him as soon as anything did.

Herbert knew something was wrong. As soon as he hung up the phone, he rang Seamus Flannery, hoping he might know more. Flannery only confirmed his fear that the investigation was going nowhere.

Follow-up phone calls to O'Malley were fruitless. Herbert left messages which were never returned. After several days of this, he filed a formal request through channels to see the file on the investigation. His request was refused.

Desperate, Herbert decided to risk suspension by retrieving the investigation file himself. He entered the Robbery Detail's area in the precinct house during a shift change and located the cabinets where active files were kept. Hurriedly he began leafing through the folders before detectives on the next shift arrived. A file folder with the bank's name, together with the names of the victims, was near the back. As he pulled it from the drawer, it felt surprisingly thin. Anxiously he looked inside, finding but one single sheet of paper on which it was noted that the file's contents had been delivered to the State's Attorney's office. That, he knew, was a lie. With no suspects and no one charged, a file would never be sent to the State's Attorney. There was no use inquiring further. Someone high up had made the file disappear. He slammed the file drawer shut with a force that rattled the whole cabinet.

He broke every speed limit driving to the Flannery's home. Mrs. Flannery greeted him, her face tired, her eyes vacant. Seamus Flannery sat at their kitchen table, a half-empty bottle of Irish whiskey in front of him.

"Get yourself a glass, Herbert, and have a bit of my friend here." Flannery's hand trembled as he pointed to the bottle. "It's about the only thing a man can trust these days."

Herbert got a glass from the sink and sat down. Flannery filled his glass.

"I went to get the file a little while ago."

"I thought you would, sometime."

"It wasn't there." Herbert felt himself start to tremble. "At least the contents weren't. Only a note saying it had been sent to the State's Attorney."

Flannery, staring at his glass, was slow to answer. "The investigation's dead. As dead as my daughter. You can be sure it ain't goin' nowhere and nobody's gonna tell us nothin'."

"We're not gonna let this rest, are we? I'll *make* those Robbery guys talk to me. I'll be on them like a blanket until they find out who did it," Herbert exclaimed, his trembling voice rising. "And if they don't, Hell, I'll do it myself."

"Herb, they *know* who did it."

"They know? What do you mean, they know?"

"I mean they know who killed Selma. They found out before they quit talkin' to us. They're made guys, guys that can't be touched." Flannery took a long swallow of whiskey.

Herbert stared at him in disbelief, the color draining from his face.

"Like I told you when your Da was killed. I've seen this before. Just never happened to me. The first time was after I was assigned to Homicide years ago. We was workin' a bad one, young girl in her mid-twenties. She probably'd been pretty before her face was kicked in. Her boyfriend went nuts when she dumped him. He was sloppy, made him easy to make. Some minor numbers boss who was a comer in the mob. It was a lay down murder one or two. After we took the case to the captain, we never heard of it again. Oh, I asked some questions but was told to keep my nose out of it if I wanted to keep my job. And if I played my cards right, maybe I could get some of the action before long."

"You mean protection? Even for murder? Like buying death insurance, for Christ's sake?" Herbert blurted out. "Even for murdering a policeman's daughter?"

Flannery gulped another swallow of whiskey. He didn't answer.

"Well, what the hell are we going to do? We can't

just let those people get away with it."

"I wish I knew, Herb. God, I wish I knew."

"Well, Goddamn it, I'll find the bastards myself!"
Herbert drained his glass of whiskey and stalked out of
the house.

He began in a straightforward fashion, directing
questions to everyone he could think of who might have
information. Few dared talk with him, and those who
did said they knew nothing. He never reached O'Malley
again, learning he had been given an indefinite leave of
absence and left the city. After his lieutenant told him
bluntly that he'd better cool it if he knew what was good
for him, Herbert turned to the street, spreading money
around to every contact he had. But the word was out.
It was an organization matter and talking to a cop,
especially Herbert Siefken, was dangerous, maybe even
lethal.

He seethed with rage. The system he served so
faithfully had shown him its underside. But there were
other ways of making sure punishment was meted out
where it was deserved. He knew vigilante cops who
levied their own sentences and delivered them in
darkened jail cells and back alleys. They had always
sickened him, but now he saw them in a new light.
Perhaps he should become like that. The thought
tormented him the night of a radio call: robbery in
progress.

Herbert and his partner, Sean O'Brien, were
cruising South Halsted Street when the call burst
through the static on their car radio. It was a liquor
store on West Madison, a few blocks from the
intersection where they had stopped for a red light.
O'Brien gunned the engine and the car lunged forward,
picking up speed rapidly on the deserted street. Herbert
didn't turn on the siren or flashing lights, knowing, on
some level, that the robbers would still be in the store.
He unfastened the 12-gauge short-barrel shotgun from
its holder near the dashboard and loaded the magazine
with the maximum five shells.

O'Brien brought the car to a rocking stop in front
of the store. He and Herbert leapt out without slamming
their doors. Herbert looked into the store through the

liquor advertisements painted on the windows. Two men were leaning over the counter on the customer side. No one else was in sight. One of the men looked familiar. The recognition was like an alarm going off in his head. Where had he seen him? Herbert pulled back on the shotgun's slide action, loading a shell into the chamber and pushed the safety off.

"Easy with that thing," O'Brien whispered, "we don't want a shooting if we can help it. Those guys are just standing there. We should be able to take 'em easy. Do you see any sign of the clerks?"

"No. They could be dead for all we know."

"Right. So there's no hurry. Let's go in slow so we don't scare 'em into doing something crazy."

"OK. Now."

A small bell tinkled overhead as Herbert opened the door. His heart was pounding as he entered in a crouch. O'Brien followed close behind, his service revolver drawn. The man Herbert recognized turned, facing him. Suddenly he remembered. It was a man he had arrested just weeks earlier for armed robbery and attempted murder. All caution vanished in vengeful desire. He raised the shotgun to his shoulder, sighted down the short barrel into the man's midsection and pulled the trigger. The sound was thunderous in the small space. The man's shirt and chest erupted in a spongy red burst and his body jerked backwards as if yanked by a giant spring.

The second man looked on in horror as the first rolled into a grotesque heap on the floor. He turned toward Herbert, a look of utter disbelief on his face, his arms hanging by his side, a pistol in his hand. Herbert's instinct was to yell at the man, to tell him to drop his gun, but a vengeful tide swept him along. He worked the slide back and forth in a quick motion loading a shell without lowering the shotgun, sighted and fired. Again the thunder. The second man's face disappeared in an burst of red mist, his body arching sharply backward before crumpling to the floor.

The air was clouded by smoke from the shotgun's blasts and smelled sharply of burning cordite. Herbert hadn't seen the third man rise from behind the counter.

He was startled by this sudden appearance of another figure. Peering hastily into the smoky haze, he saw that the man held something. Was it a knife? Briefly it occurred to him that it should end now, that he should lower the shotgun, but the compulsion drove him relentlessly. He pumped the slide again and aimed. Even as he pulled the trigger, Herbert realized his mistake. The figure wore an apron and was bleeding from the scalp. The awareness was like a blow to his midsection, sucking the breath out of him. He wanted to stop the deadly shot, to retrieve it, to somehow stuff it back into the barrel. But he could only watch as a jagged red hole erupted in the white apron and the man folded in two. Herbert let the shotgun fall to the floor, knelt down and buried his face in his hands.

The newspapers in Chicago were split. Three called Herbert a hero for doing away with two criminals with long records while regretting that the store's owner was killed. But the fourth accused Herbert of being a trigger-happy cop, meting out frontier justice and killing an innocent victim in the process.

Ironically, the system that had failed Herbert now protected him. The Police Department instituted a routine internal investigation, after which it ruled the shooting accidental. The State's Attorney's office reported publicly that it had insufficient evidence to file charges.

Herbert's guilt consumed him like a cancer. How could he have been so reckless, so impulsive? How was that shop owner's death any different than Selma's? His despair was every bit as agonizing as his grief for her, but now he had only himself to blame. Once more he stopped sleeping or eating, living his days in a zombie-like state. The prospect of returning to work terrified him—he didn't trust himself in another situation like the liquor store, and he was sure to see one sooner or later.

In the early morning hours before he had medicated himself sufficiently with alcohol, his mirror reflected a person who had gone over the edge. What had he become? Maybe he shouldn't allow himself to live any longer. It was a question he didn't ask lightly, a question he would have to answer. But that needed some time. Time he couldn't give it here, in Chicago. He was too dangerous. He needed to leave, to find another place, somewhere calm where he wouldn't be so haunted by memories, a place where he wasn't tempted to be an executioner.

Chapter Six

The Undertaker

1846

Raston's plunge from the *Prince Nathan's* deck carried him deep into the river. The water felt cool and comforting as it enveloped him. When his downward momentum stopped, he paused in the momentary peace of the watery world, then started for the surface, kicking hard. As he broke into the air, his hands hit something firm and shoved it aside. It felt like a person. Coughing and spitting water, he rubbed his eyes to see who he had shoved. The body was floating face down, almost entirely submerged. From the clothing, Raston was sure it was a crew member. He resisted an impulse to lift the head to see who it was.

Close by a woman was screaming, waving an arm.

"Stay there. I'll get you!" he yelled.

Raston swam to her as she continued to scream and thrash the water. He looked for a way to take hold of her. It was then he saw blood gushing from the sleeve of the dress where her other arm had been. With increased determination he reached across her chest and pulled her tight against his hip. Setting his bearings on the bluffs, he started to swim with his free arm. The woman twisted violently, struggling to break his grip as if he were trying to drown her. Raston was angry. Why would she do this when he was trying to help her. He thought about hitting her, but tightened his hold and kept swimming. The river's current, practically invisible from the deck of the ship, now showed its strength, pushing them downstream. Halfway to shore, the woman still struggled and Raston felt his strength waning. He began to doubt whether he could make it, doubting he had enough energy left. With his bad leg, he had never been a strong swimmer. Why should he risk his life to save this woman who was fighting him? Just as he was about to let her go, she stopped struggling. Now he was alarmed. Calling up energy he wasn't sure he had, Raston again started swimming.

When he was finally close enough to the riverbank to touch bottom, he raised the woman's head. She looked unconscious. Two of the men standing on the bank jumped in to help and lifted the woman out of the water. A third reached for Raston's hand and pulled him onto the shore. He sat on the ground, completely spent. After several minutes, his energy began to return. He raised his head slightly and watched two men lay the woman with the missing arm at the edge of the brush a few feet from the river's edge.

"My God, man, what on earth happened out there?" The man who had pulled Raston onto the riverbank was standing over him. His question caused Raston to look out over the river. The two halves of what was once the *Prince Nathan* had sunk to the river bottom. Its splintered remnants protruding from the surface like monstrous tombstones. "It was the boilers. The starboard boiler went first."

"I thought I heard 'em go. First one, then the other. God, what a noise. I ain't never heard nothin' like it. What caused it, ya think?"

"Too hot. Should never have happened," Raston replied forlornly, mesmerized by the sight of the wreckage. In the foreground another crew member was wading to the bank. With a start Raston realized there were people still struggling to escape the river. He labored to get on his feet. "I have to get back out there.

There are people, passengers, that need help."

"That they do, but there's help comin'. Boats. Pretty soon there'll be plenty of help. Sooner'n you could ever swim out there. Better you stay put."

Raston stared back at the wreckage. Among the field of debris that surrounded the remaining parts of the steamboat, he could see people still struggling toward shore, clinging to boxes and barrels, anything to stay afloat. As he watched helplessly, two small boats arrived, men pulling hard on the oars. Immediately they began pulling people from the water. In the distance more boats were approaching from the direction of Bruders Landing. Nearby on the riverbank the crew members and passengers who had managed to swim to shore lay on the ground, some dazed, some still with their chests heaving.

"Those boats have to hurry," Raston exclaimed. "There're people drowning out there!"

"Don't you worry. They's ahurryin'. A man can only pull on those oars so fast for so long against that current. I'm afeared the good Lord's gonna receive some extra people today."

The man's words struck Raston like a blow to the chest. He had to do something. Standing quickly, he ran to the riverbank.

"C'mon!" he yelled to the man. "Let's help them on shore."

Raston waded into the water neck-deep and grabbed the arms of a person thrashing through the water. When he had him close to the bank, the other man reached out and pulled him up. Immediately Raston waded back in to help someone else. Together they pulled in five people before Raston grasped the first dead person. The limp arm and lack of resistance was his first inkling that he held a lifeless body. He had never felt a dead person before. There was no feeling of alarm or revulsion, no particular feeling at all. It simply seemed necessary. He pulled the body through the water face down. He expected the man on shore to help as before, but when Raston pushed the body toward him, the man leaped back to avoid it.

"I ain't touchin' no dead man," he yelled.

"All right, I'll do it." Raston let the body float against the bank, then reached under with his arms and rolled the dead man onto the shore. The man was on his back, face-up, except there was no longer a face. All the flesh had been ripped from the front of the man's head. With no lids to cover them, the eyes stared vacantly at the sky overhead.

Raston's former helper gazed at the body from several feet away. "Holy Mother of God!" the man said weakly and walked away rapidly, his hand pressed against his mouth.

Raston stared back down at the dead man. Sympathy and remorse welled inside him. After a few moments, he was aware of a person at his side, staring quietly down at the body.

"I'm sorry, but I'm afraid there will be several more," the newcomer said softly.

Raston turned to look at him. The man was noticeably short and slender, dressed all in black except for a high starched white collar. A round-brimmed black hat like a short stove pipe sat squarely on his head as if placed there to top him off. Longish gray hair protruded from under his hat almost to his collar, matching the neatly trimmed gray beard that outlined a gentle face lined with wrinkles. A round stomach strained the middle buttons of his black jacket as if he had swallowed a large ball. The man's dress, his total appearance, seemed so strangely out of place among the chaos on the riverbank, Raston thought he might be hallucinating.

"I take it you are a member of the *Prince Nathan's* crew," the man said, looking kindly at Raston. "My name is Harman Hanzfig. What is yours, if you don't mind?" The man extended his hand to Raston. He spoke with a German accent, reminding Raston of the way people talked in Pennsylvania.

"Uh, Raston. Raston Bruhl." Raston took the man's hand and rose to his feet.

"Ah, Raston Bruhl. Interesting name. German, like mine. I take it you are surprised by my clothes. Let me explain. You see, I am a mortician, undertaker, if you will. Actually, the only mortician in Bruders

Landing at present. People have certain expectations of those who do what I do, so I wear what I wear."

"Sorry. I shouldn't have stared. I'm just . . ."

"No matter. I came to help. Maybe we can help together for a while. That man there. I know it's hard to tell given his injury, but did you know him?" Hanzfig asked, sounding energetic and businesslike.

Raston made himself look more closely at the man's damaged face, then at his wrecked body. "It's probably Silas Rashid. He is . . . was the engineer. I couldn't tell until I saw that tattoo on his arm." He pointed to a large image of a sea serpent on the lifeless forearm. "I remember it."

"Good. That's a start. What we have to do as bodies are found is to collect them in a private place and identify those we can. There's a little clearing in the woods over there at the foot of the bluff where I've got my wagon and team. That will do for now. We can just lay them in the grass until I can take them into town. Will you help?"

"Yeah. Sure, Mr. Hanzfig. I guess so," Raston replied numbly, not at all sure he could.

"All right. Good. I'm going to need you. Now let's pick up Mr. Rashid and take him back to the clearing. I have a device over here that will help."

Hanzfig walked into the trees and returned with a gray canvas stretcher. He unrolled it beside the dead man.

"All right, Raston, let's lift him on."

Hanzfig bent down over the dead man's head and reached under his shoulders, motioning Raston to take his feet. Together they lifted the body onto the stretcher. Facing away from the body, the mortician picked up his end and led them into the woods. After walking several yards through the undergrowth, they arrived at the clearing. At the far end stood a team of two black horses attached to a dark carriage with a flat bed in the rear. The horses were chewing noisily on the grass that grew tall at the clearing's edge.

"Put him down here, Raston," Hanzfig instructed, pointing to a shady area by the trees. "The shade will keep him cooler. It may be a while before we can get him on ice."

They laid the body down gently on the grass. Hanzfig straightened the dead man's arms by his side and pushed his feet together. Then he stood back up looking at Raston. "That was good work you just did, Raston. Not everyone can handle the dead like that, especially when a body has been damaged like this one. Now let's get back to the river. There's more to do this day."

Activity along the river had increased as more of the crew and passengers had made it to shore. Most were suffering from shock and exhaustion, some sitting, some lying, gasping for breath or crying. Many had injuries and lay on the ground moaning. The townspeople had begun to arrive in force, some to rescue, some to help and some to satisfy a morbid curiosity. Many had started to tend the survivors. Raston studied the faces of each person with wet clothes. There were two crew members that Raston called friends, both men close to his age, Tim Gallante and Claude Munson. He wanted to find them.

"Raston, let's get farther down the river," the mortician directed. "There won't be anyone else coming ashore here. By now the current will have taken them all further downstream."

Belying his age and physical appearance, Hanzfig plunged vigorously through the brush and young trees that grew in thick patches along the bank. Raston had to walk quickly to keep up. They hadn't gone far before Hanzfig stopped, peering down at the water's edge. Raston followed his gaze. A face surrounded by a spray of red hair bobbed up and down against a log, moving with the waves. It belonged to a woman, one of the passengers, Raston remembered seeing her board. The glazed green eyes stared lifelessly, water spilling over them like a pool of tears. Her clothes held the rest of her body submerged.

"She must have been a passenger. Do you recognize her?"

"Yeah. I think she boarded a few days ago at Hannibal, Mr. Hanzfig."

"Unlucky for her. Come now. Let's get her out of

74

the water and back to our forest morgue." Hanzfig stepped over the log into the water, sinking ankle deep into mud. As he readied himself to pick the woman up, he looked for Raston.

Still on the riverbank, Raston was gazing intently at the woman's face, trying to absorb the reality of her death. He was grateful that the mortician didn't rush him.

"The important thing to remember, Raston, is that the dead need taking care of just like the living. Especially at a time like this. There will be plenty of those who will care for the ones who survive, but there will be only us who take care of the dead. It's a solemn duty that few people are willing to perform."

"I'm willing, Mr. Hanzfig," Raston answered firmly. This was the second dead person he had confronted in a span of minutes and there would be more. He was sure he could handle it as well as most.

"You're a good boy, Raston. Now let's get her out."

As bodies were found, the rescuers, horrified by the mutilation, called for Hanzfig. With Raston at his side, he dutifully responded, sometimes on foot and sometimes by boat, gathering the ruined remains. As the bodies and parts of bodies were laid by the trees, the mortician carefully arranged them, pushing bulging organs and intestines into torsos and matching limbs with bodies. Raston meanwhile undertook to identify all those he could. Unflinchingly he examined even the worst of them, attempting to find some clue as to who they had been. In the course of the next several hours, the population of Hanzfig's morgue grew to twenty-one. Seven had suffered the fate of the first woman they found: drowning. From their appearance, most of the others were victims of the explosions, crushed by the force of the blast or torn by shrapnel from the iron boilers. A few looked uninjured, their lungs burned out by the super-heated steam. Nine were missing limbs, including the woman Raston had pulled to shore. One was merely a torso, its limbs and head torn off by the blast.

Late in the day Raston rested on a fallen tree in the forest morgue, waiting for another call. Visions of what he had seen in the past few hours flashed through his mind. He pressed his eyelids tight together, trying to force them away. His exhaustion was a godsend, numbing his mind. Bodies ringed the edge of the clearing covered by blankets. At least fourteen passengers and six crew members were still not accounted for, including Raston's two friends and the pilot, Evan Musser. He shuddered to think that one of them, or maybe all three, might lay within a few feet of where he was sitting, bodies that were impossible to recognize. For the first time that day he felt the horror of what had happened closing in. He had warned Musser about the boilers, which had only infuriated him. Now people had died, a lot of people. Maybe his two friends. And maybe the pilot had paid for it with his life.

Pushing aside branches with a flourish, Hanzfig entered the clearing, breaking the dark spell that embraced Raston.

"They are going to call off the search for the night, Raston. Will you help me load these people on my wagon? I pulled it as close as I could. We have to get them on ice soon or they'll start to spoil."

"Sure, I'll help." Raston forced himself to stand.

"After we get them back and unloaded, I want you to stay at our house. We've an extra bed and my wife will have supper for us. We've done uncommon work here today. You surely have earned my gratitude."

It was the first time Raston had thought about where he would go now that his home lay in pieces at the bottom of the Mississippi River.

"Thank you, Mr. Hanzfig. I'd be right pleased to accept your hospitality."

As they drove the wagon and team toward Bruders Landing with the victims carefully loaded and tied down in the rear, Hanzfig continued to praise Raston for his work. "My boy, no one I've met in many a year could deal so comfortably with the dead as you did today, especially ones who were killed so cruelly. You worked beyond the capability of most men, let me tell you. I haven't met many whose sensibilities could stand what yours did. You have a knack for sure. It's important work caring for those people and a good business as well, I might add. I'll sure need your help until this is finished. After that there's a job for you if you want it."

"I'll help as long as it takes, Mr. Hanzfig." Raston thought again about his two friends and the pilot who had once encouraged him. "After that, well, I'll have to see. I've been trying to get a place as a cub with a river pilot for over three years now, but . . . ." Raston swallowed hard. "Anyway I'm much obliged for your offer."

They talked little during the rest of the ride to Bruders Landing. Raston sat in silence as the events of the day raced through his mind like a nightmarish parade. For the past several hours he had felt like a spectator, observing a horrible event unfolding before his eyes. At times he had felt sure he was asleep, experiencing a horrible nightmare while he slept in his hammock aboard the *Prince Nathan*. Only it wasn't a nightmare. He was sitting high on a wagon he had helped load with twenty-one broken bodies stacked in piles and tied down with ropes like sides of beef. He felt the tears start to come. Hanzfig put his arm around his shoulders.

The road into Bruders Landing was little more than a dirt path along the river filled with ruts that became mud pits with every rain. A low dirt levee bridged by plank walkways every twenty or thirty yards ran along the river side. Between the river and the levee was a mud plain dotted with weeds. At the water's edge were the steamboats, sitting quiet and still in the mist like enormous apparitions.

On the opposite side of the the road were merchants' shops, every one closed and dark, and several taverns, each glowing with lights and voices.

Hanzfig turned the horses into an opening between the shops onto a narrow road. Here the storefronts became sparse, giving way to small houses and cabins. He brought the horses to a halt in front of a two-story building. A sign hung out from the front door.

In the dim moonlight, Raston could make out one word: UNDERTAKER. Through one of the second-story windows, he could see lantern light and someone moving about.

"Climb down now, young man. Stretch your legs a bit. I'll need a hand getting these people on the ice under my shop."

They worked over an hour carrying the victims down to a cellar where blocks of ice cut from the river during winter were stored. When they were finished, Hanzfig led Raston to the second-floor living quarters he and his wife shared. A small, efficient woman, Mrs. Hanzfig greeted him warmly with a surprisingly firm handshake. On the table in the center of the room, she had laid a generous meal of thick bacon, green beans, mashed potatoes and biscuits. As soon as he saw it, Raston discovered how hungry he was.

Often with his mouth full, Raston told as best he could what had occurred on the steamboat. When at last he finished eating, Mrs. Hanzfig insisted he go straight to bed. With a candle she led him down a narrow hallway to a small room at the rear of the building which contained a feather bed. As soon as she closed the door, Raston fell into it without undressing.

Deep in a dreamless sleep Raston heard his name called. As he opened his eyes in the pitch black room, he was startled by a face lit by a dim candle looming over him.

"Time to rise, my good young man. We've more work to do this day, I'm afraid. Dress quickly and come for breakfast."

They left Bruders Landing in the wagon just as a sliver of sun appeared over the eastern hills. The searchers found four more bodies that morning. One was Raston's friend, Claude Munson.

Late in the afternoon as Raston rested his back against a tree, a man he didn't recognize approached Hanzfig who was leading the horses to the wagon.

"Hello, Mr. Hanzfig. Are you headin' back to Bruders Landing anytime soon?"

Hanzfig brought the horses to a halt. "Yes, we are, Hiram. There don't seem to be more victims nearby. We'll go back now and to see if any have been taken to town by the people searching further south."

"We thought we'd found another one for you out on Big Tow a few hours ago, but turns out he's alive.'

At the mention of Big Tow Island, Raston's interest was aroused.

"That's good news, but what in the world persuaded you to search Big Tow Island?" I didn't think you would *ever* set foot there."

"Um, we didn't exactly search it. We, uh, me and Herman and a couple others, were lookin' for bodies along the banks when we saw this body lyin' right out on the sand at the southern tip. So we headed over, figurin' to pick it up quick and skedaddle. But we get there and the guy's still alive."

"You picked him up, I assume."

"Sure we did. That's why I'm askin'. We're gonna keep searchin' the banks all the way back to Bruders Landing, but this guy won't go back on the river. So I'm wonderin' if you'd give him a lift ta town?"

"Of course. What's his name?"

"Bump, I think. Thaddeus Bump. When we found 'im, he was in shock or somethin'. Mumblin' all the time about old men he seen on the island. Considerin' all the stories about that place, we didn't waste no time in gettin' him off, let me tell ya."

With the mention of old men, Raston walked toward the man, not wanting to miss anything more that was said.

"Can he walk or should I drive the wagon where we can load him?"

"He's kinda wobbly but he's awalkin'."

"Good. Bring him over and we'll get underway."

As they began hitching the horses to the wagon, Raston could no longer contain his curiosity: "Mr. Hanzfig, I hope you don't mind my asking, but as we were coming into Bruders Landing, the pilot talked about Big Tow, about strange old people and evil spirits that lived there. Do you think there's anything to it?"

"Well, now, I can't say for sure whether the Old Ones as they're called exist or not, but there are a lot of people in these parts think they do."

As they talked, a pale, disheveled man ambled through the trees toward them. His arms and face were lined with scratches.

"Maybe, just maybe, Raston, we're about to find out." Hanzfig turned to the man. "Mr. Bump?"

"Yes, that's me." The voice was low, barely audible. His eyes moved rapidly from side to side as if expecting some surprise.

Raston recognized him from the *Prince Nathan* but said nothing.

"Good. Come with us now. We'll get you settled in town so you can get some rest. I can offer you a seat up front with us or you can lay down in the back if that will feel better. But I should warn that you'll have company. There are four others already there who weren't so fortunate as you."

"Hmm, I'll try the seat."

Raston and Hanzfig helped Thaddeus Bump onto the wagon, then sat on either side of him. Thaddeus sat hunched over, his elbows on his knees, rocking slightly. Harman Hanzfig released the brake and jiggled the reins. Immediately the team started at a walk.

"Are you all right there, Mr. Bump?"

There was a pause before he answered. "Yeah, just very tired."

"It's no wonder. Suffering through an explosion like that. Raston Bruhl here was part of the *Prince Nathan's* crew and has been helping me with the recovery."

Thaddeus turned warily toward Raston and gave a thin smile.

"Fortunately for Raston he made it to shore. He didn't have to experience Big Tow Island as you did. The men who found you said you spoke of seeing the Old Ones. May I ask if that is so?"

"Yes, I guess that's who I saw."

Raston saw Harman Hanzfig's eyes widen.

"Very interesting, Mr. Bump. I should tell you that stories about the Old Ones on Big Tow have been with us since the Indians occupied this land, but few people living claim to have actually seen them. And it's no wonder since it's rare that anyone goes there.

Legends have it that people who have gone to Big Tow Island and seen the Old Ones never return to tell about it. Apparently that's not true, at least not in your case. So you may have been quite fortunate."

"I guess I was."

"Do you mind telling us what you saw?"

"Some old men dressed funny, but I really don't want to talk about it now, all right?" Thaddeus' voice was weary.

"Very well, of course. I understand. Maybe we can talk later when you've rested." There was no mistaking the disappointment in Harman Hanzfig's voice.

"Yeah, maybe we can."

Hanzfig and Raston delivered Thaddeus Bump to the makeshift shelter for survivors in Bruders Landing. It was the last time they ever saw him.

Chapter Seven

The Closet

1948

By age seven Henry had become bored with his grandfather's den and decided it was time to find a new adventure. He began in what to him looked like a dark cavern right there on the first floor of the farmhouse—the den's closet. One Saturday when his grandparents had both gone outside to work in the garden, he armed himself with a flashlight he hoped wouldn't be missed, cautiously opened the closet door and stepped into the small room. When he closed the door so he wouldn't be caught, the darkness promptly overwhelmed him. The pang of fear he felt was unfamiliar, nearly causing him to run back outside. But his determination held him long enough to switch on the flashlight, and in its beam he saw a treasure-trove of old hunting and fishing gear. His fear of the dark was quickly forgotten.

He played the beam around the floor and wall, mesmerized by his new-found booty—two half-filled tackle boxes, several rods and reels with heavy, black line, a dented camp lantern, a mound of duck-hunting jackets with holes, shooting vests that had rips, worn rifle and shotgun cases, duck, goose and turkey decoys (some with missing heads), several metal ammunition boxes, one filled with marbles in a myriad of sizes and colors, even an old canvas wall tent with ropes and stakes. So much to examine. Henry was ecstatic.

He returned to the closet on every visit to his grandparents, unless Sheila was there. He didn't want to share his secret place with anyone, certainly not a girl. He liked turning the handles on the reels, listening to the tight metallic click and pretending he had landed a huge catfish. Several of the rods still had their bobbers and barbed hooks which Henry learned were needle-sharp after puncturing his thumb. He also liked the basket with the slotted lid his Grandpa called a creel. It had a curved shape with leather straps at each end and a buckle as if it should be worn around your neck. Henry thought it would be perfect for holding the snakes he would catch when he could explore outside.

The den closet occupied Henry the entire winter. But by early spring the things inside which had so excited him in the fall had become routine, and he began looking for a new adventure.

The closet at the end of the back hallway beckoned him next. It looked bigger than the den closet and, situated as it was in the back of the house, even more mysterious. One time when his grandfather was gone and his grandmother busy baking, he crept down the hallway to the closet. Pausing only briefly to look back toward the kitchen to see that all was clear, he opened the door and stepped in. Instantly he was struck by a powerful odor—mothballs, momentarily making him light-headed. He switched on the flashlight and steadied himself as he slowly became accustomed to the smell.

The closet was narrow. All he could see in front of him were boxes lining the walls and clothes hanging down the center. To explore the closet, he would have to crawl under the clothes. His nerve wavered momentarily and he considered waiting to ask Sheila to come with him. But that would mean letting someone—a girl—in on his secret. Besides, his curiosity was tormenting him as much as his poison ivy had last summer.

Deciding at least to go part way, he got down on his hands and knees and began to crawl under the clothes, shining his light from side to side as he went. Cardboard boxes lined the walls as far as he could see. Peering cautiously inside one, he found more clothes and the mothball odor became stronger. Not very exciting. Gaining confidence, he crawled on. After several more feet, he felt sure the end of the closet was near.

Pushing aside a heavy, wool coat that hung nearly to the floor, he came to an open space. Raising up on his knees, the flashlight's beam fell on a dusty wood cabinet with an intricate iron base sitting at the end of the closet. He had never seen anything like it. The beam highlighted intricate designs carved into the wood on its front and sides. On the top of the cabinet was a lid which sparked his curiosity. He had to find out what was inside. He looked on the lid for a handle without success, then ran his fingers around its edge, looking for a hold. He found one and pulled. The lid wouldn't budge. Suddenly his imagination ignited. What if there was something dangerous inside? Something awful no one was supposed to see? Could it be a coffin? It kind of looked like one, but it was so small. What if it's a baby's coffin? What if someone had killed it and hid the coffin way back in this closet so no one would find out? Frightened by the thought, he dropped back down to his knees and crawled for the door as fast as he could.

For days Henry's thoughts dwelled on the cabinet, but it was three weeks before his next visit to the farm. The occasion was the Gerdes monthly Sunday dinner, dutifully attended by both his parents and Sheila's. He expected her to be there but still was delighted and a little relieved when she arrived.

After eating second helpings of fried chicken and strawberry shortcake, Henry squirmed impatiently, half-listening while the adults talked endlessly about moisture levels in the soil and the chances of the Russians launching an atomic bomb attack. His mind was on the wood cabinet. What was it doing back there and what was in it? It was a mystery he had to solve, but he needed someone to help open the lid.

Across the table, Sheila was shifting in her chair. When she saw him looking, she rolled her eyes. Henry asked to be excused as politely as he knew how and slipped from his chair, signaling Sheila to follow with an impish smile on his face. She caught up with him as he stood by the back hall closet door.

"Henry, what are you doing?" Sheila demanded.

"Shh, we have to whisper."

"Why do we have to whisper?" she asked in a whisper.

"Because we're going to explore this closet and I don't want anyone to catch us."

"In the closet? I'm not going in that closet. It's dark and it's dirty and, besides, I've got good clothes on. So do you. Why do you want to go in there anyway?"

Henry began to think he had made a mistake in inviting her. All girls do is ask questions. But he needed her. "Because closets are gobs of fun to explore. They're full of neat stuff you can play with all you want and nobody tells you to stop. You'll see. Besides, they're not so dirty."

"You've gone in Grandma and Grandpa's closets before? Weren't you scared?" Sheila sounded impressed.

"Naw, but they're awfully dark when you close the door so I bring a flashlight. I think this closet's the biggest one. I went way back in a couple weeks ago, but I didn't finish exploring it." Henry hoped he sounded fearless.

"Gosh, Henry, what's in there?" Sheila began to show interest.

"There's a bunch of clothes hanging up in the front and a lot of cardboard boxes along the side. The ones I looked in just had more old clothes. But way in the back is this really strange wood cabinet. I tried to open the lid but I couldn't do it. It was too heavy. I think there must be something secret in it, something nobody's supposed to know about. Anyway, I thought if the two of us lifted, we could get the lid open and find out what's inside."

"What do you think's in it?" Sheila, beginning to sound excited.

"I don't know, but there could be a dead body in it. It's small, so maybe a dead baby somebody wanted to keep secret."

"Don't say stuff like that. There wouldn't be a dead body in Grandma and Grandpa's house."

"If you're so sure, come on and help me look."

"All right, you've got your flashlight, so I'll go. But I better not get too dirty."

As soon as he opened the door, Sheila scrunched up her nose and started to retreat. "Ick. I hate mothballs."

"It's not so bad when you get used to it. Just hold your nose."

"OK, but you're going to get it if it makes my clothes stink."

Henry led the way as they crawled on their hands and knees under the hanging clothes to the back of the deep closet. The prospect of opening the cabinet was as exciting as opening presents on Christmas morning. When he neared the end of the closet, he waited until Sheila was kneeling beside him. With a flourish he shined his light on the cabinet, proudly showing her his mysterious discovery.

"There, that's it, what do you think?" Henry whispered excitedly.

Sheila giggled.

Henry was irritated. "What's so funny?"

"Oh, nothing really."

"OK then, let's see if we can open it."

Together they put their hands under the front of the lid and pulled. As he strained, Henry felt the lid start to rise slowly and a heavy, dark object emerged. When they had the lid resting against the wall, Henry picked up his flashlight and shined it on the cabinet. Sitting on top was a black and chrome sewing machine covered in gold designs with wheels, levers and little rods protruding everywhere. He was crushed. This was his best discovery and Sheila knew what it was as soon as she saw the cabinet.

Utterly deflated, Henry still held his light on the

sewing machine when he noticed something bulky attached to its base. He moved closer. It was a canvas sack tied to one of the machine's pedestals. Henry squeezed it to see if he could tell what was inside. Two metal objects clinked dully together.

"Here, Sheila, hold the flashlight." The bag was tied to the pedestal by the drawstrings at its top. After some fumbling, Henry untied the knot and pulled the drawstrings open. When he reached inside, the coldness of a metal object startled him.

"Well, Henry. What's in there? Come on, tell me."

"Hold your horses. I'm trying to get it out." Henry could feel what it was. A gun, maybe a real one. His expedition might be a success after all. Gripping the barrel, he pulled it from the bag. The gun was bigger than he expected, and heavier, its dark blue surface flecked with rust. The old wooden grip was worn smooth as if it had been handled a great deal. His grandfather had let him aim a rifle and a shotgun, but Henry had never held a pistol before. It looked like a revolver the cowboys used in the westerns he sometimes went to on Saturday mornings. He had an urge to cock the hammer with his thumb to hear the clicks and watch the cylinder turn like they did.

"Wow, look at this! A gun just like in the movies," he exclaimed in a loud whisper.

"Gosh, is it real?"

"Yeah, I think so. Let's see."

Nervously Henry turned the revolver to look at the hole in the end of the barrel. It looked bigger around than the ones in his grandfather's deer rifles.

"Be careful, Henry, it might be loaded."

Henry gave a long-suffering sigh and looked past the end of the barrel into the holes in the cylinder. In the dim light he saw the tips of bullets pointed at him. Henry's muscles went limp and he nearly dropped the gun. "This thing really *is* loaded."

"Put it back, then. And be careful," Sheila whispered loudly.

"I will, I will. Don't worry!"

Henry laid the revolver on the sewing machine.

"There's something else in the bag, let's see what it is first." He reached his hand in again and pulled it out. "Look!"

"What is . . . oh, it's a key, a big key."

"Yeah. And I bet it's to something important or it wouldn't be hidden in here."

"It sure looks important." Sheila held it between her two fingers. "I've never seen a key this big before, have you?"

"In the westerns, you know, when the sheriff locks the crooks in their cells. I wonder what it's to. Can you think of any door with a lock this would fit? I sure can't."

"Me either. Why do you suppose it was hidden in the sewing machine with that gun?"

They both stared silently at the key and gun for a moment, trying to think of an answer. Finally Sheila spoke. "I think there's something pretty creepy about this we're not supposed to know. Grandma and Grandpa better not find out we opened that bag."

"They won't; don't worry. But I'd sure like to find out what that key fits. I mean, who knows what it might be. Maybe a treasure room . . . or a secret burial place." Henry discovered he had given himself the chills.

"Yeah! Let's look together, OK?"

"Sure, you can come with me, but you know that door's not on the first or second floor or we'd have seen it, so we'll have to look on the third floor, or in the cellar," Henry said, trying to sound scary, hoping he would also give the chills to Sheila.

"But we're not supposed to go there."

"We're not supposed to be in *here* either. How do you think I get to explore these places? In secret, that's how."

"Well, smarty-pants, have *you* ever gone to the cellar or the third floor?"

"No, not yet, but I will. What about you?"

"Well, I might. But let's get out of here before they find us."

Very carefully, Henry placed the revolver and key back in the bag and retied it to the sewing machine.

Chapter Eight

The Mayor's Wife

1874

Raston Bruhl paused in his walk to Bruders Landing's Town Hall, staring wistfully at the four dusty-white steamboats tied side by side along the riverbank. The *Rob Roy* and the *Davenport*, both side-wheelers, were loading barrels of salt pork, smoked hams and lard. The *J. H. Johnson*, another side-wheeler, was loading passengers while the *S. S. Thorp*, a stern-wheeler, sat unattended. Before the railroad came, the riverbank would be crowded with steamboats, a half-dozen or more anchored out in the river, waiting for a place to tie up. There were times when he had taken body after body off those boats, people killed by cholera, the deadly disease that stalked boats coming from New Orleans. Cholera had swept through Bruders Landing as well, taking nearly two hundred people a few years after he came, and over a hundred just the year before. Like the Civil War, cholera epidemics had brought him far more business than he needed.

The afternoon was unusually warm for April. A bright sun beat down on Raston's navy-blue serge jacket, making it feel as if a hot iron was resting on his shoulders. Beads of sweat formed on his face, pooled, then streamed down his neck, wetting the top of his stiffly starched collar. He unfastened the four front buttons of the jacket and took off his black, wide-brimmed hat. It was as casual as Raston ever allowed himself to be in public. He had become the town's busiest undertaker, in no small part due to the dignified and austere image he inherited from his predecessor, Harman Hanzfig.

As often happened when he walked alone by the river, the memory of the wreck *Prince Nathan's* explosion arose vividly in his mind. Although it had been nearly thirty years, Raston could remember it as if it happened yesterday. The thought of how it had changed his life caused his head to twitch, as it did these days whenever he concentrated.

Raston stayed in Bruders Landing after the tragedy, working for Harman Hanzfig until he was killed in 1859, crushed when the hearse he was driving turned over as he drove the team down a steep road in the town cemetery. Raston took over the business but gave it his own name: Bruhl's Mortuary. Business was good from the start, then got even better during the war as dozens of local boys began returning home in Army boxes. To handle his growing business, Raston hired a helper and started looking for a larger building. It was then that Wilhelm Storzbach turned up dead in the river.

Strange affair, Raston mused. Big Willie, as they called him, was playing poker on one of his steamboats anchored on the east side of Big Tow Island. The cards had been bad for him all night. Big Willie, who had a temper that was legendary, grew more and more angry, drinking more and more of his whiskey. The last straw was when his full house was beaten by four Jacks. He promptly overturned the card table and rushed out of the room, bellowing and screaming, tripped on a water bucket and somersaulted over the railing. The other players heard the splash, but the night was black as ink and no one could see him in the water. He didn't answer the crew's shouts, but they thought they heard swimming toward Big Tow so the crew lowered a boat and rowed to the island. They found footprints that showed he had waded ashore, and footprints showing he had run back into the river. It was nearly a week later that a fisherman found Big Willie tangled in his net just north of Bruders Landing and brought him to Bruhl's Mortuary in the back of a wagon. No one could figure out for sure why he ran off the island into the river that night. Some said he was just drunk as a skunk. Others believe he was running for his life from the Old Ones.

After he buried him, Raston bought Wilhelm Storzbach's mansion and turned the first floor into his mortuary. But business wasn't his only reason for the purchase. Raston had taken a fancy to a young woman in town, Sophia Thye, and was planning to propose as soon as he got his nerve up. Nearly a year later he did. After the wedding they moved onto the second and third floors of the big house and the children started coming.

Raston was proud to own the Storzbach place but maintaining it proved expensive. Also he and Sophia now had four children to raise. The thought of all those expenses brought an end to his daydreaming.

He wanted to be on time for his meeting with the mayor, Herman Goelzer. The town's old high school was bursting at the seams with students, and there were more to come with the railroad. Bruders Landing needed a new school building and the mayor's wife, Amanda, had a location firmly in mind. And when Amanda had her mind set, the mayor never disagreed. The place she had chosen was a grassy field on a hill overlooking the town and the Mississippi River beyond. The problem was that the field was already occupied by the town cemetery.

Three days earlier, Mayor Goelzer had asked Raston to figure what the cost would be to move the bodies from the town to the site for a cemetery Amanda had chosen. Raston wasted no time in visiting her choice, a virgin acreage along the river bluffs north of town. He had been there before, but for a different purpose: to view the burial mounds that lined the bluff's crown. It was rough, uncleared land crossed by streams which had carved deep ravines through the limestone. Casting shade over the ravines were scores of majestic walnut and oak trees. On the patches of level ground, wispy prairie grasses and brilliant wild flowers were in abundance. All along its eastern edge were the burial mounds. Raston was well aware that the mounds and the ravines would be troublesome for laying out grave sites, and the limestone just below the surface would make hard work for his grave diggers. But with the undergrowth cut and the trees thinned, he had to admit it would be an unusually beautiful spot. Amanda had made a fine choice, inspired even. Whatever difficulty the terrain presented could be overcome, but at a price.

Raston stared at the town hall from front to back as he had so many times, shaking his head in disgust as always. It was constructed of wood in the shape of a schoolhouse but without a belfry or any other architectural feature. He thought it looked like a bloated barn. The town fathers had certainly got what they wanted, he muttered—cheap space. Now their sons and daughters and all the rest of us have to live with it. Why do only the good buildings have fires? He said a quick prayer for his house.

After climbing the stairs to the front entrance, Raston took off his hat and rested for a moment, catching his breath. Steps had become more of a problem lately as he lost more and more strength in his bad leg.

As he entered the mayor's office, he wasn't surprised to see Amanda Goelzer seated beside his desk. Herman Goelzer didn't do much as mayor that his wife didn't instigate. Raston knew them both well, well enough to know the town was fortunate to have Herman Goelzer married to someone like Amanda. The mayor was a short, round man, red-faced, always breathing hard as if every movement was an effort. Taller than her husband by nearly a head, Amanda Goelzer was slender and attractive, with large brown eyes she focused so intently few could maintain eye contact with her.

"Raston, m'boy, glad you came by. Good to see you," Mayor Goelzer said in a booming voice, circling the desk with his hand extended. Herman Goelzer had a habit of calling everyone "boy", something Raston particularly disliked. Amanda would take over from here, Raston thought as he shook his hand.

"Hello, Raston. I'm so glad you were able to come. Please sit down," Amanda Goelzer said, giving him a warm, efficient smile. "I saw Sophia last night at church but we missed you."

"Yes, well, I was sorry to miss the dinner, but I had work to do that couldn't wait, if you catch my meaning."

Raston sat down in one of the wooden chairs facing the desk.

"Oh, I do. You must have to deal with many difficult situations, with the families and all, I suppose," she added, "but you're so good with those things, which is why we're anxious to talk to you."

"Yeah, we sure got us some problems with the new school," Mayor Goelzer said in an exasperated tone, "putting it right where the cemetery is."

"What Herman means is that we're concerned for the families of the people buried up there." Amanda Goelzer spoke in a calm voice, neutralizing her husband's exasperation, "Still, some things have to get done if we're going to have progress in this town. What we need is someone to relocate those poor souls, someone their families have confidence in, someone who knows how to talk to them if they get distressed."

I'll bet you do, Raston thought, otherwise Herman is serving his last term as mayor. "I understand completely," he said.

"Fine, then. So shall we get down to business? I take it you've been out Bluff Road to look at the site for the new cemetery."

"Yes, yesterday morning. You picked a lovely place. And the view out over the river and Big Tow Island is very attractive, but it presents problems."

"Oh? And what are those?" she asked, much too innocently.

"Well, for one thing it needs to be cleared."

"Yep, we know that. We're already talkin' to the Gobles about that," the mayor interjected.

"Good. And you know the property contains several deep ravines. If you want to use the land well, you'll have to put a large number of graves along the sides and hope they don't wash out. Then near the bluffs, the rock is close to the surface, which makes tough work for my diggers. Could be a lot of the land just won't be usable for graves at all. We just won't be able to dig into it."

"What you're saying is that you'll have to increase the pay for your diggers," the mayor said.

"Yes, that, too. It'll take them a lot more time and effort than in the old cemetery."

"Well, then, what do you think it will cost to move those people from the old cemetery, Raston?" Amanda Goelzer asked. "I assume you've done some thinking about it?"

"Yes, I've done some figuring. If the space is cleared and ready where it's not solid rock, I could move each body for eight dollars. If there's a stone grave marker to move, it would be two dollars more."

Mayor Goelzer scribbled on a sheet of paper. "Let's see, the city records show 937 graves out there, so . . ."

"Pardon me, Mayor, but more people are buried than the records show. Families have been known to bury their dead without getting a permit from the town when they couldn't afford the fee. This happened often during the cholera epidemics when families lost several members and simply couldn't pay for them all."

"Well, we wouldn't want anyone left behind, would we?" Amanda Goelzer said with a smile. "We don't want any surprises for the people digging the foundation for the new school. But I think eight dollars is a little high, don't you? We'd be grateful if you could lower it some. Then we wouldn't need to go looking for anyone else."

Raston could feel his profit melting away. "All right, I'll do it for seven, but that's as low as I can go. I don't know what I'm going to have to pay to keep diggers when they get a taste of what they're in for."

"Oh, you'll do fine at six-fifty, Raston. Just fine," she said warmly, finality in her voice.

"I'll consider it." Raston knew he was being told to take it or leave it. He would take it but he wasn't ready to give them the satisfaction just yet. "But there is another thing that troubles me. You know there are Indian burial mounds at that site."

"Yes, we know. But I don't see any problem. It

seems to us that those mounds make it an especially appropriate place for our new cemetery. If they're in the way, you can always level them," Amanda Goelzer responded.

"A lot of people think disturbing those mounds is bad luck. Some even talk about curses." Raston was well aware that it was common for early settlers to bury their dead among the Indian burial mounds. But leveling the mounds, a practice followed by some farmers, disturbed him.

"I sure hope *you* don't hold any of those notions, Raston," the mayor commented. "I hear a lotta farmers just plow 'em under."

"I wouldn't recommend it."

"It doesn't seem to me that digging up some old Indian bones is any different than digging up bodies in our town cemetery," Amanda Goelzer said.

"Maybe not, but I won't touch those mounds."

"Very well, if you're worried about curses." Her voice dripped with disdain. "You do the work at our price and you can lay out the grave sites any way you want. Just be sure there are enough."

Chapter Nine

The Upper Floor

1948

Henry could hardly wait to begin looking for a door with a lock the large key would fit, but two Saturdays came and went before his mother agreed to take him to the farm. Then it was a day when Sheila had to go shopping with her mother. But Henry was determined. He would find the lock with or without Sheila.

Henry had been in the cellar only twice, both times with his grandmother. The first time he had ventured down by himself when she was washing clothes. She had been angry and made him go back upstairs. The other time had also been brief, his grandmother holding his hand while she fetched a jar of tomatoes from a storage closet. He remembered what it was like: dirt floor, musty smell, no windows, dim light, darkness at both ends. A place far more forbidding than the closets.

On the other hand, he had never seen the third floor. He knew no one had used it since his great-grandparents died after hearing his mother and grandparents talk about them more than once. His great-grandmother, whom his mother described as "not quite right", disappeared from the house sometime in the 1890s and was never found. His grandfather said she must have wandered down the bluff to the river and drowned. His great-grandfather shot himself, accidentally they said, a few years later.

The lock had to be for a door in the cellar or the third floor, of that he was sure. The fact that he would have light from windows on the third floor made his decision. This Saturday *he* would search there. The cellar could wait for Sheila.

Henry's mother was late to a beauty appointment and prepared to drive away as soon as she had given him her final instructions: remember the rules about where he could play, don't give his grandmother any trouble, look for her by 5:00, say hello to Grandma and Grandpa. Henry hoped she didn't see him rolling his eyes. As soon as she stopped to kiss him on the forehead, he rushed from the car.

"Hi, Grandma," he shouted as he burst through the kitchen door and threw his winter coat on a chair.

Emma Gerdes turned from her ironing board, the iron still in her hand, and produced a warm, welcoming smile. "Henry, I'm so glad you came. I just love it when your mother brings you. She's always so busy."

"I wanted to come, Grandma. It gets pretty boring at home sometimes. Sheila and I planned to play today, but Aunt Alice made her go shopping."

"I know, I know, Henry. But you'll find plenty to do, like always. Besides, your Aunt Alice said they might stop by later if they get finished in time."

"They never finish early. Aunt Alice always wants to shop until the stores close, and they stay open late on Saturdays."

"I know, dear, that's the way she is. It's fun for her. Anyway, you're here, so you go right ahead and enjoy yourself. Grandpa's out in the barn working on the tractor. Go on out with him if you want. I've got to finish all this ironing but as soon as I'm done, I'll need some help baking cookies. How does that sound?"

"Great, Grandma, great! I'll just go in the living room and listen to the radio and read 'til you're ready."

"All right, I'll be done in a little while."

He strolled to the living room as nonchalantly as he could and turned on the Zenith console radio. It seemed to take forever to warm up. When a station finally came on, he dashed for the stairs. As soon as he reached the second floor, he walked as quietly as he could to the door that led to the third floor. It opened stiffly with a slight squeak. He stood for a moment staring up the narrow staircase. It was longer and darker than he expected. Specks of dust hung undisturbed in the light coming from above. I'll bet no one's been up there for a long time, Henry thought to himself, raising goosebumps on his arms. A light switch was on the wall to his left. He pushed the button, which gave a sharp click, and a bulb hanging from a cord high overhead came on, shedding a weak light. He took a deep breath like a swimmer about to plunge into the deep end and started up the stairs.

The first step creaked under his weight, the shrill sound echoing faintly up and down the staircase. He stopped and listened for his grandmother, half-expecting and half-hoping to hear her calling after him. There was no voice from below. He took a second step. Another creak, but he continued to climb, stepping close to the wall in an attempt to quiet his steps. When he reached the top, he found himself looking down a long, barren hallway. Everything was completely still. The air felt cold and he wished he had worn his coat. Through the dusty light he saw several doors, two on each side of the hallway and one facing him at the end where the light faded to dark gray. All the doors were closed and he began to fear that one of them would suddenly open. The quiet and emptiness of the hallway was somehow more frightening than the closets he had explored. He had an urge to retreat back downstairs to wait for a day when Sheila could come with him. No, he told himself, he couldn't be chicken, he had to look at the locks on those doors.

The boards in the hallway floor seemed to moan as Henry forced himself to walk to the first door on the right. Leaning over slightly, he peered at the keyhole under the doorknob. It looked ordinary. Probably works with a skeleton key, he thought. Was there *another* door inside the room, he wondered? He put his hand cautiously around the doorknob and turned. There was a low, grating sound that made him stop. When he heard nothing, he turned the knob further. Then he hesitated. What if the body of his great-grandmother was in the room? He told himself this was crazy and pushed on the door. It was stuck. That was enough for one door, he told himself, and moved to the next. It had an identical doorknob and keyhole. When he tried to turn the knob, it wouldn't budge, so he moved to the door at the end of the hall. The keyhole was the same, as was the keyhole in the door next to it. He wasn't able to turn either doorknob.

Finally he reached the last door. A thin layer of perspiration covered his body despite the cool air. The keyhole was identical to all the others. He made a perfunctory attempt to turn the knob and was surprised to find it turned easily. The door opened part way with a low squeal revealing a bedroom bright with sunlight streaming through two dust-coated windows across from the door. Two single beds sat against one wall and a tall armoire against the other. A straight chair was located by one window and a rocking chair by the other. The sunlight highlighted the thick, gray film of dust that covered everything. Spider webs hung from the window frames and the corners around the ceiling.

Through the dusty windows Henry could see tree limbs. Emboldened by the sunlight and the sight of the trees, he crossed the room to the window. At this height he could nearly see over the sycamore tree that stood at the side of the house. He looked through its leafless branches at the farm buildings and the fields and the timber beyond. It was exciting to see the farm from this height. He pressed his nose against the glass, stretched out his arms and pretended he could fly. Squinting his eyes against the sun, he picked out things he recognized: the barn, the chicken coop, the storage sheds. Beyond the farmyard he could see a pasture. In places where the snow had melted, cattle grazed on the remnants of last summer's grass. Farther on was the creek with ice still lining its edges, then another field and, in the distance, the timber at the edge of the bluff.

Henry stared out the window for several minutes, fascinated by the view. Then he made up a goal for himself: to identify everything he could see. He roamed across the landscape with his eyes, gradually looking farther from the house, proud that he could recognize everything, until his eyes fell on a pile of rocks at the side of the hill by the creek. He looked closer. It wasn't just a rock pile, it was some kind of structure. It was hard for him to make out, but it looked like it might have an entrance big enough for a person. But why would it lead into the hill? Could it have a door with a heavy lock? Or was it a cave? He tried to see into the opening, but a rock wall had been built where the opening should have been. Had the entrance had been sealed up? Where had it led? A tingle of excitement ran over his skin.

Suddenly Henry realized he had lost track of the time. His grandmother could be looking for him right now. Quickly he walked back into the hallway and crept down the two flights of stairs. From the kitchen he could hear the ironing board groan as his grandmother worked. Henry slid into a chair by the radio, changed the station from a farm report to the Lone Ranger and opened a Captain Marvel comic book. As he stared absently at the color pictures, he imagined discovering a huge underground cavern where an ancient tribe of Indians still lived.

Chapter Ten

The Sheriff

1949

Herbert Siefken wrote nearly a hundred inquiries to sheriffs and police departments in towns all through the Midwest. Few responded. He wondered if publicity about the liquor store shooting had reached all those places, and began to worry that it had. As his discouragement deepened, a letter arrived from the sheriff of Eagle County, Iowa. He would consider Herbert for a deputy job if he was willing to come for an interview at his own expense.

Herbert wasted no time consulting a map. The county seat of Eagle County was Bruders Landing in southeast Iowa, on a bend in the Mississippi River. While he remembered learning to spell its name in a sing-songy way in grade school, Herbert had never seen the river. He was intrigued.

With his policeman's instinct for background, he drove seven hours to Bruders Landing the day before the interview. He had been in small towns many times, but had never looked at one from the point of view he did now. Herbert's first impression came as he crossed the river bridge. Slowing his aging Hudson, he saw a large cluster of brick buildings, all well-dressed in stately facades, nestled in a wide valley through the steep bluffs. The downtown was surrounded by hills with buildings and houses clinging to their sides. Sprinkled throughout were churches, their spear-like steeples jutting upward creating a jagged skyline. He drove at random through the streets, marveling at the steepness of the hills after the flatlands of Chicago and western Illinois. The town seemed a bit frayed at the edges but with a definite old-world charm.

Late in the afternoon, Herbert checked into the Bruders Landing Hotel, a surprisingly large building in the center of the downtown. After putting his bag in a room with a view over the river, he went to the cocktail lounge for a beer. The room was dark but he could see the walls were knotty pine. An impressive mahogany bar occupied one entire end of the lounge with a series of tables around a small dance area at the other. Nondescript linoleum that had begun to curl at its edges covered the floor. The air was cool with a familiar smell of stale cigarette smoke and beer. A Wurlitzer juke box next to the dance floor played Duke Ellington's *Black and Tan Fantasy*. Small groups of people dressed for business sat at tables, engrossed in conversation. The room had sights and sounds and smells of bars all over Chicago's South Side. Satisfied, he took an open stool at the bar.

The bartender, a heavy black man with striking gray hair, approached immediately. "What can I do you for?" His voice conveyed genuine friendliness and a trace of southern accent.

"Beer, please. Whatever you've got on tap."

As the bartender drew a Blatz beer, Herbert thought it was time to start his homework.

"Are you from here?" he asked when the bartender placed the frosty stein of beer in front of him.

"Mostly. Lived here nearly fifty years. Bruders Landing's a great little place. Never saw a reason to go anywhere else. Where you from, if you don't mind my askin'?"

"Don't mind a bit. Chicago. Lived there all my life."

"Great place, Chicago, but too big for me. Been

there once to see my cousin. Took the train. Saw the Cubs play at Wrigley, went to a couple blues bars. Man, those bars there never close. Had a great coupla days visitin', but I'll leave the livin' to you."

"You may be right about the living. It's not easy sometimes. And about the bars. They do close, at least they're supposed to."

"Yeah, like the bars across the river. Illinois closin' hours just kill the bar business in river towns. The only way a place like this can stay open even in a hotel is to serve hard liquor."

"You do? Isn't it illegal in Iowa?"

"Oh yeah, it's illegal as hell, 'cept in private clubs. But no bars on this side of the river could make it if they didn't. The sheriff, he helps us out. Long as we keep it out of sight and don't serve no drunks, he lets us alone."

Herbert was suspicious. "As simple as that? Nothing changes hands?"

"Yep, as simple as that. I ain't never seen no money sent his way."

Herbert didn't respond. Could it be true that the sheriff was protecting businesses just as a favor? It was puzzling.

His interview with Sheriff Jack Schoof had lasted all morning. Now the sheriff was ready for lunch. It was none too soon for Herbert. He liked the old sheriff well enough, but couldn't shake a nagging feeling that there was something important the man wasn't telling. And his vague talk about evil and Indian legends and burial mounds and people dying badly had left Herbert unsettled.

As they left the sheriff's office, the prospect of food brightened Herbert's outlook considerably. The sheriff was a regular at Bucher's diner on Front Street next to a Texaco station. It was only four blocks away, but the sheriff drove, parking at a curb painted yellow. The store-front diner was nearly full when they entered. A large fan near the back wall moved the air enough in the hot, smoke-filled room to make it bearable. It appeared that the sheriff knew everyone . He walked through the tables and down the counter shaking hands and slapping backs as if it were the last week before the election. He introduced Herbert to everyone close enough to shake his hand.

They took the only open table. Herbert sensed the sheriff virtually owned it, with seating by his invitation only. There were four chairs but the sheriff asked no one to join them.

"No need to look at the menu, Herb. I know everything on it and I can tell you what to try. A tenderloin. Something I bet you never get in Chicago."

"You're right about that. I saw it on a menu last night but I can't say I know what it is."

"Well, you're about to find out."

Herbert stopped himself from telling the sheriff he always ordered two sandwiches. When the tenderloin came, Herbert found himself staring at a huge sandwich with a thick, golden brown crust protruding over an inch all around the bun. The Sheriff unceremoniously reached over and lifted off the bun's top, then lathered a layer of catsup on the crust. After setting the bun back in place, he eyed Herbert expectantly. Herbert picked up the sandwich with two hands and took a large bite. To his relief it was tasty, and he was able to report to the sheriff that he liked it with a straight face.

While they ate, the sheriff recited the history of several customers, pointing out things Herbert was sure they would rather the sheriff didn't know. He talked rapidly and the names and faces became a blur, except for one. With the sheriff deep into a story about Bucher's owner, a tall, slender man with a decided stoop and unusually long white hair walked stiffly through the door. It was mid-summer, but his face had not a hint of color. Although he looked as if he could have been well into his seventies, there was a sense of strength in his movement. Herbert may have noted little more about him but for his eyes which gleamed from deep sockets so dark they looked as if they could have been painted with charcoal. Several customers nodded to the man as he came in but he sat at the counter by himself, speaking to no one.

"Excuse me, Sheriff," Herbert said, interrupting his story. "Who's the man with the white hair that just came in? The one sitting at the counter."

The sheriff looked in the direction of the white-haired man, catching his eye. They nodded to each other without smiling. Then the man turned toward Herbert with a penetrating stare. After a long minute he turned away. Herbert sensed the man played some important role in Bruders Landing, and not a pleasant one.

"That's Old Brinter, Boris Brinter. He's not real social."

"A lot of people seem to know him, though. Has he lived here long?"

"Yeah, a long time. He works at Bruhl's Mortuary. Does most of the embalming."

Oddly, Jack Schoof said no more about the man.

By the time they left Bucher's, the August sun had pushed the temperature well into the 90s. As he opened the door to the sheriff's car, Herbert was greeted by a cloud of sun-baked air.

"Whew, she's a hot one today for sure. Hop in there, Herb, and we'll take us a tour of the county. It'll feel good to get some air."

The sheriff took a road to the south that gradually climbed out of the valley. When they had left the town behind, the sheriff turned off the hard road, as he called it, onto gravel. It had been a dry summer. Trucks and farm machines had ground the gravel into thick layers of dust that raised billowy white plumes behind every passing car or pick-up. With no wind the dust hung in the air like fog, coating the weeds beside the road in white powder. A crust began forming in Herbert's nose and grit crunched between his teeth.

"If you're into huntin', we got most everything here. Ducks and geese on the river, pheasants and quail in the fields, and rabbit and squirrel in the timber. And if you got a good dog, you can get plentya 'coons after dark."

"To be truthful, I've never hunted anything that didn't walk on two legs."

They spent nearly an hour circling Bruders Landing on dusty roads while the sheriff pointed out landmarks, accident scenes, family cemeteries and farmsteads, telling a story about each one. Near the river the sheriff pointed out levees built to protect the low farmland from flooding during the spring run-off and pumping stations that lifted water from the drainage ditches into the river.

Their country tour ended north of Bruders Landing. As the sheriff headed back toward town, Herbert saw that the bluffs, which had retreated from the river both north and south of Bruders Landing, now loomed in front of them. The highway rose gradually until they reached the crest. The sheriff turned off the highway onto a road that paralleled the bluff above the Mississippi River. They were surrounded by fields of corn and soy beans ripening in the sun. Dotting the fields of green were occasional farmsteads and stands of timber where the land was too rough or hilly to clear.

At a place where the road wove close to the bluff, Herbert saw three large grassy mounds that were not part of the natural landscape.

"Would those be the Indian burial mounds?"

"Yeah, a few of 'em you can see from the road."

Herbert was interested. "Will we be getting closer to any of them?"

"Not along here. Most of them are back on farmland. Some of 'em been plowed under. It's illegal but people do it anyway. Up ahead we can see some up close if you want."

"I would. It'll be something to tell people back in Chicago."

They had driven less than two miles further when the fields ended abruptly at a long stone wall that ran along the east side of the road. Ahead Herbert saw a large stone archway. As they approached, the sheriff slowed the car. The entrance arch was massive. Herbert thought it could have led to a medieval fortress. Embedded in its base was a wrought iron gate decorated with a row of spear points at the top. The gate stood open.

"That there's the main entrance to Walnut Grove Cemetery. That entry way is local limestone. The town built it in the late 1800s after Senator Grimes was buried here. He was from Bruders Landing, ya know.

They thought the place should look more grand since it held somebody so famous. It's a big place, over 300 acres. Goes all the way back to the bluff."

"At that size, it must hold a lot of native sons and daughters."

"Yeah. Anyway I hope they're still here," the sheriff answered without laughing.

Herbert thought the remark puzzling but said nothing.

"We'll drive back to the bluff where we can see some mounds without having to hoof it too far."

As they passed under the arch, the cemetery unfolded before them. As far as Herbert could see, towering elms and oaks spread over hillsides dotted with grave stones. The trees were so numerous they blocked all but scattered patches of sunlight. The deep shade made Herbert strangely uncomfortable, as if he should be alert to something—something dangerous. Cut it out, he told himself; it's only a cemetery.

The sheriff followed a winding cinder road that led past several ravines where the shade was even deeper. Herbert gazed through the car window, fascinated by the extent of the manicured lawns and shrubs and the hundreds of headstones in as many shapes and sizes.

At last the sheriff stopped the car. "They're all along here on the other side of those trees." He pointed to a thick stand of timber at the side of the road. "Want to get out and take a look?"

"Sure."

The sheriff led the way along a narrow path through the trees that was barely visible. After several yards they came to a clearing at the edge of the bluff. Arrayed before them were large earthen mounds stretching in both directions. They were all roughly the same size, approximately ten feet in height and round, roughly thirty feet in diameter. The ones nearest to them were covered in grass cut to the height of a lawn. The ones at a distance were thick with weeds.

"Well, here they are, Herb. There's over a hundred of 'em."

"Do they have an entrance?"

"They did once, but the Indians filled 'em in and

now they're grown over. No way in I've ever seen."

"How many people do you suppose are buried in these?"

"Thousands's my guess. Over centuries."

"Has anybody ever dug into one?"

"Not here." The sheriff answered firmly. "It's against the law. Other places farther south some archeologists got permission. And there've been some grave robbers over the years. But no one would touch 'em here."

Herbert wondered how he could be so sure. Suddenly a noise close by made him flinch. He didn't realize he was so tense.

"Don't worry; it's only some animal. There's no problem here in the daylight and people won't come at night. Too many old stories, I guess." The sheriff didn't say what the stories were about.

Before Herbert left for Chicago the next day, the sheriff had offered him the job and he had accepted. He felt good about his decision. Still, as he drove back to the city, a strange unease gnawed at him, as if there were something more he should know about Bruders Landing. Maybe he should have asked about the old stories the sheriff mentioned. But any serious trouble in the town was unlikely, he told himself. Everything looked peaceful and orderly, no warning signs of underlying tension or anxiety. The people seemed normal enough, except, perhaps, for Boris the embalmer. And the sheriff appeared to be about as honest as anyone he had ever dealt with. It had to be his big city paranoia, believing that everyone and every place has a dark side.

As he began his duties in Bruders Landing, Herbert held himself aloof as he had in Chicago, afraid that getting too close to people could interfere with things he would have to do as a deputy sheriff. But his instincts, so well-honed by the big city streets, had prepared him for things he never saw in Bruders Landing. It was the kind of place he had wished for—quiet neighborhoods, quaint shops, brick streets, old-fashioned buildings, tidy homes and yards, friendly people living in slow motion. But his adjustment came slowly. In his eagerness to be successful, he went about his duties with an intensity and edge that had worked in Chicago, but people in Bruders Landing were wary of him. It didn't take long for the Sheriff to see it.

"Herb, I don't want you to take this wrong now," the sheriff said during a Sunday barbecue at his home. "People are gettin' a little nervous when you're around, thinkin' you're a little stiff. You're a good man, a real asset to this department and the whole town. And I don't want you to lose the things you picked up in Chicago, but folks here're a lot slower than you're used to. You're not gonna see people doin' things here that needs much muscle from us."

"But I've got to be ready, Sheriff. Isn't that what you're paying me for?"

"Yeah, but it's not the people you got to be ready for. Hell, I ain't even drawn my gun but once when George Belger came to my house drunk one night after huntin', and I had to threaten to shoot 'im before he'd put his .22 away. And that was fourteen years ago."

"Then you have to tell me what to do. I need this to work out."

"First thing is to relax. Take things nice and slow. We're not at war with these folks. You can be one of 'em and still do your job. The kind of trouble you might see here ain't gonna jump out at you on the street."

Herbert thought hard about the sheriff's message. He had told him to relax, blend in, be a part of things. It was probably good advice. But the sheriff hadn't told him there wouldn't be *any* trouble, just that it wouldn't be the people. Curious thing to say. Anyway, he'd take the sheriff's advice. He'd even try making some friends.

It took months for Herbert's old instincts to subside. Then a calmness began to set in and the periods when he felt comfortable and secure grew longer. He began to see people differently, no longer instinctively seeing everyone as a suspect but rather as friends and neighbors he was there to protect.

As he became more relaxed, a painful loneliness

surfaced. He began to realize how the shield he had built from his pain had isolated him. Now he needed to lower the barrier, to let people in, but he hardly knew where to start. As it turned out, the beginning was as simple as accepting an invitation to join the Wednesday night bowling league. After a few tense nights, he became one of the regulars and began to look forward to the night out. So much so that in the spring he joined a golf foursome. Well into his second year in Bruders Landing, Herbert had acquired a circle of friends and began to have a sense of belonging.

But there was one step on his road which Herbert hadn't taken and wasn't sure he ever could. Friends' wives frequently offered to introduce him to women, but he couldn't bring himself to accept. Feelings of loss and betrayal were still too close to the surface. He was also terrified of the prospect of getting close to another person, terrified of suffering another loss as he had with Selma. It was something he was sure he wouldn't risk again. Until he met Norma Bergstrom.

After boasting at lunch that he had never been sick a day in his life, Clifford Paisely collapsed while teaching a lesson on Andrew Johnson to his high school history class. The wood pointer he held suddenly clattered to the floor and Paisely pitched forward onto his desk, his head resting on his chin facing the class, his eyes staring blankly ahead. Slowly he slid to the floor, his mouth open as if to explain. The kids watched the slow-motion drama first with amusement, then horror. Finally a girl sitting close to the door began to scream, and the entire class ran for the door.

Herbert was on patrol and got the call. He arrived before the ambulance and entered the classroom at a run. The walls were lined with posters of foreign countries and famous people from history. The room was stuffy, smelling of young bodies. Sunlight streamed through the large glass windows onto the circle of teachers staring down at two figures. A siren wailed in the distance.

"Stand back now, folks," Herbert told them. "The ambulance will be here in a minute."

At the sound of his voice, the teachers turned toward him practically in unison, looks of helplessness and distress on their faces.

"Make some room now, please. The medics will need to get through," he said forcefully.

With shuffling movements, the group parted, revealing a young woman holding the head of a man who looked peaceful with his eyes closed. The man was sprawled limply next to the desk, his arms draped on the floor.

Herbert was struck by the tenderness of the woman as she stroked the man's pale face with a towel. He knelt down next to her.

"How is he?" he asked, lifting the man's arm to feel for a pulse.

"In a better place. I think he's dead," she said gently.

Herbert felt for a pulse. There was none.

After the fire department medics had removed the body, the young woman stayed behind. Throughout the whole episode, he had been aware of her, constantly stealing glances. When she relinquished the man's head to the medics and stood, he saw a tall, slender body wrapped in conservative gray dress. Her dark blonde hair was pulled back from her face in a tight bun, a face strikingly fresh and open but with a pensive expression as if remembering some elusive fact. In spite of her wistful aura, there appeared to be a vigorous and jaunty manner about her. As she stood by the window staring out over the schoolyard, her arms folded tight against her chest, Herbert found the courage to speak.

"Pardon me, ma'm, but I need some information for my report on the deceased, and I'm afraid I don't know your name."

She turned toward him and gave a wry smile. "It's Norma, Norma Bergstrom."

"You're a teacher here?" What a dumb question, he told himself as he fought the nervousness that had suddenly come over him.

"Yes. My classroom is next to this one."

As soon as he heard her voice, he knew the official interview was over. He was far more interested in her as a person than as a witness. "I guess this must have been pretty upsetting to you, but you handled it real well. You were a comfort to him, I'm sure."

"Thanks, but I doubt if he even knew I was there."

"Well, maybe not, but on some level he might have. Did you know him very well?"

"Sort of. He was my history teacher when I was in high school. Actually he was a pretty good teacher but sort of a dirty-old-man kind of guy. He seemed so alone when I came in, just lying there with people standing over him, looking up, sort of nonchalant like he knew he was dying and didn't want anyone to know. He always had a secretive side. Always wanting to keep up appearances. It must have really upset him to go out like that in front of his whole fifth period class."

Herbert stifled a grin. "Well, it *was* pretty public. By the way, your principal said he has a brother in Chillecothe. Is there anyone else you know we should call?"

"Not that I know of. He lived alone, never seemed to go anywhere. I don't know who his friends were. Actually, I wouldn't be surprised if he didn't have any. The only people I saw him with were other teachers here at school, and I don't think any of them would claim Clifford as a friend. Not that anyone particularly disliked him, it's just that he talked so incessantly and was so boring and so, well, flatulent."

"Oh, I see," he answered, nearly choking. "What about any other relatives?"

"I don't know of any of those either. I heard he was married once, although it's a little hard to imagine. If he was, it probably wasn't long. And I haven't heard about any kids, which doesn't surprise me. After all, he was a *history* teacher, which ranks right down there with teaching English."

"And you teach . . .?"

"English."

Herbert chuckled. He was enjoying her irreverent manner, so different from Selma. "Have you taught here since college?"

"No, just since last fall when I moved back from the outside world called Omaha."

"Oh? I moved here pretty recently, too." Herbert swallowed hard. He couldn't believe he had told her something about himself. It was unlike him to be so unprofessional. Maybe he was getting too loose in this new, relaxed style of his. Even worse, he wanted to tell her more.

"I know. I've been living with my parents on their farm south of town. You're Herbert Siefken, the deputy from Chicago. I've heard them talk about you. You know how word gets around in a small town."

This personal twist to what should be a witness interview began to make him uncomfortable. His face started to warm. The fact that she already knew things about him added to his discomfort, and he was suddenly worried that he might start stammering. "Uh, maybe, but then why didn't I see, uh, you know, hear anything about *you*."

"There's no reason why you would unless the sheriff keeps files on everyone new in town, or one of us is just not getting out enough."

"Well, I haven't been, until the last few months. What about you?"

"Oh, I've been trying to remain this invisible person since I came back. It's easier for me that way right now. So you have to promise not to tell anyone about me."

"Don't worry, I'm sworn to uphold the law *and* keep secrets," he answered. And he would surely keep this secret to himself.

The following day, Herbert tried to sort out what had happened to him in that classroom. Norma had aroused feelings he thought were dead, feelings he had wanted to avoid. She was constantly in his mind, and he began to feel guilty. How could he be attracted to another woman so soon after Selma died, he wondered, and began berating himself. Disloyalty was a trait he despised, yet wasn't his attraction to Norma exactly that? He didn't think he could be so despicable. Soon his head began to ache.

That night he dreamt about Norma. They were walking hand in hand along the railroad tracks below the bluff south of Bruders Landing. A steam locomotive came toward them and they stopped to watch the smoking behemoth. When it was close, a man suddenly ran screaming from the trees and knocked Norma onto the tracks. The locomotive wheels cut her in half while Herbert watched helplessly at the horror. As the mysterious man ran to escape, Herbert tackled him from behind. They rolled in the dirt, Herbert in a frenzy, raging and crying as he hit the man over and over. As the man lay barely conscious on his stomach, Herbert unholstered his revolver and fired two shots into the back of his head. When his rage subsided, Herbert rolled the body onto its back. Part of the man's face was missing where the bullets had exited. Still Herbert recognized him—the owner of the liquor store he had shot in Chicago. The shock woke him in a sweat, and his sorrow and guilt came flooding back.

He lay awake the rest of the night and by morning he knew he had to get Norma out of his mind. The only solution he could think of was to keep busy. For the next several days, he concentrated on his job, working all the extra hours he could. When he still had free time, he called friends to bowl or play golf. If he didn't find a partner, he played by himself. Anything to keep busy. But nothing helped. Her picture remained an indelible imprint on his mind, and his desire to see her again grew until it practically became an obsession.

At times he could only shake his head, unwilling to believe this was happening to him. The fact was that he didn't really know this woman. Perhaps his mind had created a fantasy, some wonderful person who didn't actually exist. What he had to do, he reasoned, was to see her, to talk with her, get to know who she really was. Then it would become clear she wasn't nearly the person Selma had been, and he could put all this behind him. But the prospect of phoning her completely unnerved him. Several times he rehearsed what he would say, lifted the phone from its cradle ready to give the operator her number, only to hang up before the operator answered.

Norma ended his torment when she called him. He was at home when the phone rang.

"Deputy Siefken? Herbert Siefken? This is Norma Bergstrom from the high school. Do you remember?"

"Uh, yes, sure," he answered, "but Herb, uh, please call me Herb." His palm grew sweaty as he held the phone.

"All right, Herb. I hope I'm not bothering you."

"No, uh, you're sure not."

"Good. You'll probably think this is presumptuous of me, but I was wondering if you would come and talk to the Civics Club at school. I'm their advisor and it would be wonderful if the students could hear first hand what you do in your job. It might make them feel a little better after what just happened."

"Well, I could, but, um, wouldn't you rather have the sheriff? I'm sure he'd be glad to . . ."

"No, Herb. I'd like you to do it." The tone in her voice made it clear it was him she wanted. His heart was pounding.

"Well, then, I guess it's OK. Sure, I'd be glad to."

"Good. Let me treat you to coffee tomorrow so I can give you the details."

As he hung up the phone, Herbert was glowing. He made himself calm down, trying to take stock of what he was feeling. Undoubtedly he was making too much of her call. It was an invitation to speak, nothing more. The thought depressed him.

They met the next day after school at Bucher's. Norma's appearance was conservative, much as when he'd first seen her. Her manner was cool and efficient. She ordered coffee almost as soon as she sat down, then fished a note pad and pencil from her large brown purse and began to discuss his talk at the high school. Between sips of the bitter coffee left over from the lunch hour, they outlined a plan for Herbert's talk. It took less than fifteen minutes for Herbert to convince himself that Norma was not the person he had imagined. She was cold and stiff, and her purpose in seeing him was strictly school business. But when the plan was settled, her demeanor softened. She rested her shoulders against the seat in the booth and cupped the coffee mug in her hands.

"Herb, I want you to know that people in Bruders Landing are very fortunate that you decided to come here." Her voice had lost its hard edge, sounding warm and endearing. A small smile crossed her face as she held his gaze.

Herbert's face got warm. "Well, uh, thanks." He began stirring his coffee rapidly, the spoon rattling in the mug.

"Mostly though, I hope it's working out for you," she continued quickly, "after growing up in the big city and all. You see, I know something about why you left Chicago. I really didn't mean to pry, but my father is Jack Schoof's first cousin and he's talked to us about you a little."

Herbert was startled that she this knew about him but was also somehow pleased that she did. "That's all right. It's nothing I've tried to keep secret. I just don't talk much about it."

"And you shouldn't unless you want to. I only told you because we have something in common. You see, I came back here after my husband died." Norma paused, taking a deep breath. "He committed suicide two years after we were married."

Herbert stopped stirring his coffee. "I'm sorry, I didn't realize . . ."

"No. How could you? Very few people know. My parents don't like me to tell people. Harold . . Hal and I met in teacher's college. After we graduated, we were married and got jobs in Omaha, where he was from. I taught in junior high and Hal went to work for an insurance company. He was fine for a year; then he started getting depressed—really depressed. I had no idea what to do. He wouldn't see a doctor and started drinking more and missing work. Things just got worse and worse. I was at my wit's end. I even told him I'd leave unless he got help. A few days later as we were getting ready to drive here to see my folks for Christmas, he left the house in our car . . ." Norma paused as she struggled with her composure, then went on, "and he drove off the highway into a tree. It might have been an accident, but I don't think so. He was going awfully fast. Anyway, it was just too painful for me to stay in

Omaha after that, so I came back here."

Listening to her talk, Herbert saw in Norma a kindred spirit, someone wounded like him. He wanted to comfort her, but words came hard. "That's awful. Your husband, I mean."

"Yes, thanks. It was awful. But I'm better now, getting over it finally. I hope you are, too, Herb."

"I think so. It's been over two years for me, too. Then there was the shooting . . . anyway it's better now."

"I hope so, for your sake. It looks like we've each had more than our share of tragedy. But I'm determined not to wallow in it anymore. It's time to get on with things. And I'm starting to, really starting."

Norma's optimism was infectious, energizing Herbert, lowering his guard. "I've started to do some things, too, just bowl and golf with some guys, though. I haven't gone out yet. I mean, with someone. What about you?"

"No. I haven't either. It just hasn't seemed right. Like it's disloyal somehow."

"That's how I feel." Suddenly his defense evaporated. "Maybe you . . um . . . do you think we might, say, have supper some night? Not like a date or anything like that. I mean, would you like to?" He could scarcely believe what he had asked. His skin grew clammy and he held his breath, waiting for her answer.

"I'd like to."

Herbert heard himself finally exhale.

Their first dinner together was a disappointment. Herbert's nerve began to desert him early that morning. By the time he drove to the farm and was introduced to her parents, he was so nervous he could scarcely complete a sentence. After they left the house, he was sure they thought their daughter was in the hands of a person with a serious speech impediment or an imbecile. All evening he tried to will his nervousness away with no success. As a result he became irritable. When the evening ended, Herbert was sure she would never want to see him again.

The next day he couldn't concentrate on anything without thoughts of Norma interrupting. The more he remembered the evening, the more embarrassed he became. He needed to see her, to apologize, to somehow try again. Several times he made up his mind to call, growing angrier each time over how shy and nervous he became around her, and each time he changed his mind. For two days he fretted. He was still in a quandry when he stopped to buy groceries at Minnie's Market. As he left his car and walked toward the store, Norma appeared in the doorway carrying two large bags in her arms. Herbert stood in her path like a statue, unable to think what to do or what to say.

"Herb, what good timing! Would you mind opening my car door for me?"

"OK, sure," he said at last and took one of the bags.

"Thanks so much. These bags are heavier than I thought. My car's over there."

Herbert's mind raced as they walked with her groceries. What should he say to her? This was silly, he thought, he was a grown man. He would simply tell her the truth.

"Norma, I have to tell you something." His voice sounded formal as if he was beginning a speech.

"Sure, but let me put this bag down first."

"Sorry," he answered, instantly feeling sheepish.

After they had put the groceries in her car, Herbert's determination returned. "Norma, I need to tell you something." He paused, realizing he had repeated himself, then cleared his throat and started again. "When I'm around you, I feel like, well, a kid, all nervous and shy-like. I don't know why it is, but I do."

Norma smiled impishly. "I'm glad you told me that. It probably took a lot of courage. I should tell you that I feel shy talking to you, too. And I've been trying to figure it out for days."

"Really?" he answered, his eyes opening wide. "Have you figured out why yet?"

"Maybe, maybe not. I don't know for sure."

"Will you tell me what you think it might be?" Herbert leaned his elbow on the roof of the car only to have it slide off. He recovered as nonchalantly as he could.

"Well . . . you see, I feel kind of shy about that, too," she said, casting her eyes to the ground.

"I don't mean to force you."

"You aren't. Actually it probably would be good for me." Norma sighed, then looked directly into his eyes. "What I think is that we're . . . that is you're a good person and I'm . . . well, I must be attracted to you."

Herbert's eyes started to water. "Oh, Norma. That's wonderful. I mean, um, that's exactly what I think, attracted to you, that is I am, I mean."

A sudden desire to take her in his arms came over him. He hesitated until he thought there was an invitation in her eyes, he did just that. When he felt her respond, he looked into her face and, with no more hesitation, kissed her lips.

Few places in Bruders Landing provided a more public place for displaying affection than the sidewalk by Minnie's Market. Their embrace attracted Minnie and her five customers to the window at the front of the store and entertained several more townsfolk in passing cars and nearby houses. By the next day, Herbert and Norma were the talk of the town.

Any barriers to their relationship that Herbert still harbored were erased the following weekend when he and Norma drove fifty miles to a supper club in Illinois. Their dinner was intimate: a darkened room, a lone candle lighting their table, holding each other close as they danced. For the first time since their encounter at Minnie's Market, they were out from under the scrutiny of Bruders Landing's microscope. He spent the evening in a dream-like state, scarcely aware of what he was eating. As they walked arm-in-arm from the restaurant, Herbert was glowing. When they were seated in his car, he put his arm around her gently and she raised her face to his. They kissed passionately, their tongues meeting, and he gave in to a desire to caress her breast. Almost as soon as he touched her, he felt ashamed and drew his hand back, certain he had offended her.

"It's all right, Herb," she said softly, "I want us to touch."

He felt like a teenager again. Gently he put his hand on her breast again, trying not to breath too heavily as he unbuttoned her blouse. They kissed feverishly while he gently caressed her. When Norma rested her hand on his upper thigh and began moving it higher, he lowered his hand to her knee. As he began to caress the bare skin above her nylon, she pulled away.

"I'm being too easy, Herb," she said in a low voice. "I'm never this fast, really."

Herbert swallowed to make sure he had control of his voice. "Don't worry. Me either, but I'm really crazy about you." He spoke fervently, eager to reassure her.

"That's what's going on with me, too. Should we go some place really romantic?"

"Yeah, sure . . . where?"

"Would you take me to a cheap motel?"

Chapter Eleven

The Messenger

1874

The day after his meeting with Mayor Goelzer, Raston Bruhl was in his ice house busily arranging Tilden Mertz for display to his grieving family when Sophia shouted from the back of the house.

"Raston! Raston, dear. There's a man here to see you. He's from out of town. Can you stop long enough to see him?"

"All right. I'll be there. Just give me a minute."

The body lay naked on the stone slab Raston used for washing. For a moment he considered leaving it right where it was, then thought better of it. He deftly rolled the body back onto the ice, covering it with a canvas shroud. After taking off his work apron and putting on a dark jacket, Raston walked through the old mansion to the front foyer.

A short, balding man was waiting. He was well-dressed in a suit that plainly had been purchased in the East, well tailored to help conceal his large stomach. The man stood nervously, shifting his weight from one foot to another, rolling and unrolling the brim of his hat. There was a package tucked under his arm. Raston didn't have the slightest notion who he was.

"Hello. I'm Raston Bruhl. What can I do for

you?" he inquired in his professional voice.

"I'm real sorry to bother you, Mr. Bruhl. I'm Carl Stottelmeyer and I represent the Hentzler Dry Goods Company in this area. But don't worry, I'm not here to sell you anything."

"Well, I'm glad to know you, Mr. Stottelmeyer. Would you like to come in and sit?"

"No, oh no. To be honest, these places, um, funeral homes, make me kind of nervous."

"Well, that's all right. It's not uncommon, Mr. Stottelmeyer."

"Please call me Carl. Anyway, Mr. Bump, Thaddeus Bump, was my boss until he died about six months ago. Good man, great salesman. Could sell whiskers to a catfish, as they say in your parts."

Raston hadn't given a thought to Thaddeus Bump for years but remembered him as soon as he heard the name. "Oh, I'm very sorry to hear that. Real sorry. I didn't know him very well or very long, but we shared something."

"I know. You were both on the *Prince Nathan* when it exploded. I heard him tell about it many times. He said he left Bruders Landing right afterwards and never saw the Mississippi again. Said he never wanted to, and I guess he never did."

"I guess not. Least I never laid eyes on him."

"He said there were bad things here, around the islands and the river bluffs. Actually, I never knew there were islands in the river. Anyway, he talked about one island in particular, the one he was washed up on after the explosion. He said some strange people lived on it. Scary people. Big Stow Island, I think he called it. He always hated water, you know."

"No, I didn't know."

"Well, that's not important. After he died, his wife found a letter addressed to you and a Mr. Harman Honzie, or something like that, and an old journal. Said it was important. She asked me to stop here on my next trip through and give it to you or Mr. Honzie. And if I couldn't find either of you, she asked me to give it to the mayor."

"Well, that's real kind of her."

"I asked around when I got off the boat and no one knew Mr. Honzie, but a man told me how to get to your place."

"Harman Hanzfig died several years ago. I worked for him. We met Thaddeus Bump at the same time."

"Well, then, if you'll just give me a note saying that I delivered this journal, I'll be pleased to give it to you and be on my way."

"All right," Raston answered, somewhat mystified. "My desk is in the parlor. Come with me."

Stottelmeyer followed Raston down the hall, looking from one side to another as if he expected something to jump out at him. "If you don't mind my asking, where do you prepare the bod . . . excuse me, the people?"

"I don't mind. For embalming there's a room in the cellar. For those who won't be embalmed, we have an ice house in the rear where we keep them cool."

"Cool? You mean so they won't . . . um . . ."

"Yes, smell. It wouldn't do for loved ones to be offensive in their last hours."

"Is there any. . . uh, one in here now?"

"Yes, in the ice house."

"Oh." Carl Stottelmeyer said nothing more.

Raston entered the parlor and sat at the chair behind his large walnut desk. With the drapes pulled, the room was cool and dark. The messenger waited, rolling and unrolling the brim of his hat even more rapidly.

When Raston had finished the note, he handed it across the desk. "Now that I've given you a note saying I received a journal, I'd better be sure I've received one."

Stottelmeyer took the package from under his arm and handed to him. Raston picked up a knife from his desk and cut off the paper wrapping. Inside was a thin journal with a blue leather cover.

"Have you read this?" he asked, casually opening the front cover where there was a letter.

"No. Matilda . . . ah, Mrs. Bump . . . asked me to keep it wrapped until I delivered it. She was very anxious to have it delivered unopened. All she said is that one of you should have it."

"Well, tell her thanks when you see her."

Raston watched Stottelmeyer walk briskly back toward the river. Shaking his head, he laid the journal on his desk and returned to finish Tilden Marcor.

Chapter Twelve

The Old Stone Entrance

1949

After searching the third floor unsuccessfully for a door the key would fit, Henry knew there was only one other place in the farmhouse to look—the cellar. However, he wasn't about to go down there by himself, and Sheila had balked. Winter passed to spring. When school was out, his summer was filled with baseball and a family vacation on a lake in the Ozarks. There was little time to visit the farm. Then it was back to school in the fall. Snow came early in November and kept falling until the countryside was blanketed in white. Henry and Sheila had started visiting the farm again, but sledding replaced exploring as the main attraction. The best run was down the hill in front of the farmhouse. With a good start, Henry could almost make it to the main road. On the third straight Saturday together at the farm, they built a snowman which they dressed gaudily in old clothes their grandmother gave them. Later, as they sat in the kitchen eating oatmeal cookies over mugs of steaming hot cocoa, Henry admitted he had gone to the third floor without her.

"There's not much up there," he said. "The doors

are to bedrooms mostly and that key couldn't begin to fit in any of them."

"Did you go into the rooms? There could be other doors in the rooms, you know."

"I could only open one of them and didn't see a closet door or anything." He reached for another oatmeal cookie.

"Just the same, I'm not going down to the cellar. It's too creepy."

"I thought we agreed to be partners."

"We did, but you already went to the third floor by yourself. Now you can just go down the cellar by yourself, too."

"Then you'll be welching on me. I never thought you'd be a welcher."

"I am not a welcher," she said emphatically. "I never said I'd go down the cellar."

"If that's where we need to go to find the door you agreed to help me find, then you're a welcher."

"I am not. Maybe I will go . . . later . . . sometime . . . maybe."

Early in April there were three warm days during the week when Henry's mother had let him go outside without a coat. He looked forward to more of the same on Saturday at the farm, but when Henry woke up that morning it was snowing. It was still snowing large, wet flakes when his mother dropped him off at the farm. As soon as he was out of the car, he picked up a handful of snow with his bare hands and squeezed it. It was heavy and solid. Good to make snowballs that hurt when they hit you, but not deep enough for sledding. He threw the snowball at the old bell that stood on a pole in the farmyard and missed. He wanted to try again, but his hands were too cold so he headed for the house.

He burst through the kitchen door, interrupting a conversation between his grandmother and Sheila as they peeled potatoes. They were both glad to see him, particularly Sheila, who looked relieved. His grandmother must have been asking about her grades, he thought.

"Henry, dear, you came just at the right time. I

was just going out to get a chicken for dinner. Grandpa's over at Herb Bruntmeier's, so you two play in the house for a little while, now," his grandmother said as she put on galoshes and a long coat stiff with heavy, dark stains.

As soon as she was out the door, Henry whispered to Sheila: "You want to sneak out and watch?"

"I suppose you think I'm chicken."

"Are you?"

"Of course not."

"Well, if you're not afraid to, let's go." Henry grabbed his coat and started toward the door.

"Wait, what if Grandma catches us spying on her?"

"She won't. I know where to go. C'mon, Sheila, it's not scary like the cellar."

"Don't worry, I'll go to the cellar with you . . . sometime."

"I'm not holding my breath. Now do you want to come or not? Pretty soon it'll be too late."

"OK, OK, I'll come. Let me get my coat on."

They ran out the back door over the snow. Henry led them behind a thick bush growing against the side of the chicken coop.

Henry spoke softly: "Be real quiet now, Grandma's in there. You can see through one of those cracks between the boards."

"Have you ever seen Grandma do this before?" Sheila bent down to the widest crack.

"Yeah, sure, a couple times," Henry lied.

Emma Gerdes had closed the door to the chicken coop behind her and stood in the center while the chickens eyed her warily from hay-filled boxes stacked against two of the walls. Henry imagined the chickens wondering whether his grandmother was there to collect eggs or heads. His grandmother was looking them over carefully as if she needed to find a particular one. When at last she made her choice, the victim seemed to know immediately and tried to make its escape. But Emma Gerdes would not be denied. With her coat and skirt swirling, she chased it from corner to corner until she was finally able to grab its feet.

Henry nudged Sheila's shoulder. "Grandma's going to take it outside. Let's go over to the corner where we can see."

Emma emerged from the chicken coop with the chicken hanging upside down squawking, its wings flapping frantically against her leg. She walked briskly to a large stump cut flat on top that served as a chopping block. An ax coated with a dark stain lay on top. She picked up the ax with her free hand and threw the chicken onto the block with a soft thump.

Henry felt a little faint as he imagined what was about to happen. Sheila took hold of his arm and squeezed it tight without looking away. Henry forced himself to keep his eyes on his grandmother.

The chicken flopped around the top of the stump, but Emma kept a firm hold on its legs in one hand, picking up the ax in the other. Henry watched her lift the ax high over her head, holding it motionless for an excruciating moment as she drew a bead on the chicken's neck. In a flash she brought the ax down sharply like the drop of the blade in a guillotine. It hit the stump with a solid thunk. The chicken's head dropped to the ground. Blood spurted from the headless carcass as she swiftly grabbed its flailing body and tied it by its legs to a nearby pole. While blood drained from the chicken's neck, Emma wiped off the ax with a rag.

Henry felt dizzy, nausea welling up in his stomach. "I don't feel so good."

"Do you feel like you're going to throw-up?"

Henry swallowed hard a few times. "I don't know. Maybe. Let's go down by the creek. I don't want Grandma to hear me if I do."

Henry skidded down the hill slippery with wet snow. When he reached the creek, he sat down on a large rock.

"Bend your head down, Henry. That's what mom tells me to do when I feel sick."

Henry bent his head forward and kept it there for a few minutes. He was humiliated. He *would* have to get sick in front of Sheila! Now she would think he was a sissy. How could he face her after she had seen him almost puke while she seemed just fine? Sheila sat down next to him, touching his shoulder gently. He scooted away, keeping his head down. Then he heard her gagging. Right away he began to feel better.

"I'm so embarrassed." Sheila turned her head away and spit. "I only felt a little sick up there, but all of a sudden it got worse."

Henry put his hand on her shoulder. "It's OK. I almost threw up, too. I guess we're just not used to seeing things all bloody like that. Do you feel better now?"

"Yeah, I do. How about you?"

"I'm better, too."

They sat for a few minutes watching the water ripple over the rocks. The creek came from the low hills in the west, winding its way through the bluffs to the river. It was a small stream, barely ten feet across, usually at its highest in the spring, sometimes disappearing entirely in the fall. But on this day melting snow had made it vigorous.

"Grandma's in the barn taking the feathers off that chicken so she won't go back to the house for a while. There's something down here I want to see up close. Do you want to come?"

"Yeah, I guess, but what is it?"

"Something I saw from the window when I was up on the third floor. C'mon."

Henry led the way, picking his way through the rocks lining the bank. He'd never gone this way before and wasn't sure how far they would have to go. After they had walked several minutes, the creek curved to the right. He kept looking ahead, expecting after each step to see the old stone entryway. At last he saw it on the other side of the stream."

"There it is!"

Sheila twisted her mouth quizically as she stared at the dark stone entryway that had been sealed by a wall of rock and mortar.

Henry was anxious to get closer. "Let's go over."

He stared at the rocks protruding randomly from the creek's surface creating ripples and eddies in the fast-moving water. The rocks were their only hope for crossing without getting their shoes soaked.

"Come on, I'm going," Henry called out and started across, stepping carefully on each rock and holding his arms out wide for balance. Sheila followed close behind. With a giggle she gave him a soft push. They both began to laugh, Henry nearly losing his balance.

Across the stream they stood side by side, staring up at the stone entrance, its stone sides rising from the base of the hill to a cathedral-style arch at the top. The stones were the same used for the farmhouse but were covered with patches of dark green moss and dried weeds sprouting from the cracks.

"This thing's bigger than it looked from the house," Henry said, "and it looks so old, even older than the house. I wish we could get in to see where it goes."

"Somebody went to a lot of trouble once to make sure we can't."

"Yeah, kids like us, I suppose."

"Well, I don't know if *I'd* want to. It kind of looks like one of those mausoleums in Walnut Grove Cemetery. Do you think there might be dead bodies buried in there?"

"Could be. But don't those things in the cemetery have doors?"

"Yeah. Maybe this did, too . . . once. A big door with a lock that needed a big key."

"Then all they'd to do was lock it to keep people out. Why would they need to seal it up with this wall?"

"True. It must only lead to a cellar, a root cellar, I think it's called, where they kept things cool before they had electricity. I wish we could see what it looks like inside."

"Maybe we can. That wall already has a bunch of cracks in it. Some of those rocks might be easy to get out."

Henry put his hands on a stone where the mortar was loose and tried to push it out. That was when he smelled the putrid odor seeping through the cracks. It was only a whiff, but enough to make him wrinkle his nose and back away.

"Ick! What's that smell? Something in there

really stinks. I can smell it through the cracks."

Sheila leaned close to the wall until her nose nearly touched it. "Yuck!. That *does* smell awful! I wonder what it is."

"Maybe there *are* dead bodies in there," Henry replied.

Chapter Thirteen

The Town Cemetery

1874

While Clarence Goble and his two sons cleared the site for Walnut Grove, the name chosen by Amanda Goelzer for Bruders Landing's new cemetery, Raston planned the move of several hundred bodies to their new resting place. He had agreed to the price and wanted to be sure there was money left over when the job was done.

To do the digging, Raston figured he would need at least twenty men with strong backs who weren't squeamish about digging up decomposed corpses. He knew just where to look—on River Street.

Bruders Landing's riverfront had long been stripped of its greenery, leaving a wide band of barren ground along the water's edge whose surface was either deep, sticky mud or dry, cracked dirt, depending on the length of time since the last rain or high water. There the steamboats and river ferries landed, sliding their flat bottoms firmly onto shore. Twenty yards back from the river was the levee, a dirt mound ten feet high built to protect the low-lying parts of the town from spring floods.

Wooden platforms and walkways allowed people and cargo from the boats to cross the mud and the levee. The passenger who successfully navigated one of these walkways arrived on River Street, a dirt road scored with deep wagon wheel ruts. Across this road facing the river stood an assortment of wooden buildings housing the businesses that served the steamboats—trading houses, warehouses, transient hotels, a slaughterhouse, suppliers and outfitters for the stream of settlers arriving daily, a goodly number of saloons and at least three bordellos. During the day, River Street teemed with people energetically conducting business, burly workers sweating and cursing as they hauled cargo back and forth across the levee between the steamboats and the warehouses and wagons on the other side, settlers preparing for their trek West and drifters killing time drinking and taunting the girls who leaned seductively out of second-story windows advertising their wares.

At night the activity on River Street continued, but of a much different sort and at a much louder level. Many of the day people were still there, but they had stopped working and started drinking. Drifters appeared in greater numbers, showing the effects of alcohol consumed throughout the day. Many of the girls had left their window perches and stood in doorways, beckoning passersby. Adding to those milling on the wooden walkways between saloons were some of Bruders Landing's younger and more adventuresome residents, identifiable, at least early in the evening, by their well-pressed clothes. Fights, sometimes drunken and half-hearted, sometimes ferocious and lethal, were a nightly feature.

Shortly after dawn on a cool May morning, dressed in dark pants and jacket as always, Raston stood on the back of the wagon he had driven to the old town cemetery, surveying the men he had collected. By offering a dollar a man per body dug up and the same when it was put back in the ground, it hadn't been difficult. They were a hard-looking lot, most of them red-eyed from the night before, unshaven, scruffy hair and beards, their rough denim clothing sporting a variety of rips and patches. All told Raston had talked with over fifty men on River Street before he found twenty who looked as if they might last for a whole day of work.

"All right, you men. Listen up! Any of you dug a grave before?" Raston spoke loudly, making sure he was heard.

Half the men raised their hands.

"Good. Now, how many of you have ever exhumed . . . ah, dug up a grave to, say, recover the body?" All the hands went down.

"That's no surprise. It doesn't happen all that much, legally anyway." There were a few laughs. Raston scanned their eyes, looking for a sign from those who had done some grave robbing. He thought he saw three.

"Digging up a body is harder than burying one. You have to be more careful, a lot more careful. Remember that. We'll work in crews of two. You men that have never dug a grave before, get a partner who has. Now listen to how this will go. Like I told you before, there's several hundred graves in this old cemetery and the faster teams will get more bodies. I've got each grave site here marked showing exactly where they are. When you dig in this old cemetery, the hole has to be wider than a fresh grave so we can lift out the coffin in one piece if possible. As soon as we've got four loaded on this wagon, we'll make a trip to Walnut Grove with the coffins and their crews. The grave sites at Walnut Grove will be marked, too. There's a wood sign on each one showing who goes where. The day doesn't end until every coffin dug up has been buried again. So when you get one out, you've got to get it buried the same day. Each crew needs to do at least one a day which will earn you two dollars. I'll pay everyone daily like I said, but not 'til the end of the following day. So if you don't work the next day, you won't get your money. No complaints. That's the way it's gonna be."

Raston paused, waiting for the murmurs to subside. No one spoke up.

"Now listen to the rest. When you're digging out the bodies, you'll reach the coffin three or four feet down. When you do, stop using your pick to keep from damaging things. As soon as you uncover the coffin, call me over so I can tell you what needs to be done to get it out. If it's in one piece, you'll dig around the sides until we can get a rope under it. If a coffin's collapsed, you'll dig it out in pieces. We'll take the body out in one piece if we can. If you think you'll have trouble with this, better you leave now."

There were several groans but no one moved to leave.

"All right, then. It's important that you treat all these people buried here with respect. If you're in a grave where the coffin's rotted away or caved in, I want you to talk to me before you do anything with the remains. If the coffin's intact, I don't want you opening it unless I tell you to. If you do, you'll be fired on the spot. And if you remove anything from a grave without permission, I'll have you arrested. All right, that's about it. When you've got a partner, line up over there by that wagon to get your picks and shovels and your grave assignment from Jules."

Jules Garth, Raston's longtime helper, stood behind a table on which was spread a large chart of the cemetery. There was a look of impatience on his face and a bead of sweat trickling out of his thin gray hair onto his forehead. He was a gaunt man, tall, strongly built, with a back markedly humped from years of digging and heavy loads.

Raston watched the men jostling about, trying to find partners. He would have to stay alert to be sure all the bodies they were about to unearth, as well as everything buried with them, were returned intact to the earth in Walnut Grove. Grave robbing was hard enough to prevent with corpses several feet under the ground, but that particular obstacle was about to disappear in the next few days. The Town Council and the sheriff would be watching as well, certain to hold him responsible for any stealing. He would inventory everything in the coffins as they were brought to the surface, then check again against his records as they were reburied. Raston kept meticulous records of his work.

Eager for the money, each pair hurried to their

first grave site and began to dig. As the sun climbed higher in the southern sky, the men shed coats, then shirts, sweating in the cool air. The first shout for Raston came less than an hour later.

"Hey, Mr. Bruhl, up here! We got one ready!"

The voice came from halfway up the hill. Two young men stood shirtless, shovels in one hand waving their shirts in the other.

Raston hurried up the hill towards them. It was the grave of Hannah Westerfal, wife of Klaus Westerfal, buried in August, 1850, seven years before Klaus who was buried beside her. He remembered both of them. Hannah made clothes for half the women in town. She had been one of the many cholera victims that year. Klaus didn't do well after she was gone, living the rest of his life in an alcoholic daze.

"Good work, you two," Raston shouted. "You're the first. Let's see what you've got here."

They had dug well. The hole was a neat rectangle with steep, straight sides. It smelled like dampness and soil, and something else, something decidedly unpleasant. Raston had opened many graves in his life and he knew their scents, all of them, but he didn't know this one. It was pungent, a scent that could make his nose burn and turn his stomach if it were any stronger—and sour, more like burned than rotting flesh. He knelt by the side of the hole, trying to identify the odor, until he felt the two men staring at him. He turned his attention to the lid of the coffin visible under the dust and clods of dirt at the bottom of the opening.

"This looks good so far. The coffin should come out in one piece. That'll save you time. I'll bring the ropes. Dig some space around the sides so we can lift it enough to get them underneath. Be careful to stand only on its edges when you dig so you don't put your foot through the top."

Raston walked to the wagon to fetch Garth with the hoisting ropes, still puzzled about the smell. After twenty-four years, it surely couldn't be Hannah. He had done the funeral, buried her himself. She wasn't embalmed, nobody was in those days, so there wouldn't be much left of her but dried skin and bones. Bodies in that condition don't have much smell at all. What could it be? He decided to open the coffin.

With the hoisting ropes in place, the two diggers, with Raston and Garth helping, began to pull the coffin out of its resting place. Garth wrinkled his nose and gave Raston a puzzled look. Even though the wood still looked sturdy, Raston watched closely for any sign that the coffin might break apart on its way to the surface. As it emerged from the dark hole that had held it so long, the diggers swung it to the side of the opening and brought it to rest on the ground at Raston's feet.

"All right, Jules, let's see what that odor is. Take off the top."

Garth had worked for Raston for over twelve years and had done this work before. Without any hesitation, he began to pry open the coffin's lid. Slowly the two diggers began edging away, apprehension on their faces.

"It'll come now, Mr. Bruhl," Garth reported. Raston helped him pull the top free from the nails holding it to the coffin.

Even before the lid was completely off, Raston saw enough to startle him. It was a flash of gray and white. As the lid was laid to one side, he stared open-mouthed into the coffin. Raston had seen more than enough corpses to know what to expect of one that had been buried for nearly a quarter of a century. That was not what he saw. Sprawled before him were scattered the bones of Hannah Westerfal completely bare of any flesh or skin. Her skull rested in the middle of the casket detached from its spine, its eye sockets staring emptily upward. Her burial clothes lay in tatters at the sides and ends of the coffin, looking as if they had been ripped from the body. There was a mound of hair in one corner.

Raston slowly digested what he was seeing. As he gazed at the bones, he made a quick inventory. It appeared they had once constituted a whole skeleton which had been somehow twisted and torn apart inside the casket. The strange odor had become stronger.

Gradually Raston became aware that Garth and the two diggers were standing beside him, staring wide-eyed into the coffin.

"Jesus!" one of the men exclaimed. "Maybe she was buried alive!"

"Jules," Raston said quickly, anxious to get the two diggers away from the casket. "Take these men and bring the cart so we can get this coffin down to the wagon."

"Right, Mr. Bruhl." Garth sounded as if he had just woken from a dream. "You men, c'mon with me." The men shrugged and followed Garth down the hill.

Raston continued to stare incredulously into the casket. Who or what could have done this? It couldn't have happened before her burial—he had buried her himself. Could someone have dug her up then repacked the dirt so well no one had noticed? That was unlikely, but not impossible. Kneeling to look more closely, he noticed marks on the bones. There were scratches and small gouges on all of them. He reached into the casket and lifted out what had been one of Hannah Westerfal's arms. Gently he turned the piece of her skeleton over in the sunlight to look at the marks. The bone looked as if something had gnawed on it, and it smelled so strongly of the strange odor Raston was tempted to put a handkerchief over his nose.

Garth returned breathing heavily from his walk up the hill. "Mr. Bruhl, cart's on its way and there's three more crews waitin' for you to check their graves."

"All right, but first I need your help. Come here and give me a hand." Garth knelt slowly on the other side of the coffin. "It looks like something got into this coffin, but you can see that as well as I can. And so can those diggers, so I didn't want them hanging around staring, then spreading God knows what kind of stories. You and I have to act matter-of-fact like around this casket so they don't get too curious. Now we need to see what's in here."

Raston began pushing the bones to one side. Garth reached in hesitantly to help. "What do you think coulda done this, Mr. Bruhl?"

"I wish I knew, Jules. I've never seen anything like it. Usually grave robbers leave some sort of trail."

"Do you think they's what's done it then?"

"I honestly don't know."

138

"And that smell, do you know what made that smell, Mr. Bruhl?"

"No, I don't know that either. I've been trying to place it myself. If those diggers ask, tell them that corpses give off a lot of different smells."

Raston rummaged through the coffin, pushing aside the torn clothes and bones, finding nothing until he lifted a small pile of clothes at the casket's head revealing a gold ring and a wide brass bracelet. "Look at this, Jules. Seems if we had robbers, they overlooked a few things." Rubbing the insides with his finger, he saw that both were engraved with the initials HHW.

As Raston hurriedly made notes in a large ledger, Garth continued to poke through the coffin. "Mr. Bruhl, look here. This is somethin'." He pointed to the foot of the casket. Raston bent over and looked closely. There was a hole in the coffin floor.

"Is that somethin', Mr. Bruhl? Could somethin've got in through there?"

Raston looked closer. The hole was slightly smaller than a silver dollar. Its sides were rough as if they had been chewed. "Yes, something could have, but it would have to be pretty small."

Raston stood up still mystified. "I think we found everything in here we're going to. This mystery will have to wait for now. We'd better get over to the other graves before our diggers get too restless. Help me put this lid back on. Let's not leave Hannah all exposed like this. She's already been through enough."

Together Raston and Jules put the top into place, then hammered the nails back into the wood.

"You men!" Raston yelled to the two diggers. "Stop digging and take this coffin to the wagon. Now, Jules, show me the next ones."

Garth led the way to the closest grave. The diggers stood leaning on their shovels. Raston checked his notebook. It was an older one, Luther Mussman, died March 18, 1835, more than a decade before Raston laid eyes on Bruders Landing.

"This'll be a hard one, Boss," one of the diggers said. "Have a look."

Raston peered into the grave. Rotted boards,

bone fragments and scraps of cloth were mixed with the dirt at the bottom. The coffin had totally collapsed. But why was the skeleton scattered in pieces, he asked himself? And there was that odor again. He lowered himself into the grave, taking care to stand at the edges. With a trowel from his pocket, he scraped away the loose dirt on top revealing a bony hand with a gold ring on one finger.

"This won't be too bad," Raston said as he climbed from the hole. "Jules here will give you a canvas bag for the bone fragments. Pick all of them you can find out of the dirt, and I do mean all. If you find anything valuable like jewelry or gold teeth, tell Jules or me. You'll bury the bag just as if it's a coffin." Garth untied one of several large bags hanging from his belt and handed it to one of the men.

"All right, Jules, let's get to another one," Raston said, making notes in his ledger.

He followed Garth to the next grave site. The headstone read *RIP Jana Herzberger Born June 21, 1847 Died August 23, 1862..* Jana was one of the first bodies Raston had prepared by himself. Full of life at fifteen, Jana had been climbing with her friends in one of the ravines along the river when she fell, breaking her neck. Raston remembered staring at her young body. He had never seen such an attractive girl naked before and had felt guilty for days when it aroused him. Jana's casket filled the space at the bottom óf the grave. The diggers had already dug around it. The same foul odor rose from the hole.

"Good work, you men. This one should come out nicely. Jules, bring the ropes."

When the coffin was raised and sitting beside the grave, Raston decided to open it.

"Jules, show these men where to get the cart. There's no reason they should just be standing around. Just leave the crowbar."

Garth took a sheaf of papers from his pocket and studied it for a minute. "All right, you men. It's over here."

After Garth left with the two men, Raston bent down and began to pry open the casket's lid. The nails squeaked in protest as he put his weight on the end of the crowbar. He had one side free when Garth returned.

"Here, Mr. Bruhl, I'll finish that. You ain't dressed for this kind of work."

"Don't worry about that. I didn't want those diggers around when we opened this one. Just in case."

Garth pried up the remaining nails and lifted the lid.

The scene inside the casket was virtually the same as the first one. The bones had been stripped of every shred of flesh and lay jumbled together at the head of the coffin, the skull face down at the foot. The pink dress she had been buried in was torn and shredded into piles around the sides.

"Damn, Jules! It looks like something got into this one, too!" Raston exclaimed in frustration. "What's going on here? Jana Herzberger has only been buried, what, not quite six years? There's no way she should be in this condition."

"Unless somethin' real hungry got in here." Garth whispered as if he was uttering something so heinous he didn't want anyone to hear.

Raston stood puzzled, shaking his head. "Well, if that's the case, whatever has such an appetite must be awfully small. Let's see what's in here."

Raston knelt at one end of the coffin and began sorting through the skeleton parts and clothing with his hands. Pushing aside the clothes and bones in order to have a look at the casket floor, his hands grasped a small object. It was cameo brooch pinned to a piece of ripped blouse. Under the clothing were the bones of a hand still attached to the arm. A tarnished silver band was on the ring finger. He picked up the arm. The ring rattled against the bony finger when Raston turned the arm to examine it. Why would grave robbers leave this jewelry? He examined the bones closely. There appeared to be scratches and gouges that looked as if they had been made by teeth, just as on the other body. He replaced the arm in the casket and ran his hands across the bottom. All the boards were intact.

At the other end of the coffin, Garth was working through the contents slowly, looking warily at everything he touched.

"C'mon here, Jules, let's finish up with this one. Find anything?" Even as he spoke, Raston saw a small hole in the bottom that Garth had just uncovered. "There! By your left hand. See that hole? Just like the first one."

By the time he had opened the ninth casket, Raston was becoming frantic. They had all been the same. Each corpse, regardless of how long it had been buried, stripped of flesh and skin, the bones scattered in the casket as if the body had been buried in pieces. What would the Mayor and the town think? The fact was he had buried most of them. If he couldn't find an explanation for what had happened, he would certainly catch the blame. People in Bruders Landing were good at blaming, and they surely would think of some unspeakable things to accuse him of. Until he found an answer to what had happened, he'd need to keep the condition of the bodies secret.

As Raston stood anxiously turning things over in his mind, Garth called to him. "Mr. Bruhl, over here. This is the next one."

Garth was standing near the graves of Civil War dead. Raston remembered receiving them in their plain wood containers, seeing the horror of their wounds, wounds often so horrible he had no idea who he was burying except for the Army identification papers nailed to the wood.

Raston walked to the open grave and looked down, braced for another strong whiff of the terrible odor. He sniffed twice. It was there, but very faint, so faint he thought he might be imagining it. The standard Army coffin looked in good condition. He glanced at the small, white headstone--*Cpl. Manfred Bergdorf, Co. D, 5th Iowa Volunteers, January 2, 1846 - April 17, 1864.* Manny Bergdorf, Raston thought to himself, a nasty little kid, always in trouble, but they said he made a good soldier. Probably a posthumous lie. If anyone had to be killed in the war, Raston couldn't imagine a more appropriate victim than Manny.

"This one should come up OK, Jules. Show them how to get the ropes under it."

Raston stood close to Jules as the two diggers positioned ropes under the coffin. He brushed the dust from the sleeves of his dark jacket. Taking a large red handkerchief from his back pocket, he wiped the sweat from his face, leaving faint streaks on each cheek.

"Tell me, Jules, are the men talking about what we're finding?" Raston asked quietly.

Garth thought for a moment. "Hard to tell, Mr. Bruhl. I ain't heard much. My guess is they ain't lookin' too close at what's inside the coffins."

"But the smell. What are they saying about the smell?"

"Well, they're complainin' 'bout it, all right. But they ain't got any idea what an old grave's s'posed to smell like. They prob'ly just think it smells normal."

"I hope you're right, Jules. Maybe there's nothing to worry about, unless the men that dug up the first body start telling stories. We just have to keep everyone away from the coffins when we open them. And we have to keep what we're finding just between us until we figure out what went on here. All right?"

"Sure thing, Mr. Bruhl, just between us."

Once the Army casket was out of the grave, Garth sent the two diggers to fetch the cart. Using his crowbar, he skillfully pried open both sides of the lid. Raston helped him lift it off. The interior of the coffin was filled by a moldy canvas bag draped over the outline of a body.

"Remember that's the way the Army sent them home, Jules. In a bag. We'd better open it up again before we put him back in the ground. We've seen what's left of Manny before. Actually, I think he was pretty much intact, if I remember right. And he still should be with all those chemicals in him, unless . . . just slit the bag with your knife."

Garth pulled his Bowie knife from its sheath on his belt and slit the canvas from top to bottom. Raston pushed the canvas aside and a shriveled face appeared, putrefied but still intact, save for the hole a piece of shrapnel had made in its forehead. What's this, he wondered? He had been sure they would find another train wreck of a skeleton.

"What do you make of this, Jules?"

"I dunno, Mr. Bruhl, I just dunno."

"Well, let's have a closer look."

Raston ripped the canvas wider and bent down close to the face. The skin was dark and dry, drawn tightly over the front of the skull. The eyes had sunk deep in their sockets. Raston lifted an arm and examined the hand. Placing his palm on the corpse's chest, he felt the body through the blue uniform. Fumbling at the buttons he opened the wool jacket then the shirt revealing dark, leather-like skin.

"Well, he's as he should be. Now let's lift him."

Using both hands, Jules lifted the canvas bag at the foot, then at the head, as Raston peered underneath. The hole was visible in the floor of the coffin, a third of the way down from the head. Raston lifted the side of the canvas. There was also a hole in the back of the bag.

"Help me turn him over," Raston called softly as he grappled for a grip on the uniform.

Together they gently turned the body on its face. It took Raston only a few seconds to find the hole in the dark uniform. He pushed the uniform jacket up, exposing the back. A few inches above the right hip, small pieces of the decayed flesh had been torn away. As Raston pushed the jacket higher, two lumps like dried dirt fell from the fold in the cloth.

"My God, Mr. Bruhl, it looks as if somethin' took some bites outa him. What would do that?"

"I wish I knew, Jules," Raston answered, picking up one of the lumps and rolling it between his fingers. "Do you know what these are? They're dried flesh. Probably came from those bites. It looks like whatever got in here didn't have much appetite for Manny."

Chapter Fourteen

The Tunnel

1950

Lt was a Saturday in March, nearly a year after
Henry and Sheila had watched their grandmother kill
the chicken. Henry's mother planned to take him to his
grandparents' farm for the day while she went shopping
with his grandmother and his aunt. The sky was a dull
gray. Cold, gusty winds brought periods of snow
showers, dusting the brown, frozen ground and the
lingering patches of crusty snow with fresh white
powder. Henry was bored and restless. It seemed the
cold would last forever. Even the trip to the farm didn't
brighten his mood.

Henry sat in the living room glumly staring at a
Hardy Boys book when Sheila and her mother arrived.
He listened to them talk with his grandmother in the
kitchen, discussing whether Sheila should come with
them on their shopping trip. Henry worried she might
go, and he would be left to entertain himself with his
grandfather. But Sheila held firm. She would stay.

As soon as she had taken off her coat and boots,
Sheila came into the living room, gave Henry a wave and
sat down next to him on the couch, bouncing briefly on

the springy cushion. He was glad she was there but looked up from his book as if he would rather not be interrupted.

"Hi, Henry, you grump. What are you going to do today besides reading what those goody-goody Hardy Boys did while the clock ticked?"

Forming his straightest face, Henry turned to her and said the first thing that came to his mind. "*We* are going to explore the cellar." The words had seemed to pop from his mouth on their own. He could scarcely believe what he had just said. Now there was no way he could back out.

Sheila looked shocked, which gave Henry enthusiasm. "Look, it's the perfect time. We'll be alone with Grandpa and he'll be working outside somewhere. It'll be really neat to see what's down there and there's no way anyone will know. And maybe we can find that door. Besides, what else is there to do?"

"Well, we could play in the snow . . . get out the sleds . . ."

"You know it's not deep enough. C'mon, let's do something *really* exciting. Remember, you said you'd go with me to look for the lock sometime. Well, now's the time."

"I just don't want to get caught in the cellar. You know how everybody is about us going down there. Maybe we should wait 'til they leave and ask Grandpa if we can play down there since there's not much snow outside."

Henry was spurred on by her reluctance. "He'll never let us. C'mon, don't be chicken."

Sheila looked at her shoes as she kicked her heels against the sofa. "Oh, all right . . . but we can't stay down too long."

Their grandfather stayed in the house all morning, first reading a newspaper, then leisurely looking through the Sears catalog that had arrived in the mail the day before. Henry and Sheila sat impatiently in the living room staring at open books. Twice their grandfather asked them if they wouldn't like to go outside in the snow rather than sit around inside. Sheila answered that they wanted to read. At noon, Lyle

Gerdes got out the lunch his wife had made before she left—ham salad sandwiches and milk from the refrigerator, potato chips and peanut butter cookies from the pantry.

"You kids want to come out to the shed with me this afternoon? I'll let you play on the tractor if you promise not to tell your grandma."

This was an offer his grandfather had never made before. He was tempted. He turned to look at Sheila who was looking at him with a question in her eye. Clearly she was tempted, too. But Henry's resolve returned.

"That would be great, Grandpa, but we really planned to read today," he answered firmly, wanting to send a clear message to Sheila.

"Yeah, we're going to read, Grandpa."

Lyle Gerdes looked surprised. "Okie dokie, but if you get bored, get your coats on and c'mon out."

As soon as his grandfather had closed the kitchen door, Henry went to the window and watched until he went into the shed. Then he ran to get flashlights from the pantry.

The door to the cellar was in a corner of the kitchen. Henry opened it softly, as if there was something in the cellar that might hear them coming. He found a light switch just inside the doorway and pushed the button. A dim light appeared off to one side below. Henry started down the stairs with Sheila close behind. He gripped the smooth wood railing tightly.

When he reached the bottom of the stairs, Henry paused. A bare bulb over the Maytag washing machine on his left cast a weak glow that faded into darkness at its edges. Henry turned on his flashlight and pointed it into the dark. A maze of large pipes appeared in the beam.

"That's the furnace over there."

"I know, Henry. It's kind of scary. Those big pipes coming out the top make it look like a giant octopus."

Henry looked at it again and shivered slightly.

"Shine your flashlight back there now," Sheila asked, pointing her light into the other end of the cellar.

Henry aimed his light in the same direction. The beams disappeared into the darkness.

"It must go back a long ways," Henry whispered, "I don't see anything."

"Henry, quit whispering. You're trying to scare me."

"How's this, scaredy-cat," Henry said in a loud voice.

"Better. And don't call me that," Sheila answered with a flash of anger. "C'mon, let's look over by the furnace first."

"Fine." Henry started walking as boldly as he could. "I think Grampa puts the coal in on the other side. There must be a light back there."

He shined his flashlight above them as they circled the furnace. One of the furnace pipes hung so low Henry brushed it with his head. The radiating heat warmed his skin. When they reached the corner of the cellar behind the furnace, Henry could see a flickering glow from the fire through a vent in the furnace door.

Suddenly everything was bright.

"You're right, there is a light." Sheila proudly held onto a cord tied to the overhead light.

The cement floor around the furnace doors looked as if it had recently been swept. In the wall were two doors, both covered with wide streaks of different colored paint. They were held closed by hooks.

"Let's see what's behind those doors," Sheila said.

Henry thought he knew. "All right, you open the first one."

She unhooked the first door and pulled it open. Cold air washed in. "Henry, come here and see."

Henry walked over to her and pointed his flashlight through the door. A short passageway led to a flight of stairs. Sheila crept slowly toward the stairs and looked up at a sliver of light overhead.

"This just goes outside." She sounded disappointed.

"That's what I thought. Grandpa takes the ashes out this way, through those slanty doors by the side of the house."

"Well then, let's see what's behind the other door."

They left the passageway. Henry hooked the first door while Sheila went to the next one.

"Well, go ahead and open it," Henry said, sounding smug.

Sheila tugged on the hook which opened with a short, rusty squeak. The door swung open by itself. Again cold air washed over them, bringing with it a new smell—one that was familiar. Henry shined his light inside. The room was filled with chunks of black coal, almost to the ceiling.

"It's just the coal bin," Henry pointed out.

"I'm not going in there."

Henry shrugged, closed the door and pushed the hook back through the eye with a metallic crunch.

"There's not much at this end. Let's go see what's back there." Henry pointed to the other end of the cellar with his flashlight.

With Henry leading, they walked past the staircase, through the edge of light around the wash tubs and into the dark. He shined his flashlight back and forth as they went. The dirt floor became uneven, and Henry had to step carefully to keep from stumbling. Behind him Sheila shined her light with jerks from one place to the next. Cobwebs dangled from the bare rafters overhead. Henry's skin started to tingle.

"Ick, Henry, there're spiders back here. They're going to get in my hair."

"Just duck under the cobwebs. The spiders won't jump on you."

"How do you know, smarty-pants?" she said, taking hold of his arm.

Henry shook off her hand. "I just do, scaredy-cat."

Sheila stuck out her tongue.

Deeper in this end of the cellar, the floor was piled with all manner of things abandoned by a series of Gerdes households. As he moved the beam of his light around slowly, Henry spied several battered suitcases, two wooden sawhorses, a pile of large tin pipes, a broken tricycle, four overturned chairs around a dented metal table and a dilapidated baby buggy. Mounds of dust and small clumps of dirt and mortar covered everything. His interest was immediately aroused. It was like a big closet. Further back, his beam fell on a pile of cardboard boxes and orange crates stacked against a stone wall where the cellar ended.

"Look at all that stuff, Henry. Let's see what's in those boxes."

"Yeah, let's do. I'll start on that side."

Henry was contemplating the stacks of boxes, wondering where to start, when he saw a large door partially hidden behind them.

"Sheila, look! There's a door back here. Hold my flashlight while I move these boxes."

Henry handed her the flashlight and started to lift the top box on the pile. He could barely move it.

"It's too heavy. I'll drop it."

"Here, I'll help." Sheila set the flashlights on the edge of a chair pointed to shine in Henry's direction.

Each taking a side, they managed to slide the box from the top and set it down on the dirt floor. Together they slid the remaining two boxes to the side, revealing the door. They stared at it for a moment. Henry picked up his flashlight and methodically moved the beam over the rough face of the door. It was massive, unlike any door he had ever seen except in movies.

Then he held his light steady on the lock. "Wow, it's big, like a door to a dungeon!"

"OK, smarty, why don't you tell me what's behind *this* door."

"Probably just black widows and tarantulas."

"Henry! You quit saying that stuff or you can stay down here by yourself!"

Henry decided to quit. "Sheila, look at that, where my light's shining."

Sheila leaned closer. "That keyhole looks pretty big. Do you think that's it?"

"Could be. And it doesn't look like anybody's opened it in a long time. Let's see if it's locked." Henry put down his flashlight and reached for the handle above the keyhole cautiously as if he expected it to be hot. By pulling down with both hands he managed to move it. Then he pulled out as hard as he could. The door didn't budge. Twisting his face into a horrible contortion, he pulled harder. Still it wouldn't move.

"It must be locked," he said a little breathless.

"You wouldn't expect someone to have a door like this and not lock it, would you?"

"This has to be the door. Let's go get the key and see."

"But what about Grandpa?"

"He'll be out in the shed a long time yet. I'm going to get it."

"Not without me, you're not!" Sheila headed for the stairs at a run, Henry right behind. They spurted out of the cellarway into the kitchen, and ran noisily down the hall to the closet door. Henry reached it first, skidding to a stop. He flicked on his flashlight and plunged in. A familiar smell of mothballs and old wool greeted him. Henry ducked under the clothes and crawled rapidly through the aisle between boxes. Sheila stayed right at his heels. The sewing machine cabinet was exactly where he'd last seen it. He waited on his knees in front of it until Sheila was beside him. Together they lifted the lid. Henry pointed his light at the machine. The bag was there. Sheila struggled to untie it. When the bag came loose, she reached in and pulled out the large key.

"What about the gun?" Henry reached for the sack.

"It's there, but don't touch it."

"Don't worry, bossy, I wasn't going to. Put the bag back and let's go."

Sheila retied the bag to the sewing machine. They crawled back to the closet door and ran down the hall. When they reached the kitchen, Sheila hesitated.

"Don't you think we should check on Grandpa before we go back down?"

Henry looked up at the schoolhouse clock on the wall. "Didn't he go out at one? It's quarter of two now. He won't be back in for at least another hour, maybe two. We've got plenty of time. C'mon." Henry headed for the cellar stairs. Sheila went to the window and looked into the farmyard. "Sheila, bring the key."

With a sigh she turned and hurried after him.

Henry was holding the beam of his flashlight on the locked door when she caught up. "Give it here, Sheila; let me try it."

"No, I'll do it. Hold my flashlight." She stepped to the door and tried to insert the key into the lock. She jiggled it twice and the key slid in. But when she tried to turn it, the key barely budged. Summoning more strength, she tried again. Slowly it began to turn with a low, grinding sound.

"Ataway, Sheila, it works!"

When she had turned the key as far as it would go, she put her hand on the handle and pulled on the door. It wouldn't move. She seized the handle with both hands and pulled again. Still it didn't move.

"Let's both try." Henry put down his flashlight, placed his hands around hers and squeezed. "OK, let's pull together. Ready . . . set . . . pull!"

"Ow, Henry. Not so hard. That hurts my hand."

"Sorry, but we got it started. Let's try it again." Henry tightened his grip around Sheila's hands, screwed his face into a grimace, and they both lunged backwards. The door opened grudgingly, its rusting hinges groaning under its weight. Henry was suddenly face to face with the blackness of the interior. An odor of stale air drifted out.

Sheila came alongside him with their flashlights pointing their beams through the doorway. Inside was a small room with crumbling stone walls. Lines of moisture ran down the rocks where water had seeped in, forming small puddles in the hard-packed dirt floor. Except for rocks and yellowing newspapers scattered across the floor, the room was empty. Henry courageously stepped inside. The air felt moist against his skin, smelling of damp earth mixed with something unpleasant.

Without warning the door creaked closed behind him. For a moment Henry was paralyzed with fear. Then he heard muffled laughing on the other side. Putting his hands against the door, he pushed. It wouldn't open.

"Sheila," he screamed. "What are you doing?

Open the door!"

"What's the matter? Is it scary in there?" Henry could barely hear her. "Who's the scaredy-cat now?"

"Who cares." He could hear her laughing. "This isn't funny. Just open the door!"

"I'll open it if you promise not to call me that anymore."

"OK, OK, I promise."

"Hope to die, stick a needle in your eye?"

"Yes, yes!" Henry yelled, beginning to feel panicky.

Slowly the door creaked open. Sheila stood in the doorway giggling. His eyes watery, Henry glared at her. Stepping back through the doorway, he socked her on the shoulder. "That wasn't funny."

"Oh, Henry, can't you take a joke?"

"Yeah, but that wasn't a very good one. Look, if we're going to explore, we have to promise each other some things."

"All right. What should we promise?"

"I mean it. We have to promise not to trick each other like that."

"OK, but you have to promise not to treat me like a kid or call me names."

"Fine. And we also have to promise never to tell on each other. C'mon now, let's swear."

"Sure. I swear. Shouldn't we do like the Indians, prick our fingers and do it in blood?"

"We could. Do you have a needle?"

"No."

"Let's just swear then." Henry raised his right hand. "I solemnly swear not to play scary tricks on you, to treat you better, like you were a boy my own age and not a girl who's a whole year younger, and never to tell anyone about the places we go on the farm. And I won't call you names, either."

Sheila raised her right hand, looking very serious. "I solemnly swear not to play scary tricks on you, to treat you better, like one of my girl friends and not like some old cousin who thinks he's better than any girl. Oh, and I swear not to call you names or tell anybody a thing about where we go or what we do on the farm."

Henry mimicked Sheila's intent expression. They both giggled.

"Good. Now let's go in." Henry took a tentative step toward the doorway keeping his eye on Sheila.

"No, I'll go first." Sheila stepped around Henry and walked boldly to the middle of the room. She slowly turned in a slow circle shining her light around the walls. Henry followed her beam with his.

"It stinks in here," she said.

Henry had noticed the smell. An odor of something putrid and rotten, but different somehow. It seemed vaguely familiar. "I know. Maybe it's because it's been closed up a long time."

"It sure looks like Grandma and Grandpa don't come in here. I wonder why it has such a big door?"

"And with that big lock. Do you think it was to keep something out? Or something in?" Henry wished he hadn't asked the question. As soon as he had said the words, goosebumps rose on his skin.

"Henry, don't say that. I get scared. It is really weird, though. I mean with the key hidden in a bag with a gun. Maybe we should get out. There might be something dangerous in here."

"Oh, c'mon. You can see there's nothing in here. Let's just look around a little."

They began to shine their lights around the stone walls.

"Henry, look over there." She was holding her light on the wall opposite the door.

"Where?"

"In the wall. There's a hole."

A jagged opening the size of the center of a tire was in the stone wall a few feet above the dirt floor. A small pile of stones lay beneath it.

"I'll take a look. Keep your light on it."

Henry crossed the room and climbed onto the rocks.

"C'mon over with your flashlight," Henry whispered.

"All right, but don't whisper like that."

Henry stood on the stones, steadying himself with one hand on the side of the opening and pointed his flashlight inside. The light couldn't reach the end. He was excited. It was a tunnel—right there in the cellar of his grandparents' house. The walls were uneven with rocks protruding in many places. Its rock floor was worn and smooth. Cobwebs stretched between the rocks on the ceiling and walls. Everything Henry's light touched glistened with a thin coat of moisture, including the cobwebs which held tiny droplets of water. The odor he noticed when they first entered the old cellar was much stronger. Then he remembered.

"Sheila! Come up here and see this!"

Sheila climbed on top of the rocks. "Phew, that smell's worse over here. It must come from in there."

"Don't you remember it? The big stone entrance by the creek that we saw last year? I think it's the same smell that came from behind those rocks."

"I don't remember too well, but you might be right." She put her head next to his and looked inside. "It looks like a tunnel or a little cave. Look at all those spider webs. Ick! I'll bet there're bats in there, too, and that's what makes it smell. Where do you suppose it goes? Do you think it was part of the underground railroad? Remember Grandpa told us that there are tunnels around here where runaway slaves used to hide."

"I'd sure like to find out where it goes. Finally we *really* have something to explore. Look at these rocks in the cement around the sides here. They're like the ones in this pile. I'll bet this was all sealed up sometime like that old entrance. But we can get in here. It might get bigger further back. Let's go in a ways." But as he peered into the dark passageway again, Henry began to have second thoughts.

"I don't know. Look at all those spider webs. Besides, is there time? We have to crawl and we're going to get dirty, you know. Then Grandpa will guess where we were . . ."

"Maybe you're right. Maybe we should do it later." Henry felt a little relieved.

"Oh, all right, I'll go in a little ways, just to see where it ends. But you have to go first and get those cobwebs out of the way."

Henry knew he couldn't change his mind now without looking chicken. Summoning his courage, he put his head into the opening.

"Here, I'll give you a boost." Sheila pushed on his bottom until he could get a knee on the bottom edge. Then he wriggled inside.

"Give me your flashlight. I'll grab your hand," Henry said, twisting his body to look back. She handed him her flashlight, then jumped up and bent into the opening at her waist. Henry held onto her hand and she pulled her legs in.

"All right. Now let's go." Henry took another deep breath, lowered his head and squirmed into the passageway. As he moved forward, the tight quarters began to make him nervous and it occurred to him that there might be something dangerous up ahead. A vision of a hibernating bear flashed in his mind. Maybe they should get out. But he didn't dare say so. Sheila might think he was chicken. He'd go on.

He crawled ahead crab-like, trying to keep from scraping his skin on the rocks that protruded from the walls and floor. He kept his light pointed ahead, imagining that any second he might find something terrible. Gradually the tunnel widened enough for him to get onto his hands and knees. Now he could see the beam from Sheila's flashlight bouncing around him as she crawled close behind. He brushed at the cobwebs that were strung across the passageway. Some caught on his face.

"Stay close, Sheila, and watch out for the rocks."

"Just don't go too fast. My flashlight's getting dim. Do you see the end yet?"

"Not yet."

Henry crawled steadily, shining his light into the darkness, hoping to see an end to the tunnel. He was still nervous, but gaining confidence the farther they went encountering nothing. Gradually he became concerned that their only discovery might be the tunnel itself. Then he sensed the passageway begin to slope downhill, and the putrid odor become stronger. How far had they come, he wondered? And how long would it take to get out?

"Henry?" Sheila's voice sounded tense.

Henry stopped. "What?" He twisted his head back toward her.

"I think my flashlight's going out."

Henry looked at her light. It had clearly faded. "Maybe there's a bad connection somewhere. Shake it a little."

Sheila shook her flashlight. The batteries rattled inside but the light didn't brighten. She shook it again. "It's not helping. We'd better go back. I don't want to stay here without a light. Besides, that smell's getting worse."

Henry grew frustrated. His newly-gained confidence made him want to keep going. "My flashlight's fine. Let's just go a little farther. We've got to come to the end pretty soon."

"No, I don't want to go without my own flashlight that works."

"Well, *I'm* not going back." Henry was annoyed. He wanted to go on, but not without her. "Aw, c'mon, Sheila," he said in a conciliatory voice. "Just a little farther. I promise I'll go back right away if your light goes out." Henry pointed his flashlight down the passageway and started to crawl.

"Oh, all right, but remember you promised."

Henry crawled for several more minutes. The only sound came from their knees scraping along the rock floor.

"Henry," Sheila whispered.

"What now?"

"I think there's something in here with us."

A sensation like electricity ran through Henry's body. "What do you mean *something's* in here with us?"

"I mean it feels like there's something in here. And it smells like it, too."

Henry shined his light around. "I don't see anything, do you?"

"Well, no . . . "

"Let's keep going then." Henry answered, irritated that Sheila had frightened him.

"All right, just a little ways, but then I'm going back. This place gives me the creeps."

Henry started to crawl faster, anxious to find where the tunnel ended before Sheila turned back. His sudden flash of fright had passed, but he was still tense. After a few minutes he turned his head and pointed his flashlight back at Sheila. The beam fell on her face which was set in a grim expression.

"Isn't this neat, Sheila? I wonder how it got here."

"Maybe runaway slaves dug it a long time ago so they could escape from the house if somebody came looking for them."

"Could be, but it's pretty small for anybody bigger than us."

"Do you think Grandma and Grandpa even know it's here?"

"Sure they do, they must."

"But that door hadn't been open in a long time."

"Yeah, but they've lived here a long time. Grandpa probably built it to keep people out, like the stone wall in that old entryway by the creek."

"I hope you're right, Henry."

The floor felt level again, but the passageway was becoming smaller. He had to be careful not to hit his head on the ceiling. It dawned on him that it would be hard to turn around. The closeness of the walls and ceiling began to make him panicky. Then the walls seemed to retreat and he saw a fork in the passageway. The excitement of the discovery helped his panic subside.

"Sheila, look at this!" he whispered loudly.

Sheila squeezed along side him. "Oh, Henry, let's not go in either one. We might get lost."

"No we won't. Where do you think we are, anyway? I mean, what do you think's above us?"

Sheila thought for a moment. "Well, the old cellar was at the end of house toward the river and the entrance was in the wall across from the door, so we're going toward the bluff."

"That's what I think, too. We could even be further than the yard, out in the field. Which means the creek would be ahead somewhere. Do you know what else?"

"No, what?"

"I'll bet one of these goes to that old entrance by the creek. We're headed in that direction, and it smells the same way. Let's see if we can tell which one."

"No, I want to go back. Besides, you promised. And Grandpa will be coming in the house pretty soon. If he catches us down here, we'll get in trouble."

"I'm just going to look a little ways."

"Well, I'm staying here, so you've got two minutes," Sheila said firmly.

Henry looked down the passageway on his left. He could see nothing but the tunnel disappearing into blackness. If this leads to the entrance by the creek, which he guessed it did, then where does the other passageway go? He chose the opening on the right. The tunnel sloped downward, becoming gradually steeper as he crawled. The rocks along the sides seemed smoother. And there were no cobwebs. Henry had crawled barely five yards when the putrid odor grew so strong, it almost made him gag. He had nearly become accustomed to it, but now it was sharper, as if it could burn the lining of his nose.

Ahead Henry saw a wide spot in the passageway. There was an odd shaped mound on the floor. He crawled faster, anxious to see what it was.

"Oh Jeez!" he cried. In front of him was a pile of tattered clothing and bones that looked human. He caught his breath with a gasp. He pushed on the pile gently with his flashlight. The slight touch was enough. The pile collapsed. Some of the bones disintegrated into dust, others rolled onto the floor. He uttered a small cry when one came to rest against his knee. He pointed his light down to look. It was large and round—the back of a skull. Recoiling in alarm, his knee brushed against it and the skull rolled face up, its empty eyes staring up at him. Terrified, he began crawling backwards as fast as he could.

He had backed only a few yards when he heard a shriek. The sound was piercing in the tunnel. He was too shocked to realize what it was. Then he heard his name.

"Henry, Henry! Help, Henry! Come here! Come back, quick!"

Henry froze. The shrieks had paralyzed him. It took him a few seconds to find his voice. Sheila was still screaming. "What's wrong? What is it, Sheila?"

"There's something in here! Something's touching me! Oh, Henry, get it off!" Sheila continued to scream, sounding incoherent.

Henry backed out of the passageway as fast as he could and turned, banging his head sharply on the rock wall. Rubbing the spot above his ear, he pointed the beam of his flashlight toward her, afraid of what he might see. Sheila was huddled against the side of the tunnel a few feet in front of him shuddering, her arms holding her knees tight to her chest. Her flashlight was still in her hand but it wasn't on. He saw nothing else.

"What's the matter?"

"Something touched me," she answered in a hoarse voice, tears in her eyes.

"What happened? Tell me."

It took her a few seconds to answer. "My flashlight went out all the way as soon as you went down that other tunnel." Still shaking, she struggled to talk. "I saw your light for a couple minutes . . . and then you were gone . . . it got so dark . . . and that's when it happened."

"What?"

"Something touched my arm. Something soft, like skin. Then it pressed against my pants here, on my leg. Let's get out of here!"

Her fear was making Henry frightened as well. He shined his light quickly around the passageway. "Do you see anything now?"

Sheila looked intently in both directions. "No, nothing. But I want to go right now!"

"OK. Anyway it probably was just a bat that flew by in the dark," Henry said, trying to convince himself as well as Sheila. "You lead. Here, take my flashlight. Just remember to point it back here sometimes."

They crawled rapidly for several minutes without talking. Henry found it much harder without a light. Rocks seemed to protrude from everywhere. He could see nothing but Sheila's outline in front of him as she crawled into the beam of light bouncing in front of her.

When they reached the narrower part of the tunnel, his shoulder hit a sharp rock that jutted out from the wall. He stopped to rub it. Sheila kept moving. The darkness deepened around him as she crawled away.

Henry felt a puff of wind on his face and a slight change in the air on his skin. It was over in a second but made the hair on his body stand upright. He held his breath and listened. There seemed to be a small sound coming toward him from behind, a low, slurping sound, that reminded him of jello pouring into a bowl. The awful stench grew stronger again. He twisted his head as far to the rear as he could and squinted into the darkness, wanting to be convinced that nothing was there. Instead he thought he saw something moving along the tunnel floor, coming toward him in the blackness, something he could feel more than see, something steadily pushing the air and its odor toward him. Henry desperately hoped it was his imagination.

"Sheila, wait up!" He started crawling rapidly toward the dim light ahead, forgetting the pain in his shoulder. "Quick! Shine the light back here."

Almost immediately the beam was in his eyes. He ducked. "Shine it behind me. See if something's back there."

"I don't see anything, Henry. What's wrong? Did something touch you, too?"

Henry raised his head and looked back, seeing only the tunnel walls disappearing into darkness.

"No, nothing touched me, but I thought I saw something . . . or felt something behind me. I must be imagining things."

Sheila twisted forward with a jerk, scraping her hand against the tunnel wall and dropping the flashlight. Henry heard it hit the rock floor as the light went out. The blackness was immediate.

He could hear Sheila fumbling for the light. As he waited for it to come on, something brushed lightly against his leg. Startled, he yelled and jerked upward, hitting the ceiling with his head, then landing on his knee.

"Ow, Jeez, Sheila, cripes, you're right, there's something in here!" As he rubbed his knee, he felt it again, this time brushing his cheek. It was soft and moist, like skin. Then he felt something sharp like a pin prick. He yelled again.

"I've got the flashlight, Henry. Let me just get it back on."

Then the light was on. On the verge of panic, Henry tried to see what had touched him . . . but again the light went out.

Now Sheila screamed. "It's touching me! Something's touching me again! Henry, on my neck! Ow, it's still there!"

"Get the light on, Sheila! Hurry!"

"I'm trying to!"

She shook the flashlight and it came on. Henry looked all around, then at Sheila. She was holding the light, shaking. He saw nothing but the tunnel walls. "We've got to be sure the light stays on. Let me see it a minute."

As soon as Henry took the flashlight from her, the light went out again. "Dammit!" he screamed. He felt the end piece that held in the batteries. It was loose. As he tightened it, something pressed against his neck, something hard and sharp like a pin prick. He screamed just as the light came on. Again he saw nothing.

"Did it get you, Henry? Did you feel it? Are you OK?"

Henry worked to find his voice. "I'm OK. I think I fixed the light so it'll stay on. Let's get out of here. Go ahead. I'll hold the light on you." He rubbed his neck to see if there might be blood. It felt dry.

They crawled as fast as they could, ignoring the pain of the rock floor that was bruising their knees. Henry was sure something would overtake him at any second. He kept urging her to go faster, crawling so close that his hand came down on her shoe, stopping her abruptly and causing her to scream. It seemed forever until they reached the opening into the cellar. Sheila scrambled out ahead of him. Henry came tumbling out behind her, falling onto the rocks. He scrambled upright and they stood facing each other, catching their breath. Henry shined the flashlight back toward the tunnel opening. There was nothing but stones ringing a jagged black hole.

"C'mon, Henry, I want to get out of this room." Together they raced for the door. Once outside, they pushed the heavy door closed as fast as they could. Henry reached for the key. It turned slowly in the keyhole and the door locked.

Although relieved that the door was closed and locked, Henry still trembled. "What do you think was *in* there?" he asked.

"I don't know, but something was."

"Maybe now we know why this big door is here."

Sheila stared at him. She was shaking but her eyes burned intently. "I've never been so scared in my life, Henry. You'll *never, ever* get me to come down to this old cellar again!"

Going back into the tunnel was the last thing in Henry's mind. Still, he thought he wouldn't tell her about the skeleton. Just in case.

Chapter Fifteen

The Letter

1874

Late Saturday night after the sixth day of digging, Raston Bruhl sat at the large oak desk in his study rubbing his hands roughly over his cheeks and forehead while a fierce spring thunderstorm raged outside. A crystal oil lamp burned on the corner of his desk, smoke drifting from its chimney, its flickering light struggling to penetrate the darkness in the room. Sophia and the children were already in bed, and the quiet of the house magnified the sound of rain pelting the windows. As the work in the town cemetery progressed, Raston had grown increasingly troubled. His eyes were red-rimmed, contrasting sharply with the dark circles which had appeared earlier in the week.

He read his notes over and over. They kept telling him the same thing. All told they had unearthed fifty-seven bodies. Forty-four of them had been nothing but mutilated skeletons, stripped of their flesh. What had happened to them? Was it possible that something . . . or someone . . . actually ate them? What could have gotten into the coffins to do it? When did it happen? Should I tell the Mayor? What if I tell no one? Then what if someone finds out? Will I be blamed? What will they think I did? My God, they'll think I'm some kind of ghoul. Raston rubbed his sweaty palms against his pants.

Most of the bodies were people Raston had buried. He couldn't help but think the town would blame him for what happened. Raston rose unsteadily from his chair, walked to a table against the wall and poured himself another sherry, his fifth in the last hour. He felt some discomfort in his chest and rubbed it absentmindedly.

There has be a logical answer to what happened, he told himself sternly and began to go over it all again. Besides the forty-four mutilated bodies, thirteen were largely untouched—seven soldiers killed in the war and six others that had been buried in the last two years. Like the mutilated bodies, the soldiers had small holes in the bottom of their Army-issue caskets, holes that only worms and beetles could get through. Except he knew that worms and beetles couldn't do what had been done to those corpses. There was something else. The soldiers had bite marks on their bodies while the six bodies recently buried had neither bite marks nor holes in their caskets, which could mean that whatever had been in the town cemetery feeding on corpses didn't like the taste of soldiers, then stopped feeding altogether about two years ago. In which case the thing is gone and he and the town would never know what it was. If only he could believe that. A severe thunderclap shook the windows in his study, punctuating his anxious mood.

Raston rose from his leather desk chair, brushing against a pile of papers which scattered over the floor. As he leaned over to gather them, he noticed an unfamiliar leather-bound book on which the papers had been stacked. It took him a few seconds to remember what it was—the journal delivered by the dry goods peddler weeks earlier. Raston sat back down and opened the journal. An envelope slid onto his lap. The names Harman Hanzfig and Raston Bruhl were written on the front. He slit open the envelope and took out a letter. Squinting to make out the unfamiliar handwriting in the dim light, he began to read.

March 2, 1874
Mr. Harmon Hanzfig
Mr. Raston Bruhl
Bruders Landing, Iowa

Dear Sirs,

With this letter I am sending you a journal. It records
an experience in my life you know something about, the
explosion of the Prince Nathan and my rescue from Big Tow
Island. As you may remember, I stayed in Bruders Landing
only as long as it took to arrange land transportation east.
Perhaps when you read this journal you will understand why.
It describes things that happened to me on that island, things I
could not bring myself to tell you while I was there. Yet I felt I
must record what happened on that Island while it was fresh
in my mind. Thus I wrote this journal on my journey back to
Baltimore.

News of the explosion had reached Baltimore and
people were amazed that I had survived such an event out
West in the wilderness. When I arrived, I was greeted as a
hero. Never had I been treated with such care and attention.
There were celebrations and dinners and even a neighborhood
parade in my honor. And Gus Hentzler himself assured me I
would have a good position with the Hentzler Dry Goods
Company as long as I wished it.

With all this going on I made a decision for which I may
be eternally damned. I decided to tell no one what happened
on the island and hid the journal away. This was a decision
made out of pure fear and vanity. I had become deathly afraid
of losing this exalted place with my family and friends, and my
secure future with the Hentzler Dry Goods Company. You will
see that my experience was so strange, how could anyone
believe it anyway? I was afraid I would be branded a lunatic
and my new life and future would be doomed.

How this cowardly decision may have harmed you and
the innocent people of Bruders Landing has haunted me greatly
these last thirty years. It has been the source of many
nightmares. You see, there are things about Big Tow Island
you must know, things that at times will put you all in mortal
danger. I prayed regularly that you have learned of these
things some other way, that the time of danger didn't come
before you found out, or that the danger didn't come at all. In
spite of my torment, I couldn't bring myself to tell you out of

another fear, the fear of facing the consequences of withholding this information for so long.

But now this has all changed. I wish I could say the change was from my own resolve, but I cannot. My doctors have told me what they must have known for weeks, that I am dying of consumption. This sentence of death has at last given me the courage I was unable to find during my life.

I pray continually for your well-being and forgiveness. My death will have come by the time you read this. Please pray for my soul.

Thaddeus Bump

Raston laid the letter aside and stared into the darkness, conjuring up memory after memory—the ride to Bruders Landing with Thaddeus Bump after he had been rescued from Big Tow Island, the Indian legends surrounding Shoquoquon he had heard, Evan Musser's words in the *Prince Nathan's* pilot house as they approached the town, and the warnings in *Ichabod's Compendium of Troubles in the New World* which had been lost with the *Prince Nathan*. Maybe there is good reason no one goes to Big Tow Island. He began to feel chilly and the discomfort in his chest returned.

With more than a little trepidation, Raston picked up the journal and turned to the first page. The ink had faded. He pulled the lamp closer. With some difficulty Raston read Bump's entries describing his passage on the river boat, his drinking bout the night before leaving Bruders Landing, falling asleep in a chair on the Texas deck, the first explosion which jolted him from his alcohol-induced sleep, the second explosion which blew him into the water, then regaining consciousness on what he thought was the Illinois shore and starting to make his way to Bruders Landing.

On the journal's fourth page, Raston found a warning.

The rest of this account you might dismiss as the blithering of an idiot—or one who was knocked forever senseless by the explosions. Even I find it hard to believe as I look back, but I swear on all I hold dear that it is true. Take care not to treat it lightly for it may be a matter of life or death for those who venture near Big Tow Island and the bluffs of Bruders Landing.

Raston read on, deeply absorbed, oblivious to everything beyond the circle of dim light cast by the oil lamp. When he reached the end, Raston let the journal fall into his lap and stared straight ahead.

Chapter Sixteen

The Mausoleum

1956

Herbert Siefken leaned back in his desk chair, eyes half-closed, daydreaming about the night with Norma. The window next to his desk was open and a breeze with the scent of fresh earth and budding lilacs blew gently across his face. It was the first warm day of April. Herbert thought of the flower garden he intended to plant, just as he had intended every other spring since he and Norma were married five years before. After all, he reminded himself, it was a search for a place to do peaceful things like gardening that brought him to Bruders Landing in the first place, wasn't it? Well, the garden would come eventually, but he certainly had found things peaceful. Oh, there were trouble spots—cases of shoplifting, mostly by kids in their teens, occasional fights in the late night hours after the taverns closed, a few cases of domestic violence which he made sure were never repeated, and one or two robberies each year—but compared to the streets of Chicago, Bruders Landing was paradise. He was blessed with a wonderful wife and child. And he had carved a secure place for himself in the community, elected sheriff after Jack

Schoof retired, then re-elected for a second term without opposition.

The piercing ring of a telephone in the outer office roused him from his thoughts. Lester Hammond, the deputy on office duty, didn't answer until the fourth ring, one of his habits that annoyed Herbert no end. Hammond was in his early forties, of average height and thin enough to have once been called Skinny, a nickname he had managed to shed only after he became a deputy. His khaki uniform fit poorly, looking as if he had suddenly lost thirty pounds, pants bunched at the waist by a tightly cinched belt, one end hanging several inches down from the buckle. His thick, brown hair was neatly combed, held firmly in place by a liberal amount of Brylcreem. He had been hired by the former Sheriff as a dispatcher, but Herbert had also started to use him in the field.

Herbert could hear little of what Hammond was saying, but his tone conveyed a sense that the call might not be routine. The conversation was over in a few moments. Herbert heard a chair scrape sharply across the bare wood floor, which meant Lester was about to appear in the doorway.

"Sheriff, that was Walter Lippert out at Walnut Grove Cemetery. He said they found something out there this morning that he needs us to see."

"Some kids tipping over tombstones again?"

"No, I asked him that. He says it's worse, but didn't want to get into it on the phone. He said we have to get out there and look. Shall I call Gus in his car and send him over?"

Herbert saw an opportunity to enjoy the spring weather. "No, I'll go. Walt probably expects me to come and Gus should be in the south end of the county about now. Besides it's too nice a day to stay in the office."

Since its founding, Walnut Grove Cemetery had grown to over three hundred acres. Its natural setting on the bluffs, stately oak and maple trees, well-tended landscaping and intriguing headstones had made it a source of local pride. In the early 1900s the cemetery became the resting place of a former vice president so the town decided to replace the original wooden entry gate with one that would befit its new occupant, constructing an impressive arched entrance with local limestone. At the center of the stone entrance was an ornate iron gate topped by a row of spear points which was dutifully opened each morning and closed each night. The gate's intimidating design was used for the iron fence that extended along the road. So pleased was the town with the new entrance that the old administration building was replaced with a much larger structure built with blocks of the same limestone in the style of a medieval fortress with battlements lining its roof and small turrets at each corner.

Herbert drove through the stone arch and brought his car to a stop in front of the administration building, a structure that always reminded him of a prison.

"Good morning, Sheriff." Greta Foesel greeted him warmly as he entered the reception area. He walked to her desk past a long counter where maps of the cemetery were displayed to show grave site locations to prospective buyers. "Mr. Lippert's waiting for you in his office with Clyde and Kaleb. Go right on in."

"G'morning to you, Greta, and thanks," Herbert replied, giving her a smile as he passed.

Walter Lippert rose from the chair behind his desk as soon as Herbert entered. "Morning, Herb, I'm glad you came yourself." The cemetery manager was a tall, heavily built man with a full head of gray hair. He wore a khaki work shirt and pants starched military style. Herbert thought he seemed unusually glad to see him. "You know Clyde Hostetter, head of maintenance, and Kaleb Junker?"

"Actually, yes and no." Herbert shook each man's calloused hand. He knew Hostetter slightly. He was a man about fifty with an intelligent, weathered face. Herbert also knew that he was the person mainly responsible for the impeccable look of the cemetery grounds. Junker, on the other hand, was one of the few people in Eagle County Herbert had never seen before. His reaction was that Junker looked exactly like the grave digger he was, slender and muscular, powerful arms protruding from the long underwear he wore under a blue work shirt and bib coveralls smudged with dirt. His hair was gray and sparse, his weathered face a sea of wrinkles.

"Have a seat, Herb," Walter said with hesitation. "No, tell you what, let's go on over there so you can see for yourself."

"See what?"

"Some graves, in a mausoleum. You'll need one of these flashlights."

Lippert led the way down a cinder drive to the old part of the cemetery. No one spoke. The spring sun bore down, heating Herbert's head through his wide-brimmed hat. The only sounds were cinders crunching under their feet as they walked.

"Pretty warm for April," Herbert commented, attempting to lighten the mood.

"Yeah," Lippert answered offhandedly, and said nothing more.

Since the men were clearly in no mood for talking, Herbert read the tombstones as they passed. Several family names were familiar to him. As they walked farther, the grave markers became steadily older and more weatherbeaten. Some of the inscriptions became impossible to read. They had reached the oldest section in Walnut Grove. It was then that Lippert broke his silence.

"Herb, you've seen the mausoleums that some of the town's more prominent families built back in the 1800s. Generally we never open them unless there's a burial or the family asks us to for some reason. Which means we never go in most of them because the families have either died out or moved away. But you remember Rena Schneider, the girl that died in Chicago a couple years ago?"

"Yeah, sort of."

"Doesn't matter. The Schneider family mausoleum is up ahead and her parents wanted her buried there. It's one of those that was carved into the rock on the side of a ravine. The last time we opened it before her burial was nearly ten years earlier. Well, when Clyde here went in to get a space ready for the casket, he noticed that some of the shields we use to seal the burial chambers in the walls were broken out. We cleaned it all up for the funeral, but afterwards I told Bill Schneider that they should be repaired. He said he'd let me know."

"You didn't think Bill would agree to spend money so easy, did you?" Herbert asked.

"No, but I called him every once in a while to remind him. A couple weeks ago he finally gave the go-ahead, so Kaleb went to start work on it. Now, Herb, that mausoleum's been locked tight with cast iron doors and double locks. The keys are in a safe in my office. I keep a record whenever a key is checked out and a vault is opened. No one has taken the keys to the Schneider vault since we closed it after that funeral nearly two years ago, that is until this morning. And unless you burrow through solid rock, that door is the only way in. Now, look straight ahead. That's the mausoleum."

Lippert pointed to a stone structure with a peaked roof that looked as if it led directly into the hill in front of them. Large oak trees just coming into bud framed it on both sides. At the center of the structure was an iron door with a border of rivets and a small window with twisted bars near the top. The name Schneider was carved in stone above the door. Like the entrance and administration building, the mausoleum's stone had weathered with a dark cast. Where they joined the hillside, the stone was covered with a thick green moss that had thrived in the damp shade. Around the edge of the roof, the stone had been carved with ornate swirls. A gargoyle glowered down at them from the peak of the roof. To Herbert the structure looked like the entrance to an ancient maximum security cell.

"OK, Kaleb, tell him what you saw when you went in," Walter said as they approached the entrance.

"Well, Sheriff, somethin' sure went on in there since we buried that there girl. You'll see my meanin' in a minute." Junker reached into the front pocket of his overalls and retrieved two keys. One was made of heavy brass and looked well-used. The other was much smaller and newer. He inserted the large key into a keyhole halfway up the door.

"I had a devil of a time years back when I had to unlock this thing for that girl's funeral. It hadn't been opened in so long all the works had rusted up. I had t'soak the lock with cuttin' oil for hours 'fore I could turn the key. Then I had to give it another squirt this mornin' to make it work."

As the key turned, Herbert heard a heavy bolt slide away. Kaleb then took the smaller key and reached for an oversized padlock at the top of the door.

""Bout ten years ago we put these extra locks on all the vaults that have old locks like this one," Hostetter explained. "We got worried somebody might be able to pick one and try to steal somethin' or do some damage."

The padlock was fastened to a flange on a steel rod at the side of the door. After unlocking the padlock, Junker turned the flange and raised the rod from a hole at the base of the door frame, then pushed on the iron door. It swung stiffly on rusted hinges that moaned in protest.

"Sheriff, you're not goin' to like the smell in there," Junker said. "It's not like anythin' you ever smelt before. If it gets too bad, tell me. I've got some Vicks to put under your nose. It'll help." He went in first with Herbert close behind. Lippert and Hostetter followed. The bright April sun was quickly left behind as they entered the darkness. Junker's three-cell flashlight was on and its light roamed the ceiling and walls as they went. Patches of moss coated the stones which glistened with dampness and seeping water. The air was cool and wet.

Lippert began to explain as they walked: "You see, Sheriff, what they did here a hundred years ago or so was to build this entrance to the actual burial chamber which they carved into the hill. The vault itself is a room with twenty or so holes in the wall big enough to hold a casket. When there's a burial, the casket's put in one of 'em, then it's sealed with a stone shield like a tombstone that has the person's name on it. Watch yourself now, there're steps ahead."

Herbert switched on his flashlight. He heard the sound of water dripping on stone. The place smelled musty, like wet leaves and freshly turned earth. As he

174

followed Junker deeper into the mausoleum, he became aware of another smell, a bad one, bad enough that the lining in his nose began to sting. It was sharp and pungent like the scent from a skunk, but different. He couldn't place it. It didn't come from a decaying corpse. He knew that odor all too well. Several times in Chicago he had recovered bodies that had ripened in hot apartments and trunks of abandoned cars. It wasn't a smell soon forgotten.

"What *is* that?" Herbert asked, reaching for his handkerchief.

"Your guess is as good as ours, Sheriff. We hoped you might recognize it. It gets worse farther back. All we know for sure is that it's not from the bodies. Here, use some of this." Walter dipped his finger in the jar of Vicks and smeared it under his nostrils. Herbert did the same.

Junker walked another five yards to the head of the stairs and stopped, waiting for the others to catch up. "Clyde, bring that lantern on up here so's the Sheriff can see."

The burial chamber slowly took shape as Hostetter lit a Coleman lantern and adjusted the hissing light. When he reached the top of the stairs, he held the lantern above his head.

The chamber was larger than Herbert expected. Just as Lippert had described, the final resting place for the Schneiders had been excavated from the solid rock of the hill. Even the steps at his feet were carved from stone. Water dripped steadily from several places in the ceiling. On three sides of the chamber, gaping holes lined the walls like mouths waiting to be fed. The stones which had been their seals lay beneath them, broken into pieces. The air was cold.

The chamber floor was lined with caskets, each one open, displaying its contents. It was a macabre sight, like nothing Herbert could have imagined. A tremor ran down his back. He cast his eyes across the coffins in the surreal light cast by the hissing lantern. In two of the caskets he saw whole bodies and quickly looked away. The interiors of the others appeared to be in shambles. At first he thought they were merely filled with gray sticks and branches sticking out of piles of rags. Then he saw two skulls with shadows for eyes that seemed to look from wall to wall as Hostetter moved the lantern. He focused on the casket closest to the stairs, staring at a skull resting on a mat of brown hair, its eyes, nose and mouth empty holes.

It became all too clear what he was seeing. The rags were their burial clothes and the sticks were all that was left of their bodies. The fine jackets, pants and dresses that had been their final garments were in shreds, ripped from the bodies they once covered, and their skeletons were in pieces.

For a moment they all stared in silence at the gruesome scene. Finally Lippert spoke: "Sheriff, I'll tell you what we know. When Kaleb came in to do the repairs, he found most of the burial seals had been broken out. Bein' curious, he looked inside and saw that some of the old coffins had broken open. When he saw the condition of the bodies, he came right away to see me. After I saw it, I decided we better pull them all out for a look. Now I might have been wrong legally in doin' that," he continued apologetically, "but you better have a look before you decide."

Lippert made his way down the stairs to the floor of the chamber motioning Herbert to follow. He stopped at the first casket and pointed to the skull resting on a mat of hair. "Clyde, swing your light over here."

Herbert peered inside. The skeleton had been dismantled, its bones scattered among the tattered burial clothes. A piece of a dress covered the lower part of the skull like a veil.

"This is the way we found most of the ones we opened, the skeleton pulled apart, the clothes ripped off and the bones stripped clean as a whistle. Now look close." Lippert knelt down and gently lifted out the skull. "This here's prob'ly Louisa Schneider. She's been dead eleven years. Even so, we'd expect to see a lot more of her." He tipped the skull back so Herbert could look inside.

"See? There's nothin' there. Absolutely nothin'. Not one trace of skin, soft tissue, internal organs, nothing. Now look real close." Walter brought the skull close to Herbert's face.

"See those marks?" Lippert was talking in a loud whisper, like there was something nearby he didn't want to hear. Herbert saw a series of scratches and gouges on the skull. "Those marks are on the bones of most of the bodies, Sheriff, and I think they're made by teeth."

Herbert looked at him incredulously.

"That's right, teeth marks from some pretty sharp teeth. Something's picked these bodies clean. And I'll tell you something else strange. There's no sign anything got in here or that these coffins have ever been opened until we did it."

"You're sure about that."

"Damn sure. We did find one thing though. Look here." Lippert knelt next to the coffin and pointed inside to one corner. "See that hole there?"

Herbert saw it. A small hole, not more than an inch wide, rough around the edges.

"There's a hole like this in each one of the caskets. Even the metal ones. Now look over here."

Lippert stood and took two steps to his right. Using his flashlight he pushed aside a large piece of cloth. "This is Rena Schneider, the girl we buried two years ago. We're keepin' her covered. Clyde, bring that lantern over here."

As Hostetter held the lantern over the coffin, Herbert gasped. Two years of death had done little to change the young girl's face. Framed by silken hair still held in pink ribbons, she looked as if she were merely asleep except for the sunken eyes beneath her eyelids and the speckles of mold near her hairline. Her skin had shriveled slightly, parting her lips just enough to give a glimpse of her well-formed teeth and a hint of a smile. Herbert shuddered. He would never get used to dead bodies.

"Ya see, Rena's pretty much intact."

"What do you mean, pretty much intact?" Herbert asked.

"I mean she looks like she should. That she hasn't been eaten like the others," Walter answered, his throaty whisper sounding as if he had just uttered some unforgivable sacrilege.

177

Herbert looked up at him quickly. "Eaten?"

"Yeah, eaten. It sure looks like somethin' ate the flesh off every single body in here except for Rena and a couple others. She's pretty much like you'd expect to find 'er after two years, 'cept for her arm. Take a look here," Lippert said, pointing to her side.

The girl had been buried in a light blue dress with long sleeves, one of which had been slightly ripped, exposing her right arm. The pale gray skin of her hand and wrist was dotted with small gouges.

"What the hell are those?" Herbert asked.

"My guess is those are bites. Deep ones. I'd say something took some bites out of her then quit for some reason."

"I guess whatever it was didn't like her, and she's the best lookin' one of the lot," Junker commented with a smirk.

Lippert scowled at him. "Two bodies over there are like this, too, Sheriff. Both dead about fifteen years. A bunch of bite marks on the neck of one and the leg of the other."

"Is there something different about the three bodies?" Herbert asked.

"Nothing we really know of right now, except they died out of town. I remember Rena's folks brought her body here from Chicago. They took her to a hospital there after she got some disease. She died from it. Polio, I think it was. The other two are Daniel Schneider and his wife Irma. They were buried before I was here, but the records say they died in '39. A funeral home in Bloomington, Indiana, did the arranging and sent them to us."

"I kind of remember 'em," Junker added. "They moved over near Bloomington and got killed in a car accident."

Herbert stared again at the arm, then stood slowly, shaking his head. "My God, Walt, what a friggin' mess. Unbelievable! What do you think did this?"

"I've worked at cemeteries twenty-nine years, Herb, and I've never seen the likes of it. I wish I thought this could've been done by some kids who like to vandalize these places on Halloween, but I don't.

Vandals might break in a mausoleum. They might even bust open a casket or two and dump bodies," Lippert said thoughtfully, "but what kind of person would eat rotting flesh off the bones? What are those things called? Cannibals? No, ghouls. That's what they're called. But that's just too hard to believe. I have to think it's some kind of animal that got in here somehow."

"So you don't know any way something could've gotten in here?" Herbert had begun to sweat. He lifted his wide-brimmed hat and wiped his forehead.

"We looked all morning and couldn't find anyway it could, but we're sure it didn't come through the door and the rest of the place is solid rock. But we still want to look in each of the burial slots. Maybe we'll find a hole back there," Lippert answered.

"Well, suppose you do. What kind of animal do you think we have here?" Herbert asked.

All three men shook their heads slowly.

"Frankly, Sheriff, I don't have a clue," Lippert replied. "Might be rats, maybe a badger, but I've never seen anything do such a job on bodies like this. If I believed such things, I'd say some ghoul got in here somehow. But whatever it was, I think we're still smelling it. I've never smelled anything like it in my life. And there's something more about this smell. Clyde, you tell him."

"Well, Sheriff, Kaleb and me, we both recognize the smell. We run across it before. At different places around the grounds. Faint, not so strong as in here. Just in the last month or so, since we started workin' on the grounds this spring. Me and Kaleb talked about it once or twice, wondered what it was, but we never tried to track it down."

"Where was this, around some other mausoleums?" Herbert asked.

Hostetter and Junker looked quizzically at each other.

"Let me think, now," Junker answered. "Yep, maybe so. It's real hard to be sure, Sheriff. These old rock piles are scattered everywhere 'cept in the new part."

"What do you mean, the new part?"

"I mean out in the flat where we started buryin' during the war."

"Have you opened any other of these things lately?" Herbert asked, looking at Lippert.

"No. Like I said, most of them were built in the 1800s and the families either died out or moved away. We treat mausoleums like all our graves. We take care of the outside but we don't open them up unless someone's going to be buried inside one. I can tell you that's a pretty rare thing these days."

"Well, you'd better check the others."

"Right. But what about a court order? You know we're not supposed to open a grave just anytime we want to."

"Yeah, I know. But we'd better keep this among ourselves until we figure out what went on here. Can't you just hear the rumors this would start? Jesus! I don't want people panicking. Call it a maintenance check. Go inside the things and have a look around. You know, to see if the roof's leaking or something. You can justify that. Anyway I'll back you up if anyone gets their nose out of joint."

"That's good enough for me, Sheriff. I'd just as soon not have to deal with stories about something out here eatin' bodies."

"We need to let the coroner have a look, too. I'll tell him what you found. Maybe he can give us some idea about what did it. And he'll be willing to let this stay quiet for the time being if I ask him."

"Whatever you say." Lippert looked uncomfortable. He was a stickler for rules.

"It'll be all right. I'll have the coroner call you before he comes. Now, when you start your maintenance checks, do you want me to send a deputy to stand by? You know, just to be safe?"

Lippert looked at his two workers, raising his eyebrows slightly.

"We can handle it, Sheriff." Hostetter answered. Junker shook his head in agreement.

"All right," Herbert said quickly. "Go ahead and get started. Call me after you've opened a couple and let me know if you find anything."

Herbert started to climb the stairs. He needed to get outside, his tolerance for the sight and the smell exhausted. If his stomach rebelled, he didn't want any witnesses.

Chapter Seventeen

The Red-Haired Boy

1948

Jack Powell walked slowly through the alley behind Minnie's Market holding the icy bottle of Hires root beer bought with money he had earned cutting grass for a neighbor, when he heard them coming. They were running fast, their feet crunching in the gravel. He turned as soon as he heard their steps. When he saw who it was and the meanness in their faces, he started to run. But they were too close. Lloyd Wischmeier grabbed him from behind after only a few yards and pulled him off the bike which clattered to the gravel. Lloyd's cohorts, Carl Siefert and Larry Frey, were puffing when they caught up.

For as long as Jack could remember, Lloyd Wischmeier had been a bully. He was only a year older than Jack, but several inches taller, and thick and heavy. Out of earshot, Jack had taken to calling him a fatass. Lloyd's appearance mirrored his attitude—hair cut in a flattop, broken front tooth, scruffy blue jeans pulled down over dusty engineer boots and a pack of Lucky's rolled up in the sleeve of a dirty T-shirt. The swagger in his walk and the cantankerous look on his face carried the message that he would beat the tar out of anyone who crossed him. Whether he was capable of this was unproven since the only kids he seemed to actually pick on were small.

Jack had been Lloyd's special target since the incident with Sharon Gartner's kitten after her birthday party. He wasn't sure why Lloyd had zeroed in on him, after all it had been Henry who told. Maybe it was because he was small, or because he had flaming red hair. There certainly weren't any other kids around with hair like that. Lloyd always called him Red when he taunted him, a nickname Jack hated with a passion. But most likely it was because Jack was small and Lloyd often found him alone. Jack seldom hung around with friends because he didn't have many besides Henry Starker.

Jack and Henry lived one house apart on Corse Street in the North Hill section of Bruders Landing. Jack was older by four months but they had started kindergarten together at North Park School, walking through the front door to the school hand in hand (Henry's mother still had the picture). While Henry did well with schoolwork and sports, Jack's performance in class was average at best and his size made sports out of the question. They had grown up as buddies and did everything together, when Henry wasn't visiting his grandparents' farm. Their relationship had been as equals until Lloyd and his two pals had picked on Jack in the schoolyard during recess. After Henry made them back down, he had been like Jack's bodyguard.

Jack had looked for Henry before going to Minnie's. It wasn't often he had money to buy them both a bottle of pop, but Henry had gone to the farm with his mother. With Lloyd living on the same street just two doors away, Jack was always wary when he went to the store by himself. But the combination of the hot day, a fierce thirst and four quarters in his pocket had been too tempting. He figured the alley would be safe.

As Lloyd shoved him back against a garage on the alley, Jack's shoes skidded on the gravel, but he managed to stay on his feet.

"Hey, cut it out! You're gonna make me spill my pop!"

"Oh, the little baby wants us to quit," Lloyd snarled, pushing him against Siefert. "You gonna do somethin' 'bout it, Red?" Siefert grabbed him around the neck and held on.

"Keep it up and I just might." Jack raised the bottle toward Lloyd. Siefert released the grip around his neck.

"You really scare me. Ain't ya gonna offer us a drink, Red?" Lloyd grabbed the bottle and jerked it from Jack's hand. Siefert gave him a sharp push in the center of his back that made him fall into Lloyd.

"Give it back!"

"Make me, you redheaded fruitcake." Lloyd took a swig from the bottle.

"Yeah, he's a redheaded fruit all right. C'mon, gimme some of that," Frey yelled. Lloyd tossed the bottle to him and Frey took a long drink, making exaggerated sucking sounds.

"Come on, you guys, give me . . ." Lloyd grabbed him in a bear hug before he could finish, lifted him off his feet and slammed him to the ground. Jack landed on his back. Stunned, he gasped for air.

The three boys stood over him laughing. Jack tried to get up, but Lloyd pushed him back down with his foot.

"What's the matter, ya little queer?" Lloyd stared down contemptuously. "Cat got your tongue? Aw, you're just a red-haired chickenshit."

Siefert took the pop bottle from Frey and finished it, throwing the bottle on Jack. It thumped against his chest.

"You know what I bet? I bet he's a 'morphrodite," Lloyd said with a sneer. "What do you guys think?"

"Sure he is," Siefert answered obediently. "A little red-headed fairy. Likes to do it with his homo buddies."

"Naw, I mean a 'morphrodite. Ya know, like he's got a cock *and* a pussy."

"Yeah, I know," Siefert mumbled.

"That's why all the queers like him, I'll bet," Frey chimed in.

"Maybe we'd better have a look, guys." Lloyd's voice sounded more ominous. "He's prob'ly even got red hair growin' around his balls."

The laughing stopped. Jack sensed things had just taken a turn for the worse and started to feel scared. He was still on his back, laying in some high grass at the edge of the alley. He had recovered his wind. It was time to make a run for it. He twisted quickly onto his stomach and tried to rise. Someone grabbed his shoulder and twisted him back to the ground. Lloyd kicked him hard in the ribs. Jack was more shocked than hurt by the blow.

"You ain't goin' nowhere, you fuckin' 'morph'. Come on, you guys, let's check him out. Drag him in there." Lloyd pointed to a wooden shed a few feet away.

Lloyd grabbed one of his arms while Siefert grabbed the other. Jack started kicking, but Larry managed to pin Jack's legs under his arms. When they started to lift him, Jack yelled again: "Quit it! Cut it out!"

"You shut your damn mouth, or I'll shut it for you." Lloyd spoke so viciously, Jack quit yelling for fear he'd be kicked again.

The inside of the shed was hot and smelled of old sunbaked wood. They laid him on the dirt floor, keeping him from rolling over on his stomach.

"Hold his arms," Lloyd ordered.

Siefert got a firm grip on his wrists while Frey pinned his ankles. Pain shot up both of Jack's legs.

"Ow! Ow! That hurts! Get off!" Jack tried to twist his legs free with no success.

"Shut your damn mouth, 'morph', or I'll really show you what hurts." Lloyd knelt down beside him. Jack saw the cruel sneer on Lloyd's face. "Now let's see if the hair between the 'morph's legs is red, too."

Pinned to the floor, Jack raised his head and watched helplessly as Lloyd unbuckled his belt, then unbuttoned his pants and fly. Lloyd began breathing heavily.

"You gettin' excited now, you fuckin' fairy? I know you like it." Lloyd grabbed the top of Jack's pants and underwear at his hips and yanked them down to his knees. Feeling the rough floor against the bare skin of his butt, Jack yelled, arching his back and jerking his head back hard against the dirt floor, desperate to get free. Siefert and Frey snickered as Lloyd leered at Jack's genitals.

"Well, lookie here. Guess he ain't a 'morph' after all." Lloyd spoke as if he was out of breath. "Tiniest little prick I ever seen. He's growin' some red stuff down here, too." Lloyd grabbed some of Jack's pubic hair between his fingers and yanked. Jack screamed. "Oh, did I hurt the little fairy? We just wanted some souvenirs, didn't we, guys." Frey and Siefert broke out laughing.

Then Lloyd leaned over, his face close to Jack's. "Any more noise outa you like that again, and I'll take your balls as a souvenir."

Lloyd returned to a kneeling position breathing loudly, his breath sour. Jack could feel Lloyd's eyes on his genitals again. Furious and scared, Jack started to yell as loud as he could. Lloyd tried to cover Jack's mouth with his hand. Jack felt the sweaty palm over his lips, opened his mouth and bit down as hard as he could.

Lloyd bellowed as he jerked his hand away. "Jesus Christ! That little queer bit me! I'll prob'ly get some disease."

Jack started to yell again.

"Shit, Lloyd! Let's get outa here! Somebody's gonna hear 'im!" Frey shouted, trying to be heard over Jack's screams.

"Yeah, c'mon, Lloyd. We don't want someone to catch us," Siefert chimed in.

Before Lloyd could protest, both Frey and Siefert had risen and started for the door.

"Aw, all right, if you guys are gonna be chicken." Lloyd stood up quickly, glaring at Jack who had stopped yelling. Jack returned his glare. "You even think about tellin' on us, you'd better think again, Red. And you know I mean it, don't you?"

Then they were gone. Jack pulled up his pants and buttoned them. When he stood up, he was still shaking. He tried unsuccessfully to keep from crying, swearing over and over he'd get Lloyd back—somehow.

Chapter Eighteen

The Grave Diggers

1874

A cold spring rain swept over Bruders Landing in sheets, turning River Street into a soup-like mud. The rain had started softly in the afternoon, becoming an unrelenting deluge late in the evening, drenching those who were determined to finish their Saturday night shopping. Heavy gray clouds rolled low over the town, covering it in a shadowy pall. As the air cooled, fog rose from the waters of the Mississippi, at times obliterating what little visibility was left. River Street was deserted except for the occasional person running from the shelter of one doorway to another.

Sam Binder and Leaford Wentzel sat at a bare table in the rear of Haller's Social Club, a large saloon sparsely furnished with battered tables and chairs and a bar made of boards supported by saw horses. Most of the tables were filled, but the mood was unusually subdued. Bert Haller had lit the Club's lanterns in the middle of the afternoon because the day was so dark. A haze from burning oil and cheap tobacco hung heavily in the dim room. Binder and Wentzel had been drinking beer with an occasional shot of whiskey since eating the saloon's free lunch of dried beef sandwiches and pickled pigs' feet.

Binder had lived in a nearby rooming house off and on for several years, working only when his money ran low, periodically signing on a riverboat heading south when the weather turned cold or the law turned hot. He was a short, heavily built man, his once-hard muscles softening from alcohol and middle age. His gray eyes signaled a streak of cold meanness which surfaced regularly, often without warning. As a result most people had learned to steer clear of him. Wentzel had arrived in Bruders Landing as a deckhand on the *Fantella*, a luxury riverboat that had stopped in Bruders Landing for two days. He promptly began a binge in the River Street bars and was still drunk when the *Fantella* departed without him. At first glance Wentzel was the picture of dissipation, belying a reservoir of energy he could tap when he wasn't drunk. He was tall and thin nearly to emaciation, his bones displayed prominently against his skin. The two men had met the previous Monday morning when they started work for Raston Bruhl. On Wednesday afternoon, Raston fired them both for drinking on the job.

Binder and Wentzel had been sitting quietly for some time, Binder nursing his seventh beer and a smoldering anger. Suddenly he raised his head and yelled: "This goddamn weather! S'nuff to make a man drink all day. Then what we s'posed t'do t'night, tell me that?"

The volume of Binder's words startled Wentzel out of a stupor. "Dunno. Drink some more, maybe."

"Yeah? How much money you got left?"

Wentzel reached into the front pocket of his pants and pulled out a bill and some coins. He stretched to regain some of his senses and began counting. "'Bout three bucks, I reckon. Have to get some more work soon."

"I only got a coupla bucks left m'self. That goddamned Bruhl coulda give us a break. Hell, I just needed a few drinks to keep agoin'. That diggin' 'bout killed me."

"Me too, Sam. My back felt like it was broke sometimes."

"He's a bastard, he is." Binder banged his fist on

the table. "A God damned bastard! And you know what else? There's somethin' strange about him and what he's doin'."

"That's for sure. Diggin' up dead bodies is crazy."

"Yeah, but there's somethin' else." Binder leaned over the table nearly knocking over his drink and began talking softly. "Didya see inside those coffins, Leaford? Didya see what they looked like?"

"Yeah. I tried not to look, but I saw in some."

"I did, too. The bastard tried to keep me from seein', but I looked. There's somethin' unnatural goin' on, I'll tell ya."

"Yeah. Bones. They was just a messa bones and ripped up clothes."

"Right. Just bones all jumbled 'round. Now that's strange, Leaford. You seen dead bodies before?"

"Sure, maybe four or five, not countin' my grandma. She was buried proper like."

"And how many was skel'tons?"

"Well, uh, none was."

"That's right. None was. You never see a skel'ton 'cept a body's been in the dirt for a lot o' years where the worms and the maggots can get it." Binder spoke more and more excitedly. Wentzel looked bewildered. "All those bodies was buried in coffins. Some of 'em lead-lined. And some ain't been in the ground none too long. But the meat was all gone from 'em. You know what I think? I think they was eaten!" Binder's anger was turning into a righteous rage.

Shock spread across Wentzel's face. "Eaten? What? You mean like somethin' got in there and et 'em?"

"That's just what I mean. Somethin' . . . or someone . . . ate 'em and left their bones there in a pile."

"Hell, there warn't no sign of any animal or nothin' in those graves."

"Right. 'Twarn't no animal what done it."

"You're sayin' it was a person?. You think some crazy person dug all those bodies up and fed 'em to somethin' . . . or et 'em?" Wentzel choked. "God. Who could do all that diggin'?"

190

"Some crazy person. Yeah. But maybe he didn't dig 'em up. Who do you think does most of the buryin' here?" Binder was talking so intensely, Wentzel began to squirm.

"Old Man Bruhl, I s'pose."

Binder was spurred on by the effect he was having. "Right. So he coulda done it before they was buried. There're people like that, ya know. Do you know what they call 'em?" Binder's eyes narrowed. "Ghouls! That's what they call 'em. They's called ghouls. That's what I bet Old Man Bruhl is, a God-damned ghoul!"

He leaned farther forward until his face was almost touching Wentzel's. "I'll bet he cut up those people and ate 'em before he buried 'em! And you know what else I think? He took their valuables right off their bodies. Stole 'em, I'll betcha. He's prob'ly got 'em all stashed someplace in that mansion of his." Binder sat back in his chair, a greedy gleam in his gray eyes.

Wentzel looked puzzled, his eyes glazed.

Binder suddenly knew what he wanted to do. Perspiration began rolling down his face like rain on a window. He picked up a shot glass of whiskey and drank it down, then lifted his glass of beer and drained it as well. With a loud belch, he lurched to his feet, weaving slightly.

"Listen up, you guys!" His shout startled the other drinkers, many of which had also been digging for Raston Bruhl. "There's somethin' y'all gotta know for your own good. And for your family, if any of you got one."

All eyes turned to Binder.

"Me 'n Leaford here been workin' for Ol' Man Bruhl like some o' you, diggin' bodies outa the old cemetery. We found out somethin' 'bout him. Y' know all those bodies we been diggin' up? They all been cut up and not a piece of meat left on 'em. And you wanta know why? 'Cause they's been *eaten*, that's why!"

The room went deathly quiet.

"You heard me right. Eaten! After they was dead. There's only one thing that would do such a hellish thing. A ghoul! That's right, a damned ghoul. And we know who it is." Binder paused, relishing the limelight, sizing up the looks on faces around the smoke-filled room.

"There's only one person coulda done it, the one what buried them, that undertaker, Bruhl. Raston Bruhl. The man is a Goddamned ghoul!"

An agitated buzz swept the room. The listless boredom of a few minutes earlier had changed to a growing anger.

"How do you know that?" someone called out.

"Ya got us tellin' ya, me and Leaford. We been there and we know damn well what we saw. How 'bout you other men workin' up there? You saw the bodies."

A tall man with a stoop stood up. "I saw 'em. But they weren't bodies, just bones, all in a pile, in each one we dug up. It was kinda weird. And Ol' Man Bruhl tried to keep us from seein' 'em."

"That's what I'm tellin' ya. He cut those poor people in pieces, then et 'em and stole their valuables. Hell, he prob'ly took gold teeth right out of their mouths, and buried what was left. Ol' Man Bruhl's been feedin' on people like us, you 'n me. And women and little kids, too."

Another man stood. "I saw the same things. But they ain't all like that. We dug up a soldier what was all there."

"Well, maybe Ol' Man Bruhl had some decency. 'Sides, the Army prepares its own. But Ol' Man Bruhl, he's been feedin' on all the resta those people he buried up there." Binder sensed he had become their leader. He liked the feeling it gave him.

"Me'n Leaford here are damn well goin' to do somethin' 'bout it. How 'bout you all? You man enough to take care of this ghoul, right here, right now?" There were angry shouts of approval and the sounds of chairs roughly pushed back over the plank floor.

"Let's get on with it, then." Binder stumbled toward the door. Five men followed him shouting angrily with Wentzel bringing up the rear. High on this unfamiliar role of leader, Binder led them into the downpour outside with no idea what would happen when they reached Bruhl's Mortuary.

Chapter Nineteen

The Bike Ride

July 14, 1956

A brilliant ray of sunlight streamed through the parted curtains in Henry's bedroom onto his face. He rubbed his eyes sleepily. Gradually he recognized the sounds of birds busily chirping and two neighbors chatting that drifted through the windows in his room. A warm July breeze blew the curtains lazily. The electric fan on his dresser hummed as it oscillated, occasionally blowing a breath of air over his bed. His first thought brought him rudely awake: do I have to cut the grass? He moaned. But no, this was Saturday, and it was still summer vacation. He could cut it on Monday. Then he remembered what the week-end held in store—an overnight at his grandparents' farm. At fourteen, the prospect of a visit to the farm still excited him. Besides, Jack was going along this time and Sheila would be there. There were so many things to do—fish and swim in the river, explore the the bluffs, jump from the haymow. And there would be his grandmother's cookies.

Henry's face had become broad and pleasant, and girls thought he was fairly good-looking. However, occasional onslaughts of pimples were making him painfully self-conscious. It was his last summer before joining the incoming class of '59 at Bruders Landing High School, a prospect that bothered him more than he would admit. Fortunately, his laid-back and relaxed manner helped him make friends easily. In spite of his easy-going personality, Henry yearned to be a leader, and he liked people that allowed him that role. Jack Powell was one of those people.

Henry rolled onto his side in order to see the alarm clock on his nightstand—8:15. He pulled on an Alligator shirt and jeans, his everyday summer outfit, and ran down their narrow stairs for breakfast. As soon as he entered the kitchen, his exhilaration began to fade. Something wasn't right. It was almost 8:30 and his father was still sitting at the kitchen table reading the morning paper. His mother sat across from him polishing her nails.

"Good morning, sleepyhead," his mother said, looking back down at her nails. "You'll have to get your own cereal this morning, I'm afraid. My nails are wet."

"'Mornin', son." His father looked up from his newspaper. "I need you to do something."

'What's that?" Henry was wary. "You know I'm going to Grandma and Grandpa's today."

"Right, and I want you to ask Lloyd Wischmeier to go with you."

"Lloyd? Dad, I can't take Lloyd! Jack's going. Besides, it's an overnight and Sheila hates Lloyd!"

"No ifs, ands or buts this time, Henry." Roy Starker carefully folded the newspaper and laid it on the table. "I promised Lloyd's father that you'd ask him and I've already talked to Grandpa Gerdes. Look, I know what you think of Lloyd, but his parents say his problems are the fault of those kids he hangs out with, and they want him to find new friends. When I mentioned that you and Jack were going to the farm today, he practically begged me to let Lloyd go along. So I said OK. Now you'll ride your bikes and Lloyd can come back later in the afternoon while you and Jack stay over."

Lloyd was a notorious fixture in the

neighborhood. All the younger kids were afraid of him, and Henry knew it was for good reason. When they were both much younger, Lloyd had made Henry watch as he caught frogs at Holstein's pond, cut off their legs with a pen knife and laugh as he threw them back in the water to drown. Henry had run home crying. Later there was Sharon Gartner's birthday party. All the neighborhood kids were invited. The highlight of the party was the gift Sharon's mother gave her: a little yellow kitten that she promptly named Fuzzy. Everyone at the party was crazy about Fuzzy and waited in line for a chance to hold her. Lloyd waited as well, but when he lifted up the dress of the girl standing in front of him, Sharon's mother made him leave. That evening Fuzzy wandered away and Henry and all the neighbor kids helped the Gartners search for her. He was riding his bike down the alley behind a vacant lot next to Wischmeier's house, looking from side to side, when he saw Lloyd pushing a lawnmower erratically through the grass. The sight was so strange, Henry stopped to look. Lloyd was chasing something in the grass with the lawnmower, something small and yellow dashing in circles. It took a moment for Henry to realize it was Fuzzy, the same moment that Lloyd caught the kitten in the lawnmower's blades. There was a crunching sound as if the mower hit a bag of potato chips, one pitiful squeal, and the mower stopped. Lloyd claimed he had run over the kitten by accident. Only his parents believed him.

In desperation Henry turned to his mother who was still polishing her nails, giving her the most imploring look he could muster. But she gave him a helpless look in return, shrugging her shoulders sympathetically. Henry sulked through breakfast. He was still sulking when he telephoned Lloyd.

As Henry rode his bike to the front of his house, Lloyd was waiting in the street, straddling his bicycle with his arms folded. Lloyd's bike suited him well—a black Schwinn Phantom, big and mean looking, with bulging fenders, crossbar and tires, and sporting several of Lloyd's personal additions: white handle grips with long buckskin tassels and oversized white mudflaps pierced by red and orange reflectors.

"Hi, Henry, how're they hangin'?"

The tone of Lloyd's voice was less hostile than usual. Henry guessed the change must require a great deal of effort and wouldn't last long.

"It's a long ride, you know." Henry knew there was little hope Lloyd would change his mind, but he would give it a last try. "It gets real hot out there in the sun, and it's pretty dusty on the road by the cemetery."

"You're not worried 'bout me keepin' up with you guys, are you?" Lloyd laughed, but only one side of his face was smiling.

Before Henry could answer, Jack appeared on his bicycle, staring at them with a puzzled look. Henry was afraid he might refuse to go.

"Hold on a minute. I've got to go talk to Jack."

"Don't make the little 'morph' come if he doesn't want to."

Henry rode to where Jack stood twisting his bike's handle grips around in his hands. "What's Lloyd doing here? He isn't going, too, is he?"

"I'm afraid so. My dad went bowling with his last night at Olivier's. Mr. Wischmeier talked Dad into it. Believe me, I don't want him to come any more than you do."

"You know why he wants to come, don't you? To get at Sheila. There's gonna be trouble."

"That's why you have to come, Jack. In case he tries to do something, there'll be two of us."

"Your grandma and grandpa will be there, won't they?"

"Grandma's going shopping with my mom and my aunt, but Grandpa should be."

"All right, I'll go. But Sheila's really gonna be mad."

As the two rode to where Lloyd waited, he glared at Jack. "What was you tellin' him, Red?" Lloyd's voice had more of the menace Henry was used to.

Jack glared back at him. "Nothin'. It's none of your business anyway."

"It better be nothin' or I'll make it my business." Lloyd turned to Henry and his voice softened. "OK, I

know my dad and yours cooked this up. But I really
wanta see your farm. I ain't seen farms much. You
guys lead the way and I'll do whatever you want." Henry
stifled his urge to tell Lloyd exactly what he could do.

As soon as they set out down the street, Lloyd
began to talk. "Lookit, there's Ol' Lady Koske's house
behind those bushes. Ain't she weird? I used to be kind
of scared of her when I was little but now I just think
she's nuts. One Halloween me and Carl and Larry put a
bag fulla dog shit on her porch and lit it. Man, I wish I
coulda seen her tryin' to stomp it out."

Lloyd laughed hilariously at his own story. Henry
forced a smile. Sonia Koske *was* scary. Every kid in
their neighborhood grew up with stories that she was a
witch. Henry still avoided her. Carl Frey and Larry
Seifert were a little scary, too—when they were around
Lloyd. They were his only friends as far as Henry knew.
Seifert had spent time in reform school and Frey had to
repeat sixth grade after he was expelled.

Henry and Jack rode silently while Lloyd
chattered away. When they reached Walnut Grove
Cemetery, Lloyd began talking louder. "Man, you guys
shoulda been around on Halloween last year when me,
Frey 'n Siefert came out here. See, we brought some
paint, a gallon of black paint and some brushes to do
some decoratin' in the cemetery. I had this railroad flare
with me, see, and wanted to find a good place to set it
off. Then on the way we saw this dumb ol' dog tied up
in this yard, and I got an idea. So I snuck up and
untied the dog . . . it was lickin' my hand and everything
and I stuffed it in the saddlebag on my bike . . ."

As Lloyd told the story, Henry remembered what
he was talking about, his father had shown him the
article in the *Bruders Landing Gazette.* Whoever did it
hadn't been caught. Henry wasn't surprised to find out
it was Lloyd.

". . . we went in those gates over there, see, and
rode back to one of those underground things,
mossoleums or somethin' like that, they're called. Then
we took out the dog and painted it all over with black
paint, see, so when anybody touched it, they'd . . ."
Lloyd began to giggle or snort, Henry wasn't sure which.

". . . then I threw the clothesline around a bar stickin' out above the door and pulled the dog off the ground a couple o' feet by it's collar while Larry lit the flare. That fuckin' dog just hung there, didn't howl or nothin'. Man, I thought it was gonna croak right then. But it sure came to life when I stuck that flare under its ass . . ."

Lloyd grew more and more excited, talking faster and louder. ". . . Jesus, what a fuckin' sight. Ya shoulda seen it! That flare lit up everythin'. The fuckin' dog was yowlin' and swingin' and bouncin' against that door. It was really somethin'. I was hopin' somebody'd come along so I could see the look on their face. It woulda scared the crap out of 'em! And if they tried to take that fuckin' dog down, the paint . . ."

Lloyd had started laughing too hard for Henry to understand any more. Jack looked furious. Henry continued to pedal his bicycle quietly, remembering the rest of the news story. The howls of pain coming from the cemetery frightened people living close by who called the sheriff. By the time a patrol car arrived, the flare was out and the dog was dead, its hind quarters burned away.

As they rode up the gravel driveway to the Gerdes farmhouse, Sheila came onto the front porch. After her father drowned on a duck hunting trip three years earlier, she and her mother had moved in with her grandparents. At thirteen, Sheila was nearly as tall as Henry and had developed from skinny to slender. Her brown hair grew almost to her waist. She had smooth, tan skin that fit her tightly, a clue to the time she spent outdoors. Henry noticed that boys had started giving his cousin second looks.

Sheila smiled and waved until they were close to the porch. Henry guessed that no one had told her Lloyd was coming. When she saw Lloyd, her smile turned to a scowl.

They rode their bikes to the foot of the front steps and got off. Sheila stayed on the porch, glaring at Lloyd, then looked angrily at Henry. Fluffy, Sheila's gray Persian cat, rubbed against her leg, purring. She picked up the cat and began stroking her back. Sheila's hair was pulled back in a pony tail and she wore an over-sized shirt tied above her waist and close-fitting denim shorts, her summer uniform at the farm.

Lloyd put one foot on the first step and leaned forward, his eyes roaming over her body. "It's great to see you on your farm, Sheila, 'cause I don't see you much 'round school anymore." He gave her a wide, toothy grin which didn't alter the leer from his eyes.

"That's right, Lloyd, you don't because you and your stupid friends can't keep your hands to yourselves."

"Aw, Sheila, we was just foolin'. Can't you take a joke?"

"It depends. What are you doing here, anyway? Who said you could come?"

"Henry asked me, didn't ya, Henry?"

Henry nodded. "Lloyd can only stay until dinner."

A tense silence followed. Jack began to kick at the dirt.

"OK, come on inside," Sheila answered at last, sounding resigned. "Grandma baked chocolate chip cookies before she left."

Henry glanced at the garage as he climbed the porch stairs. He expected to see his grandfather's pickup truck, but the garage was empty.

Inside the house the smell of something freshly baked hung in the air. A plate piled with cookies sat in the center of the kitchen table. Sheila brought a bottle of milk from the refrigerator, shaking it to mix the cream that floated on top. The four of them sat at the table under a temporary truce, eagerly devouring the warm cookies, washing them down with cold milk and finally licking the sticky chocolate from their fingers.

The cookies had a pacifying effect. Even Sheila became calm enough to speak normally. "Henry, are you going down to the river today, or what? I've got to do some chores out in the barn first, so I can meet you later. Just tell me where you'll be."

"I'd sure like to see if we can catch some fish before it gets too hot. What about it, Jack? Do you want to do some fishing?"

"Yeah, sounds great!" Jack answered, then

glanced warily at Lloyd.

"Me, too. I'll go with you guys if you have an extra pole."

"I'll find you one." Henry got up and headed for the den.

"I'll help you." Sheila followed him from the table.

Sheila cornered him as soon as they reached the den. "Why did you bring Lloyd here? You know I hate that guy. I don't trust him for a minute after what he did to me last year at school."

"What did he do?"

Sheila paused. "You promise not to tell?"

"Sure . . ."

"Well, one day when I left school by one of the rear doors, Lloyd and his little gang, Frey and Siefert, were hanging around outside. There wasn't anyone else there and when I walked by them, they pushed me against the wall and Lloyd put his hands all over me. You know . . . places. When I screamed, they just laughed and called me dirty names." Tears started to form in Sheila's eyes.

"Did you tell anyone, go to the principal's office or anything?"

"No, I was too embarrassed. I haven't even told Mom."

"You should have. If my dad knew, he wouldn't have made me bring Lloyd."

"Oh, so that's why he came with you. I get it. Well, don't tell anybody yet. I need to think about it. I should tell Mom first."

"Maybe we should tell Grandpa. He'd make Lloyd leave. Is Grandpa here? I didn't see his truck in the garage."

"No, he left just before you came. He had to get the pickup fixed some place in town. Then he's going to meet Grandma and Mom at some church supper."

"Jeez! Lloyd's not planning to leave until late this afternoon. We should try to get him out of here sooner."

"Good. I don't want him around me. Keep him down at the river. I'll give you the sandwiches to take with you so you don't have to come back for lunch."

"That might work if the fish are biting. Let's find

him a good pole."

Henry led the way as the three of them trudged single file from the farmhouse on a narrow path that led to the bluff. They each carried a fishing pole, line dangling from the pole's tip to the hook stuck into the cork handgrip. Henry had his grandfather's straw creel slung over his shoulder. Jack was behind him carrying a trenching tool in his other hand. Lloyd was a few steps back with a bait bucket filled with sandwiches and cold bottles of Grapette.

Henry could feel the hot sun in his hair. He followed the path through the pasture and across the creek where he and Sheila had piled stones for steps. When he reached the cornfield, the path disappeared. The corn stalks were up to his waist, their wide leaves drooping in the warm sun. He walked into them without pausing, using his pole to push the leaves aside to prevent the tiny cuts they could make on his skin.

For several minutes they were surrounded by corn. Henry could hear Jack and Lloyd behind him as they thrashed through the stalks. At the end of the cornfield, Henry took a path that led through the woods. The distant Illinois bluffs were visible through the branches.

Suddenly Jack yelled: "Dammit, Lloyd, stop it."

Henry turned. Jack and Lloyd were facing each other, Jack swinging the trenching tool in front of his body like a pendulum while Lloyd used his fishing pole like a rapier, jabbing at him between his legs.

"What's the matter?. Ya didn't mind a little goose, did ya? Ya used to like it." Lloyd thrust again hitting Jack just below his belt buckle. The pole bent almost double.

"Ow! Quit it, Lloyd! I mean it!" Jack dropped his fishing pole and grabbed the shovel with both hands like a baseball bat.

"C'mon, you guys. Quit it!. You can't stay if you fight and I mean it! So cut it out now!" Henry shouted.

"OK, OK. I was only foolin' around, just goosed him a little. Thought he might like it, for all I know," Lloyd snickered.

"He doesn't, so cut it out."

Jack still held the shovel ready to swing. "Don't mess with me any more or so help me I'll . . ."

Lloyd scowled. "Or ya'll what, ya little pissant. Go ahead, tell me what ya're gonna do."

"Look, I said cut it out. Both of you!"

"I will, but he'd better leave me alone." Jack lowered the trenching tool to his side.

The two remained toe-to-toe, Lloyd continuing to scowl at Jack, Jack defiantly scowling back.

Henry thought some movement might help and started to walk away. "C'mon now, let's get down to the river. We've still got to dig worms before we can get our lines in." Jack shrugged his shoulders and followed him. Seconds later Lloyd did the same.

After walking several yards into the timber, they reached the start of a deep ravine that had been carved through the bluff by the creek that crossed the Gerdes farm. Although his grandfather had assured him it was true, Henry had found it difficult to believe that a stream usually so lazy could have accomplished such a feat. That was until last summer when he watched a cloudburst transform the little creek into an angry river that cascaded down the bluff in a torrent.

The ravine began nearly a hundred yards from the edge of the bluff, gradually widening as it sloped down to the river. Tall trees grew thickly along the sides creating a cool shade. Its walls were dotted with shrubs and ferns that grew between the moss-covered rocks.

As Henry entered the ravine, the air felt cool, almost as if he had walked into a movie theater. He knew to step carefully. The water flowing over the rock made the surface smooth and slippery.

"Son of a bitch!" Lloyd shouted just before a loud clattering of rocks and metal. "Oof . . . God dammit!"

Henry turned to see Lloyd sliding on his back through the rocks and water straight toward Jack. A collision would have been inevitable if Lloyd hadn't hit a tree stump butt first. His fishing pole and the bucket holding their lunch continued bouncing down the rocky stream.

Henry struggled to stifle his laughter, but Jack

was doubled over roaring.

"What are you laughing at, pissant?" Lloyd shouted venomously as he struggled to stand. "You fuckin' queer, wipe that shit-eatin' grin off your fuckin' face or I'll cut it off!" Once on his feet, Lloyd reached into the pocket of his mud-streaked jeans and pulled out a pearl-handled knife. He pushed the button on its side and a blade leaped out, snapping in place.

Jack stopped laughing and clumsily took a step backwards.

Henry watched the scene anxiously. He wanted to yell some threat at Lloyd, but realized that could make things worse. "Lloyd, c'mon now," he pleaded instead. "Jack didn't mean to laugh at you. Put that knife away." Lloyd moved to a crouch as if he was preparing to spring. "Lloyd, put that away. My grandparents don't let us have knives here. If you don't put it away right now, I'll have to tell Grandpa and he'll make you leave.'

Lloyd shifted his glare to Henry. "Oh, so you're gonna be a fuckin' tattletale. A squealer, is that what you are? I knew it all along. You know what squealer's get, don't you?"

"No, I don't know what squealer's get, but I know what you'll get if my grandpa finds you with that knife." Henry was afraid Lloyd might suspect his grandfather was gone.

But Lloyd relaxed. With a smirk, he closed the blade and put the knife back in his pocket. "All right, let's go fishin'. I wasn't gonna do nothin' anyway. But you, pissant, don't ever let me catch you laughin' at me no more."

Jack sniffed and began to gather up the sandwiches and bottles of Grapette that had fallen out of the bucket.

As they came to the bottom of the ravine, the steep slope began to level out. Henry picked up his pace. As suddenly as he had entered, Henry emerged from the shade onto the broad shore of the Mississippi. In the early spring, the river, swollen by the melting snow and spring rains, had covered the place where they walked. The evidence was there—dried mud cracked into squares that curled upward at the edges, and long strips of sand formed by the water into wavy ridges. In the weeks since the river had returned to its banks, weeds and grass had taken root, making a home for the grasshoppers that jumped with a whirring sound in the hot sun.

Henry could smell the river—an earthy scent from the soil, plants, fish and animals it had digested as the river wended its way south. Henry had come to know the smell. He liked it. He thought the river smelled friendly.

The three walked across the caked mud side by side. A few large trees grew near the river bank, stubbornly surviving their annual submersion, providing shade coveted by both the fish and the fishers. Henry headed for a large willow directly in front of them.

"Let's set our stuff under that tree," Henry suggested.

"Hey, Henry, do you guys swim here?" Lloyd walked to water's edge.

"Not here, the bottom's too muddy. There's a sand bar up a ways. Me and Sheila go swimming there once in a while."

"Man, I bet she looks tough in a bathing suit. Or does she even wear one? What about it, Henry?"

"Of course she wears one."

"Bet you can still see her tits. Have you seen 'em, Henry? Does she have nice ones?"

"I guess I didn't notice." Henry blushed. He *had* noticed.

"Aw, don't give me that bullshit. Just because she's your cousin doesn't mean you're blind. Shee-it. I'll bet you even seen her without her bathing suit, haven't you? C'mon, you can tell me."

Henry's face reddened more. He hoped it didn't show. "I wouldn't tell you if I did, Lloyd. It's sure none of your business."

Lloyd laughed.

"C'mon, Jack. Let's dig the worms." Henry picked up the bucket and walked toward a grassy area where the stream had finally made its way to the river. Jack followed with the trenching tool.

Worms were easy to find that day. Jack picked up two rusty tin cans and put several strands of wriggling bait into each one. He handed a can to Lloyd then sat back against a tree to watch him bait his hook.

Lloyd stared into the can and pulled out a worm. He held it out in front of him, letting it dangle between his thumb and index finger. "Did ya know that worms can live when you cut 'em in two? Watch."

Lloyd pulled his knife from his pocket. With a snap of his hand, the blade clicked into place. Holding the worm in a loop, Lloyd inserted the knife and sliced it in half. Jack winced.

"Here, Red, think fast." Lloyd flipped the worm's parts toward Jack. One half hit his cheek, the other landed on his shirt.

"Dammit, Lloyd, cut it out!" Jack brushed at the pieces of worm.

"Oh, sure, I'll cut it out. Think fast again." Lloyd raised his arm rapidly and threw the knife. It stuck up to its hilt in the ground between Jack's legs who stared at the knife, disbelief on his face.

"You're crazy, Lloyd, you know that?" Jack's voice trembled. "You're crazy and everybody knows it."

"Don't call *me* crazy, you red-headed queer!" Lloyd screamed. He flung himself on Jack, forcing him onto his back. He mounted Jack's chest, sitting heavily, pinning Jack's arms to the ground with his knees. Jack lurched upward, trying to free himself, but failed. Lloyd reached over and pulled his knife out of the ground.

Henry watched with alarm as Lloyd waived the knife in Jack's face. Somehow he had to stop this. "Lloyd, put that knife away!" He grabbed the arm with the knife from behind. Lloyd jerked his arm away, throwing Henry to the ground.

"All right, you little queer, call me crazy and see what happens." Lloyd reached behind his back with his free hand, grabbed Jack's pants between his legs and squeezed. Jack screamed.

"I'm gonna cut your nuts off, you fuckin' queer, right after I carve my initials in your chest." Lloyd pressed the blade of his knife against the skin on Jack's chest above his shirt. Jack held his head up and stared wide-eyed at the blade.

Henry leapt to his feet as blood appeared under the point of the knife. "Stop it!" Henry lunged at Lloyd with his shoulder lowered, hitting him on his side as solidly as he had ever hit anyone playing football. Lloyd flew off Jack's chest and landed on the caked mud. Jack bounced to his feet quickly. Henry stood with his fists clenched as Lloyd rose to his knees glaring at them. He waved the knife threateningly.

"God damn you, Henry. You're chickenshit, you know that? Hittin' me when I wasn't lookin'. All right, c'mon on, you guys. It's two against one."

"What were you trying to do? You cut his chest. You could have really hurt him. Killed him even."

"If I wanted to kill him, I woulda," Lloyd said coldly.

Henry shuddered. He needed to get Lloyd out of there, away from the farm. "You're lucky you only pricked him. You'd better get out of here, Lloyd. Go on home and maybe Jack won't tell."

"I don't give a shit if he tells."

"You will if he tells the sheriff."

Lloyd became quiet.

"What do you say, Jack? Would you promise not to tell if he leaves?"

Jack looked down at the small cut on his chest. "Maybe."

"Look, you fruits, if you *do* tell anyone, you'll really be in for it. Understand? If I go on home, it's 'cause I'm sick of you chickenshits, not 'cause I'm scared of a couple o' queers like you."

"Go on, Lloyd. Get out of here," Henry shouted. "If you don't, I'm going to tell my grandpa and he'll *make* you leave. Then he'll call the sheriff and your folks will find out, too."

"OK, you shitheads, maybe I will. But I ain't forgettin' this, believe me," Lloyd muttered, his teeth clenched. Slowly he rose from his knees and stood. For a moment Henry was sure Lloyd was about to charge him with his knife. His muscles tensed. But Lloyd simply smirked, closed the blade on his knife and put it back in his pocket. Then he kicked the fishing pole and bucket aside and started walking toward the bluff.

Henry and Jack stood without talking as Lloyd swaggered into the ravine. When he was out of sight, Jack turned to Henry with a look of gratitude on his face, his eyes glistening.

"Thanks, Henry. Really, thanks. That knife . . . I can still see it . . . still feel it on my chest. It was great, you knockin' him down like that."

"Aw, that's OK." Suddenly a thought flashed into his mind. "You know what? Sheila's up there by herself. If Lloyd figures out Grandpa's gone, she could be in trouble. Grab the stuff."

Henry had never climbed the ravine so fast, even with the two fishing poles, the creel and the trenching tool. As he neared the top, he stepped on a loose rock that rolled under his foot and fell, still clutching everything in his hands. Quickly he scrambled to his feet and set off at a run through the trees and into the cornfield. Jack followed a few yards behind.

As Henry ran across the pasture, he could see the three bikes standing in front of the farmhouse where they had left them. So Lloyd was still there—somewhere. Where would Sheila be? His apprehension produced another charge of adrenaline and he kept running until he reached the porch. Neither Lloyd nor Sheila were anywhere in sight. He dropped everything he was carrying onto the porch floor, opened the screen door and ran into the front hall.

"Sheila! Sheila! Are you in here?" Henry shouted as loud as he could while he tried to catch his breath. There was no answer. When he heard Jack's steps on the porch, he turned and ran back out the front door.

"Sheila's not in the house. C'mon, let's look in the barn."

They raced side by side across the yard. As they approached the barn, his grandparents' dog Mutt was scratching at the large double door. He pushed Mutt aside with his foot and pulled on the iron ring attached at one side. When the door wouldn't budge, Henry became panicky.

"Sheila! Are you in there? Are you OK?" Henry

shouted.

A muffled noise of something falling came from inside. He heard Sheila scream. "I'm in here. Damn you, Lloyd. Get out! Get out of here! Get your filthy hands off of me! Don't touch me! Don't you ever touch me!"

Henry was about to run to another entrance when there was a rattle behind the double-door. One side swung open, hitting the side of the barn with a bang. Sheila burst out. She was shaking. Her hands were behind her neck, tying the strings to her halter. Pieces of straw clung to her clothes and hair. Lloyd walked out behind her, holding the side of his head and smirking. Mutt approached within a few feet of him, growling. Lloyd aimed a kick that was well short. "Damn dog," he muttered.

"Don't you dare kick him!" Sheila shouted. "Damn you, Lloyd! You're such a pervert. I'm going to call Grandpa. You're not going to get away with stuff anymore." She started to sob.

"Lloyd, what did you do to her?" Henry demanded.

"Nothin' she didn't want me to." Lloyd laughed, then lowered his hand from his head. Blood covered his fingers and Henry could see more in his hair. The smirk left Lloyd's face when he saw his blood. "You bitch, you hit me. You dirty little bitch. Lookit, I'm bleedin'." He held out his hand with the blood on it. "You're really gonna get it, now," he said coldly.

"If anybody's going to get it, Lloyd, it'll be you," Henry answered angrily. "Now go home."

"Don't sweat it, I'm goin'. But you'd better not forget our deal. Anyway, it's too bad you guys came back when you did. Me and Sheila were gonna have some fun, weren't we, sweets."

"Get out of here, Lloyd." Sheila shrieked. "Just you wait 'til you see what happens."

Lloyd's eyes narrowed to slits. "I hope you're not thinkin' about tellin' people a buncha lies about me, bitch. That wouldn't be too good for you, if you know what I mean." Lloyd patted the pocket where he kept his knife. "Ask the queer there. He knows, don't ya,

Red?" Jack said nothing. "See, Sheila, those chickenshits know what's good for them. They promised not to tell."

"That was different, Lloyd. It had nothing to do with Sheila." Henry stiffened, his hands on his hips.

"It better not be any different if you want to stay in one piece." Lloyd glared first at Sheila, then at Jack and finally at Henry.

"We're not scared of you," Henry said at last.

"You oughta be," Lloyd replied icily. Then he turned and walked toward his bicycle.

They stood silently watching Lloyd pedal out of sight.

Chapter Twenty

The Mob

1874

Raston Bruhl yawned and rubbed his eyes, eager to join Sophia in their warm featherbed. With several glasses of sherry blunting his anxiety, he had made up his mind. First thing Monday morning he would see the Mayor, tell him what he was finding in the graves and show him Thaddeus Bump's journal. When they read it, neither the mayor, his wife Amanda nor anyone else could blame him for the condition of those bodies. As a precaution, he decided to hide the journal so it would be safe until Monday. Carrying an oil lamp to light his way, Raston descended the wood stairs unsteadily to the cavernous cellar beneath the old mansion. His footsteps echoed through the stone chamber as he walked across the uneven stone floor, searching in the shadows cast by the flickering lamplight for a safe hiding place.

As he passed the arched entrance to a small side chamber, he found the place he was looking for. He pulled a wooden box next to the archway and climbed onto it. Stretching his arms high over his head, he felt around the stones above the arch. There was a ledge, just as he thought. With one hand gripping a stone, he laid the journal on the ledge well out of sight and stepped down awkwardly.

As he emerged from the doorway at the top of the cellar stairs, he paused to catch his breath, feeling pain in his chest. Suddenly he heard muffled voices coming from the front of his house. People were shouting his name over and over. With the oil lamp in one hand and massaging his chest with the other, he walked to the front door more curious than alarmed. Just as he reached the front hall, something heavy struck the door. Alarmed, he opened it cautiously. A tree limb lay on the porch. More shouts rang out.

"There he is. The ghoul!"

"Come on out here, Bruhl. We wanta ash you sumpin'."

"Bruhl, the ghoul! Whatcha have for your supper tonight?" A round of drunken laughter followed.

Raston opened the door wide and walked onto the porch. He could see several grizzled men holding torches. From the the sounds of their voices, it was clear they were drunk. He tried to make out their faces to see if anyone was familiar.

"What do you men want here this time of night?"

"We want you, ya damn ghoul! That's what we want," one of them yelled.

"You men are all drunk. You'd better go somewhere and sleep it off. Now get out of here before I call the sheriff."

"Don't think you want to do that now, Mr. Bruhl," Sam Binder said, stepping out in front of the others. "Not with what we seen up there in that cemetery."

Raston thought the face of the man speaking was familiar, probably one of the diggers. "So some of you've been digging up graves for me, have you? Sounds like you don't have the stomach for it. You'd best get on back to Front Street where you came from and maybe you'll still have work come Monday."

"We got the stomach for the work, don't you worry. It's *you* we ain't got the stomach for. You and what you done to those bodies b'fore you buried 'em."

Now Raston recognized him. It was one of the men he had fired in the middle of the week for being drunk.

211

"You were just seeing things after all you'd been drinking. And you don't know what you're talking about because you're drunk as a skunk right now."

"Takin' a drink don't mean we don't know what ya are, Bruhl. You're a God damned *ghoul!* You been *eatin'* those bodies before you buried 'em. We all seen 'em, ya know. Weren't nothin' left but their bones."

Raston tensed. This was exactly the kind of rumor he was afraid might start. Now here was someone in front of his house shouting it. He hesitated, not sure what to say.

Binder turned to face his cohorts. "There! Ya see? He don't deny it."

Raston felt a growing tightness in his chest. "Not deny it? Of course, I deny it. It's ridiculous."

He thought he saw one man holding a coiled rope. The tightness in his chest increased followed by a flash of pain below his shoulder that ran down his arm.

"We also know ya been stealin' from the dead before you plant 'em, takin' their valuables b'fore you stuck what was left of 'em in the ground. We think you ought to share some o' that with us or we'll be tellin' the whole town what we seen up there."

"Oh, now I get it. You've come to blackmail me. Well, I'll have none of it, you hear?" A pain gripped his chest making him wince.

"Well, whaddya know," Sam said in a sarcastic but softer tone, "sounds to me like he needs a little persuadin'."

The pain came again, white-hot and stabbing, nearly taking him to his knees. It made him light-headed and dizzy. He turned to retreat through the doorway, reaching for the doorknob to steady himself.

Suddenly there was an eruption inside his chest followed by excruciating pain. He swayed unsteadily until his legs no longer supported him, and crumpled into the doorway. Raston's last thought was that he had been shot, then his eyes rolled to the top of their sockets. The back of his head hit the stone threshold with a sound like a ripe melon, but he felt nothing. The oil lamp fell from his hand. It exploded on the porch floor showering Raston's body with glass, oil and flame. In seconds his skin and clothing were on fire. Raston lay still and unfeeling as the fire burned his hair and blackened the skin on his face.

The seven men watched open-mouthed as Raston's body lay burning on the porch. One vomited where he stood. When the first man turned and ran, the stampede back to Haller's Social Club was on.

Chapter Twenty-One

The Deaths

July 14, 1956

The three friends ate lunch quietly on the porch of the farmhouse, ignoring the peculiar odor the sandwiches had acquired from the bait bucket. Henry sat on the steps, brushing at flies and frequently glancing down the driveway. Sheila and Jack sat in the porch swing. Henry could see that both of them were taking occasional looks down the driveway as well.

"Hey, look you guys, he's not going to come back, so let's quit worrying," Sheila said. Henry wondered whether she really was as confidant as she sounded. "Let's go down to the river. You can do some fishing and I'll get some sun. What do you say?"

"Whatever we do, this time we better stick together. Maybe we shouldn't leave the house. If Lloyd comes back, who knows what he might do to it," Henry replied.

"He's not coming back, Henry. So come on. What about it, Jack? You want to go down to the river?"

"Yeah, I'm goin' wherever you guys are goin'."

"It'll be fine. I'll get my suit on. Do you guys want to take suits or are you just going to fish?"

"Let's take them. We might want to go in if we get hot."

"OK. I'll borrow your green one again," Jack said, "but I'm gonna change in the bathroom up here."

They picked their way gingerly down the ravine with towels around their necks, their hands full of fishing gear. Sheila led with Henry following while Jack made his own way down the other side of the small stream. Suddenly Henry slipped on a moss covered rock, flailing at the air to keep his balance. He hoped no one had seen him looking so awkward.

"Ooo, Henry, you all right?" Sheila called from below.

"Hey, Henry, way to go! Pretty fast footwork there," Jack called from the other side of the ravine.

"Just watch where you're going your own self. These rocks are slippery."

"You're tellin' us!" Jack chuckled. Then he called out again. "Hey, what's in that little cave up there?"

Sheila and Henry both stopped.

"What cave? There's no cave up there." Henry was sure Jack must be seeing things.

"Yes, there is. Just below those rocks." Jack pointed at the rock wall beyond where he stood.

Henry looked where Jack was pointing, expecting to see nothing. But there it was—a dark hole at the base of some large rocks, partly hidden from where he stood. Henry could hardly believe his eyes. He and Sheila had explored this ravine dozens of times and had never seen it.

"Hey, Sheila, look up there. Have you seen that before?"

"No, never. I see it but I don't believe it."

"C'mon, let's take a look." Henry gingerly crossed to the other side of the stream. Jack was already climbing toward the hole.

The three of them gathered in front of the opening. It was at the base of an outcropping of limestone, less than three feet in diameter at its widest point with a jagged rock protruding from one side.

"We've been up here a jillion times. How did we miss it?" Sheila asked, looking at Henry.

"You got me. I'm sure we've been here."

"Hey, how 'bout some credit, you guys," Jack interjected, "maybe I've just got good eyes."

"Yeah, maybe, but maybe there's another reason," Henry said. "Look at the dirt in front of it. It looks pretty fresh." He turned to Sheila. "Maybe the reason we didn't see it before is that it wasn't here."

Sheila looked puzzled. "Maybe that's right."

"So, what are you sayin', that you think somethin' dug its way through solid rock a few days ago? Prob'ly not. I think you guys were just blind."

Henry looked inquiringly at Sheila, wondering whether she was thinking the same thing he was—could this somehow connect to the tunnel they found in the cellar years before? He wanted to ask her right then what she thought, but stopped himself.

Sheila had been staring at the opening deep in thought. "I wonder how far back it goes."

"Maybe I can see far enough to tell." Henry got down on his hands and knees and looked inside the opening.

"Henry, don't!" Sheila cried out. "There might be something in there like in that tunnel!" As soon as she said it, her hand flew to her mouth.

Jack looked at her quizzically. "What tunnel? Is there a tunnel here someplace?"

"Uh . . . not here, exactly," Sheila answered, fumbling at what to say. "We'll tell you later. Now Henry, come on, stay out of there!"

"Don't worry, it's too small to get into anyway. I just want to see something." Henry squeezed his head and shoulders into the opening, blocking the light from outside. He tested the air. It smelled of fresh earth—and something else. A hint of something foul and pungent. He recognized it immediately. His curiosity was satisfied—the tunnel could lead to the farmhouse cellar. A vivid flashback of his experience in that place appeared in his mind's eye. As he tried to blot it out, a black shape seemed to form out of the darkness in front of him. Just my imagination, he told himself, and blinked to erase the sight. But an instinct told him there *was* something there, something crawling toward him. He quickly pushed himself backward to let in light from outside.

"What's wrong, Henry? Did you see something?" Sheila asked as soon as he was out.

Henry rested on his hands and knees for a moment, then started to stand, bumping his head on the top of the opening. "Ow! Darn it!" He took his time rubbing the spot to make sure his voice would be calm. He didn't want Sheila and Jack to think he had been scared. "I couldn't see much, but there was that awful smell again. Like the one in the cellar."

"All right, now, what is this about another tunnel?" Jack asked. "Are going to tell me, or is it some big secret?"

Henry gave Sheila a questioning look. She answered with a shrug of her shoulders.

Henry looked back at Jack: "It *is* a big secret, so if we tell you, you have to give your word not to tell anyone else, not even your parents."

"Sure, I promise, cross my heart." Jack's voice was quivering with curiosity.

"OK, then." Henry proceeded to tell Jack the story of how they had found the key and the pistol in their grandparents' hall closet and how they later discovered the entrance to the tunnel.

"Jeez, did you really go in?"

"Yeah, but it was pretty small like this one."

"Really? How far did you go?"

"I don't know for sure. We went quite a ways until we came to a place where it split. That's when Sheila's flashlight quit working, so we crawled back out."

Sheila gave him a disgusted look.

"Did you ever go back in to see where it went?" Jack asked excitedly.

"No, but we've looked for places where it might come out."

"Why didn't you go back? It sounds like a really neat place."

"Because Henry didn't tell you the bad part, that's why," Sheila exclaimed. "There was something in there. Something awful."

"There was? Cripes, what was it?" Jack was bouncing up and down on his toes.

"We don't know," Sheila continued. "We couldn't see it, but we could smell it. There was this sickening smell. Then it touched me. It touched *both* of us!"

"You mean it was invisible?"

"No, I mean it only touched us in the dark, when our flashlights were off. As soon as Henry got his on, it disappeared."

"That's pretty scary." Jack no longer bounced on his toes and his facial expression had turned almost grim. "Did you tell your grandma and grandpa?"

"No," Henry answered. "They'd be mad if they found out we were in the cellar. And they probably wouldn't believe there was something in there anyway."

"What about this opening then? Do you think it's connected to the tunnel in the cellar?"

"It might be. There's that same awful smell in there. There's another place, too, at the entrance to an old fruit cellar along the creek. It's all sealed up with rocks, but we could smell it through the cracks."

"Do you think whatever's in there dug its way out here?" Jack asked, backing away from the opening.

"Yeah, I think it might have."

"Come on, Henry," Sheila said. "Don't say things like that. You're always trying to scare people."

"This time it's true. It might have dug its way out." Henry was thinking of the pile of human remains he had seen in the tunnel. "It could be something dangerous."

"If you really think so, you should tell someone," Jack insisted.

Henry thought for a minute. "Maybe, but they'd just think we're crazy. Besides it's been five years."

"Will you at least show it to me?" Jack pleaded, up on his toes again.

Henry looked at Sheila. "Well, I don't . . . "

"You can show him, but I'm sure not going *in* there again."

"It would be hard to get in now anyway. We were smaller then, you know."

"Cripes," Jack exclaimed, "I don't want to go *in*,

but I'd really like to see it."

"OK, when we go back up to the house."

As they started down toward the river again, Henry stole a last look at the strange new opening in the bluff. Maybe they *were* making a big mistake by keeping these things a secret.

Jack walked beside Henry and Sheila along the river toward the sandbar. Like his two friends, he was wearing only a swimsuit, feeling the warm, hard-packed earth under his bare feet. He loved being part of the world Henry and Sheila had on their grandparents' farm. His own was so different—a father who was a tyrant even when he wasn't drunk, which he was most of the time, and a mother who never defended him and had started drinking herself. He had an older brother, Karsten, but he'd run away from home two years before. And there was Lloyd, always lurking somewhere, wanting to do dirty things to hurt him. The brightest spots in his life were Henry and Sheila. At that moment he didn't think he had ever been happier.

When they reached the sand, Jack's thoughts were interrupted by an irresistible impulse. Giving Sheila a knowing look, he shoved Henry toward the water. Taken by surprise, Henry had nearly sidestepped the dunking when Sheila joined in with a push and he dove into the water laughing. Whooping and splashing, Jack and Sheila plunged in behind him just as his head emerged. The cool water came as a shock on Jack's sunburned skin. He stood up exhilarated, not only by the water but by Sheila's willingness to team up with him. His confidence at a high level, he watched Henry and Sheila swim out from shore into the river current, letting it pull them several yards downstream before swimming back to where they could touch bottom again. Although he had never been a good swimmer, he dove in to follow them. After a few strokes underwater, the current swept over him, slowly but forcefully carrying him with it. For a moment he was terrified, afraid he couldn't swim well enough to get back to shore, when something grabbed his arm. Startled, he jerked his head out of the water and saw Henry beaming at him.

"What are you doing out here?" Henry asked. "I

thought you couldn't swim."

"What d'ya mean? Of course I can swim. Just watch." Jack jerked his arm away. Certain Sheila was watching, he dove toward shore and began flailing at the water as hard as he could. Before long his arms became so heavy he could hardly lift them. He thought he must be close enough to touch bottom. Pausing, he lowered his foot. There was nothing there. Desperately he stretched his leg further, toes pointed down. With great relief he brushed the sand.

"See!" he yelled back at Henry and Sheila.

When he turned to look, Henry was no more than six feet behind him, treading water and laughing. "You were right, I *guess* that was swimming."

They played in the water until Henry decided it was time to do some fishing. Since they already had dug the worms, Jack agreed to join him, but Sheila said she would rather lie in the sun and watch.

Poking through the dirt in the coffee can, Henry plucked out a worm and handed it to Jack. Baiting a hook was not Jack's favorite part of fishing. Holding the slippery creature firmly between his thumb and index finger, he began skewering it with the sharp point of the hook in a series of loops while it squirmed in protest. After Henry and Jack had cast their fishing lines into the still water behind a submerged log, they stretched out on the warm sand. Periodically Jack would sit up, look for some movement from his bobber, steal a glance at Sheila, then lie back down. When he began to feel the beginning of a bad sunburn, Jack moved a few feet into the shade from a low-hanging willow tree.

"You know what's *really* scary, Jack?" he heard Sheila ask.

"No, what?" Jack answered, immediately all-ears.

"That island over there, Big Tow, the one people tell those stories about. It's always given me the creeps."

Jack raised his head to look, squinting into the bright sun reflecting off the water. The island stretched as far as he could see in either direction. Trees grew thickly along its shore making the island appear to be surrounded by a furry green wall. "I thought that was

Illinois."

"No, it's the island all those stories are about. You know, how a tribe of weird old people live on it, and that people who go there end up disappearing."

"Yeah, Grandpa said he won't *ever* go there," Henry added.

"I've heard my dad say he won't go there either," Jack added.

"I've always wanted to explore it," Henry replied, his voice rising, "but I can't figure out a way to get there. If we could just borrow somebody's boat. What about your dad's, Jack. Do you think sometime you could use it?"

"Not a chance. My dad would never let me."

"Too bad. It'd be fun."

Henry became quiet. Sheila already was still. With no one talking any longer, Jack laid back down in the warm sand and drifted off to sleep.

He dozed fitfully. Lloyd Wischmeier had entered his house in the dark, slicing a screen in the back door with his knife, and was stealing up the stairs. Even though he was asleep in bed, Jack could somehow see him coming up the stairs, rage on his face, a vicious look in his eyes. He appeared in the bedroom doorway, eyeing Jack with an evil grin. His switchblade knife glittered in his hand, the blade curved like a fish hook with a barb at the end. Jack was petrified. Lloyd was about to skewer him like he had skewered the worm.

"C'mon, you guys, the fish went home and your worms've drowned. Let's go back to the house," Sheila called out. "I've had enough sun."

Jack heard Sheila's voice as Lloyd stalked across the room toward him. He raised up with a start, perspiration covering his forehead, expecting to see Lloyd lunge at him, to feel the blade pierce his chest. It took him a moment to realize he was sitting by the river.

Sheila stood a few feet away brushing sand off the back of her swimming suit and her legs. Her tan skin glistened from a mixture of suntan oil and sweat. The one piece suit she wore was faded red and fit her snugly, hugging the developing curves of her hips and breasts. Jack took in each part of her with his eyes, settling on the fabric between her legs. He felt a stirring under his swimming suit.

He caught himself and looked away. His face grew flush. Jeez, what a dirty mind, he thought. I'm as bad as Lloyd. What if she saw me looking at her there? She'd never talk to me again. He looked guiltily at her face. She was gathering her fishing pole. There was no sign she had seen him staring. His cheeks started to cool.

"Jack, Henry, c'mon now. Let's get those lines in and give the worms a decent burial."

Henry picked up his pole and started to reel in the line, watching the bobber skip across the water. Sheila did the same with Jack's pole and they raced their bobbers to shore. As Jack started to stand, he discovered that the impact Sheila had on him wasn't over. The stirring he felt in his tight-fitting swim suit resulted in a protrusion that he didn't know how to eliminate or hide. He glanced down at it, overwhelmed with embarrassment. There was no way he could let Sheila see him like that. Subconsciously he uttered a moan. Henry and Sheila both turned to look.

"Hey, Jack, something wrong?" Henry asked.

"Nah. Just sort of a stomach ache all of a sudden." He had to think of something quick. He couldn't continue sitting there much longer, and the protrusion wasn't going away. Then he remembered his towel. It was skimpy but it might work. He stood up keeping his back to Henry and Sheila and wrapped the towel around his waist, holding it tightly at his hip. Jack hoped he could now face them. But when he looked down to check, he was horrified to see that his problem was still visible. In desperation he jabbed at it with his hand, pushing it awkwardly between his legs, hoping he could hold it in place with his thighs. But when he tried to move, his thighs lost their grip and a blunt point appeared again in the towel.

"Jack, what are you doing?" Sheila asked. "It won't help to push on your stomach. We'll get you something at the house."

Jack still had his back to her but he knew she was looking at him. His knees almost buckled from mortification. Oh my gosh, she saw me playing with it! What did I do to deserve this? It's my dirty mind, that's what. I'm being punished for my dirty mind. He collapsed back down on the sand.

"It's OK," he muttered, "you and Henry just get the stuff together. I'll be there in a minute."

He was afraid that Sheila would come to where he was sitting and see it. If that happened, she would never speak to him again. Then he remembered hearing once that if you snapped the end with the tip of your finger like people flicked cigarette butts, it would go away. He turned to see if they were looking. Both Henry and Sheila were busy with the fishing gear so he pulled the waist band of his suit out in front and, with an angry snarl, gave it a hard snap on the end. He winced, then sat still, praying for a miracle.

"You ready, Jack? Do you think you can you make it up the bluff?" Henry asked.

This is it, Jack thought. He wasn't going to be able to hide it much longer. As a last resort he decided that his only hope was to have an appendicitis attack. Just when he was about to throw himself on the ground and writhe on his stomach, he felt a relaxation. He looked down. The miracle had come to pass.

"All right, I'm better. Let's go. I can help carry now."

When they reached the farmhouse, Sheila went to her room to change out of her bathing suit. Henry and Jack changed in the living room, strewing clothes across the floor.

"Hey, you were acting kind of weird down there. Are you sure you had a stomach ache or were you just fooling around?" Henry asked.

"Well, no . . . I mean yeah, I had a stomach ache sort of sudden like, but it's gone now, really."

"All right, it's just that it looked like you were trying to hide something."

"Can I come in now?" Sheila asked from outside the door.

"Hold on a minute," Jack yelled in alarm, frantically pulling on his underpants.

"OK, but just for a minute. Honestly, boys are so

modest."

"Nice talk, Sheila. And who just changed in her own room? You're just trying to embarrass Jack."

"Beware scaredy cats, I'm coming in." Sheila, wearing shorts and a work shirt tied at her waist, strolled into the room smiling and threw herself into her grandfather's deep leather chair. Jack fumbled at the buttons to his jeans.

"So, what do you guys want to do now?" Sheila asked. "It's getting all dark outside like a storm's coming, so we better stay in."

"How about something to eat?" Henry suggested.

"I'll tell you what I'd like to do," Jack said. "You said you'd show me that tunnel in the cellar."

"What do you think, Sheila? It's been an awful long time since we were down there."

"I'll go down with you to show Jack, but remember, I'm not going in."

"All right, then. Find a couple of flashlights and let's see if the key's still there." Henry had a twinge of anxiety at the thought of going back to the old cellar.

Sheila returned carrying three flashlights. "I think these all work. Let's go get the key."

The closet seemed smaller than Henry remembered. A cardboard box blocked his path under the hanging clothes. He pushed it aside and crawled to the back. Jack followed closely, while Sheila waited outside.

"The sewing machine's still here."

"Is that where it's at?"

"Yeah, it was in a bag tied inside." Henry lifted the lid. "There's the bag. Shine your light on it." Henry untied the bag and reached inside. "It's still here." He lifted the key out with a flourish.

"Wow, it *is* big, just like you said."

"I'll show you something else that's in here, but you have to promise not to tell."

"Sure, OK."

Henry gingerly lifted out the revolver. "See?"

"Jeez, it looks like a six-gun. Is it real?"

"It sure is, and it's loaded."

"Can I hold it?"

"OK, but you have to be really careful."

Jack took the pistol and aimed at the ceiling. "I shot a pistol once. My uncle let me. It had a lot of kick, and it wasn't even as big as this one. I'll bet this really kicks."

"Let's not find out. Put it back and we'll go down to the cellar."

Jack handed him the revolver and Henry placed it back in the bag. "I'll leave it open for now. We'll be back in a few minutes. Let's go. You first."

When they emerged from the closet, Sheila was waiting for them impatiently. "It's about time. I see you found the key. What were you doing back there, anyway? I hope you weren't playing with that gun. Remember, it was loaded. It *is* still there, isn't it?"

"Yeah, it's still there. Just like I remembered it."

With Henry leading the way, they descended the steep stairs into the cellar cautiously. They were quiet, as if they wanted to avoid warning something below of their approach. When he reached the bottom step, Henry pointed his flashlight toward the darkest end of the cellar.

"The door's back there, Jack. We'll have to use flashlights."

Beams of light bobbed chaotically across the dirt floor and stone walls as they made their way. Sheila's light found the door first.

"There it is, behind those boxes," she exclaimed.

"It's just like I remember," Henry said, shining his light on it. "I think those are the same boxes we moved before."

"Maybe, but I remember them as bigger."

"Funny, very funny. C'mon, let's move them. Here, Jack, take a side."

The two boys pushed the boxes away from the door while Sheila held the flashlights. When the door was clear, Jack stood in front of it staring. "Cripes, it looks like there's a dungeon back here."

"Let's see if the key still works." Henry inserted it into the keyhole and tried to turn it. When it wouldn't move, he used both hands and tried again, grunting and straining. A sound of grinding metal came from inside the lock. Very slowly the key began to move. When he could turn it no further, Henry stepped back.

"I think I got it. Let's see." He pulled on the handle. The hinges moaned and the door moved slightly.

"Here, Jack, grab hold."

Sheila kept her light on the door as they both pulled. It opened grudgingly.

"Phew, there's that smell already." Henry let go of the handle. "That's far enough. Boy, I don't remember that it smelled so bad."

Sheila shined her light through the doorway. "Henry! Look at this!" Her flashlight was pointed at a shallow hole surrounded by fresh dirt at the threshold. "It looks like something was trying to dig out!"

A high-pitched wail suddenly came from the distance. They stood staring at each other. No one moved. Then it came again, distant and muffled.

Jack spoke first. "What *is* that? It sounds like an animal!"

"Yeah, like something's being hurt outside," Henry exclaimed. Then he heard the faint barking of a dog. It must be Mutt, he thought to himself.

"Oh my God. It could be Fluffy. Something's hurting my cat!" Sheila screamed and ran for the stairs.

"C'mon, Jack!" Henry yelled. "There's something out there!"

Sheila burst through the front door onto the porch, Henry and Jack right behind. It was as if night had suddenly come while they were in the cellar, an early darkness created by the dense, black storm clouds rolling across the sky. Strong gusts of wind whipped through the farmyard, blowing dust in Henry's eyes. Thunder rumbled in the distance. The large trees in the front yard bent and sighed as the wind rushed through their branches.

They stopped at the top of the porch steps to listen. Mutt was still barking out of sight in the direction of the barn. The temperature had dropped so much the wind felt chilly.

"Fluffy! Fluffy!" Sheila called.

A gust of wind caught the screen door, banging it closed.

"Do you see anything?" she asked.

"No, but Mutt's out by the barn," Henry answered "Let's go look. If it was some animal, he's probably scared it off by now."

"We've got to find Fluffy. I know she's out here hurt someplace."

They raced down the steps toward the barn. Henry led the footrace, worried that Sheila was right about Fluffy. Mutt suddenly ran from behind the barn, barking relentlessly, and scratched at the door on the lower level. A brilliant flash of light lit up the sky.

"Mutt's trying to find a way in!" Sheila cried. "There must be something in there . . ."
A giant clap of thunder drowned out the rest of her words.

Henry lifted the wooden handle on the door and pulled it open. Sheila rushed to the doorway calling her cat's name. She stopped calling and they all listened. The only sound was wind howling through the farmyard and thunder rumbling in the distance.

Mutt ran between their legs and through the door. Henry felt on the inside wall for the light switch and pushed it. The barn door blew closed behind them. Inside, protected from the gusting winds, the barn seemed eerily calm. Three dust-coated light bulbs cast a weak glow, illuminating doors to the cattle and horse stalls that lined both sides. Mounds of straw littered the floor. A coat of tan dust covered every surface: the walls, the ledges, and the tools and tack and horse collars hanging on rusty nails in the walls. Cobwebs hung from floor joists overhead, weighted down by the dust caught in their webbing. Henry noticed he was still carrying his flashlight.

Mutt trotted down the hallway, sniffing from one door to the next, his nose close to the ground, occasionally burrowing into a pile of straw then pushing it aside. Henry watched, expecting him to find something at any moment.

"Good boy, Mutt. Find Fluffy," Sheila said as if she was talking to a child. "Stay close to him. I think he's picked up a scent."

Sheila crouched as she followed the dog. Mutt stopped at the boards nailed to the wall that led to the hayloft, then put his front paws on the first rung and stared up at the dark hole overhead. As he started to bark, a bolt of lightning cracked outside, its flash penetrating every opening in the barn's walls. An explosion of thunder followed that shook the barn and caused the dirt floor to vibrate.

"Wow, that was close," Jack struggled to say.

Just then a small, furry object flew out of the darkness at the top of the ladder and landed near Mutt. Startled, the dog jumped sideways with a yelp. Henry quickly aimed the beam of his flashlight into the opening, expecting to see who had thrown it, but saw nothing. After hitting the floor, the object rolled, picking up straw and dust which stuck to its sides. At first Henry thought the object was an odd-shaped ball smeared with something sticky. He went closer. The thing still glistened. He was thinking that for a ball, it wasn't very round when Sheila screamed.

"Look! Oh my God. Oh, no. Henry! Jack! Oh my God, no! It looks like . . . it's Fluffy." Sheila hands flew to her face, covering her eyes.

Henry looked at the "ball", saw two eyes and a pink nose surrounded by fur matted with blood.

Sheila screamed as she collapsed against one of the stall doors and slid to the floor. Jack stared at the furry head, his mouth open wide.

Henry was afraid he was going to throw up and turned his face away. His mind went numb. He stood motionless, not knowing what to do when a sound came from overhead. A mound of gray fur with legs and a tail fell from the darkness, landing with a fleshy thud. This time Henry knew exactly what it was. He began to feel even sicker. Sheila's shrill scream made him forget his stomach.

"It's Lloyd!" Henry ran to the foot of the ladder and shouted. "Lloyd, you sick son of a bitch! We'll get you for this! I mean it." He waited, expecting an answer of some kind, but there was none.

"Lloyd, you chickenshit, I know it's you. This

time you're really gonna get it!" He waited again. Still no sound from the hayloft.

Jack knelt awkwardly by Sheila, trying to comfort her. She was racked with sobs and shaking. Henry took her hands. She raised her head to look at him. Her eyes were red and wet, but Henry could see the anger.

"I'm going to fix him for this, really fix him," she said, her voice unsteady. Resolve began forming on her face and she stood up.

"I'm with you, Sheila," Jack said emphatically. "Let's get that son of a bitch."

Motioning up at the haymow, Henry spoke softly. "He must still be up there. Let's get back to the house and call the Sheriff."

"You go on, Henry. I want to stay here and make sure he doesn't get away." Sheila's voice was firm.

"You can't stay here. What if he came down all of a sudden? Besides, he might go out another way."

"All right. You and Jack stay here. But don't let him get out. I'll go call the sheriff."

Sheila gently picked up the remains of her cat and ran out of the barn.

Henry stood at the bottom of the ladder with Jack next to him, staring up at the opening.

"Lloyd, come on down!" Henry called out. But the only sound from overhead was the wind.

"I don't hear anything," Jack said softly. "Can he get out from up there?"

"Yeah, there's a door to unload the wagons but we'd hear it open. There's also the door where they lower the hay to the wagon, but it's up high. He must still be up there. Let's go look."

Jack had two metal bars in his hand. He held one out and Henry took it.

Climbing the ladder was difficult with his flashlight in one hand and the metal bar in the other. He went slowly, drawing closer to the darkness of the haymow overhead with each rung. His throat tightened. As the initial rush of excitement and adrenalin subsided, he began to wonder whether Lloyd was waiting for them with his knife. There was a flash of light and another crack of thunder, nearly as loud as the one before. Henry made himself climb another rung.

"Is there a light up there?" Jack asked softly from below.

"Yeah, but the switch is over by the door."

One more step and he could put his head into the dark hole above him. He crouched and stepped onto the next rung. Taking a deep breath, he held the iron bar over his head for protection and raised up quickly, thrusting his arms and head through the opening to the haymow. He shined his light around quickly, convinced he would see Lloyd about to swing something at him. But Lloyd wasn't there. A sudden fluttering almost made him lose his grip on the sides of the opening. A bat flew through the beam of his flashlight, nearly causing him to drop it. He pulled himself through the opening, afraid he would see Lloyd appear from the shadows at any minute. He climbed the rest of the way into the haymow and stood. With only the light from his flashlight, the haymow looked cavernous. The wind was making a low, whistling sound as it blew between the warped boards of the walls. Jack climbed through the opening a moment later.

They stood next to each other playing the beams from their flashlights around the room. The sweet smell of dry hay was strong. Jack sneezed. Henry aimed his light at the high arched ceiling. The beam appeared to have substance as it reflected off the dust stirred by the wind. He could barely make out the timber at the roof's peak through the haze. As he stood waiting for his heart to slow, he heard a sharp squeak above the sound of the wind. It came again. He looked at Jack. From the frightened look on his face, Henry knew Jack had heard it, too. They remained still, listening. The sound came again.

Jack nudged Henry's arm, pointing his light toward a pile of hay bales stacked at the far end of the room. "That's where it's coming from. He's back there," Jack said in a whisper.

"Yeah, it's the only place he could hide up here." Henry's voice drowned in a roll of thunder.

"All right, c'mon out, you chickenshit!" Jack

yelled, waving the iron bar. "We know you're back there. You better get out here if you know what's good for you!"

Henry was surprised how loud Jack's voice sounded. They waited. He motioned to Jack and they walked stealthily toward the hay bales. Henry squeezed the iron bar tightly, feeling sweat in his palm. When he was near the pile, he lunged onto the bales holding his flashlight out in front of him. But the light revealed only an empty space behind the hay and the small set of double-doors used for loading hay. One of the doors was open, swinging in the gusts of wind. A heavy pounding began on the roof overhead as the rain arrived. The large drops quickly progressed to a downpour which sounded like a waterfall inside the barn.

"Dammit, Henry, he's not up here." Jack sounded disappointed.

"Yeah, but I'll bet he was." Henry shined his light on the floor near the hay bales. "Look at that." A large red stain colored the hay, wet and glistening in the flashlight's beam.

"This is where he did it." Henry caught the sob in his throat. "That poor little cat. And Sheila. She feels so bad. How can Lloyd do things like that? He's going to pay for it this time."

Jack walked to the double-doors, pushed both sides open into the rain and looked down. "He might've jumped after he threw Fluffy down. That's some jump, though. He coulda broke somethin'."

Outside Mutt started barking again. Henry stuck his head out the door and looked. "Where's Mutt?"

"Sounds like he's up by the house."

"Oh, jeez, maybe Lloyd saw Sheila leave. We better get up there. See the rope hanging on the pulley out there? We can slide down. I've done it lots of times. That's probably what Lloyd did." Henry crouched at the door, shielding his eyes against the rain, and pointed at a wood beam jutting out above the opening. A pulley at the end of the beam was silhouetted against the dim light. A line of rope ran through it, one end tied to the barn, the other hanging nearly to the ground. "Grab the rope then loosen your hands and slide. It'll be slippery in the rain so grab it tight at first."

"OK. I'll follow you. Go ahead." Jack seemed unsure.

Henry jammed his flashlight into the waistband of his jeans, wiped the water from his face and threw the iron bar down to the ground. "Shine your light on the rope. OK. Here goes!" Henry reached for the rope. The rain had made it feel almost slimy. He seized it tightly in both hands, leaned out the doorway and began sliding. In a second he had landed in a puddle.

Henry pulled out his flashlight and shined it up the rope. "All right. Can you see it? Come on." A thump sounded several feet behind him as Jack's iron bar hit the ground. Then Jack appeared in the light clutching the rope.

"OK, now just let go a little and slide." As he watched, a bolt of lightning made a jagged arc across the sky.

Jack slid slowly at first, gaining speed as he neared the ground. His knees buckled when he hit, but he managed to stay upright by hanging onto the rope.

Henry gave Jack no time to recover. "Let's go!" he yelled as soon as Jack's feet touched the ground, then racing for the farmhouse as thunder rumbled around the sky.

"Wait! I don't have my club," Jack called out.

"Forget it. We've got to get up there." Henry had forgotten his iron bar as well but the urgency he felt wouldn't let him go back. He dashed headlong through the muddy puddles forming in front of the farmhouse and took the porch stairs two at a time. Jack was only a step behind. Mutt was barking furiously at the front door. The fact that the door was closed increased Henry's concern. Without pausing, he pulled open the screen door, gave the doorknob a hard twist and hit the door with his hip. It wouldn't open. Why would Sheila lock it? He banged on the door with his hip again.

"Is it locked?" Jack stood with his hands on his hips gulping air.

"Yeah, maybe Sheila locked it because of Lloyd." Henry hoped he was right. He started to pound on the door with his fists.

"Sheila! Sheila! Open up. It's us. Me and Jack."
He stood and waited. No answer came.

"I'll go check the back door." Jack ran down the porch steps and disappeared into the downpour.

Henry pounded on the door again and called Sheila's name over and over. The only response was the sound of rain and distant thunder. The small glass panes in the door were fogged over. He cleared one of them with his shirt and peered inside. There was a light in the kitchen but nothing moved. Suddenly he heard a voice in the distance. He stood and listened anxiously. It was only Jack calling Sheila's name at the rear of the house.

A minute later Jack bounded onto the porch, water dripping down his hair and clothes. "The back door's locked and I couldn't get any answer. I checked the cellar door on the way. It's locked, too. The house is all dark back there, but I saw a light on the third floor."

"That's strange. All of this is strange. What's going on here?" Henry called out in frustration. "I'm afraid Lloyd's in there with Sheila."

"Jeez, maybe that's why there's a light on the third floor."

"If we want to help her, we'll have to break in."

"How do we do that?"

"We'll have to break the glass. I wish we had those iron bars, but I guess I can break it with my flashlight." He looked at the front door, guessing which pane would be closest to the lock on the other side. He hit it with the end of his flashlight. The glass cracked. He hit it again. This time the glass shattered. With several quick blows, he broke out the glass around the frame to make way for his arm. When the shards of glass stopped falling to the floor, Henry was sure he heard a muffled shout.

"Did you hear that?"

"Yeah, the glass broke."

"No, something else, like somebody shouting."

"Maybe . . . but I don't think so."

"OK, let's see if I can get the door open now. Hold the light where I can see." Henry reached through the window frame and groped for the knob that turned the lock. "Ow! I cut myself!"

Jack shined his light on Henry's arm. There was a small cut near his elbow. "Yeah, you did. It's bleeding but not bad."

"There, I've got it." Henry found the knob and twisted. He pulled his arm back from through door and pushed it open. "Sheila! Sheila! Answer me! Where are you?" He thought he heard another muffled shout. "It sounds like she's upstairs."

Henry raced to the stairs to the second floor, Jack right behind. At the top they stood in the dark hallway listening. Muffled thunder came from outside. All the doors were closed. Suddenly a scream came from overhead.

"How do you get to the third floor?" Jack asked.

"This way!" Henry shouted as he ran to the door that led to the stairway. When they reached the third floor, Henry was greeted by a shriek and shouts from a deeper voice. The hall was dark but a light came from under the door to one of the bedrooms.

"There, Jack. He must have her in there!" Henry shouted. "Oh God! What's he doing to her?"

Henry ran toward the door and twisted the knob. It was locked. He hit it with his shoulder, but the door didn't budge. He turned the knob and hit it again. The result was the same.

Inside, Sheila's screams became more shrill, more desperate. "Lloyd, don't. Stop it! Please stop! Henry, help!"

"Lloyd!" Henry shouted at the closed door. "Open up and let her go. We've called the Sheriff. Open this door. He'll be here any minute. If you don't open it, we'll bust it in!"

"I know how to fix him!" Jack said. Then, to Henry's surprise, he ran noisily back down the stairs.

Henry turned his attention back to the door. "Lloyd, you better open up." He kicked at the door with his foot. "The sheriff will get in if we don't."

He could hear a struggle inside and Sheila screamed again. He had to get in somehow. Frantically, he glanced around the hall for something he could use

to break in. Nothing. Maybe in one of the rooms, he
thought. He looked desperately at the other doors,
wondering where to start. Instead, he leaned back and
gave the door a kick with the bottom of his shoe. The
wood by the lock cracked.

"Henry. Jack. Break . . ." Sheila's shout from the
other side of the door was cut short.

As he prepared for another kick, Henry heard feet
pounding up the stairs. Jack came up behind him,
breathing hard.

"I've got it, Henry."

Henry barely heard what he said. "Jack! Come
on! We can kick it in!" He gave the door another kick
with all the strength he could muster. The doorjamb
splintered with a loud crack. He kicked again and the
door sprang open. Henry rushed in with Jack right
behind.

Sheila was lying on the bed almost naked. Lloyd
was leaning over her, struggling to tie her hands to the
brass headboard with her brassiere. Red welts stood
out on her arms. Her work shirt was pushed up around
her neck, baring her small breasts. Her jeans and
underwear were down around her ankles. Henry
averted his eyes from between her legs.

Lloyd released his grip on Sheila's wrists and
straightened up. Sheila rolled away from him onto the
floor. Lloyd's pants were around his ankles, his
enlarged penis protruding from between his shirttails.
For a split second, Henry had an urge to laugh. Lloyd
hurriedly bent over and pulled up his pants. As he
struggled to button his fly, he sneered first at Henry,
then at Jack.

"I told you fuckers to keep out of here. It looks
like you're gonna have to learn to listen better." He
gripped the heavy metal buckle of his belt and pulled it
from the loops in his pants. Slowly the belt slid through
his hand until he held it at the end. Then he reached
into the front pocket of his pants and brought out the
pearl-handled knife which opened with a sinister click.
A bright flash of lightning lit the window behind him.

There was no doubt in Henry's mind that he was
in for the fight of his life, maybe *for* his life. He wished

he had that iron bar. Lloyd came toward him swinging the belt, his knife pointed at Henry's stomach, his eyes narrowed to creases. Sheila stared wide-eyed from behind the bed. A crack of thunder erupted, but Lloyd showed no reaction. Escape was still possible if he ran, but abandoning Sheila was unthinkable. The buckle at the end of the swinging belt was mesmerizing. He had to be ready to dodge it. Barely two steps away, Lloyd swung the belt behind his back, preparing to strike. Henry's muscles tightened and a cold sweat broke out on his skin. His plan was to dive at Lloyd's legs at the last minute, knocking him off his feet. As he prepared to lunge, he imagined the knife plunging into his back. With a vicious look on his face, Lloyd had started to swing when Henry saw his eyes suddenly grow wide.

The explosion behind him was so loud that Henry was amazed to find himself still upright. It seemed to enter his right ear and burst inside his head. He was too stunned to move. His ear rang painfully. A blue haze hung in the air and the smell of something burning stung the lining of his nose. He rubbed his eyes, trying to see clearly, afraid that any second he might feel a blow from Lloyd's belt or the blade of his knife. But Lloyd had retreated against the far wall, his belt and knife on the floor. Through the ringing in his ears, Henry heard Jack raging.

"You homo! You goddamn homo! I owe you this! You stay right there or the next one won't miss. Move and I'll shoot your dick off! I'll teach you, you lousy bastard!" Lloyd cringed, holding his palms up as a shield. Sheila stared open-mouthed.

The revolver from the sewing machine looked huge in Jack's hand. Smoke still curled out of the end of its barrel. Jack had it pointed squarely at Lloyd, his thumb on the hammer. Henry wondered where the bullet had gone. Had Jack actually tried to hit him? If so, it looked like he had missed, but he must have given Lloyd the scare of his life.

"Don't move a muscle, you fucker. Shit, I ought to shoot even if you don't."

Henry couldn't tell whether Jack was yelling or crying. "Jack! Great! Now be careful. Don't shoot him by accident."

"What should we do with him? Maybe we oughta make him jump outa that window." Jack sounded somewhat calmer.

"Just keep it pointed at him and I'll go call the Sheriff."

Sheila, struggling to pull on her clothes, spoke for the first time. "You can't. He pulled the phone out of the wall."

"All right. Grandma and Grandpa have to be home soon. We'll just go downstairs and wait."

"We should tie him up and use his belt on him!" Sheila came from around the bed, her voice sounding venomous.

"Yeah, use his belt on him. Maybe carve on him a little with his knife. What do ya say, you homo?"

Still hunched over, Lloyd didn't answer.

"Let's take him downstairs and tie him up with some clothesline," Henry said.

"OK. Come on, Lloyd. Downstairs. That belt and knife stay on the floor. And if you try to touch 'em or come near any of us, so help me I'll pull this trigger." Jack sounded very convincing.

Lloyd walked slowly around the bed, past Henry and into the hall. Jack followed a few steps behind, pointing the revolver at his back. Henry hurriedly picked up the knife and belt.

"Watch him, Jack. He might try something. Don't get too close," Henry said in a low voice.

"Look, I ain't gonna try nothin'." Lloyd spoke for the first time since the shot. "Just keep that fuckin' 'morph from pullin' the trigger."

"You shut your Goddamned mouth! Call me that one more time, and I'll shoot your ugly head off."

Sheila finished straightening her clothes and touched Jack's arm. "Give me the gun, Jack. I owe him something." Her voice was calm and cold.

Jack gave her a questioning look.

"Just give me the gun."

Henry had never heard Sheila sound so icy. He watched her take the revolver from Jack. In Sheila's hands the gun looked even bigger. The thought occurred to him that she might be planning to shoot. So what if she did, Henry told himself.

Lloyd stopped walking while the gun was exchanged. Sheila pointed the gun at the back of his head, brushing his hair with the tip of the barrel. Three metallic clicks sounded as she cocked the hammer with her thumb.

"You'd better head down those stairs," she said evenly. Her hands were steady on the revolver.

"OK, OK. Just be careful with that thing."

"Go on down those steps and don't turn around. If you do, so help me I'll blow your brains out!" From the sound of her voice, Henry believed her.

They walked single file down the stairs. A fierce crack of thunder startled Henry but Sheila remained cool and purposeful. He stayed close behind them clutching Lloyd's belt and knife, expecting him to try something at any moment.

"Where shall we put him?" Jack asked when they reached the first floor.

"The kitchen." Sheila answered without taking her eyes off Lloyd. "We'll tie him to a chair. The clothesline's by the back door."

Lloyd walked through the door from the hallway into the kitchen. On his right the door to the cellar stood open. Lloyd hesitated, then suddenly crouched down, turned swiftly and hit Sheila's arm with his fist. Henry was again rocked by an explosion and stumbled backwards, tripping over a chair. As he fell he saw Lloyd with a disbelieving look on his face tumbling backwards through the door to the cellar, grasping in vain at the sides. Then he disappeared. As he sprawled on the kitchen floor, Henry heard Lloyd tumble down the stairs. Sheila stood in the cellar doorway holding the revolver with both hands, pointing it down the stairway. Jack stood next to her, staring over her shoulder. Henry watched her cock the hammer again and take aim. There was another explosion and Sheila's arms jerked sharply upward.

Henry got to his feet quickly and ran between Jack and Sheila to look. He saw nothing but darkness at the bottom of the stairs. "Jeez, Sheila. Did you . . .

Did you hit him?"

"I think so." Sheila voice quivered. "When he tried to hit me. Down the cellar, I don't know. I thought I saw him at the bottom of the stairs for a second. It looked like he was getting up. I was afraid he might come back so I shot."

"The homo deserved it," Jack said firmly.

Henry switched on the cellar light. There was no sign of Lloyd. "Well, he's not there now. If you shot him, he must not be hurt too bad."

"Then he'll try to get out. I'm going to find him," Sheila answered, her voice no longer quivering. "I don't want him to get away."

"You know, if we go down there and he's not hurt too bad, he'll try to get the gun," Henry said.

"He won't get it away from me any more than he did a minute ago."

"I'll come with you. We'll get that homo." Jack looked ready to plunge down the stairs.

"No, I'll go with Henry. You check the storm doors at the side of the house and make sure they're locked outside." Sheila's voice was firm again.

"Oh, OK." Jack was clearly disappointed but went out the kitchen door.

Henry took another flashlight from a cabinet and handed it to Sheila. "Here. I'll go first so he can't grab the gun."

He began edging down the steps sideways, expecting to be grabbed any second. Halfway down fhe ducked his head under the floor joists at the cellar's ceiling and switched on his flashlight, shining it around swiftly. To his relief Lloyd wasn't anywhere to be seen. Then he shined the beam into the darkness beyond the circle of light from the bulb above the wash tubs.

"I don't see him," he whispered.

When he reached the bottom, Henry spied a small crimson pool on the floor. He stooped to touch it, then rubbed his fingers together. It was wet and sticky. Just like Fluffy's, he thought. "There's blood down here."

Sheila stood two steps above him. "That means I hit him."

"Maybe, or he could have cut himself when he

fell."

"Do you see blood anyplace else?"

"No. Not right here, anyway."

"I wonder which way he went?" Sheila said in a low voice. She looked around cautiously, moving the revolver and her eyes together. There was no sound but their breathing.

"I don't know," Henry finally answered.

"Let's look over by the furnace."

They walked toward it on tiptoes, Henry in front shining the beam of his flashlight from side to side, imagining Lloyd leaping from the darkness at every step. When they reached the furnace, he turned on the overhead light. "He's not here and the doors outside are closed."

"He must have gone back there, then." Sheila pointed to the far end of the cellar. "We left that door open, remember. Maybe he'll find the tunnel and try to go through it."

"I don't think he could."

"He might try."

Henry started toward the old cellar room, walking stealthily. He could feel Sheila's breath on the back of his neck. When they had gone several steps past the stairs, he saw another red spot on the floor. "Here, Sheila. Look!"

Sheila stood beside him and looked down. "He was here, all right. Let's . . ."

Sheila's words were interrupted by a shriek that pierced through the darkness in front of them. There was a look of terror on her face as she raised the revolver. The shrillness of the sound penetrated Henry's body as if he had been stabbed. He stared straight ahead, expecting to see Lloyd materialize. Instead the shriek was followed by another, and another. Henry was bewildered, undecided whether to run or stand their ground.

"Henry! Make them stop!" Sheila cried. "I can't stand it."

The screams didn't stop. Henry covered his ears but it did little to help. He felt himself growing faint. It must be Lloyd, he thought to himself, but they were so high-pitched it was hard to be sure. What could be happening to him? After standing in place for what seemed like hours, the screaming began to grow fainter, then stopped as abruptly as it had started—and the cellar became fearfully quiet. Sheila lowered the revolver, her arms shaking.

"That must have been Lloyd," Sheila whispered breathlessly. "Should we go see what happened?"

Henry's curiosity nearly let him say yes, but somewhere in his head a red flag waved, stirred by his memory of the tunnel.

"I don't think that's a good idea."

Chapter Twenty-Two

The Body

July 14, 1956

Herbert Siefken drove through the darkness and rain as fast as he dared, the Ford cruiser's headlights dimly illuminating the narrow blacktop road. Driving to the Gerdes farm usually took fifteen minutes. Herbert had set out to do it in ten. He glanced warily from one side of the road to the other as he drove, worried something might appear in the road ahead too late to avoid. Overhead the red light spun relentlessly, its beam casting a pulsating glow on the rain-drenched trees lining the road. He knew the asphalt was slick. The year before he had skidded off this road rushing to the site where Orville Hemie had rolled his '39 Packard. He didn't want to suffer that embarrassment again. Ordinarily he should be using the siren, but it was late and residents in the north part of Bruders Landing didn't like to be disturbed at night The siren stayed off. Besides, he might soon have enough trouble as it was.

The phone call had been a shock. In a town rarely touched by violence, Herbert had listened to Lyle Gerdes, normally a calm, thoughtful man, describe hysterically not just one but two violent crimes. Herbert was annoyed when the call first came. He hated working Saturday nights and was about to go off duty. Lyle had talked so fast and in such a strange, high-pitched voice, Herbert first thought he was on something. But when he heard the word "rape" in Lyle's rush of words, he bolted upright in his chair. Lyle had said Lloyd Wischmeier attacked his granddaughter. Not only that, he said Lloyd was lying dead in his cellar. Herbert had slumped back down and groaned, afraid Lyle had taken care of things himself.

It had been hard to get much information over the phone. Lyle's answers to his questions were sketchy. Usually he wasn't much of a talker but tonight he had talked a mile a minute, a torrent of words containing little information. The man was horrified. His granddaughter had been attacked. And he had found her attacker's body, Lloyd Wischmeier's body—at least what Lyle *thought* was Lloyd Wischmeier's body—part way inside a hole in their cellar wall. Mutilated. Impossible to make out the features. Herbert told him to keep everyone out of the cellar, he was on his way.

He wasn't surprised to hear that Lloyd Wischmeier might have attacked someone. He'd been trouble as long as Herbert had been in Bruders Landing. But Lloyd had also been clever, careful not to be caught. And when he was, his parents had bailed him out. After pushing little Dickie Steingraber down a flight of steps at school, breaking his arm, Lloyd had avoided reform school only because his parents agreed to pay the Steingrabers' medical bills, and the judge was aglow after a liquid Christmas lunch. That Lloyd would end up behind bars sooner or later Herbert had been certain. The signs were all there. It was only a matter of when and for what. Lloyd seemed capable of anything. But to hear that Norman and Blanche Wischmeier's only son Lloyd might at this moment be lying dead in Lyle Gerdes' cellar was too ironic. It didn't figure. Herbert had experience with killers and why people kill. He didn't know of many candidates for killer in Bruders Landing, except perhaps Lloyd himself. And now it appeared Lloyd was the victim. Life certainly had its strange twists. Lyle Gerdes certainly didn't fit the profile of a killer, but Herbert would have to take a close look. Revenge was a powerful motivator.

As the cruiser's lights picked out the southern edge of Walnut Grove Cemetery, the dilemma Herbert had wrestled with for nearly two months moved to the forefront of his mind. He still had no idea what had been feeding in the cemetery. At least three mausoleums had been invaded, bodies picked clean of every piece of flesh, their skeletons in pieces. Other corpses bore marks where the flesh had been bitten but otherwise left intact. For all he knew, the thing had also gotten into coffins buried in the ground, but he hadn't wanted to start digging up graves. That would become a sideshow. And what had he learned so far? Precious little. No sign of forced entry at the entrances to the mausoleums, which seemed to rule out anything as large as a human. For that much he was grateful. But no sign of entry had been found anywhere else, at least no opening large enough for anything bigger than a small chipmunk. Did this thing act out of anger, some demented instinct or simple hunger? Whatever had invaded that cemetery behaved like nothing he had ever heard of.

The coroner, Reuben Blustein, confirmed that the bites and marks found on the bodies and bones were made by small teeth, but he couldn't identify what made them. He wouldn't even guess. But he *did* have a hunch.

Herbert had been sitting on the affair for weeks to avoid upsetting the surviving families with the knowledge that something so unspeakable had happened to a deceased parent or child, at least until he knew how to put a stop to it. But he still didn't know how, and for all he knew it was still going on, in the mausoleums and underground in any of the thousands of graves. The facts and questions smoldered inside him like hot embers.

So far no word had leaked out. How long could he keep it quiet? What if a family wanted to use one of the mausoleums? That could happen at any time. He wondered what would happen when Harry Berghoff, reporter, editor and owner of the *Bruders Landing Gazette*, the town's weekly newspaper, learned that the sheriff had kept the information from the public for more than two months and still didn't know diddleyshit about what was going on? Berghoff had never been one of Herbert's fans and he would have a field day with this story. When that happened, Herbert could forget about being re-elected. He was beginning to feel like *he* was the one about to be eaten.

And now this. An attempted rape and a murder. In the same night. And a body mutilated to boot. At the Gerdes farm. The farm next to Walnut Grove Cemetery.

The blacktop ended and the cruiser's tires struck gravel when Herbert passed the cemetery, crossing the city limits. His mind focused back on driving. Water gathered in low spots in the road. He hit the pools without slowing, spraying water high over the ditch at the side of the road. Before leaving he had told a deputy, Lester Hammond, to send the coroner with an ambulance. But it could be another half hour before Reuben Blustein arrived, depending on how long it took Hammond to find him on a Saturday night.

The entrance to the Gerdes place appeared in his headlights. He braked hard, wheels skidding in the gravel, to make the sharp right turn into the lane leading to the house. Trees grew close together on each side, their branches intertwining overhead. It was like driving into a tunnel. Ahead, centered squarely between the trees, was the Gerdes house. Lights burned in the downstairs windows all across its front. On the second floor, lights glowed from two rooms facing front at each end of the floor. The effect gave the house a face which seemed to leer at him as he approached.

Herbert stopped directly in front of the porch, headlights beamed at the front door, the cruiser's overhead light still throbbing. Lyle Gerdes hurried onto the porch. As soon as Herbert reached the steps, Lyle seized his hand and began pumping.

"Sure glad you came so quick, Sheriff. Sure glad." Lyle was still talking a mile a minute, but Herbert noticed his voice had lowered an octave since their phone conversation. "Thanks a heap. We sure do need you. There's been some bad trouble here tonight."

"Sounds like it, Lyle. I'll sure do what I can. Just take it easy now. It'll be all right. Now, you told me on the phone that your granddaughter was attacked, right?"

"Yep, that's right. Sheila. Uh, we was all gone to town . . ."

"I'll get the story later. I want to have a look at the girl first. See how she is. You think Lloyd Wischmeier did it. And he's down in your cellar, dead?"

"I guess it's him. Uh, it's . . . it's just real hard to tell, Sheriff. You'll see. The kids seen him go into the cellar."

"You mean Lloyd Wischmeier?"

"That's right. Sheila said she and Henry were in the cellar lookin' for him when he started yellin'. When he quit, they didn't feel like goin' to see what happened to 'im. Can't say as I blame 'em. We got home around 10:30, and Sheila and Henry told what happened. I got a flashlight and m'Winchester 12 gauge and went . . ."

"OK, slow down a little."

"Yep, sorry, it's been one hell of a night. So I looked all over down there. Finally, I found this fella stickin' halfway outa this hole in the old cellar. His butt and legs sorta hangin' there, like he got stuck tryin' to get in. I yelled for him to get on outa there. When he didn't move none, I walked over and poked 'im in the ass with my shotgun. Still he don't move." Lyle paused and took a deep breath. "So I grabbed holda 'im by his belt and pulled."

"Uh, did he come out?"

"Yeah. When he started to pull free was when I saw blood run out from under 'im. A lot of it. All down the wall. Just like a dam broke. Then he flopped out. Yep, just flopped out on those rocks on the floor." Lyle started to talk softly, almost in a whisper, and his voice raised to a higher pitch. "I ain't seen nothin' like it, Sheriff." He swallowed hard. "There wasn't nothin' left on the top o' him. Nothin' but bones."

Herbert swallowed hard. "That's enough. I'll go have a look. The coroner will be along in a few minutes, too. I'd better go have a look at your granddaughter."

"There's one more thing, Sheriff." Lyle began to speak softly in a voice that was nearly back to normal. "My grandson Henry's friend, Jack Powell, was here avisitin' when all this happened. They tell me Jack got the drop on Lloyd with an old pistol and squeezed off a round to scare 'im. That's when Sheila got loose. Then they say Sheila took the pistol and marched the Wischmeier kid to the kitchen where he swung at her and tried take it." Lyle suddenly paused, sighed, then went on. "Well, Sheila says she shot at 'im, maybe hit 'im. The kid fell down the cellar steps. That's the last they saw of 'im."

My God, it only gets worse, Herbert thought. "Where'd they get the pistol?"

"It's an old one Emma had hid away. It was my daddy's. I'd forgot all about it. Them kids musta found it sometime."

"OK. I'll be talkin' to them, too. Let's go on inside."

Lyle led Herbert into the living room. Alice McQueen sat on the couch, her arm around her daughter's shoulders. Although she had gained weight since her husband's death, Alice looked small as she sat consoling her daughter. Sheila's face was a blank. Across the room Henry and Jack slouched in chairs, looking subdued. They both stood up when Herbert entered the room. "Evening, everybody."

Emma Gerdes came in from the kitchen, wiping her hands on her apron. "Sheriff, I'm so glad you got here. This evening's been a nightmare for everyone, let me tell you, especially these kids. An absolute nightmare."

Herbert shook the boys' hands. "You all sit back down now and relax. I'm just here to help. To do what I can to sort things out. I'll need to talk to each of you."

Herbert walked to the couch and knelt down in front of Sheila and her mother. "Sheila, your grandpa tells me that Lloyd Wischmeier attacked you. Is that right?" His voice was gentle, full of concern.

"Yeah, he tried." Sheila's eyes were watery but she looked angry.

"OK, now can you tell me whether you're hurt?

Whether we should get you to a doctor?" Herbert turned his eyes to Alice as he finished the question.

"No, I'm OK. Lloyd tried to do stuff, but Henry and Jack stopped him."

"All right, good. There's a doctor coming in a few minutes anyway, Doctor Blustein, and he'll talk to you and your mom in private. Then I'll want to talk to you some more to find out exactly what Lloyd did, OK?"

"OK." Sheila suddenly became animated, her voice rising almost to a scream. "But Sheriff, he killed Fluffy! He killed my cat!"

"Who, Lloyd Wischmeier?" Herbert asked, caught by surprise.

"Yes. Out in the barn."

"I'm really sorry, Sheila. I'll have a look out there as soon as we're through in the cellar."

"And there's something else. I shot him."

Herbert was nonplused at the bluntness of her statement. "You mean you shot him or you shot *at* him?"

"Well, I shot at him when he tried to hit me. I think I hit him. Then I shot at him again at the bottom of the cellar steps. I don't think I hit him that time, though."

"Oh, Sheriff, she's not going to be in trouble, is she?" Alice asked in alarm. "She was just defending herself."

"We'll see, Alice. It sounds like Lloyd certainly did plenty to provoke her." Herbert stood and turned to the boys. "I hear that one of you fired the pistol earlier. Was it you, Jack?"

"Yeah, it was me."

"He only did it because Lloyd was hurting me," Sheila said.

"So I understand. Right now I just want to know where the pistol is."

"There on the table." Lyle pointed to a table at the side of the room.

The revolver was lying on a handsomely embroidered cloth that covered part of the table top. He went for a closer look. It was a vintage Colt .44, probably dating back to the turn of the century. He leaned over and sniffed the cylinder. A sharp smell of cordite told him it had been recently fired.

"OK," Herbert said, straightening up, "leave the revolver here for the time being. Nobody touch it. I'll need to have a close look at it later. Now, Lyle, has anyone been in the cellar since you found the body?"

Lyle shook his head. Their faces told Herbert everyone else agreed. "All right. Let's go on down and have a look."

Herbert steeled himself. He had no doubt Lyle had reason to be shocked by what he had seen, which meant there was something gruesome waiting below.

Lyle led the way down the narrow stairs, his lips set in a straight line. "You're gonna need your flashlight, Sheriff. There's no light back in the old cellar where he's layin'."

Herbert switched on his powerful three-cell flashlight and followed Lyle closely as he walked out of the light over the washtubs into the darkness. After several steps, he was surprised to see an oversized wooden door with a large lock and heavy iron hinges standing part way open.

"My God, Lyle, what's a door like that doing down here?"

"Daddy and me built it for Emma when we was first married. Seems that her kitten came in here and got its legs bit off by somethin'. We didn't want nothin' like that happenin' again so me and Daddy built that door to seal off this old part from the rest of the cellar. Mainly, though, we wanted to close off the hole in the wall the cat got into."

"The hole where you found the body?"

"Yep," Lyle answered quietly, "the same hole. Sheriff, that door's been locked ever since we built it, far as I know. Then those kids found the key in the same place they found Daddy's old Colt. Careful where you step, there's a hole in the doorway."

Herbert pointed his light at a hole at the threshold at the other side of the door. It looked freshly dug. "What did this?"

"Don't know. Never seen it 'til tonight."

Herbert followed Lyle through the door, stepping

over the hole. The smell struck him as soon as he
entered the old cellar. It was sharp, putrid. He stopped
where he stood, shining his light around the room,
instinctively looking for a source. It was a mere second
before he recognized the odor from the mausoleums at
Walnut Grove.

"Do you know what the hell is causing that
smell?"

"Nope, I sure don't, Sheriff. It comes outa that
hole. Always has. I remember it from when I was a kid
before Daddy and some men from town sealed it up. It
seems real strong now, stronger'n I remember."

Herbert would have liked to cover his nose with a
handkerchief but didn't have one. He stopped in the
center of the room. "Where did you find the body?"

Lyle pointed his flashlight to the opposite wall,
illuminating a hole about four feet above the dirt floor.
Beneath the hole was a pile of stones. An object was
draped across the top. A quick glance told Herbert what
it was. He aimed his flashlight and walked slowly
following its beam, his eyes focused on the pools of
blood, not looking at the object until his foot touched
the base of the rock pile.

"Careful, Sheriff. The floor's slip'ry from the
blood."

The object was, or had been, a person. Near the
tip of Herbert's shoe the skull was lying face up, eyes
vacant, the jaw opened wide as if still screaming. Now
there was another odor, like the smell of fresh meat in a
butcher shop. The scene sent a shock through his body
and he fought to remain calm, objective. His eyes
traveled slowly down the body. The bones of the skull,
neck, arms, and ribcage were bare, glistening white
covered with patches of blood and thin strands of pink.
The left arm was detached. The skull and chest cavity
had been emptied of all their vital contents—eyes, brain,
lungs, stomach. From the waist up, nothing remained
of what had been a person. He couldn't help thinking of
the scene at Tiny's Butcher Shop after Tiny had finished
boning a carcass for hamburger. The bones looked
fresh, moist, not dried-up like those in the mausoleums.
A lone beetle crawled over the skull's face and into an

eye socket. From the waist down, the body still wore clothes. The pants looked as if they still held legs. Herbert could see skin above the socks.

He moved the beam of his flashlight slowly up the wall. There was the hole—small, dark, ominous. A crimson stain ran down the wall from the opening. Herbert peered inside. Blood pooled in the depressions in the rock. The stench was stronger.

Herbert backed slowly away from the wall toward the center of the room shaking his head.

Lyle had stayed back by the doorway. "Some awful mess, huh, Sheriff?"

"My God, Lyle, it's horrible. Just horrible. I've never seen such a thing done to a human being." He stood staring for a moment, then added: "Let's hope the kid was dead before whatever it was started eating."

Herbert sat with Reuben Blustein on he front steps of the Gerdes farmhouse watching Bruhl's ambulance drive away with the mutilated body. It had taken them most of the night to finish their work. The star-speckled sky was beginning to show a hint of gray in the east, reminding Herbert there would still be a dawn, no matter what terrible events had transpired that night.

"What now, Herb?" Blustein thrust his hands deep into the pockets of the blood-stained smock he still wore.

"I don't know at the moment, I just don't know. The fact is I don't have a clue as to what the hell's back in that tunnel." Herbert gave the bottom stair a kick.

"If you lost about 180 pounds and narrowed your shoulders by half, you could crawl right in there and find out."

"Sure, like crawling into a cave with a sleeping bear, only it doesn't look like this thing is sleeping."

"When do you plan to talk to Berghoff?" Blustein's voice sounded weary.

"As soon as he calls, which you can bet it will be this morning. Ol' Harry'll get wind of this before the dew's dry. He'll probably even have his headline written before he picks up the phone."

"What do you think it'll say?"

"I'm afraid to guess, to tell the truth. But whatever it says, you can be sure the story'll keep people out of their cellars."

The Gerdes house was dark except for a light on the second floor. The family had decided to leave. Herbert looked at the rocking chairs sitting on the porch, wondering whether to move to a place more comfortable than the step he was sitting on. Reuben sat with his chin resting on his fists. They both stared straight ahead for several minutes.

Blustein was the first to speak: "First, we have some ghoul loose in Walnut Grove. Now we have a cannibal attack just north of there. Tell me this is all a bad dream."

"It *is* a bad dream. Trouble is, when I go to sleep and wake up, I'll have to dream it over again." Herbert's face suddenly took on an intense look. "The girl, Sheila, is she all right?"

"Yeah. I examined her. Talked to her and her mother, Alice. Physically she's OK. She says Lloyd only touched her breasts and crotch with his hand before the boys broke in. As far as I can tell, that's true. She was lucky. Apparently he had his pants down ready to do her."

"Well, we won't have Lloyd Wischmeier out there assaulting people any more, looks like."

"He sure as hell won't be. I've never seen a body in worse condition. I mean one that's been dead such a short time. Not a piece of meat left on him above the waist. The skull and chest cavity completely cleaned out. Every major organ gone. If he hadn't got stuck halfway into that hole, there might not have been *anything* left."

Blustein rubbed his hands along his smock and coughed. "Frankly, I don't think we have both a ghoul *and* a cannibal. The marks on the kid's body looked a lot like the marks on those bodies in Walnut Grove. My guess is we have something here that just put some variety in its diet." His body stiffened as he spoke.

"If that's the case, it looks like there's something with a peculiar appetite in these old bluffs."

252

They both sat quietly for a minute, listening to the creak of a chair on the porch rocked by the breeze.

"So you think the same thing that chewed up those bodies at Walnut Grove did this?" Herbert finally asked.

"Yeah, it looks like it. The same thing or things. I can be more definite after I examine the body back at Bruhl's."

"That doesn't surprise me. I talked to those kids some. Two of them, Sheila and Henry, said they crawled into that hole in the cellar years ago. They said it goes back a long ways, then branches in two directions. I'm afraid there could be a network of tunnels through these bluffs the thing is using. If that's the case, who knows where all it could go . . . where it could hide. And there's something else. From what Lyle tells me, it sounds like the thing might have come around before, years ago."

"How so?"

"Just that his dad and some others tried to seal up that opening back then. They might have been trying to keep out more than the smell."

"So the thing might've come back?"

"Either that or it's been here all the time and just got hungry."

"I guess you've got your work cut out for you, then. I'm glad I just do bodies."

Leaning back on the steps, Herbert focused again on Blustein. "What I have to do is to make sure you don't have more of them. Anyway, I guess this couldn't happen to a better guy. Did you see what the Wischmeier kid did to that cat out in the barn?"

"No, I don't do cats. Somehow people killing animals bothers me more than people killing people."

"Now I know why you're a doctor and not a vet. The cat we can handle, but I think we ought to downplay the condition of the kid's body for his parents' sake, don't you?"

"Yeah, giving the parents all the gory details about their kid won't serve any purpose. Besides, Berghoff might get ahold of them and put them in print to sell more of his papers."

253

"What about the cause of death? Any sign at all of a bullet wound on the body?"

"Not that I saw. There's a possibility the bullet hit soft tissue in his upper body, but there's no way to tell for sure one way or the other."

"That gets us to the hard part. What am I going to say *did* kill him? When this story hits, I'm going to have a lot of scared people to deal with." Herbert stood and began to pace in front of the steps. "Christ, half the town might pack up and leave. And I wouldn't blame them. They aren't used to thinking of themselves as food. I'm going to need some answers."

"I'll do a full autopsy on what's left of the body this afternoon. But honestly, Herb, I don't think it'll tell me more than I found out from those bodies at the cemetery."

Herbert stopped pacing and looked down at Blustein. "And have you found anything useful yet?"

"Nothing for sure. I'm still trying to track down what made those bites, but I also have a hunch that embalming might play some role here. We're about the only place in the world that does it routinely, you know. Makes a corpse look better. Vanity in this country knows no bounds."

"I guess not. What about your plan to send bone samples or close-up shots of the corpses to the university to see if someone there can ID those bites?"

"I got the close-ups back yesterday. I had a little problem stealing body parts without the family's permission. I don't want to be known as Doctor Frankenstein."

"Oh yeah, that *other* doctor." Herbert turned and looked out toward the river bluffs. "Frankly, it bothers the hell out of me to keep that business at the cemetery under wraps, but there's not much choice unless we want a panic on our hands. Especially now with the Wischmeier kid getting torn apart. I'll have to go public with it soon, though. Did you see that hole near the old cellar door?"

"I saw it. You know what I think?"

"Let me guess. You think that whatever's been in that hole in the wall was trying to get out."

"Bingo, but it really doesn't need to get out, does it? It might have a regular highway system down in the bluffs, which could lead beyond the cemetery. Something I'll keep it in mind every time I go down to *our* cellar."

"That's exactly the kind of talk I don't want to get started." Herbert picked up a rock and threw at the school bell hanging in the yard, missing.

"I understand, Herb, believe me. Just tell me what you say to Berghoff after you talk to him and I'll stick with your story. After all, I've always got my medical license to fall back on, if I can just keep it." In the distance birds had begun their morning chirping.

"Well, Reuben, I'll leave you with just one more question to puzzle on. If the thing in the cellar is the same thing that chewed up the bodies at Walnut Grove, what gave it an appetite for live food?"

Chapter Twenty-Three

The Stakeout

July 15, 1956

Lying in bed with his eyes closed, Herbert couldn't get the scene at Lloyd Wischmeier's autopsy earlier that day out of his mind—three men, Reuben Blustein, Hilder Bruhl and Herbert, hovering in the shadows around the brightly lit examination table, an aroma of formaldehyde and raw flesh permeating the room. With half the boy's body reduced to a skeleton, the formal part of the coroner's procedure had gone quickly, but Blustein took his time examining marks on the bones and remaining tissue. In the end he was convinced that the bite marks were identical to the marks found on the corpses in Walnut Grove Cemetery.

As images of the half-eaten body laid out on the steel table coated with a pale red liquid ran through his head, a long, lizard-like creature slithered out of the drain in his cellar. Freed from the confines of the narrow pipe, its body began to shorten and swell. Dripping with grease and excrement from the sewer, its forked tongue darting constantly from its mouth, the black creature made its way up the stairs into the kitchen. It slithered across the floor leaving a foul trail of glutinous fluid. At the bottom of the stairs to the second floor it hesitated as if to get its bearings, then began to wriggle upwards. When it reached the bedroom, it pushed the door open noiselessly with its head. Its tongue relentlessly darting ahead to feel its way, the creature entered the room. At the side of their bed, the creature rose to a surprising height, its head swaying over Herbert's waist. Slowly its mouth opened wide, revealing rows of brown teeth ending in dagger-like points. Then the creature struck, clamping its mouth around the area between Herbert's legs.

His scream woke him. After thrashing once, Herbert bolted upright. A cold sweat covered his skin. His hands were clasped protectively around his crotch.

"Jesus!" he cried out loud as he felt himself to make sure he was intact.

"Herb, you OK?" Norma called from downstairs.

"I just had a dream." It was almost 8:30, the time his alarm on the nightstand was set to go off. The sun was beginning to set, leaving a dim evening light. He dressed quickly in his tan uniform and picked up his short boots. Leaving the bedroom he walked toward a closed door at the end of the hall.

Herbert turned the knob and gently opened the door to his son's darkened bedroom. The Mickey Mouse nightlight produced just enough light for him to navigate across the room without running into the rocking chair he enjoyed sitting in with his son. He walked to the crib, stepping gently to keep the old wood floor from making a squeak that might wake Albie. Putting his large, calloused hands on the side rail, he bent over, listening in the silence of the room for his son's breathing. Relieved and grateful when he heard slow, steady breaths coming from the child's open mouth, he leaned close to Albie's face. Suddenly he pictured himself as the lizard from his nightmare. As if to provide an antidote to the gruesome thought, he gently kissed him on the forehead. The child stirred at the touch, giving a soft moan. Startled, Herbert raised up quickly. Albie continued to sleep peacefully. After retracing his steps carefully back to the door, Herbert paused. Hearing no sound, he closed the door and went downstairs.

As Herbert entered the living room, Norma raised her eyes from the book she was reading. "Is Albie sleeping?" she asked.

"Sawing logs like a trooper."

Norma closed her book. "Herb, I heard you yell from down here like you were having a nightmare. Are you feeling OK?"

Herbert sat down on the footstool at the end of her chair and began putting on his boots. His throat was tight. "To tell the truth, I haven't had a nightmare as bad as that since Chicago. Something with serious teeth crawled into my bedroom in the dream and took a big bite at, um, the family jewels. God, Norma, it was so real after I woke up I checked to be sure they were OK."

Norma leaned forward and felt between his legs. "You seem to be all there. It was probably a man-hating female."

"Very funny. It's pretty scary to think of losing valuable parts like that, you know." Herbert leaned forward and cupped her breasts gently in his hands. "I mean, what if you were to lose these?"

"We'd both be devastated, of course. Maybe I better check your parts again?"

"You do and I'll end up being late." Herbert kissed her. "I told Gus I'd meet him at 9:30 and I have a stop to make on the way. Did anyone call?"

"The mayor. She said to call her back tonight, even if it's late. And Harry Berghoff. He said he'd call back."

"No doubt he will. The mayor will have to wait until morning."

"I have to tell you I hate it when you work two nights in a row. Why are you doing a stakeout tonight anyway? You were out at the Gerdes farm all night last night."

"I have to move on catching whatever's out there in those tunnels. It was one thing when it was feeding on corpses in Walnut Grove. It's something else when it chews up a live citizen, even if it was Lloyd Wischmeier."

"But you don't know what you're looking for. How can you do a stakeout?"

258

"Unfortunately, you're right, which is all the more reason for the stakeout. The mayor and the newspaper are looking for some answers and I don't have any."

Norma took his big hands into hers. "I've got a creepy feeling about you doing this tonight. Can you at least tell me where you'll be?"

"Walnut Grove Cemetery. We've got to get that thing to come out in the open somehow."

"Does it have to be at night?"

"I'm afraid so. Seems like it doesn't like daylight much."

"If you're determined to go, I'll wrap the sandwich I made for your dinner."

When Norma returned from the kitchen, she also brought a thermos.

"There's some hot coffee left from this morning you can take, too. I've been thinking. Wouldn't it be better if you did this in the Gerdes cellar? After all, that's where the thing was last night."

"I figure there's a connecting tunnel so one place should be as good as the other. If we don't get it to come out at the cemetery, we'll try at the Gerdes place." Herbert took the bag and thermos, then rose and started for the front hall.

"What makes you think it'll come out?"

"Bait. We're going to use bait."

"Oh great. I suppose that's you."

"Maybe, but that's not the bait I had in mind."

Herbert reached onto the high shelf in the front hall closet and retrieved his pistol belt. He fastened the chrome buckle and patted the holster for his revolver, an old habit.

Norma faced him, looking up with a pout. "If I'm asleep when you get home, wake me up." She put her arms around him and pressed the length of her body against his. He could feel her full breasts through his shirt. She rubbed hard against him. "Come back safe, ya hear?"

He held her tightly and kissed her, his hands rubbing her butt while his finger traced the deep crease. After a long moment, he dropped his arms and cleared his throat. "I'm too old for this."

"Yes, you are, Herbert Siefken, but come home anyway."

Two deputies were on duty in the office when Herbert arrived. Lester Hammond sat at the radio, his hand around the microphone as if he was about to break into song. Gustav Mecklenberg slouched in a chair thumbing through a well-worn copy of *Sports Afield*.

"Evening, guys. Anything happening?" Herbert gave Hammond's shoulder a pat as he walked by.

"More 'n I'd like," Hammond answered. "A couple calls from the usual bars, and there's a ruckus at the Powell's again. The neighbors called. Second time this month. Sounds like they're both drunk as usual. You'd think they'd lay off the stuff at least for a while considerin' what their boy went through last night."

"That boy Jack's got a tough row to hoe at home. His parents probably scare him more than that thing out at Gerdes's did. Did you send a car?"

"Yeah, Howard's there now. He left the car a minute ago headed for the house. Tell me, Sheriff, you really goin' to do a stakeout at Walnut Grove t'night?"

"Yes, at the Schneider mausoleum. That's where this all started, so we'll start there as well. Gus, come on in my office. We need to talk before we go."

Gustav Mecklenberg had been a deputy sheriff since serving with the Marines during World War II. He was a large man, well over six feet, and growing larger each year. When he sat, his once taut stomach now rested on his knees. Topping him off was his bald, shiny pate, something he seemed to take pride in. Mecklenberg had enlisted in the Marines after the Japanese bombed Pearl Harbor, and lost a leg to a grenade on Guadalcanal. The Marines gave him a rack of medals and an artificial limb, then discharged him. Jack Schoof took him on as a deputy shortly after he returned to Bruders Landing. Mecklenberg wouldn't tolerate anyone setting limits on his duties because of his leg, and no one dared suggest any.

Mecklenberg followed Herbert into his office and closed the door. "Sheriff, now I know you don't like t'use 'em, but I'd feel a whole lot better if we was packin' somethin' extra tonight."

Herbert felt a catch in his throat. Even the thought of a shotgun could make him break out in a sweat. Three Winchester 12 gauge shotguns had come with the office, but Herbert hadn't let any them out of their rack except for an annual cleaning. There hadn't been any reason to, and no deputy had asked to carry one, until now. He wanted to refuse, but he couldn't think of a good enough reason.

"I suspect you're right." Herbert went to the tall vault door in the rear of his office. The dial on the vault's door gave off small, solid metallic clicks as he turned it. Squinting, he found the last number in the combination, then pushed down on the lever protruding from one side of the door. There was the sound of tumblers sliding and the thick door opened. He pulled out two shotguns, handing one to Mecklenberg. Reaching in again he brought out two boxes of ammunition.

"I'm not big on these, as you know, but I'm also not sure what we might run into. Lets load 'em up." Herbert pulled the pump back and began loading shells into the breach. When he had loaded five shells, he took another handful from the box and stuffed them into his shirt pocket. Mecklenberg did the same.

Simply holding the shotgun made his hands sweat. Could he trust himself? Had he come far enough from that night in the liquor store? Tonight there was no choice. He couldn't let Gus go into that place short on firepower.

Mecklenberg sighted down the barrel. "What makes you think the thing'll show up tonight?"

"I'm not sure it will, so we may be doing it more than once. Think of it as a long Halloween party." Herbert forced a small laugh. "I thought we'd try taking a little something it might like. Then if nothing happens, we'll move on. Maybe to another mausoleum, or maybe out to Gerdes's. Make sure you bring your flashlight."

A full moon was rising as they started for the cemetery. Herbert drove the patrol car in silence, anxious about what the night might have in store. Mecklenberg contented himself by staring out the window, keeping a firm grip on the thermos of coffee. As they turned into the drive leading to Walnut Grove, their headlights illuminated the massive stone pillars on each side of the entrance. The ornate iron gates stood open. Herbert felt a chill as they entered the old cemetery.

Tombstones reached into the distance on each side of the road. To his left in a grove of walnut trees, rows of narrow stones marked the cemetery's oldest graves. On a long field to the right, larger gravestones rose like apparitions, casting long shadows in the moonlight across the well-kept lawn. The cruiser's tires crunched into the black cinder road which seemed to absorb the beams from the car's headlights. When they came to the top of a hill overlooking a deep ravine formed by a stream flowing at its floor, Herbert slowed the car. "We'll go the rest of the way without lights."

"Good idea. We don't want to scare it off as long as we're out here.'

Herbert switched off the headlights. In the moonlight the cinder road looked like a broad, black ribbon winding in front of them. He drove cautiously for several minutes then stopped. "We have to walk from here."

Mecklenberg took their shotguns from the car, closing the doors softly.

"Hang on to my gun, Gus. I've got to get something from the trunk." Fumbling through his keys, he found the one he wanted and opened the trunk. A smell of fresh meat drifted out.

"What you got in there?" Mecklenberg shined his flashlight over Herbert's shoulder. The beam fell on sheets of heavy brown paper soaked in a red fluid which outlined a long, bulky object. "Jesus, Herb, did you bring a body?"

"Sort of." Herbert lifted the paper revealing part of a large, skinned animal oozing juices like diluted blood witha stump of a leg protruding from one end.

"What *is* that?"

"Bait," Herbert answered matter-of-factly. "Something to draw that thing out of its hole. It's a cow, part of one anyway, a front quarter, just butchered. Got it from Tiny's on the way to the office tonight. If the thing isn't too picky about its meat, this just might tempt it to come out."

"I'm glad to hear you didn't get it from Bruhl's. Are you sure it's not too fresh? Maybe we shoulda dug somethin' up."

"It's not as fresh as Lloyd Wischmeier was. Give me a hand getting it up on my shoulder, will you?"

Herbert lifted one end of the carcass by the stump and pulled it from the trunk. Mecklenberg boosted it onto Herbert's shoulder. He gave a short grunt when the full weight came to rest. "Christ, it *does* feel like a body. All right, here we go."

Herbert started toward the mausoleum, his flashlight pointed at the ground in front, his eyes darting warily in all directions. Mecklenberg was right behind. The sound of their feet on the crushed cinders seemed amplified by the darkness. The carcass pressed heavily on Herbert's shoulders. From the corner of his eye he watched the gravestones as they passed, standing silently like shadowy specters. He felt as if they were intruding in a peaceful community which had closed for the night, its inhabitants watching silently, waiting to come out as soon as the intruders passed. He found himself glancing at the larger gravestones, wondering what might lie behind. An image of skeletons dancing in the moonlight came to his mind. He was getting the creeps, just as he had as a young boy walking in their neighborhood cemetery. He told himself to act his age.

When they reached the bottom of the hill, Herbert could see the faint outline of the mausoleum on the side of the ravine opposite them. Suddenly he remembered Mecklenberg might be struggling to keep up. He slowed his pace as they crossed a wooden bridge over the stream and started to climb the hill. The carcass grew heavier on his shoulders with each step. The path to the mausoleum led through a field of tombstones. He gave each one a wide berth, remembering the old admonition about stepping on a grave. When at last they reached the mausoleum, Herbert stopped to rest by its iron door. Mecklenberg, breathing heavily, leaned the shotguns against the wall. Herbert let the carcass slide from his shoulder. allowing it to land heavily on the ground in front of him. With a deep breath, he placed his hands on the iron door and pushed. It moved.

"Looks like Lippert remembered to leave it unlocked," he said. "Let's have a look inside before we take this in. Bring the shotguns. It might be crazy to even think of firing one of these in here, so think twice before you use it."

Herbert led the way through the doorway into the old structure, shining his flashlight around the stone wall which glistened with moisture. He smelled the air carefully. It was damp, musty, stale, a slight odor of decay, nothing more.

"Damn!" Mecklenberg suddenly hissed in a loud whisper.

"What's wrong?"

"Nothin', Herb, sorry. A drop of water fell on my face."

"OK. Relax," Herbert answered sympathetically, starting to walk again. "I don't think we have to whisper. In fact it might help to make some noise, let the thing know we're here. Remember there were gunshots in the Gerdes house before it got Lloyd Wischmeier." Their voices produced a hollow echo that made Herbert feel confined. "Careful, there are stairs right ahead, see them?"

"Yeah, I see 'em."

"Let's go down to the burial chamber and have a look."

Herbert pointed his light into the vault area below and started down the stairs. Unlike his first visit, the stone floor was bare except for a marble bench in the middle of the room. Somehow the burial chamber looked much larger than he remembered—and more ominous. All the burial spaces in the walls had been sealed except one.

"It sure looks a lot different in here now than it did when I first saw it. There, they left that tomb open. They found a hole in the back where something might have burrowed in. It looks too small for something that did all the damage it did, but all the other burial spaces were tight as drums." Herbert walked to the opening and shined his light inside. It was a long, narrow cavity drilled out of rock. In the rear, toward the bottom, he could see the small hole. "No sign of anything now. Gus, come over here and tell me if you smell anything?"

"Like what?"

"Anything strange . . . different."

Mecklenberg smelled the air carefully. "It smells like a cellar that's been wet for a long time. I don't smell nothin' else."

"Me either. I think that means the thing's not around. It's got a special odor. You'll know it."

"So you've said."

"I'm going back to get that meat. Then we'll wait, me on that bench and you at the bottom of the stairs."

When he had placed the carcass on the floor of the vault in front of the open burial space, Herbert stretched his back to get out a kink. "Better get ready for a long night. I don't think it'll bother the thing if we talk, in fact it might help get its attention, but we'd better not use the flashlights much after this. Keep yours handy, though. We'll need to see the thing if we hear it. I'll take the first watch and you get some sleep."

Herbert sat down on the stone bench and turned off his flashlight, laying it next to the shotgun which touched his leg. He shifted a little so he wouldn't have to feel the weapon. Gradually the coldness of the stone crept through the seat of his pants. It was a good feeling in the airless room. He could hear Gus shuffling as he settled in on the stairs. Seconds later his flashlight went out as well. The darkness was sudden and absolute. The chamber seemed smaller, as if it had closed in on them. Herbert waited, wondering whether he might be able to see as his eyes adjusted. After several minutes, he peered at his feet, then in the direction of the open hole, attempting in vain to see through the darkness.

Moving his hand on the bench, he brushed the flashlight and picked it up. His mind drifted back to the autopsy. Got to stay alert, he thought. Inhaling slowly through his nose, he analyzed the air as if he was tasting it. There was no change.

After a half hour, a pain had developed in his butt that was growing worse. He decided to try lying down. Finding the shotgun with his free hand, he laid it on the bench and stretched out on his side facing the hole, his head resting on his hand. For twenty minutes Herbert was comfortable. Then the aches began. First his shoulder, then his hip. Time to change positions. He was tempted to merely roll to his other side, but he wanted to remain facing the hole. Slowly he pushed himself upright and returned to a sitting position. When he stopped moving, the room again became deathly still. A minute later he heard Mecklenberg moving.

"You awake, Gus?"

"Yeah, just bored."

"You should try getting some shut-eye. See if you can find a way to get comfortable."

"I tried but this stone's too hard. Damn it, anyway. We shoulda brought us some sleepin' bags to lie on."

"You're right. There's a blanket in the back seat of the car. Do you want to get it?"

"Naw, I'll be all right."

There were sounds of more shuffling in the dark, then it was still. Herbert raised one foot onto the bench and smelled the air again. Nothing. Maybe the mausoleum was a bad choice, he told himself. The thing could be back in the Gerdes cellar looking for more live food. It's been over two months since the thing was here. Why would it come back? For the bait, of course. What's left of that cow . . . or *us*. As questions swirled in his head, his chin fell onto his chest. He snapped his head up with a jerk.

"Hell!" he said out loud, instantly thinking he must have woken Mecklenberg. He heard soft snoring then a snort. Had it been an hour yet? He couldn't see the numbers on his watch. When he bought it two years before, the numbers glowed in the dark. Now there was nothing. He didn't want to turn on his flashlight to look. It must have been over an hour. Time for a change.

"Gus!" he called. "Wake up. Let's switch."

"OK," came the mumbled response.

"Bring your stuff and come on down here. But don't turn on your flashlight."

"All right. Give me a minute. I can't see a damn thing."

"Take your time." Herbert heard him come down the stairs. There was an extra tap at each step as Mecklenberg used his shotgun to feel his way, He shuffled across the floor until he bumped into the bench.

"OK. Find a way to make yourself comfortable here, but keep facing the wall with your flashlight and shotgun handy. Wake me in about an hour. Can you read your watch in the dark?"

"Yeah. It's quarter of one."

"Good. Wake me about two. But if you have trouble stayin' awake, go ahead and wake me up."

"I'll be fine, Herb. I've had a hell of a lot more sleep in the last twenty-four hours than you have."

"That doesn't mean you won't get sleepy. After all, it's way past your bedtime."

"Yeah, tell me about it."

Herbert felt his way toward the stairs. Touching the bottom step with the toe of his boot, he began to climb, planning to lay on the floor at the top. Suddenly he stopped. Had he caught a whiff of the odor? He smelled the air again. Nothing there.

"Gus! Do you smell anything down there?"

"Nope. Nothin' new anyway."

"Well, stay alert. I thought I might have."

"Don't worry, I will."

Herbert laid down on the stone floor and closed his eyes. The sound of Mecklenberg moving woke him with a start. He sat up quickly, realizing he had fallen asleep.

"Gus! What's going on?"

"I thought I heard somethin'."

Herbert recognized the smell immediately. It was faint but there was no mistaking it. He snapped on his flashlight and played the light over the room. Gus was sitting on the edge of the bench, his shotgun at the ready, but nothing looked amiss.

Herbert made his way down the steps into the

burial chamber. "What did you hear?"

"Just a tiny sound, soft like."

"Smell that?" The odor was much stronger in the burial chamber.

"Sure do. Hard to miss it. Whew!"

"When did you first notice it?"

"Just before I heard the sound."

Herbert went over to the beef carcass and knelt down, shining his light across its surface. "Come here and look at this."

Mecklenberg knelt beside him. "Jesus, are those bites?"

"They sure are. And they weren't here when I put it down. The thing was here, Gus. It must have run back in there when you moved, or when I turned on my flashlight."

"Maybe it'll come back if you turn it off."

"We'll see. This time we both stay on the bench. You be ready with your shotgun, I'll do the light. If we hear something, I'll yell before I turn it on. If you see anything, shoot it. Understood?"

"Understood."

"Good. Here goes."

Herbert switched off the light. A second later Mecklenberg pumped his shotgun, loading a shell in the chamber.

They sat perfectly still, neither of them moving, barely breathing. Herbert listened, tense with the anticipation. The thing had actually been there, right in front of him. What was it? It came and went with barely a sound. So fast. Was he right in telling Gus to shoot? Or should they wait and try to catch it? How could they do that? The damn thing was dangerous. He was tired of asking himself all these questions, but at least they helped his anxiety. Or did they fuel it? He turned his attention back to listening.

The putrid odor was getting stronger, he was sure of it. His muscles were so tense he felt paralyzed. He focused on relaxing them one by one. First his right arm. There was a pain in his hand from gripping the flashlight so tightly.

Suddenly he heard a sound—soft, fleshy. He

hesitated, wanting to be sure. The odor was nauseating. Something was there, right in front of him.

"Now, Gus!" he yelled, switching on his flashlight, aiming it first at the carcass, then shifting quickly to the burial hole in the wall.

Both of them stared perplexed. There was nothing there.

"Dammit!" Herbert yelled. "Where the hell is that thing? How can it just disappear like that? Did you hear it?"

"I sure did. Smelled it, too. Started makin' me sick."

"How the hell does it move so fast?" Herbert walked to the carcass and knelt down. "Strange. There're no more bites out of it, but it must have been here." He walked back to the bench and sat down with a sigh. For a moment he sat quietly, thinking.

"Let's try something else. Draw a bead right on the carcass and hold it after I shut off the flashlight. If the thing comes back, I want you to fire a round before I turn it on. Do it when I yell."

"All right, it might work."

"Good. Got your bead?"

"Yeah, I got it."

"OK, here goes." Herbert moved to sit cross-legged on the bench, then switched off the light.

It was only a minute until a wave of putrid odor swept through the chamber. Again he hesitated, his head filled with second thoughts about asking Gus to fire at something they couldn't see. A dreadful image had formed in his mind, one that hadn't haunted him for months. He was in the liquor store again, aiming his shotgun. He couldn't bring himself to yell at Gus. If only he had waited in that store, he told himself. Maybe he should just turn on his flashlight again.

"God damn it!" Gus shouted. "Somethin's touchin' me. There're things on m'legs. Ow! Dammit! They're bitin' me!"

Without warning there was a bright flash and deafening roar. The shock of the ear-splitting noise made Herbert's body jerk and his hand hit the flashlight, knocking it to the floor. Tiny pellets

269

ricocheted around the stone walls with a sound like sleet on a slate roof. Hurriedly, Herbert fell to his knees and groped across the cold stone floor for the light.

"Jesus Christ! They come right back!" Mecklenberg screamed. Herbert heard him pump another shell into the chamber. A flash and roar came again.

As soon as the long echo diminished, Herbert heard Mecklenberg yelling: "The light, Herb. Quick. They're bitin' me all over!"

As his hand at last fell on the flashlight, he felt a touch under his pants leg, then another against his neck, soft like loose skin. Suddenly a sharp pain like a needle prick pierced his leg. He kicked at the place and swatted his neck with his left hand. A split second later he had the flashlight on. His ears ringing, Herbert peered through the cloud of blue smoke ready to tear the thing off his clothes, but nothing was there except for three small holes in his pants.

"You OK, Gus?"

Mecklenberg stood with the smoking shotgun in his hand, looking down at his feet and rubbing his neck. "I don't know, my leg sure burns."

Herbert shined the light on Mecklenberg's legs. One of his pants legs below the knee was perforated like swiss cheese and covered with crimson spots that were growing.

"Christ, Gus, did you shoot yourself?"

"Hell, no, I didn't shoot myself. Those things did it. I shot out in front of my feet, tryin' to scare 'em off me. Did they come after you, too?"

Herbert rubbed the sore spot on his leg. "Yeah, they started to. Let's have a look."

Herbert knelt in front of Mecklenberg and pushed up his shredded pants leg. From the top of his boot to his knee, he was bleeding from several small gouges in his skin.

"Dammit!" Mecklenberg shouted, studying the wounds on his leg. "It's a good thing my other leg isn't real or they woulda got that one, too."

"Did they get your neck? Let me have a look." Bringing his flashlight close, Herbert saw three bites on

270

one side. Blood oozed slightly from two of them. "You got a couple bites there but nothing too bad."

"That's good. I guess we got 'em stopped in the nick of time. One thing's for sure, Sheriff. There's more than one of those things."

"There sure are. A lot more." Herbert stood up and pointed his light at the carcass. "I'll take a look and see if you hit anything."

Rising quickly, Herbert walked to the carcass. Part way he found the result of Mecklenberg's second shot—a rough, white scar several inches wide in the dark stone floor. His first shot was just as easy to spot. It had torn through the top of the carcass, blowing apart several rib bones and plastering chunks of meat against the wall. Otherwise, the carcass seemed untouched.

"You put that first round in the right place, Gus. The trouble is, I don't see any dead critters."

Gustav limped over to his side.

"The fact is, it doesn't look like they were as interested in this cow as they were in us."

Gustav stooped over, looking closely at the carcass. "My God, I'll bet you're right."

Herbert trained his beam on the burial hole. "It's time we got out of here. This flashlight's probably the only thing keeping us alive."

Chapter Twenty-Four

The Funeral

July 17, 1956

T he day of Lloyd's funeral started hot. Henry ate breakfast listlessly. As he lingered at the table staring at the back of the cereal box, his mother asked him to run to Minnie's Market for eggs and milk, with a bottle of pop as a reward. He didn't have the energy to put up his usual resistance. Besides, a root beer sounded good.

After paying Minnie for the groceries, Henry bent over the pop cooler and reached into icy water for one of the squatty bottles of Dad's Old-Fashioned Root Beer. He was sorting through the bottles when he heard a voice behind him.

"Hey, Henry. How they hangin'?"

Henry looked up to see Larry Frey and Carl Siefert walking through the store's front screen door. They let it close with a bang. Frey's hair was slicked back with Brylcreem into a ducktail. He wore a dirty yellow T-shirt with the sleeves rolled up onto his skinny shoulders, one roll containing a pack of Camels. Frey was about the same height as Henry, Siefert was shorter and much heavier. Siefert also wore a T-shirt which was too short, displaying a hairy belly-button above his blue jeans. Their mouths were stretched into forced smiles. Shit-eating grins if I ever saw any, Henry thought. Thumbs hooked in the belt loops of his Wranglers, Frey swaggered toward him, scraping the wood floor at each step with the metal cleats on his engineer boots.

"We didn't think we'd find you, Henry. Thought you'd be gettin' ready for the funeral. Ain't you goin?" Frey was trying to speak normally, but his voice reeked with hostility.

"Yeah, I just had to run an errand."

"Looks like you're done. C'mon outside, we wanta ask you somethin'."

"If you want to ask me something, ask me here. I'm getting a bottle of pop." Henry was determined to stay put. He glanced quickly around the store. Minnie had been standing behind the counter a moment earlier. Now she was nowhere in sight.

Siefert stepped toward him. "Wherever you want it, then. C'mere, chickenshit." He reached forward and grabbed Henry's arm.

Henry jerked free. "What are you mad at me for?"

The blow on the side of his head from Siefert's fist came suddenly. Henry's head jerked sideways, but he felt no pain. As he straightened up with his ear ringing, Frey pushed him against the counter. His back struck the narrow edge and he fell to his knees. Something hard hit his shoulder.

"Ow, dammit you guys!" Without thinking he lunged at Seifert's legs with a tackle, bringing him to the floor. Immediately Henry pounced on his chest, pinning his arms under his knees. Frey wrapped his arm around Henry's head from behind, trying to pull him off. Henry reached back and grabbed Frey's legs, pulling them out from under him. He fell on his back and started to gasp for breath. Henry leaned over and put his face close to Seifert's, keeping him firmly pinned. "I asked what're you mad at me for? Now will you answer me?"

"What's going on here?" Minnie called out as she rushed from the back room.

All three boys scrambled to their feet. Siefert and

Frey raced for the door. As he was about to run out, Siefert turned and shouted: "There's gonna be more where that came from, you bastard. Tell it to that little cunt Sheila, too. For what happened to Lloyd. And tell that red-haired homo we're gonna bust his nuts again."

Henry rushed after them but stopped outside the door and watched them run down the street. He had to get on home; the funeral would start in an hour. Seifert and Frey would surely be there and might be laying for him. Surprisingly, he found he could care less. With Lloyd gone, they weren't so scary anymore.

Henry skidded his Western Flyer to a stop at the side of Bruhl's Mortuary, leaving a thin black trail of rubber on the sidewalk. Jack slid his bike to a stop behind him. Ordinarily they would be quick to compare skid marks, checking to see whose was the longest, but today was different. A winning skid mark seemed unimportant. Henry got off his bike slightly disoriented and had to work to get his thoughts together.

"Over there, Jack, let's put our bikes behind those bushes. Nobody'll see them in back."

"Boy, I hope not. I can't afford to lose my bike."

"Aw, they'll be safe there. I heard the funeral won't last more than an hour anyway."

Jack squeezed his bike between the branches and the brick wall of the old mansion. Henry pushed his in behind. As they emerged from the bushes, Henry brushed off his shirt and tried to smooth the wrinkles from his pants with his hand. He was hot again. The moist air pressed against his face like a warm washcloth. Beads of sweat ran down his chest and legs, causing his clothes to stick to his skin.

"Wait a second, Jack, you've got stuff on the back of your shirt." Henry brushed off several small pieces of evergreen. "Now tell me if I have any."

"Jeez, I hate wearin' good clothes." Jack took two half-hearted swipes at Henry's back.

"Thanks. We'd better go in or we'll be late."

Jack didn't move and his lower lip had begun to tremble. "Henry. I've never been to a funeral before. I'm kinda scared . . . and I feel terrible anyway."

As Jack's eyes started to water, Henry's nerve started to falter. He *had* been to a funeral before. It was his uncle's, three years earlier. He didn't like the experience one bit—in fact it had given him nightmares for weeks. And he thought today would be worse. This funeral was for someone he had grown-up with, someone he had known all his life, someone he had heard die! But he had to be there. He and Sheila and Jack had made a pact the day after Lloyd died. They would come to the funeral. They would see Lloyd buried. Then it would be over.

Henry's parents didn't think he should come. They said it wouldn't look right, considering what Lloyd did before he died. Sheila's mother and Jack's parents felt the same way. But the three of them persisted. After all, it still was unclear to everyone just what happened. In the end Henry and Jack were allowed to come together, but Sheila came with her mother.

"That's OK, Jack, nobody likes funerals. I was at my uncle's a couple years ago. They make everyone feel bad. People cry. I felt like crying myself there for a minute."

"It's not just the funeral." Jack spoke quickly, choking back a sob. "I've felt awful since he was . . . since it happened. I don't sleep good either, and when I do, I have these dreams, bad dreams."

Henry hesitated for a moment, then decided to be honest. "Me too. I've had some nightmares of my own."

"You have?" Jack asked, surprised. "I was afraid I was the only one." He let out a breath.

"Well, you're not. My mom says Sheila's woken up screaming a couple times. We've got a right to have nightmares. Mom says it's natural when something like that happens."

"I didn't feel bad at the time, but now, I don't know. I can hardly believe that Lloyd's dead. Really dead. We heard it. We heard him gettin' killed. Sometimes I think I can still hear him screamin' when I close my eyes." Jack was trembling. "Do you ever hear him?"

"Yeah, I can still hear him when I think about it, so I try not to." Henry put his hand on Jack's shoulder.

"When I start feeling bad about that night and the stuff that went on, I think about Lloyd when he was alive and all the crummy things he did. Even when we were small. Like the time he pushed me off my bike and I had to have stitches."

Jack's trembling eased. "Yeah, I remember things, too. Really bad things. Some things I haven't even told *you*. Just because he was bigger and older he used to do stuff to kids." Jack choked back another sob that seemed to catch him by surprise. "He did some stuff to me, bad stuff I've never told you or any one else about."

"That's it. That's what you need to do. Think about things he did that made you mad!" Henry gave Jack's shoulder a soft punch with his fist. "C'mon, let's go in and see if we can find Sheila."

Four generations after his death, Raston Bruhl's mortuary business survived in the hands of his great-grandson, Hilder Bruhl. He had spent a good deal of money renovating the old brick mansion, but hadn't been able to alter its gloomy countenance. The old turrets still stared at each other from each corner, their round, peaked roofs towering above the house itself. Stretching along the roof between the turrets were stone battlements. On the second and third stories, Hilder Bruhl retained the tall, slender windows while on the first floor he installed new windows that were nearly as wide as they were tall. The unfortunate result was to make it appear as if, over time, the weight of the second and third floors had squashed the first. At the center entrance were massive oak doors with burnished brass handles and center panels of dark stained glass, giving the visitor a hint of what to expect inside.

Henry approached the entrance nervously and turned the brass doorknob. The door opened easily, revealing a large, dimly lit foyer with ornately-carved wood covering the ceiling and walls. Across from the entrance a tall man stood solemnly. He was slightly stooped with stringy white hair growing down over his collar. Heavy, dark circles surrounded his eyes. The black suit he wore was noticeably small, revealing part of his forearms and the tops of his short, unmatched socks. His appearance so startled Henry that he stayed in the doorway staring for several seconds. Without a word, the man motioned them inside, then pointed down a hallway toward the chapel.

"That's old Brinter," Henry whispered after they had walked out of earshot. "I hear he's the one that fixes up bodies before the funeral. You know, embalms them and makes them look better for people to see in their casket."

"Jeez, do you think he was able to fix Lloyd?"

A chill like ice water ran through Henry's body. "Are you kidding? It gives me the creeps to even think about it."

As Henry stepped into the mansion's grand living room that served as the chapel, he couldn't help remembering his uncle's funeral. Dim pictures of big people in dark clothes, standing with their heads bowed, flashed before his eyes. Gradually the visions grew more vivid. He saw his aunt and could almost feel her hugging him again so tight he could hardly breathe while she sobbed, wetting his cheek.

As the vision faded, the room's odor nearly overwhelmed him—the same sweet, smothering smell that sickened him at his uncle's funeral. It seemed to permeate every brick and beam in the old funeral home, a syrupy smell that thickened the air, giving it a substance that was unnatural and offensive. His stomach started to churn.

The chapel was brightly lit by two glittering chandeliers, but the deep purple carpet and matching drapes covering the windows made the room feel oppressive. As Henry looked at the people already seated, he tried to avoid the casket, but his eyes were drawn to it irresistibly. It was in front as he knew it would be, surrounded by flowers. He forced himself to look away. Was it open, he asked himself? No, it couldn't be. He was determined not to look again.

Jack nudged him, pointing to kids from their neighborhood sitting near the front. They were like an island in a small sea of empty seats separating them from the adults in the rear.

"Look how grownups take the back seats first,

just like church," Jack whispered.

"How would you know?"

"I've been to church. I just don't go all the time. Maybe I'll start after this."

As Henry stood wondering where to sit, a bony hand suddenly gripped his arm and he found himself looking into the wrinkled face of Sonia Koske—the old woman who all the kids said was a witch. He had never seen her so close and found himself staring at a large mole covered with thick black hairs that grew from her chin. Clamping his jaw, he barely managed to stifle a cry. Around the neighborhood he had kept his distance, hoping she would never know he existed. He had been successful until the day he had to climb over her back fence to retrieve a baseball and had seen her watching from a window. She was a medium-sized woman, slightly stooped, of an age that Henry thought of as "real old". Occasionally he saw her as she made her weekly shopping trips, walking briskly to Minnie's Market, looking neither right nor left, as if to say to anyone within eyesight that she minded her own business and expected others to do the same. Invariably she dressed in baggy house dresses in the summer, covered by a baggy coat in the winter, her stockings rolled down to the top of her shoes. Her gray hair usually fell long and loose to her shoulders, looking half-combed.

But not this day. Today Sonia Koske wore a long, black dress buttoned at the neck with lace at the wrists, her hair in a braid twisted on top of her head. Henry thought she looked like an old-time school marm.

"You're Henry Starker, Delores and Roy's boy," she said in a voice slightly above a whisper. "You were out at the Gerdes farm when it happened, weren't you."

The gaze from her eyes inquired but did not threaten, and her voice had a calming effect. She smelled faintly like the clothes in his grandmother's dresser drawers, a smell of sweet spices and dry flowers.

"Yeah . . . yes, I was there." Her grip on his arm softened.

"You heard him screaming, I hear. A terrible thing for you."

Henry managed a nod.

278

"The sheriff's trying to find out what happened to that boy. Maybe he will and maybe he won't, but *I* know what happened. And it's going to happen again, maybe to a lot of people. Listen to me carefully, now. There's something special about you and me, something that can help people at a time like this. You come and talk to me, at my house. I want to tell you some things, some things you need to know."

Henry could only stare at her blankly.

A frown crossed her face as if she had thought of something that concerned her. "There's only the two of us. There was another once, they say, but that was a long time ago. You come on over to my house and we'll talk." She turned away and walked to a seat on the side aisle.

Jack shuffled over to Henry. "What did *she* want?"

"She wants me to come to her house to talk about what happened to Lloyd. Into her house, can you believe it?"

"Holy smoke, you're not gonna go are you?"

"Are you kidding? C'mon, let's go sit down. There're a couple seats by Dennie."

They walked slowly down the center aisle and sat next to an older boy from the neighborhood, Dennis Lutenegger. To avoid looking at the casket, Henry first stared at his feet, then looked over his shoulder to see who else had arrived. He saw Sheila with her mother two rows behind near the side. He waited until she turned her head toward him and caught her eye. She gave him a forlorn smile, looking as if she had been crying.

Henry slouched down in his seat. The sound of whispers and soft crying came from behind him. When the organ began to play softly, he started to doze, then quickly caught himself. He didn't want to have one of his nightmares right there in the chapel. The worst had been the night before last. He dreamt he was back in his grandparents' kitchen with Sheila and Jack. Terrible screams were coming from the cellar, then they heard footsteps climbing the stairs. He knew it had to be Lloyd, coming for them. Sheila pointed the revolver toward the door. The steps came slowly, steadily. When the cellar door burst open, a torso supported by two legs stood in the doorway. Sheila fired, hitting the thing between the legs, but it started walking again. They ran out into the farmyard screaming. When he woke up, he was still screaming.

The pain in his butt helped him stay awake. His gaze was now drawn irresistibly to the coffin and his skin grew clammy. It was closed, unlike his uncle's. With the top half of the casket open, he remembered his uncle lying in full view. Squeezed into the front pew between his mother and father, Henry had been mesmerized by the the dead, waxy face. He had tried to look away then, too, but his eyes kept drifting back. When the minister finished the long eulogy, his parents whispered that he was to accompany them to pay their last respects. Henry knew what this meant—he would have to walk up to the casket, only inches from his uncle's body. He was sure there would be a putrid odor and mold growing on his skin. He shrank down in his seat, but his mother seized his arm and dragged him out of the pew. He had survived by closing his eyes and holding his breath when she made him stand by the casket.

At least I won't have to face that today, Henry thought with relief. They'll never open it. Lloyd was so mutilated even old Brinter couldn't fix him. The thought of the mangled body triggered his imagination. As he slowly became fixated by the coffin, its bronze exterior seemed to dissolve, gradually revealing the contents. Henry's eyes grew wide as parts of Lloyd's body became visible—gray bones protruding from pieces of bloody flesh, then a head with its face shredded, eyes hanging from their sockets. Beads of sweat formed on his forehead and ran down his back. He rubbed his eyes and squeezed them closed again and again, trying to force the horror out of his mind. Nausea sprouted in his stomach and began to creep into his throat.

I've got to get out of here, Henry told himself. I can't puke in front of all these people. He decided to make a run for it, but his stomach was quicker than his feet. He turned his head toward Jack in desperation and spewed cereal and Dad's Old-Fashioned Root Beer into Jack's lap.

Chapter Twenty-Five

The Doctors

July 18, 1956

It was nearly 2:00 on Wednesday afternoon when Beryl Piffin, Bruders Landing's busiest dentist, steered his cabin cruiser away from its slip in Flint Cliffs Marina and headed for the main channel of the Mississippi River. His passengers were two doctors, Fred Tarkenhoff and Sidney Parish, following a tradition of longstanding in the local medical community—taking Wednesday afternoon off. Beryl had met the two at Crystal Springs Country Club and the three discovered a common passion. They all hated golf. Each Wednesday they took turns selecting the afternoon's activity and it was Beryl's day to choose.

He still wore his sandy hair in a short, military cut, a carryover from his years in the Army during the Korean "Police Action", a style which gave his stocky body a look of outdoor vigor. That Beryl chose fishing as his Wednesday activity, as he so often did, was ironic. Growing up in Bruders Landing, he had barely noticed that he lived alongside one of the world's great rivers. While the river had been merely irrelevant in his young life, the idea of trying to catch its fish had become repulsive after his introduction ended badly. On his fifth birthday his parents had given him a small fishing rod and reel and his father promised to take him to the river the next day. Beryl was thrilled. He had never gone fishing and it sounded terribly exciting. To start, they would catch nightcrawlers for bait. That night after dark, his father took him into their yard and showed him how to catch them. Beryl caught on quickly. As they combed the dew-soaked grass, he would spot a worm glistening in the beam of his flashlight, grab it quickly between his thumb and index finger before it could squeeze back into its hole, then drop it into his dirt-filled coffee can. He liked the feel of their rough, slick skin and narrow, muscular bodies squirming between his fingers. But he was puzzled about how they caught fish.

The next morning on the riverbank, Beryl watched his father prepare his new rod and reel, stringing the line and attaching a hook and bobber. That done, his father reached into the dirt-filled coffee can and pulled out one of the large nightcrawlers. Holding it firmly, he picked up the line with the other and, as if he was threading a needle, plunged the barbed hook into the worm over and over until it was completely impaled. Beryl stared in horror, stifling a scream. He began to feel weak. Not wanting his father to think he was a sissy, he made himself keep watching. He saw the worm writhing on the hook, imagining it shrieking and pleading for help. When his tears started, he couldn't stop. His father bundled up their gear and took him home. It would be over twenty years before he went fishing again.

The afternoon was typical for mid-July—hot, humid, no wind to speak of, temperature in the low 90s, high overcast sky, possibility of a thunderstorm in the forecast. Beryl steered the boat slowly through the narrow passageway between the marina's docks that led to the river. He was sweating profusely by the time they reached the open water. As the boat picked up speed, a cooling wind swept over him, drying his skin.

Beryl's destination was the slough on the east side of Big Tow Island. He was four years old when he first heard the island's name, imagining an island that looked like a big toe. Not until high school, when he saw the name written on a map, did he realize his mistake.

As a child he had been petrified by stories about Big Tow, how people who dared go there had disappeared, victims of strange old men who lived somewhere deep in the island's interior. Beryl was skeptical, but he had never dared set foot on the island.

The main channel of the river carrying the barge traffic ran to the west of Big Tow, allowing the slough on its east side to remain quiet and undisturbed. Once the slough had been wider, nearly two hundred yards for the entire length of the island, but when the dams were built, the river rose but the current through the slough slowed. Silt gradually built up, allowing reeds and lily pods, then shrubs and trees, to grow farther and farther from each shore, narrowing the slough to as few as twenty yards in places. Hidden among this vegetation were the stumps of trees which had died after the rising water, posing a serious danger to any boaters who ventured close to the island.

White egrets and blue herons standing gracefully on spindly legs while they fished were the slough's most visible inhabitants. Where the current flowed close to the bank, trees and bushes crowded the river, their branches growing over the water. Here and there were small inlets, many hidden by overhanging trees, that were passages for the river to enter the island's interior. Dead trees and branches were stacked against the bank in many places, carried by high water in the spring, then stranded as the water receded. In Big Tow slough, Beryl believed he saw the Mississippi River as it should be—untouched by the world he had left at the dock.

As the head of Big Tow Island came into sight, the sun broke through the clouds. Beryl's neck and shoulders grew hot. He turned the wheel leisurely, steering the boat out of the main channel, staying clear of the sand bar which jutted out from the island and lurked invisibly beneath the water's surface. A few moments later they entered the slough, the high pitch of the motor announcing their arrival. Beryl slowed the boat and the motor noise fell to a low rumble.

"Ah, that's better. Some peace and quiet at last, but I don't mean to be critical. This sure beats looking up someone's ass. Can you believe it? I've had eight patients with hemorrhoids and given seven prostate exams already this week," Fred said as he slouched low in the lounge chair, his feet resting on the railing. When he opened his medical practice in 1925, Fred Tarkenhoff was the only Jewish doctor in Bruders Landing. Thirty-one years later what was left of his curly red hair had turned to a blend of white and faded orange. Although well short of six feet, he looked taller because of his Ichabod Crane build. Every pound he gained after age eighteen had come to rest in his stomach which protruded under his belt like a round shelf on which he had the habit of resting his folded hands. Like Beryl Piffin, Fred had been born in Bruders Landing and thought that this birthright would assure the success of his practice, underestimating the latent anti-Semitism in the community. His practice foundered until he took pity on a prominent Methodist banker and his wife who had sought him out in desperation, needing help out of the public eye for their fifteen year-old daughter who was pregnant. And Fred had helped. After the girl returned to school, recovered from her bout with the "flu", the banker became his first gentile patient and his wife the second. After that it had been as if a dam had broken.

Sidney Parish had risen from his chair and was leaning over the railing, staring at the island. "Congratulations, Fred. It sounds like your practice is going great guns, assuming those people pay your outrageous bills. Y'know, you could be developing a specialty here. Maybe we can work out some kind of trade. Tell you what, I'll send you all my patients that have problems with their anus and you send me all yours that don't."

Sidney was tall and dark-complected with such distinctly Southern Mediterranean features that he would occasionally attend the Congregational church to counter rumors that he was Jewish like his partners. As with Beryl, Sidney was a veteran of Korea, a doctor in a MASH unit that had been overrun soon after the Chinese entered the war. When the truce was signed, Sidney was released after two and a half years in a prison camp near the Yalu River. He returned to the states unsure about anything except that he didn't want to practice medicine in his native New York City. In the middle of a cross-country odyssey by train, he got off in Bruders Landing to have a close look at the Mississippi River and stumbled onto a woman who had infatuated him years before on the transport ship taking them to Korea. Sharon Stiefel was a nurse working in a local hospital. After a late evening together, she offered the couch in her apartment. Three years later Sidney had yet to use the couch or the balance of his train ticket. He and Sharon lived together from that night on, an eye-popping arrangement in Bruders Landing.

"Very funny, Sid, very funny. For that, you can crack the first beer." Leaning forward, Fred opened the ice chest and fished out two beers. "Beryl, do want one or are you too busy keeping us afloat?"

Beryl kept a firm hold on the small, spoked wheel. "You'd damn well make sure I got to be one of your patients in that new specialty of yours if we hit a log out here, so I better have one to steady my nerves."

"That's the ticket. Steady as she goes, eh Beryl? Like in the office when you're inflicting pain on those poor slobs who actually pay you to do it."

"Oh yeah, they pay, but not as much as you two charge for all your rear entries."

"Ah, professional jealousy rears its ugly head." Fred fished another beer from the chest, leaned back in his chair and rested his feet back on the railing.

With the boat moving slowly, the afternoon sun felt stronger. Beryl looked for a spot to anchor close to shore in the shade. He heard the opener pop twice. Sidney handed him a can of beer dripping slivers of ice and cold water. He took a deep drink. It tasted heavenly. The first one is always the best, he thought. He sipped the beer as he steered the boat through the slough, still keeping close watch on the water ahead. It was another ten minutes before he found a spot that looked ideal, an area next to the shore under two large willow trees that shaded the water like great green umbrellas. But he didn't know how deep the water was, and there might stumps as they got close to shore.

"All right, you guys, time to get serious. You see those two trees over by the shore? I'm going to anchor this thing under them to keep us cool. There might even be some good fishin', but I'm going to need some help."

"No problem, Beryl ol' buddy." Sidney looked out over the water toward shore. "Which end of this thing do you want Fred and me to carry?"

"I need something a little less strenuous, like making sure we have enough water and checking for stumps in our way. So one of you take an oar up on the bow and check the depth as we go."

"Come on, Sid, we'll both do it, one on each side. Grab an oar." Fred stood and drained his can of beer.

"OK, OK, I'm comin'. I need the exercise anyway."

As Sidney and Fred kneeled on each side of the bow holding an oar, Beryl steered the cruiser toward the island.

"Now, you guys, stick the old oar in and see how much we've got," Beryl called out.

"All right, Beryl, but only because you make it sound so sensual," Sidney replied.

They both stuck their oars into the water as far ahead of the bow as they could reach and pulled them out.

"Looks like there's plenty," Fred yelled. A faint echo answered from the shore.

"Good. Keep checking, but you both don't need to do it at the same time. Take turns."

"OK, I'll go first." Fred stuck his oar deep into the dark water. "Still can't find the bottom, Beryl."

"All right, I'll go." Sidney thrust his oar enthusiastically into the dark water. It reached the mud bottom and sank in. "The bottom's about three feet down," Sidney shouted and gave a pull on his oar. It was stuck. He pulled again. It stayed in the mud. The boat continued slowly forward, forcing Sidney to reach farther back to keep his hold on the oar. He tried once more, pulling with both hands. The oar budged a little, but Sidney, holding tight to the oar, was now suspended between the oar and the boat. And the boat was moving on.

As soon as he saw Sidney's predicament, Beryl threw the motor into reverse, but the boat couldn't stop quickly. He felt as if he were watching a Laurel and Hardy movie in slow motion. Sidney's face was a combination of dilemma and panic, silently pleading for a last-minute reprieve from what he knew was coming. The boat slid out from under him and he fell feet first into the river, still gripping the oar which tipped over from his weight. Sidney and the oar disappeared beneath the muddy water.

Within seconds he resurfaced, standing in water to the middle of his chest, spitting and wiping his eyes with the back of his hands. Fred was laughing hysterically.

"Sid, you numbskull, why didn't you let go?" Fred yelled, still laughing.

"Because I was practicing my pole vault," Sidney shouted back, "why the hell do you think? Now get me out of here before I sink any deeper in this muck. Christ, it must be up to my balls."

"All right, Sid, I'm gonna throw you this . . ." A noise like muffled lawnmower blades hitting the hull silenced him. The boat shuddered and the motor died. Fred lost his balance and nearly joined Sidney in the water.

"Shit, we hit something." Beryl turned to look at the controls. The shift lever was still in reverse. Quickly he went to the stern and leaned over, looking into the murky water. "I think we hit a stump. Dammit, I hope to hell it didn't damage the prop."

"Hey you guys, what's goin' on? I'd like to get out of here, if you don't mind," Sidney shouted.

"Hold your horses, Sid, we got trouble here." Unable to see anything through the muddy water, Beryl returned to the boat's controls, shifted to neutral and punched the starter button. The motor started on his first try. "So far, so good. Now let's see if we can move. Sid, give us a push away from that stump." He shifted the gear lever to forward and pushed on the throttle. The engine raced, but the boat didn't move. "Shit! We must have sheared a pin." Beryl slapped the side of the wheel.

"Guys, I don't want to be a nag, but would you mind getting me the hell out of here!" Sidney shouted, his voice growing louder. "You might also look over to the west. Those black clouds don't look too friendly. So whatever you're doing, do it quick!"

Beryl looked to the west. A bank of teeming black and white clouds was rolling toward them across the entire horizon, undulating menacingly. He cursed himself for knowing so little about boat repair. "Damn. Sid's right. Looks like we're in for a doozy." The air had become deathly still and the humid heat more intense. They could be in trouble out here when the storm hit. He needed to get the boat to shore, which was still some thirty yards away. Not much of a distance when you have a motor, he thought, but it could be a tough paddle.

"Well, since you fix teeth all day, I assume you can also fix boats," Fred commented.

"I'm afraid I missed that course in dental school."

"Oh fine, Beryl. So how do we get back, swim?"

"It might be a little far for an old goat like you, Fred. Tell you what. I'm going to jump in and play African Queen with Sid, hopefully without the leeches. We need to get the boat on over by shore so we don't get blown to hell and gone when the storm hits. You stay on board and steer a little while Sid and I pull us in."

"I heard that," Sidney said, a crooked smile curling his lips. "Come on in, the water's fine."

"No sweat, hey Sid? It's not far. If Bogart could pull that old steamer through the jungle by himself, the two of us sure as hell can pull this thing over to shore. Here, catch." Beryl threw a line to Sidney, picked up another and jumped. The water was cool. He felt his feet sink deep into the soft mud. It seemed as if he would never stop sinking. With water up to his chest, he attempted to walk, discovering that it took a good deal of effort just to pull his foot out of the mud.

"How do you like it so far, Beryl ol' pal?" Sidney asked.

"It'll be slow goin', but there's no turning back

now."

Beryl and Sidney pulled the slack from their lines and started to struggle toward shore. Each step was an effort, the mud bottom clinging to their feet as if it were determined to keep them. After several minutes, Beryl was drained and stopped to rest. The top of his head, which the sun had continued to scorch, suddenly felt cool. Instinctively, he looked up. The sun was gone, covered by black clouds that were rolling more quickly across the sky than he expected. The gray light filtering through the clouds had a greenish cast. Tornadoes are made of stuff like this, he thought to himself.

"Let's hit it, Sid; we can finish this little trip in no time," Beryl shouted.

The wind began to pick up. Ripples appeared on the water and a rustle came from the trees lining the shore, their limbs starting to sway.

Several yards to his right Beryl noticed a thick, dark line wriggling on the water's surface. As he concentrated on the effort to reach shore quickly, his mind was slow to react. It was only a few feet away when he became aware that the "line" was changing shape as it moved toward him.

"Look out, Sid," he called out. "I think there's a snake headed our way!"

Unable to move his feet quickly enough to get out of the way, Beryl leaned back and watched the snake wriggle past him. From the shape of its head, it looked like a water moccasin.

"It sure as hell is a snake, and a big one!" Beryl felt like he had just dodged a speeding car.

"Dammit, Beryl, hit it with something," Sidney as the snake headed toward him. "Keep it away from me. I hate those damn things!"

Beryl watched the snake curling and uncurling its long body as it swam toward Sidney who was screaming and beating the water wildly with his arms. The snake swam straight into the churning water around Sidney and disappeared.

"Ow! Ouch! Shit, holy shit! The God damn thing bit me!' Sidney yelled, holding his right forearm.

"Come over here and let me have a look," Fred

called from the boat. "Hold your arm up."

Sidney did as he was told.

Fred turned his arm over and examined the inside of his forearm. "It looks like it got you, all right." He looked down at Beryl. "What kind do you think it was?"

Beryl struggled over to Sidney and took his arm. As he examined the marks, large drops of rain began to fall. "I can't say for sure. It might have been a water snake. They're harmless. On the other hand, it might have been a moccasin. I don't think we should take any chances. What do you guys have in your bags?"

"I didn't bring my bag," Sidney replied.

"Mine's here," Fred said. "I never go anywhere without it, but I don't carry serum to neutralize snake venom. Sid, we have to get you to the hospital to do the precautionary treatment. Meanwhile, you have to stay quiet and we need to get a tourniquet on that arm."

Sidney started to shiver. "I know, you don't have to remind me of the drill."

"Whatever we do, we can't stay here," Beryl interjected, starting to take charge. "The boat's dead in the water and nobody's going to just happen along here with that storm coming. We have to try to get somebody's attention on a passing boat or on shore, which means we have to get to the other side of the island. I can pull the boat the rest of the way. Sid, you float on over to the bank. It should be shallower there and we can get you back on the boat under some cover. Fred, get the tool box from under the wheel and the tarpaulin from that compartment in the rear."

Beryl had only taken a few steps before Fred came back onto the bow. "I hate to be the bearer of more bad news, Beryl, but your boat's taking on water. When I opened that compartment, it looked like there must be two feet in the bottom."

"Shit, what next! You'll have to start the pump. Make sure the shift lever is in neutral, give the throttle some gas and push the starter. When it starts, look for the switch that says pump and flip it up."

"I got it." Fred returned to the rear of the boat.

Beryl heard the motor start, then the low throb of

the pump. He started for the shore again with the boat in tow.

When Sidney reached the shore of Big Tow Island, Beryl was close behind. Rain now fell in earnest, drenching his hair and dripping into his eyes. A distant flash lit up the sky, followed by a deep rumble that rolled through the river valley. Beryl grabbed hold of a branch hanging over the water and pulled himself out of the muddy bottom onto shore. As the wind started to blow the cruiser downstream, he secured it to a tree with his line, then went to help Sidney who was still standing in the water.

"Out you come, Sid." Sidney held out his hands and Beryl took hold. The rain had already turned the bank's surface into slippery mud and Beryl nearly stumbled back into the river trying to pull him up. Finally on shore, Sidney found a dry place beneath a tree and propped himself between two large roots. He then pulled the belt from his pants, buckled it around the biceps of his right arm and pulled it tight.

Fred was still in the boat, struggling to get the tarpaulin and the tool chest onto the bank. Beryl took them and helped him over the side, then climbed back into the boat to arrange a place for Sidney. Suddenly he realized both the pump and the engine had stopped running. Alarmed, he pulled open the hatch to the engine compartment. It was flooded. The water had risen faster than the pump could handle, and it was still rising. The reality that his boat was sinking struck home.

"Believe it or not, my beloved cabin cruiser is headed for the bottom," Beryl told them when he joined Fred and Sidney on shore. The rain, aided by rising winds, had started to penetrate the leaves overhead. "Sid, unless you want to go down with the ship, our plan to get you back on the boat is over. So we need to find a place to string this tarpaulin where you can stay dry and off your feet while Fred and I go for help." A bright flash followed by a sharp thunderclap came like an exclamation point.

Fred stared at the dense trees and underbrush in front of them. "Do we just dive in there and try to find a place to rig this tarp?"

"I sure don't see any path. You look here and I'll try over there." Turning toward Sidney, Beryl shouted: "We're going to find a place to set up the tarp. Stay still, Sid, ol' buddy. And remember to loosen that belt every ten minutes or so."

Fred plunged through the rain into the underbrush. Beryl did the same several yards to his right. As he entered the tangled brush, he recalled the stories about strange old men that supposedly inhabited the place, but his more immediate concern was keeping the driving rain and branches out of his face. He hadn't walked far before the undergrowth began to thin and the ground became rocky. Ahead he could see large stones among the trees, and he had to step carefully to avoid the rocks protruding from the mud under his feet. Strange terrain for a river island, he thought. Peering through rain which was now making its way unimpeded through the branches, Beryl saw a low hill directly ahead. He decided to climb it rather than go around. At the top was a thick patch of thorn bushes. As he pushed his way carefully through them, he was startled to find that the hill dropped off sharply, creating what looked like an overhang below.

"Fred, over here. I think there might be a place," he shouted.

"All right, I'm on my way," Fred yelled back from the distance.

Beryl walked to one side of the dropoff and carefully picked his way down. When he reached the bottom of the hill, he pushed through the wet brush to the point below where he had been standing. He was right. There was a deep indentation in the rocky hillside, a shallow cave about the size of a small room. He walked beneath the rock overhang out of the rain. Judging by the smooth rock of the walls and the floor, he guessed the room must have been carved out of the hillside by the river. In the rear near the floor he noticed a small opening that could be a natural drain. It seemed like a good spot for Sydney to wait out the storm.

Beryl went back out into the rain. "Fred, you up

there?"

"Yeah, I'm here. How'd you get down?"

"Over at the side, but don't try, I'm comin' up. There's a place down here that should work."

Beryl climbed back to the top of the hill and found Fred crouched under a tree, out of the worst of the rain. For a minute the two men stared at one another, their faces hanging as heavily as their drenched clothes. The light had grown so dim, it seemed like dusk.

"There's a shallow cave down there that's pretty dry. Let's go fetch Sid."

They tramped back through the underbrush, Beryl in front, Fred lagging behind. When they reached Sydney, he was lying in a puddle. The tree above him had long ceased providing any protection from the rain. The sky had grown so dark Beryl could hardly make out the horizon over the water. Suddenly the sky was pierced by a jagged bolt of lightning. He held his breath until the thunderclap came.

"How're you doin', Sid?" Beryl asked as the thunder rumbled off.

"Oh, fine. Just sittin' here in my shower takin' in the light and sound show."

"The arm, Sid, how's your arm?" Fred asked.

"It's just fine, Doctor, I can't feel a thing."

"You'd better loosen that belt for a minute and let a little blood in."

"There's a place we found just a ways from here that ought to keep you dry. Do you feel like movin' on?" Beryl asked.

"Yeah, let's go. I'll just take it easy."

They pulled Sidney to his feet, one on each side. Beryl gathered up the tarpaulin and tool box. Fred carried his black medical bag.

By the time they reached the shallow cave, the wind had become a gale, blowing the rain ahead of it in sheets. The tree limbs overhead bent and swayed, groaning from the wind's abuse. Beryl spread the tarpaulin over the rock floor.

"All right, Sid. Nice and dry. You can ride this out under here." Beryl tried to sound nonchalant as he looked closely at Sidney's face. The loss of color and the glazed look in his eyes concerned him. He knew Fred saw it as well.

"Fred, I think I'll do better without having to drag you along. You huddle here with Sid and keep an eye on him."

Sidney started to protest, but a loud crack of thunder drowned him out.

"I'm not nearly as old as I look, Beryl, but go ahead. Just shake a leg. We don't want to be here all night," Fred answered.

Beryl opened the tool box and took out a flashlight and matches. From the bottom he picked up a revolver, held it momentarily, then put it back.

"God, Beryl, is that what you use when you can't get your fish with a rod and reel?"

"Damn right. Scares'em to death. I'll leave Mr. Smith and Mr. Wesson for you. Watch him, Fred. I'll be back as quick as I can." As Beryl was about to leave, he caught the scent of something foul and an ominous feeling crept over him. Then, just as suddenly, the odor was gone, disappearing in a gust of wind. He hesitated, sniffing the air. Nothing more. He walked out into the storm.

Once more on top of the hill, Beryl peered through the rain to make sure of his bearings. Watching the trees bow in the wind, he imagined what it must be like on the open water. Any boater in his right mind would have long since headed for shelter. There would be no one to see a distress signal unless some hapless tugboat pushing a barge had failed to find a safe mooring. The only hope would be to try signaling the Iowa shore with the flashlight, hoping to catch someone's attention. Even if he were successful and the person understood that they needed help, no one would risk setting out in a boat until the storm had died down. Anyway, people at the marina knew they were out here somewhere. When the storm passed and they didn't return, a search would begin. How long would that take?. And how long did Sid have before the venom started to do some real damage? They sure could use some luck. As soon as they got back, he vowed to buy a marine radio.

He set off toward the western shore of the island. Progress was slow. After several minutes, the trees and undergrowth abruptly ended, replaced by thick reeds like those that grew in shallow water. Could he have reached the river already? He didn't think it would be so close.

Out from under the cover of the trees, he was hit by the full force of the storm. As a long streak of lightning crossed the sky, he squinted into the rain to see what was beyond the reeds. Open water—then more reeds and a line of leafless trees with limbs reaching towards the black clouds. It was a pond or small lake, not the river.

With the next lightning flash, Beryl thought he saw a figure standing at the far side of the pond. Startled, he squinted his eyes tighter. Was it really a person or just dead tree trunk, he wondered? As the flash lost its strength, the gray light descended and the figure vanished. Then came another jagged flash and the figure reappeared. It *did* look like a person, standing at the edge of the reeds. As the light faded again, he continued to stare at the place where the figure stood. He must be mistaken. Surely it was a tree trunk. Why would someone be standing out there? A flash came again, this time a long streak. The figure was still there. It *was* a person—tall, unusually tall, and strangely thin. And the peaked hat it wore made it look even taller. Dark clothes hung loosely from its narrow shoulders like a full length robe. There was something in its hand, a long staff or spear. And it had a beard, white and full. The light dimmed again.

The ominous feeling he had as he left Sidney and Fred rose inside him much stronger. Old stories about the island raced through his mind. Nonsense, he told himself. If there was someone out there, he had to make contact for Sidney's sake.

"Hey! Hey! Over here. Hey!" Beryl shouted.

Another jagged flash of light. This time he saw two more figures standing a few yards from the first. Each looked like the other, the same odd dress, the hat, the staff. Surely he was hallucinating. A distant flash lit the scene again. Yes, there *were* three figures. Standing perfectly still, unaffected by the driving rain. He shouted again. They didn't answer. The first hint of real fear began to take hold. He wanted to run, but he forced himself to turn and walk in the direction that would take him around the figures and the pond. He walked several yards then looked back. The figures were gone. Stories about the island came rushing into his mind again. He shuddered.

I must have been seeing things, it's just those damn trees, he thought, trying to calm himself. "Damn this storm!" he shouted.

He plunged ahead . A sharp-edged bolt of lightning crossed the sky. He stopped cold. In the reeds not twenty yards in front of him was one of the figures—a tall, thin man. Old, very old. A face with eyes glowing from under his peaked hat. The light faded. No, it couldn't be, he told himself. It has to be one of those tree trunks. Lightning flashed again. The figure was there, standing completely still. It *wasn't* a tree, it was a person, an old man. His eyes seemed pierce into him, speaking to him, telling him something, something he couldn't understand.

"My God, those stories are real!" he said under his breath. All he could think to do was to call out again.

"Hey! Who are you? What are you doing out here? We've got a sick man. Bit by a snake. Can you help us get back?" he shouted. Silence. With the next lightning flash, the figure was closer. Its eyes had grown fiery. Once more there was a burst of lightning and the figure was closer still, not more than ten yards away. Beryl panicked. He turned and began to run wildly back the way he came, his mind on the small cave and the revolver in his tool box.

He ran headlong through the brush, branches whipping his face. From up ahead he heard a scream. A second scream made him slow down, out of breath, wanting to be sure where it was coming from. Then another scream. This time it sounded like Sid. More screams, high-pitched. From two people. Then a gunshot. My God, what's happening? He started to run again toward the sounds. As he glanced quickly over his shoulder to see if he was followed, his canvas shoe twisted on a root. An excruciating pain ran through his ankle into his leg. He fell forward. Too late he tried to catch himself. His head slammed into the rock which hit between his eyes. He felt nothing as he was dragged away.

Chapter Twenty-Six

The Island

July 18, 1956

By late afternoon it seemed as if night had already come. The thunderstorm had lingered, growing more severe and casting a pall over Bruders Landing. Rain fell relentlessly, driven by fierce gusts of wind that howled through the streets. The town's ancient elms and oaks bent and swayed at the limit of their endurance—sometimes beyond. Limbs gave way and lay twisted and broken on streets and sidewalks. Jagged bolts of lightning regularly pierced the black sky, followed by frightening thunderclaps that rattled windows before rumbling into the distance.

Herbert Siefken sprinted through the downpour from his car to the front door of his house. A sudden burst of wind nearly blew him through the doorway, wrenching the slippery knob from his hand and flinging the door against the hallway table. He watched helplessly as the ceramic lamp teetered, then fell to the floor bursting into pieces. Rain and leaves swirled in behind him until he could reach the knob and pull the door closed.

"Dammit! Dammit!" Herbert yelled as he stood in the hallway wiping his shoes on the rug. Water from his black raincoat dripped to the floor, forming a wet circle around his feet. The driving rain pelted the windows sounding as if it were hail.

Norma came into the living room at a run. "My God, Herb. What happened? Are you all right?"

"Yeah, it's that wind. It's ferocious. This storm just won't quit! There're limbs down all over the place. The power's out on the west side and we'll be damned lucky if ours stays on." Thunder rumbled in the distance.

"I'll take care of the lamp. Hang your coat up in the cellarway so it can dry off."

"Where's Albie?'

"In the kitchen. He was playing on the floor while I was making supper. Why don't you bring him in here and put him in his playpen while I clean this up."

Herbert walked down the short hallway to the kitchen and hung his dripping raincoat in the the cellarway. An image of the Gerdes cellar was in his mind as he peered down the stairs into the darkness. He switched on the cellar lights and left them burning.

When he returned to the front room, Herbert carried a mop in one hand and their two-year old son in his arm. Albie had one arm around his father's neck and the other around a fire truck. Norma was emptying the last pieces of the lamp into a waste basket. Herbert set Albie down in the wood playpen, kissed him on the top of his head and started to mop the water off the wood floor.

"This is situation normal for my day so far. I can't just have a storm outside, it has to follow me right into our house."

"Well, then, let's compare days. Dinner's not ready yet, anyway." Norma led him to the sofa. "Let's see, now, was your day worse than seeing Hermie Sandburg lift up Sally Kesselman's dress during recess, then having to drag him by his arm to the principal's office while he's crying his eyes out?"

"Maybe not that bad, but close. All I've had to deal with are trees falling on houses and cars all over town, and more questions from the mayor and Harry Berghoff about the Wischmeier kid." The antique clock on the mantle chimed six times. Herbert began to pace across the living room. "God, I hate this. It's so damned mysterious. Why can't I be dealing with a simple shooting, something straightforward? Depending on how Berghoff writes his story about the Wischmeier kid, we could have a panic on our hands."

"You're doing everything that anyone could, I'm sure. Maybe you can get some sleep tonight. You're not going to do another stakeout, are you?"

"Not tonight."

Norma looked over at Albie who was pushing his firetruck around the floor of the playpen. Turning her head, she stared back at Herbert. "Tell me the honest truth now. Are we in any danger? We have a cellar, too, you know. Is there any chance those things might get in, any chance at all?"

Herbert stopped pacing and shoved his hands in his pockets. "Honestly? I don't think so. There's no sign they've come beyond Walnut Grove, at least since the old cemetery was emptied out." He sat down beside her, concern spreading across his face. "But if they get hungry enough, I . . ."

The sharp ring of the telephone startled them .

"I'll get it." Norma reached past him for the phone. "Hello, Siefken's . . . yes, just a minute, Lester. Herb, it's for you." She handed him the phone.

"What's up, Lester," Herbert asked curtly.

"Beryl Piffin's wife just called. Seems he went out fishing in his cruiser this afternoon with two docs, Tarkenhoff and Parish, and they aren't back. She's worried sick with this storm and all. Can't say that I blame her."

"How long have they been out?"

"Since about 1:00, she said."

"Better get ready for a search. Round up some volunteers. I'll meet you at the marina in a few minutes." Herbert hung up the phone with a sigh.

Norma looked at him quizzically. "Well?"

"Seems that some of our medical community's missing out on the river, Tarkenhoff, Parish and Beryl

Piffin. They took Piffin's cruiser out this afternoon and haven't come back. Piffin's wife called worried sick."

"I'll bet she is, but this storm didn't come up all that fast. I'm surprised they didn't get back."

"I am, too. Maybe some trouble with the boat, or they just weren't paying attention. We'll have to go look for them.'

"You can't take a boat out in this."

"Don't I know it, but the three of them could all be dead if we wait. I'll meet Lester at the marina and we'll see how the Old Man looks in this storm. It might be possible and it might not. With the wind the way it is, the waves on that river could be rollin' like the ocean. But if it lets up some, we'll go. This is no time to have people saying all over town that the sheriff won't even go out in the rain."

Herbert retrieved his raincoat, which was still dripping, pulled on his boots, then kissed Norma on the lips. As he opened the door, the sky was lit by a jagged bolt of lightning. He waited, counting the seconds until the thunder, then walked into the storm.

The red light on top of Lester Hammond's cruiser pulsated through the downpour. Taking care to stay on the gravel to avoid sinking in the mud, Herbert pulled alongside, opened Hammond's door and threw himself in. Immediately he was engulfed by cigarette smoke.

"Evenin', Sheriff. Don't look like the storm's lettin' up much."

"Doesn't look like it. I suppose they're still out there."

"Yep, their boat's not back, I checked. Sorry to bother you, but Mrs. Piffin just wouldn't let up. The other two women were polite and nice, but that Piffin woman kept on. I told 'em I'd call soon as we could begin the search."

"Good, Lester. Did you call the weather service?"

"Yep. They said the storm's s'posed to be lettin' up a little, but it won't blow over 'til sometime after midnight."

"What about volunteers, did you make the calls?"

"We got seven boats lined up to search for sure,

probably three or four more, but to hold on 'til it looked safe to go out. Soon's I got here I went out on the pier for a look. The waves look to be over three feet, way too rough for a small boat. We'd be swamped as soon as we left the harbor. It'd be suicide to go out there."

"You're probably right, but I'd better have a look for myself. You'd better come along."

Flint Cliffs Marina was enclosed by a levee built with rock and dirt to protect the boats from the worst of the river's waves, but the force of the storm had whipped up the normally placid water inside. Waves washed over the piers and floating docks, causing them to buck and pitch. Boats rocked from side to side in their slips, straining against the ropes that secured them.

The Sheriff's Department's boat was moored in a slip close to a twenty foot gap in the levee that provided access to the river. Herbert stepped gingerly onto the heaving dock, Hammond close behind. Rain stung his face like sand pebbles. As he carefully made his way along the ramp, a heavy gust of wind caught his raincoat, blowing it tight against his body. He felt as if he could be blown off the pier at any minute. When he was close to the break in the levee, he shielded his eyes and peered out into the river. It was as Hammond had described. Tall waves topped by white foam were crashing into the levee. He signaled Hammond to turn back.

They sat impatiently in the steamy interior of the cruiser, waiting out the storm. Hammond chain-smoked one Lucky Strike after another. Periodically Herbert would roll down his window for fresh air, receiving a gust of wind and rain for his effort. Frustrated, Herbert would crank the window closed again. Seemingly unperturbed, Hammond would light another Lucky Strike.

"Dammit, Lester, suckin' on those coffin nails all day the way you do is gonna kill you."

"You might be right, Sheriff, but my old man's smoked all his life, three packs a day, and he's still healthy as a horse. Anyway, I probably couldn't quit even if I wanted. How long's it been since you stopped now, Sheriff, 'bout two years?"

"Five. After I had my appendix out. Couldn't stand them after that. But if we don't catch whatever killed that Wischmeier kid soon, I might start again."

"It's all so damned far-fetched, Sheriff. What are people in town gonna do when they hear some strange critters livin' in the bluffs eat people dead or alive? They'll go crazy, that's what. They'll be scared to death. It's like the stories about Big Tow Island, only worse. Hell, nobody in town'll go near that island, and those're just old Indian tales."

"You don't believe those stories, now, do you, Lester?"

"'Course not."

"OK, just checking."

In the distance Herbert saw the headlights of a car on the road into the marina, spray flying to each side as it struck the pools of water. Its headlights bore down on them as if the driver intended to hit the cruiser broadside. Herbert edged away from the door. At the last minute, the car turned sharply and skidded to a stop close alongside. He rolled down the steam-coated window, letting in a shower of wind and water. The other driver did the same. He recognized Jane Piffin.

"You ought to drive more carefully in weather like this, Mrs. Piffin," Herbert called out to her across the small gap between the cars.

"My driving is the least of your problems, Sheriff," she shouted back. Her voice dripped with anger. "I want to know just when you're going to get your butt out of that car and start searching for my husband."

Herbert was tempted to shout a barbed protest, but he reined himself in, reminding himself of the despair and frustration she must be feeling. "Soon, Mrs. Piffin, very soon, but it's too dangerous for anyone to go out there right now. The weather service says the storm should be easing up before long. As soon as those waves are down, we'll go, even if it's still dark."

"My God, those men've been out there in this storm for hours. How long do you think they can hold out?"

"There's no choice but to wait. We've got more than a dozen volunteers lined up and ready to search in their boats, but I couldn't ask anyone to go out in this. We have to hope your husband found some shelter when he saw the storm coming. My guess is that's what he did."

Jane Piffin was quiet for a moment. "Can I at least wait here with you?"

Herbert pushed opened the back door of the cruiser and Jane Piffin hurried between the cars and climbed in. A lithe woman, she fit easily into the small back seat. After removing her close-fitting rain hat, she shook her head like a puppy, loosening her dark hair. Herbert turned on the overhead light.

Jane Piffin's attractive face wore a determined look. "Well, Sheriff, just what happens when the storm *does* die down?"

"When we see it easing, I'll radio the office and tell them we're going. Then they'll call the volunteers. There'll be at least five boats with radios. Each one will search the section of the river that we assigned. When they find your husband, they'll radio back to us and I'll let you know right away."

Jane Piffin was quiet. Herbert thought she might be crying.

"We'll find them; don't you worry. They're probably holed up on shore or an island someplace. But we won't really have much chance until it's light. I know it's hard, but you'll have to be a little patient, Mrs. Piffin."

"I'll be patient, Sheriff, when you're out there doing your job."

They waited for over an hour. Hammond dozed, snoring softly. Jane Piffin sat silently, but Herbert could feel her scowling at the back of his head.

At last he sensed the wind lessening and rolled down his window to see if he was right. The rain was letting up. His watch read 1:35. He opened the car door quietly and stepped out. The wind had fallen to a stiff breeze and the rain was now a foggy drizzle. He could hear the ropes groaning as the boats still rocked in their slips.

Herbert walked around the cruiser and knocked on the driver's window. After a moment, Hammond rolled it down.

"C'mon, let's go have a look."

Lester rubbed his eyes sleepily and stretched, his hands pressing on the roof of the car. "Right, Sheriff. Has the rain stopped?"

"Almost. The wind is down, too."

Jane Piffin opened the back car door. "Can you start now?"

"It looks promising, Mrs. Piffin. You just wait in the car for a minute. We're going to have a look at the waves."

Herbert led the way down the dock. High overhead the marina's after-hours light cast a faint glow through the gathering fog. There was barely enough light to see where to step. The dock still moved, rocked by ripples remaining on the waters surface. The mist in the air felt wet against Herbert's face. The wind had nearly vanished. Now the only sounds were the soft groans of the mooring lines.

When he reached the end of the dock, Herbert stared out into the dark expanse of the river. A thick fog was gathering, but the waves were diminishing rapidly. Satisfied, he walked back to the Department's boat, a twenty-foot Jon boat with a Johnson 35 motor. As he feared, the bottom was filled with several inches of water.

"Lester, start bailing this water out. I'm going to call the office and tell them to roust the volunteers."

"Wait a minute," Hammond said, wrinkling his forehead. "You're not thinkin' about goin' out before sunup, are you?"

"Yeah, I sure am. Soon as we get it bailed out. We don't need much light to get started."

"Sheriff, that's crazy, if you don't mind my sayin' so. In the first place we could get within ten feet of those guys in this soup and never see 'em. You shouldn't let yourself get pressured by that woman."

"In the first place, I do mind you saying so, Lester. In the second place, I'm not letting myself be pressured. Even if we can't see them, we can hear them, and they might see our lights. I also have a hunch where they might be. In the third place, I think you're scared to go out on the river in the dark and I don't blame you. I'm scared myself and I wouldn't be asking you to do it if I didn't need you with me. You know the river a hell of a lot better than I do."

"OK. OK. You're the boss. I'll go. I just won't like it."

Herbert walked back down the dock carrying a full gas tank. Hammond was scraping the last of the water from the bottom with a can.

"Good work, Lester. Looks like you've got it. Give me a hand with these, will you?"

Hammond took one of the cans and put it next to the motor. Herbert came over the side with the other.

"Things are all set with our search party. Gus'll get them started. Now let's see if that motor'll start after standing in a rain like that."

"I'm sure it will, Sheriff. It always does when you don't want it to."

Herbert gave the starter rope a hard yank. The motor coughed then caught, running roughly. Herbert twisted the throttle and the engine smoothed out.

"That's a break. OK, go ahead and untie us."

Hammond fumbled with the knots in the mooring lines, muttering as he untied them one by one. Herbert made his way to the bow of the boat where a spotlight was fastened and turned the switch. A brilliant beam of light hit the water.

"You handle the searchlight, Lester, and keep your eyes peeled for snags. There'll be a lot of stuff floating out there after a storm like that one."

Herbert steered the boat at low throttle toward marina's entrance. Hammond pointed the spotlight in front of them, steadily sweeping the water's surface. As they approached the break in the levee, Herbert's began to feel uneasy. He had come this way many times, but never had he been so apprehensive. Staring at the opening before them, it looked as if they were approaching the gateway to some shadowy abyss. He shook his head to turn off his imagination.

The levee rose steeply out of the water on both sides of the boat as they passed through. Then they were in the open water of the river. The air was suddenly cooler. In the beam of the searchlight, the fog was a bright gray, making it nearly impossible to see anything other than the water directly ahead of the bow.

Hammond peered intently out over the black water. "I can't see much in this damn fog, Sheriff. Better not take 'er any faster." His voice sounded hollow and strangely close.

"OK, I'll hold her steady." Herbert turned the boat north.

"You said you had this hunch, Sheriff. Mind tellin' me where you're takin' us?"

"Big Tow Island." Even though Hammond was facing forward, Herbert could feel his eyes widen.

"Big Tow! Why there? Nobody goes *there*!"

"Not on the island. Around to the slough on the backside."

"Jesus, that slough's fulla snags and stumps. It's no place to be goin' in the dark."

"That's why I want to look. They might have gotten caught in there. That would explain why they didn't get in before the storm hit and nobody saw them."

"We got way over an hour 'til sunup You're not goin' in there before we got light, are you?"

"We'll see how it looks. At the rate we're goin', it'll take us a good half hour just to get there. At least I want to be close so we can go in as soon as there's light."

When Herbert quit speaking, the only sound was the motor, a high-pitched drone muffled by the fog. As they moved north, the fog thickened, wrapping the boat in a gray shroud. Lights from the shore disappeared and a feeling of isolation came over him.

Suddenly Hammond shouted. "To the left, quick! Steer left! Snag!"

Herbert pulled sharply to the left. A split second later the boat was buried in a mass of leaves and branches. "What the hell? There's a whole damn tree floating out here." He pushed a branch away from his face. "Untangle us up there, Lester. I'll back us out." He pulled the shift lever into reverse and applied power gradually. Branches scraped the hull as the boat came free. The mound of branches drifted slowly into the fog.

"Christ, that was close. I don't want to say I told you so," Hammond said.

"Then don't. Just try to give me a little more warning," Herbert answered curtly, attempting to cover up his embarrassment.

"I'll try, but this fog is like duck soup. There could be a barge out here and I couldn't see it 'til it ran us over."

"OK. Much as I hate to admit it, we'd better hold off. I'll head us over to shore until it gets light. Radio the office and tell the volunteers to hold off until visibility gets better."

There was a rustling sound from his rain coat as Hammond shifted his position, took a last drag on his Lucky and flicked the glowing butt into the water.

"Lester, that's number nine, just in the time we've been tied up here."

"Yeah, well, I'm trying to cut down. I gotta get down to three packs a day. Save a little money."

"That's some goal," Herbert answered, leading to another period of silence.

It was wet and uncomfortable on the boat's metal seats, yet Herbert dozed on and off. As the sky lightened, he shook himself fully awake, expecting to get underway. Still the dense fog clung to the water, a white veil hiding everything more than a few yards from where they were anchored. Herbert was aware the families would be gathering, frantic with concern, putting their hopes in his search. A search that hadn't even begun. He stared in frustration at the the billowy gray mist surrounding them, as if he could somehow cause it to part. Maybe it was his imagination, but it appeared the fog was slowly growing thinner.

"Another 15 minutes and we're going, fog or no fog."

"I can't wait." Hammond sounded tense.

"So you're not looking forward to Big Tow. Have you ever been on it?"

"Never had a reason to. Fact is, I've stayed away from the place. When you've grown up here like me, you hear stories about it from the time you're a little kid. Hell, you know, Sheriff, hardly nobody goes there. Those stories and all, old Indian legends I guess they are, 'bout strange people there, people disappearin' and what have you. They scared the crap out of me when I was little. Guess I never got over it completely, like most people here."

"Technically, Big Tow's part of our responsibility, you know. We probably should be taking a look out there every once in a while, but from what I hear, Jack Schoof hadn't set foot on it for years either."

"That don't surprise me none. I think the law has a tradition of lettin' *all* these river islands alone, not just Big Tow."

"Sometime we'll have to break tradition, I guess."

Herbert stood up. "I think the fog's lifted enough to try it again. I'll radio the office and tell them we're headed for Big Tow. The others can start as soon as they think they can see well enough."

He started the motor and headed the boat back into the main channel, gradually increasing their speed. "Keep the spotlight on, Lester. It won't do us much good, but the docs might see it."

They traveled steadily north, passing two small islands that loomed darkly through the fog. Herbert scanned the shore of each one as they passed, seeing nothing.

After nearly twenty minutes, Hammond shouted over the sound of the motor: "I think I see Big Tow up ahead now. Bear to the right. You want to stay away from the point. There's some bad currents there and a sandbar that's always shiftin'."

Herbert watched the island emerge from the fog.

"It looks OK so far, Sheriff. I can see maybe forty or fifty yards out. Keep 'er headed straight. The slough's dead ahead now. Better take 'er easy."

Herbert throttled the motor down and the bow settled into the water. "Here we go, Lester. You concentrate on what's ahead of us in the water, but keep sweeping that spotlight from shore to shore. You might try using your binoculars to see if they're any help."

"If those guys're in there, you can bet they'll be on the island side 'cause that's where they'd be fishin'. The fish love all those reeds and stumps."

As they entered the slough, the air thickened with an odor of water-soaked vegetation. Over the sound of the motor, Herbert heard the high-pitched croaking of tree frogs and the frequent splash of fish leaping for their breakfast. He raised the field binoculars that hung from his neck and scanned from side to side, looking through the light gray mist for anything unnatural, any flash of color that could mean a boat.

"I don't think they'd 've tried to get in along here to fish, Sheriff. Too many reeds to tangle up a prop. They clear out a ways ahead."

"You're probably right, but keep a sharp eye out."

As they glided steadily through the slough, Herbert worked to stay alert, continually shifting positions and readjusting the life jacket beneath him, his only protection from the hard aluminum seat. Gradually the reeds thinned out and the banks along the island's shore became visible.

"There're stumps all along here, now," Hammond pointed out. "You can't see 'em but they're there, just below the water. It's good fishin' near the shore, but I wouldn't want to try gettin' back in there with Doc Piffin's cruiser."

"That could be the problem," Herbert replied, hoping he wasn't mistaken about searching for the men in the Big Tow slough.

Hammond saw it first. "Hold 'er a minute, Sheriff. I think I see somethin'. There, next to bank."

Herbert throttled back the motor and brought the binoculars to his eyes. Lester did the same. As they stared at the shore, a band of fog rolled gently across the water, blocking their view. Herbert waited impatiently for it to clear. In a moment the shore emerged and he saw it.

"Do you see that, Sheriff?" Hammond exclaimed.

"Yeah, it looks like the top of the cruiser. Damn, they must have gotten in there and sunk. I just hope to hell they got off. Let's check it out. You guide us through the stumps."

Herbert headed the boat toward shore, moving slowly as Hammond bent over the bow with a short wooden oar that he regularly plunged into the brown water. Twice Herbert felt a soft bump as they glanced off stumps that Hammond missed.

They hadn't gone far before before it was clear that the object next to shore was indeed the top of a cabin cruiser. Herbert pulled the boat alongside. The cruiser's cabin was below the water's surface and he bent over, trying to peer inside.

"Damn, I can't see a thing. I hope to hell nobody's in there." He straightened back up and blew five long blasts from the boat's horn. When the echo faded, he cupped his hands around his mouth and shouted into the island: "Beryl! Fred! Sidney! It's Herb Siefken. We're by your boat! Call out if you can hear us!"

He stared at Hammond as they listened for some response. There was none.

"Wherever they are, they can't hear us. Let's get on shore and see if there's some sign of them."

With the top of the sunken cabin cruiser for leverage, they pulled their boat against the riverbank. Hammond climbed on the shore and tied a line to a tree.

"Hey, Sheriff, there's a blanket, some clothes and other stuff here. It looks for sure like they got off. There's a bunch of tracks in the mud, too. Looks like they headed into the island."

Herbert stared into the underbrush where the tracks disappeared. Fog drifted through the treetops, clinging to the leaves. The heavily-leafed branches created a thick canopy blocking much of the already dim light. The air was deathly still, heavy with the smell of wet and decaying vegetation. It felt like the inside of a tent after a heavy rain.

Herbert studied the footprints in the mud. "There's three sets of footprints here, so they all got off. We'll try to follow their tracks. There's one set of prints over there; then it looks like they all went this way. You follow those tracks, and I'll do these. Try to stay in shouting distance."

The trail of footprints Herbert followed grew faint in the heavy underbrush. At that point, bent and broken branches helped show the way. The mist-like fog hanging in the air kept the brush wet. Herbert's shirt and pants were soon soaked. As he walked on, Herbert felt the soft ground give way to hard clay and rock. Then, directly ahead, was a hill. He halted, listening to Hammond forcing his way through the undergrowth a short distance away.

"You OK over there, Lester?" Herbert shouted.

"Sure. Fine," Hammond shouted back.

"You notice anything strange about this place yet?"

"You mean like any old people?"

"No. What you're walking on."

"You mean the rock?"

"Yeah. The island's rocky. How many island's have you been on in this river that're rocky?"

"None I remember."

"Me neither. And look ahead, that hill. How many island's have you seen with a hill?"

"None, I guess."

"So already we've found something strange about Big Tow."

"That's strange enough for me, Sheriff."

Herbert reached the hill and started to climb following the broken branches. At the top, he paused to get his bearings. Around him the treetops rose out of the ground fog like bushy plants. He was sure that the western shore of the island lay straight ahead. At his feet, in an area of clay between the rocks, were scuff marks . He was still on their trail. Straight ahead, a branch had been pushed aside. There was another like it on his left. To his right there seemed to be a slide mark made by a shoe where the hill went down steeply. He was about to follow when he heard someone coming in his direction through the brush. In a few moments Hammond appeared between two saplings.

"So you decided to join me?"

"No, just following the tracks. This is where they go."

In the brief silence after Hammond talked, he

heard something—a low sound, like a moan.

"Did you hear that, Lester? Sshh."

Hammond's mouth was open wide. "I . . I don't hear nothin'. Shit, Sheriff. This place gives me the creeps."

"I'm sure I heard something. Let's have a look down there." Herbert pointed down the hillside where the tracks led. "They could've fallen."

The sound came again. A soft cry, almost a word, from below.

"I hear it, Sheriff. I'm right behind you. Careful. I'll bet it's slick as hell."

"Can anybody hear me?" Herbert shouted.

A hoarse voice came from a cluster of trees at the bottom to his left: "Here. Down here."

"We're coming!" Herbert climbed down the hillside as fast as he dared, grabbing onto branches to keep from falling. When he reached level ground, he rushed through the trees in the direction the voice had come from, nearly stumbling over Sidney Parish lying under a tarpaulin at the edge of a shallow cave.

Herbert knelt down and saw a face so lacking in color it hardly looked human. Then the face opened its mouth, forming a word.

"Taken."

"My God, Doctor Parish!" Herbert blurted out. "What happened to you?"

The doctor struggled to say more. "Fred gone. In there."

Herbert raised up on his knees and stared into the cave, casting his eyes around the rock floor and walls. Fred was nowhere in sight, but he saw the small opening at the rear. Then he smelled it—that putrid odor. It was all too familiar.

"Oh my God!" Herbert exclaimed and knelt back down. "We'll get you out, don't worry. Can you tell me where you're hurt?"

"Snake. Bit me. Arm. In there. Took my hand."

Herbert shuddered. "OK. Let's have a look." With apprehension he lifted a side of the tarpaulin. Sidney Parish's right arm was folded across his chest, a belt tied around his bicep. The skin below the belt was blue. But it was the hand that made Herbert gasp. It was still attached to the arm, but only bone was left. The skin, the muscle, even the tendons, were missing up to the wrist. The bone had been stripped clean except for a few speckles of pink. Sidney stared at it pitifully, tears forming in his eyes. Herbert felt nauseous. Behind him Hammond swore softly.

"Fred's in there." Sidney nodded toward the cave.

Herbert rose and walked inside. A sheen of moisture covered the rock walls. The water which had gathered in an indentation in the stone floor was red. Blood mixed with rain water. A great deal of blood. He shook his head and moved on to the opening at the rear. It wasn't large, twenty inches at most. He knelt down and pointed his flashlight inside. Streaks of blood lined the floor as far as he could see. The smell was nearly overpowering. Fred Tarkenhoff wasn't a large man. Herbert had no doubt about what happened to him.

Herbert went back to where Sidney Parish was lying. Hammond was trying to make him comfortable. "Can you tell us where Doctor Piffin is?"

"Don't know. Left to get help. Never came back."

Chapter Twenty-Seven

The Old Woman

July 19, 1956

It was a few minutes after 8:00 in the morning when Henry came downstairs, at least an hour earlier than normal. The kitchen was empty. When he looked out the back door, he saw his mother pulling weeds in their vegetable garden. Without bothering to tell her he was up, he took a box of Kix from the pantry and a bottle of milk from the refrigerator. He ate while staring blankly at the spy ring offer on the back of the box, searching his mind for some way to get to Big Tow. After several minutes his cereal bowl was empty and he was no closer to a solution than he had been the night before. Maybe if he went outside he could think of something. With a shrug of his shoulders, he drank the sugary milk remaining in the bowl and rose from the table.

"Bye, Mom. I'm going outside for a while," he yelled in her direction, then went out the front door without waiting for her response.

The day was overcast and cool for July. He looked up and down the street, surprised to see no one. The only sound was someone chopping a tree in the distance. A city truck filled with broken tree limbs was parked on the other side of the street in the next block. With no particular plan in mind, he crossed the street in front of the house owned by Sonia Koske. A thick hedge grew high in her front yard blocking a view of the house itself. Nearly oblivious to his surroundings, Henry continued toward the chopping sound thinking about Big Tow Island.

As he passed the opening in the hedge leading to Sonia Koske's front door, she suddenly appeared, her face not three feet from his, as if she had materialized out of thin air. His whole body jerked, his eyes opening wide. She stood heavily, a larger person than he remembered, dressed as he always saw her in summer: a print apron over a shapeless house dress with a faded, flowery pattern. Her cotton socks were tightly rolled down to the top of her black shoes. She carried a straw broom in her hand as if she had been sweeping her sidewalk. Maybe she just rode in, Henry thought to himself.

"Good morning to you, Henry Starker. I was beginning to think you were never going to come see me." The gaze from her brilliant blue eyes froze him in place.

"G'morning, Mrs. Koske," Henry stammered, trying to avoid staring at the hairy mole on her chin. "I wasn't exactly . . . I was just walking by and . . ."

"Nonsense," she sniffed. "It's time for us to have our talk. You come on in now and we'll spend a few minutes. I just baked cookies."

Henry didn't move. There was something different about Mrs. Koske today. She looked concerned, worried, the way his mother did when he would come in late after dark.

"What's the matter, Henry, cat got your tongue? You don't have to be afraid of me. I'm just a harmless old lady."

The gentle tone of her voice reassured him. "Oh, I'm not afraid, Mrs. Koske. It's just that you, well, surprised me."

"Off wool-gathering were you? Well, there's certainly a lot to think about these days with that killing out at your grandpa's farm and now those people dead over on Big Tow Island. Anyway, that's what we need to talk about. Come along inside, now."

Her soft voice was compelling and Henry was curious, so he followed her as she walked stiffly up the small sidewalk toward her house.

They climbed the steps to the large, wrap-around porch. The house was wood frame, a sturdy two-story with large windows and cream-colored paint that had started to peel. Henry noticed the front shades were pulled. The boards creaked as they crossed the porch to the front door.

She let the screen door close behind them with a bang that nearly made him jump. In the darkened interior, it looked as if he was confronted by a room full of odd-shaped ghosts. Gray shapes loomed everywhere. As his eyes adjusted to the dim light, he saw that sheets covered every object in the room—chairs, sofa, tables, shelves, even pictures hanging on the walls. He had never seen anything like it, except in a spooky Abbott and Costello movie. The room smelled musty as if it had been closed a long time.

Sonia Koske turned back toward him as he stood staring. "Have to keep the dust off. Come on in the kitchen. We can sit better in there."

She led him between the shrouded furniture into what looked like the dining room. Shades were pulled in its two windows as well. Boxes and chairs lined the walls. In the center of the room was a large table piled with dishes, pots, pans, several mounds of eating and cooking utensils and more boxes. A set of tall crystal candelabra rose from the center. A layer of dust coated everything.

When Sonia Koske pushed open a door on the far side of the dining room, Henry imagined she was leading him into some inner sanctum from which he could never escape. To his relief, the door led into a tidy kitchen and he was greeted by a mouth-watering smell of something freshly baked. Instantly, his mouth started to water.

"There, Henry. Sit down at the table. I made some chocolate cupcakes this morning. Just had a taste for them. Don't suppose I could interest you in one or two, could I?"

The thought that they were drugged occurred to him and he was about to decline when he inhaled the irresistible aroma again. "Yes, you sure can."

As Mrs. Koske busied herself extracting cupcakes from the baking tin, Henry gazed around the kitchen. Unlike the other rooms he had just seen, this room was neat and orderly. The large porcelain sink was so white it almost glowed. On the wall opposite the sink he saw a Roper stove with gray enamel trim identical to his grandmother's. On the counter next to it was a wooden box with the word "Bread" carved in front. The counter also held a large crockery jar with the words "Cookie Supply" in yellow. A tall wooden cabinet with two doors, top and bottom, both with gleaming brass handles, sat against the wall behind him. He had to stare for a minute before he realized what it was—an icebox, one that used real ice. He remembered waiting for the ice truck to come down their street on hot summer days, delivering ice to her house and two others on their block. When the truck stopped, he and Jack would run to the rear and wait for the driver to throw back the heavy canvas curtain, releasing a burst of cool air. The ice came in huge blocks and the driver used an ice pick to chip them into smaller ones, producing a shower of ice slivers. When he finished, the driver would pick up the blocks with ice tongs and deliver them to the houses with red cards in their front windows showing how much was needed that day. As soon as the driver left the truck, he and Jack would climb into the back and collect as many of the ice chips as they could stuff into their mouths and hold in their freezing hands. On especially hot days, they would put the chips under their shirts and rub them against their chests for as long as they could stand it. For years he had begged his parents to trade their refrigerator for an icebox so the truck would bring ice to their house.

Mrs. Koske put a plateful of warm cupcakes in colored baking papers on the table. "There, Henry, I hope you like them. A growing boy needs his strength so you better have at least three."

As Henry picked up a cupcake and peeled off the paper, Sonia Koske went to her icebox and brought out a quart of milk. The bottle was unopened, the cream collected at the top. She shook it to mix the cream, then poured a glassful and set it in front of him.

"Milk tastes real good after you've had a couple of these," she said, picking up one of the cupcakes. Already Henry was reaching for his second. He stared at the glass of milk before drinking, making sure there were no lumps of cream floating on top. He hated getting those in his mouth. While Sonia Koske ate silently, the pleasant expression on her face slowly turned to one of great seriousness.

"Henry, I'm going to tell you some things that very few people know," she said somberly. The cupcake sat unwrapped on the table in front of her. "In fact there's only one other person left in Bruders Landing that knows what I'm gonna tell you and he's as old as me. Years ago we all swore a blood oath never to tell these things to a living soul. And there's a terrible price to pay by anyone who does." She paused, seemingly to gather resolve.

"Now the rest of them are dead except him and me, and we aren't going to be around much longer. It looks like the trouble has started again, sooner than I thought. Trouble too terrible for me to stay quiet. So I have to tell someone about it, someone who can do something."

"You . . . you mean me?"

"I need you to be my messenger."

"To who?"

"The sheriff. It's not safe for me to be seen talking to him. That blood oath I told you about is still with us. It has an enforcer, you see, someone who inflicts the penalty on anyone who breaks it."

Henry squirmed, feeling himself slipping into something much too deep. "Why don't you just call him on the phone?"

"I don't have a phone. Now look me in the eye, Henry Starker. There're things I have to tell you." She reached her hand across the table and gently tugged the end of his chin, turning his head so he was looking directly into her face. "Remember what I told you at the funeral. You and I are special. We have a gift that lets us hear the Old Ones on the island. The town will need you and your gift just like it did mine a long time ago. That's important for you to know, but there's more, much more. What I'm going to tell you now is the truth, even if it's hard to believe. Think what you will about me, just remember it's the truth you're about to hear. Pay close attention so you can remember." She paused momentarily as if she needed to catch her breath, then lowered her voice. "You see, *I know* what's doing the killing."

Henry's hand stopped in midair as he reached for a third cupcake.

"When I tell you these things, you may think I'm just a crazy old lady. That's all right. The important thing is that you repeat them to the sheriff."

As she talked, Henry believed he was hearing things that nightmares are made of. They couldn't be true, they just couldn't, but he listened closely, captivated by what she was telling him.

When she finished, Sonia Koske handed him another cupcake. He barely had the strength to hold it.

"Now you go and tell this to the Sheriff, Henry. He needs to know." She reached for his hand, gripping it firmly.

"But he won't believe me," Henry pleaded, imagining the sheriff laughing at him. "You have to come, too."

"I can't do that. I just . . . can't. *You* have to tell him. Say if he wants proof to go look at the records. The ones that Boris Brinter keeps hidden at Bruhl's Mortuary. And tell him one more thing."

"Wh-what's that?"

"Tell him the Gathering are awake."

Chapter Twenty-Eight

The Key Ring

July 19, 1956

It was approaching 6:00 in the evening when Jack Powell started for home. It was the last place he wanted to go, but there would be hell to pay from his father if he was late for supper. He had spent the day by himself, riding aimlessly on his bicycle, enjoying his freedom from the threat of Lloyd Wischmeier. Lloyd had been a nightmarish part of Jack's life for as long as he could remember and now Lloyd was dead. His buddies, Frey and Siefert, were still out there some place, but they didn't feel so threatening without Lloyd to egg them on.

Jack had left his house early that morning with an urge to see Sheila. He planned to ride to the house where she was staying with her mother and grandparents. He was sure he knew where it was. All he had to do was get up the nerve to knock on her door. But as he rode, the thought of seeing her without Henry began to unnerve him. He had never been with her by himself and doubts formed in his mind. Could he think of things to say? Would she think it was strange if he showed up alone? What if she didn't want to talk to him?

By the time he reached her house, his doubts were too strong. Instead of going to the door, he rode by slowly, staring at the windows, hoping to catch a glimpse of her. When the house was out of sight, he circled the block trying to work up his nerve. After circling the block for the fifth time, he still couldn't bring himself to go to the door. With an angry jerk on his handlebars, he pedaled away.

It was 6:30 when he arrived home. As he turned the corner of his block, he was relieved to see that his father's car wasn't there. This meant he wouldn't get yelled at or hit for being late, and it would be quiet in the house, at least for a few minutes until his father got home. He let himself hope that this might be one day his mother hadn't been drinking.

The rusty kickstand on his bicycle squealed as he pushed it down with his foot. He was careful to park his bike away from the back door so his father wouldn't kick it over as he did whenever he thought it was in his way. It had been a gift from his grandmother and there wouldn't be another now that she was dead.

"Hi, Mom, I'm home," he called out as he opened the back door, putting as much cheer as possible into his voice. There was no answer. When he entered the kitchen, he expected to find his mother fixing supper. It was his father's rule that supper was to be on the table at 6:30, period. No excuses. Jack looked at the clock above the kitchen door. It was already 6:30 and there was nothing on the table, nothing cooking on the stove. He called his mother again. Still no answer. He started to worry. Unless she was with his father, there was going to be another fight with a lot of hitting.

The way to the living room in the small house was through his parents' bedroom and Jack headed there first. The shades in the bedroom were pulled.

"Thass shoo, Zhack?"

Jack knew what it meant when she sounded like that. He could see the glow of a cigarette and a figure struggling to rise from the bed.

"Gimme a boosh, Zhack. Need to giddup and fi'sh dinner."

Jack walked to the bed and took her outstretched hands, pulling her to her feet. "Aw, Mom, why do you do this?"

She rose unsteadily, an apologetic look on her face and a half-burned Pall Mall dangling from her lips, then collapsed back on the bed.

Elizabeth Powell was not a large woman to start with and had been losing weight steadily for nearly two years. Her clothes now looked like hand-me-downs from a large older sister. Although she was only thirty-four, her dark hair had turned salt-and-pepper and on many days never saw a comb. From the look of her, Jack guessed this was one of those days. Since it appeared she was wearing a robe over her nightgown, he also guessed she hadn't bothered to dress.

"Why'd you have to go and drink so much? You know it's supper time and Dad'll be mad." Jack didn't need an answer. He knew it already. There had been another fight that morning before his father left for work. Over what didn't matter. They just fought. The fight would be especially bad tonight. He was afraid for his mother. She would get hit. One of these times he'd call the sheriff. He picked the cigarette from her lips and stubbed it out in an ashtray on the nightstand.

"Y'right, Zhack. Need to giddup. Jush gimme a hand."

"OK, but you have to hurry. Dad'll be home any minute." As Jack started to pull his mother to her feet again, he heard the familiar sound of their car turning the corner onto their street. It was a 1938 Dodge, ill-kept and bearing the scars of several accidents. Rattles sprang from the old Dodge at the slightest bump.

"Jeez, Mom, he's home! He'll be inside any minute! You gotta get up."

His mother made a valiant effort to rise before collapsing again. Jack reluctantly released her hands. It was useless. She couldn't stand. And if she couldn't even stand, there was nothing he could do. Pulling aside the shade, Jack peered into the street. There he was, closing the trunk with one hand and holding two fishing poles in the other.

Seth Powell was slender as a young man, but had

324

been adding weight steadily for years. At the army ammunition plant where he worked, Seth Powell drove a lift truck, which settled most of his new pounds in his seat and hips. He was wearing a sleeveless undershirt smudged with sweat and dirt. The thick dark hair on his arms and shoulders glistened along with the smooth skin on top of his head.

Jack watched through the window as his father bent down to pick up his tackle box and a stringer holding a few small fish. Why doesn't he ever ask me to go, Jack wondered as he had so many times? As he was about to release the shade, Jack saw his father stumble and fall forward onto his hands and knees. He started to rise slowly, his head drooping as if he no longer had muscles in his neck. Getting a grip on the fishing poles again, he grabbed the tackle box and stringer, cursed loudly, then pushed himself the rest of the way up. He stumbled toward the house.

Jack waited anxiously. He knew what happened when his father came home drunk. That was when his temper was at its worst. The back door slammed and his father came inside.

"Lizzie! I'm home." There was the sound of fishing tackle dropping on the floor. "Fishin' wasn't no good, so I went to Haller's for a coupla beers." The usual grouchiness was in his voice. Jack listened to him shuffle through the kitchen.

"Lizzie, dammit, where are you?" Silence. "Christ, it's after 6:30. Ain't supper ready?" A chair banged against the floor. "God damn it, Liz, Jack, where the hell are you?" he bellowed.

"In here. I'm in here. No, supper ain't ready." Jack's mother sat on the side of the bed sounding surprisingly sober.

Seth Powell appeared unsteadily in the doorway, staring into the dimly lit room. "Oh, there ya' are, both of o' ya'. What are ya' doin' in here in the dark?"

"I was restin', Seth. Just fixin' to get up."

"Hell, it'sh after 6:30. Why ain't dinner ready?"

"I said I was restin'. I guess I'll go put it on now."

Seth Powell took a few steps toward his wife, then stopped, swaying slightly. "You been drinkin' again?"

"It ain't none of your damn business."

"I asked you a question, dammit. You been drinkin'?" While he still spoke at a normal volume, his voice was taut and ominous.

"So what if I have? What you doin' gettin' home this late? You been at Haller's for more than a couple, that's for sure."

"God damn it!" he shouted and took a step toward her. "You can't be settin' here in the house drinkin' all day!"

Things were escalating as Jack feared. He could only stand and watch.

"I can if I want, Seth Powell, and there's nothin' you can do about it!" She stood and faced him, hands on her hips. "You can't go 'round tellin' me what to do all the time. I'm tired of it!"

"I damn well *can* tell you to stop drinkin'! Hell, you ain't even able to fix my supper."

"*You* tell *me*? *You*, the biggest lush at the plant. You're the last one to tell *anyone* to stop drinkin'." Jack was surprised by his mother's defiance. He was sure it would only make his father angrier.

"Who you callin' a lush, ya' drunken bitch?"

"You. Lush! Lush! Lush!"

In the dim light, Jack saw his father screw up his face, his eyes bulging out as if they were ripe grapes. He started to shake all over.

"You shut your damn mouth!" his father screamed.

"Injush try to make me. I'll shay whatever the hell I want."

Seth Powell raised his arm and staggered toward her. As he swung, he stumbled, hitting her a glancing blow on the shoulder. His momentum carried him forward and he fell sideways onto the bed, then rolled onto the floor. Elizabeth pushed the bedside lamp over on him.

"Sonuvabitch!" he yelled, struggling to untangle himself from the cord. "I'll get you for that."

"Stop it! Can't you both stop it!" Jack yelled suddenly, half screaming and half crying. "Why can't you be like other parents!"

His mother and father stopped in their tracks, staring at him wide-eyed, his father on his back tangled in the lamp cord, his mother looking as if she had been shot.

His outburst had surprised Jack as well. Now he didn't know what to do, so he stood there waiting, for what he didn't know.

His father reacted first. "Don't you yell at me, kid! Don't you ever yell at me! You're gonna be sorry for that!" he bellowed.

Jack was on the verge of shouting back at his father. Catching himself, he backed away and ran up the stairs to his bedroom. He fell on his bed and put his hands over his ears, expecting to hear his father stomp up the stairs and burst through his door. Well, let him, he said out loud. Then he'll really have a fight on his hands. He threw himself face down on his bed and hammered his pillows with both fists.

Jack waited until he was sure his mother and father were asleep. His stomach was growling. He hadn't eaten anything except a package of SnoBalls since breakfast. It had been quiet downstairs the rest of the evening. Probably they had both passed out early. He went to the top of the stairs and listened. A low, steady sound of static came from the living room and gray light flickered through the doorway. Jack crept down the steps and peered in. The blank screen flickered as the TV set produced a steady stream of white noise. Sprawled in his chair across from the TV was his father, yesterday's dirty undershirt stretched over his chest and stomach, hairy legs protruding from wrinkled boxer shorts, bare feet wide apart, head rolled to one side, mouth gaping open, arms hanging down on each side of the overstuffed chair. A beer bottle had fallen from his hand and lay in a wet pool on the thread-bare rug. A snort and a cough startled Jack, but his father merely rolled his head from one side to the other and remained unconscious.

Jack crossed the room on his tip-toes and went into their bedroom. His mother was in bed, breathing heavily. Gradually other shapes began to emerge in the room as his eyes became accustomed to the dark. It didn't take long to find what he was looking for. They were thrown over the dresser his father and mother shared. He lifted the pants gently, making sure nothing rattled, then slipped his hand into a side pocket. His fist closed around a few coins and a bill. He tried the other side pocket and only found a comb. For good measure he tried both hip pockets—a billfold and a gritty handkerchief. Shit, he muttered, where are they? As he walked over to the dresser, his foot brushed something on the floor that jingled. He froze, afraid his mother heard and would wake up. When she didn't, he reached down and picked up his father's keyring. It held several keys, but there was only one he wanted. He found it, parted the sides of the ring with his thumbnail and slid the key around until it came free. Gently he laid the key ring back on the floor noiselessly and put the key he wanted in his pocket.

The rumble in his stomach reminded him of what he needed to do next. He walked softly into the kitchen and opened the refrigerator. The sudden light from inside startled him. On the top shelf was a half-empty quart of milk. In the pantry he found a package of bread that still seemed soft and a jar of crunchy peanut butter. Holding on tightly to the things he had found, Jack retraced his steps. In the living room he paused, considered whether to turn off the TV, decided not to, then climbed the stairs to his room with gray light flickering behind him.

Chapter Twenty-Nine

The News

July 19, 1956

Henry walked through the front door with all the aplomb he could muster. His mind was still reeling from his encounter with Sonia Koske and the things she had told him. Roy Starker sat behind the newspaper in his easy chair. All Henry could see of him were his stocking feet resting on the hassock.

"You're late for dinner." The newspaper his father was holding didn't move. "Your mother's worried. Better go tell her you're home."

Henry started toward the kitchen, prepared to make a long apology, when the newspaper's headline caught his eye.

DENTIST AND DOCTOR MISSING ON BIG TOW

The words pushed any apology far from his mind. He stared at it for several seconds to be sure what it said.

"Dad, could I see the front page of the paper?"

The newspaper dropped revealing his father's face which wore an incredulous look.

"Did I hear that right? You want to see the front page? Henry, what's come over you?"

"Nothing. I don't always just read the sports and the comics."

"By all means, then, here it is."

Henry picked it up and started to read. According to the story, two prominent residents of Bruders Landing, a dentist and a doctor, had disappeared on Big Tow Island. Another doctor was in critical condition from a water moccasin bite and a hand mangled by an animal as yet unidentified. Searchers feared the two missing men had been killed by the same animal.

He was stunned. Maybe everything Ol' Lady Koske had told him that morning was true. He hadn't wanted to go to the sheriff only to be laughed at because of some crazy story from an old lady, but now maybe he should.

During dinner, the events on Big Tow were all his parents talked about. He listened to them mesmerized. His father believed the three men had been attacked by the same animal that killed Lloyd Wischmeier. He guessed it was a rabid badger that had somehow wandered into the Gerdes cellar, but had trouble explaining how it could cross the river to Big Tow Island. His theory was that the tunnel in the Gerdes cellar led through the bluff and under the river. Henry's mother disagreed. She thought the two events were a coincidence, that no animal had attacked the men. To her the attack on the island proved what people had said about Big Tow all along—that it was inhabited by some dangerous old men who do away with anyone who goes there.

When his mother and father realized how interested Henry was in their conversation, they asked him to promise never to go near Big Tow Island. Henry mumbled an answer that they heard as a promise. But Henry hadn't promised any such thing.

Chapter Thirty

The Boat Trip

July 20, 1956

The plastic cuckoo clock on the living room
wall rang eight tinny chimes as Jack crept quietly down
the stairs, an empty milk bottle in one hand, the peanut
butter jar in the other—and the key tucked in his
pocket. He touched its outline on the outside of his
pocket to be sure it was still there. The house was still.
His father always managed to leave for his job at the
ammunition plant by 7:30 no matter how much he
drank the night before. But Jack had waited until
nearly 8:00 just to be sure. He also hoped to avoid his
mother.

The living room was empty, the wet mark still
visible on rug. The bedroom was empty as well, the
bedspread pulled carelessly to the headboard.
Cautiously he looked through the doorway to the
kitchen. His mother wasn't there either. A dirty coffee
cup sat on the table by an ash tray brimming with ashes
and cigarette butts. She's either gone to the store or in
the cellar doing the washing, he thought to himself. He
crossed the kitchen, set the empty milk bottle and
peanut butter jar on the table, and went out the back

door, closing it quietly. Swinging his leg over the seat of his bicycle, he headed for Henry's house.

After his second knock, the door was opened by Henry's mother. "Well, good morning, Jack. You're certainly up bright and early for summer vacation. Would you like to come in? Henry's not up yet, but he should be pretty soon."

"Gee, I dunno, Mrs. Starker. I can just wait out here . . . or come back later." Jack was nervous around adults, and Henry's mother was no exception.

"Nonsense. You just come on inside and wake him up." She held the screen door open. "You go right on up to his room. It's time for him to get up anyway."

"Thanks, Mrs. Starker. I guess I will." Jack climbed the stairs two at a time, eager to be out of her sight.

When Jack opened the door to Henry's bedroom, a pillow struck him squarely in the face.

"What the . . ." he shouted, catching himself before he yelled something he didn't want Mrs. Starker to hear.

Henry stood on his bed laughing.

"Thanks a lot, Henry. Some greeting." Jack picked up the pillow from the floor and threw it back at Henry who was laughing too hard to duck. "Here I am, bringing you the chance of a lifetime and you ambush me."

Henry stopped laughing. "What kind of chance?"

"A chance to do something *really* exciting. Something you've never done before."

"Oh, yeah? Like what?"

Jack reached into the pocket of his jeans and brought out the key. "Guess what this is?"

"A key."

"Of course it's a key. I mean, guess what it's a key *to*."

"How would I know?"

"Well, just guess. I'll give you a nickel if you get it right."

"Um, OK. Let me see . . . it's the key to your Dad's boat."

Jack was crestfallen. "Shh, not so loud. I don't

want your mom to hear. How'd you know?"

"You mean I was right?"

"Yeah, you guessed it." Jack reached back into his jeans and pulled out a nickel which he flipped to Henry.

"Thanks. Now tell me, what're you going to do when your dad catches you with it?"

"I don't care if he catches me," Jack snapped. "I just don't care. Besides, I'll put it back tonight before he even knows it's gone. I just want it for today, to do one thing. Go to Big Tow Island."

Henry's face lit up. "Really? Will you really take your Dad's boat to Big Tow?"

"Yeah, if you want to."

"Sure I want to. But you heard about those three guys that got attacked out there. Two of them are still missing."

"Yeah, I heard. Maybe we can find out what happened to them. Maybe even find the guys who're missing."

"When do you want to leave?"

"As soon as you're out of bed. But you have to hurry."

"Oh, man!" Henry leaped out of bed and started rapidly going through drawers looking for clothes.

Jack stood near the door watching. "Um, I was, um, thinking Sheila might want to go, too. Do you think she would?"

"Sheila?" Henry answered vaguely, his head inside a drawer.

'Yeah. She talked about wanting to."

"OK. She might."

"We can ride by and see."

Henry stopped rummaging. "Yeah, let's go ask her. I have to have something to tell my Mom anyway."

When they walked into the kitchen, Delores Starker was sweeping the back porch. Henry put his finger to his lips and motioned for Jack to follow him. Quietly Henry opened the door to their pantry and held out two apples. Jack stuffed them in his pocket. Next came a box of animal crackers. Jack slipped the cloth handle around his wrist as he looked to make sure

Henry's mother wasn't about to catch him in the act.

"Here, take as many as you want," Henry whispered. Jack blinked to be sure what he saw. Henry held a newly-opened package of Oreo cookies. Jack managed to grab five in one hand and put them inside his shirt.

Henry's mother was sweeping dirt into a dustpan as they walked onto the porch on their way outside.

"Mom, we're going to ride our bikes over to Sheila's. OK?"

"Sure, that's fine." She stood up, careful not to spill the dirt. "Tell Grandma and Grandpa I'll call them about Sunday dinner. Did you boys have some breakfast?"

"Yeah. We took some apples."

"Uh, thanks, Mrs. Starker."

"Will you be back for lunch?"

"Maybe, probably not."

"OK, but be home by 5:30 for supper, Henry."

Sheila was on the porch helping her mother unpack a box when they rode up. Henry greeted his aunt and motioned to Sheila to come outside. Jack felt his shyness return, but he was determined to be the one to tell her their plan. As soon as Sheila was out of earshot of her mother, he told her in a whisper. At first she was surprised, then skeptical. Henry began coaxing her. Jack crossed his fingers. When she nodded her head, he did a little jump.

On their way to the river, Sheila rode alongside him. "Gosh, Jack, how'd you get your dad to let you take out his boat?"

Jack had expected the question. "Oh, um, he just said since I'm 14, I'm allowed to use the boat when he doesn't need it to go fishin'."

"Even out on the Mississippi?"

"Yeah, of course. That's where he keeps it."

"Gee, that's great. You must be the only kid in our class that gets to take a boat out by yourself on the river. How'd you learn what to do, where to go?'

"Oh, I just watched my Dad."

"That's enough? You *have* taken it out before by yourself, haven't you?"

"Sure, I have." Jack wasn't sure his lie sounded convincing. He waited for Henry to say something, but Henry wasn't listening.

"How many times?"

"Um, let's see, oh, maybe . . ."

"Jack, you tell the truth, now. You've never taken it out by yourself, have you?"

"I have, too."

"Well, I sure hope so. Anyway, it's a nice day so the water'll be calm."

The scattered clouds from the early morning had disappeared. The sun rose high overhead into a powder blue sky. The wind had all but disappeared and heat started to build. Jack led them down a dirt road to the south end of Flint Cliffs Marina where several Jon boats rested on the bank, their flat bows pulled onto the mud at the water's edge, looking nearly identical in their olive drab paint. Each one was secured by a long chain or cable locked to large metal eyelets that protruded from a block of concrete. Jack got off his bicycle next to the chain securing his father's boat and reached into his pocket for the key.

"Where should we put our bikes?" Henry asked.

"Behind the cement there, I guess. They'll be OK. Nobody comes here much except on weekends," Jack answered, thinking Sheila would expect him to know.

"Do you need to get some gas?" Sheila asked.

Jack almost panicked. He hadn't thought about gas. His father always filled a gas tank and brought it with him to the boat when he took it out. "I have to check in the boat," he answered as calmly as he could.

He looked in the boat's stern. A squatty, red tank sat by the motor with the gas lines attached. He almost sighed with relief. At least the tank is there. He also noticed several empty beer cans littering the bottom of the boat. That's one good thing about his drinking yesterday, Jack thought, he forgot to take the gas can home with him. He climbed into the boat, grabbed the can by the handle and lifted. It was heavy. Gas sloshed inside. He sat it back down and looked at the gauge on top. It read half full. Was that enough? It would have to be. He had no money to buy more.

Jack climbed back on shore and opened the padlock with the key. "OK. Let's go. Sheila, go ahead and climb in. Sit in the back so Henry and me can push it out."

Sheila did as he asked.

"I'm ready when you are." Henry grinned. "Let's go find those bad old guys."

"All right, let's push"

They both bent over and pushed on the bow. The boat didn't budge.

"We gotta push harder," Jack said, straightening up.

"OK. Let's try it again. On three."

They both counted to three out loud and pushed, grunting loudly. There was a grating sound and the boat started to slide. A startled blue heron standing on the shore a several yards away flapped its broad wings and rose into the air.

"Go, Henry! We got it!"

"Yeah, here it goes."

The boat slid faster. When they were about to step in the water, Jack yelled: "In, Henry, jump in!"

Henry took one last step, his feet in the water, and lunged into the boat. "Shit! I lost my shoe!"

Jack took two more steps, both in the water. He felt the boat float free and his feet sink into mud. Pushing down hard on the bow with both hands, he pulled them out and rolled into the bottom of the boat. "We did it!"

"Good for you guys!" Sheila called out. Jack was elated.

"Yeah, but I'm still missing a shoe." Henry rose to his knees. "Wait, there it is. It's floating right there. Get us back where I can grab it.'

Jack looked around the boat's bottom. He remembered a paddle somewhere. Then he saw his feet. Mud covered his shoes and socks up to his ankles.

"Here's a paddle," Sheila cried. "I'll get us back." She paddled as if the Jon boat was a canoe, first on one side then the other until the stern of the boat edged near Henry's shoe.

"Now don't fall in," she called out as Henry

stretched out over the water. "You don't have a life jacket on." Jack was surprised to see her wearing one and he began looking for two more. He found three stuffed along the gunwales, their original orange color badly faded. Two were smudged with dirt. He handed the clean one to Henry.

"That's one way to get it clean." Henry proudly held up his dripping shoe. "Guess I might as will do the other one." He took off his other shoe, leaned over the side and swished it around in the water.

Jack looked at his feet again. Just taking off his shoes wasn't going to do it. Scooting to the side of the boat, he swung his legs over and plunged both feet into the water, splashing vigorously. When Henry leaned over to watch, the top of the boat's gunwale dipped near the water.

"Hey! Don't sink us! One of you has to get on the other side!" Sheila shouted.

Jack pulled his feet out, mortified that Sheila had shouted at him. Henry jumped back to the other side, rocking the boat and nearly falling overboard. Sheila giggled.

"Dammit, Sheila, scare us to death, why don't you," Henry said.

"Guess I better take these off and let 'em dry." Jack stuck his feet into the air, letting the water drip down his legs. Sheila giggled again.

It took Jack three pulls on the starter rope to get the motor running. He was grateful his father had let him start it the few times they had gone fishing so he didn't look like a complete beginner in front of Sheila. He twisted the throttle letting the boat turn slowly and headed toward the open water of the Mississippi.

By the time they reached the main channel, Jack was gripping the throttle so tightly his knuckles had turned white. He began to think he had made a very big mistake. This was it, his first time driving a boat on the Mississippi River. And he was on his own. Henry and Sheila knew even less about boats and the river than he did. He was responsible for them, for everything that happened. This was no time to panic or act afraid.

A light wind raised small ripples on the river's otherwise smooth surface. Jack had only seen Big Tow Island from the Gerdes farm, but he assumed they could find it simply by heading north. Across the broad expanse of river to Illinois, the water looked endless and threatening. He quickly turned the boat north to stay close to shore as they headed to the island.

The Jon boat jarred them slightly as its flat bottom struck the ripples. Henry and Sheila seemed to be thoroughly enjoying the ride. Jack was envious. Sheila called out landmarks as they went by—Kotloff's boat house, Pumping Station Park, the public boat landing, the mouth of Flint Creek. As they continued north, the bluff gradually retreated from the river and they arrived at a section of shore occupied by a series of cabins, all built high on stilts. Sheila picked out the one she wanted, a white one, then asked Jack to pick. They all looked wonderful, he would have loved any of them. Finally he chose a yellow one with a stout-looking wood dock where two boats were moored. She approved.

As they continued on uneventfully, Jack started to gain confidence in his control of the boat. The sun rose higher, warming the top of his head and shoulders. Soon he was steering nonchalantly while he stared at the cabins Sheila pointed out. Soon the bluff came forward again, practically to the water's edge, towering over their heads as if it might crush them. Jack studied the trees that grew from the crevices, wondering how they did it. Henry sat stiffly on the boat seat, staring at the bluff as intently as if he was struggling with an algebra problem. Sheila was lying across a seat with her head on a life jacket letting her legs dangle over the side, her eyes closed. Jack was nearly lulled to sleep by the drone of the motor. His eyes wanted to close so he fought to stay alert by watching for fish that would occasionally leap from the water. A heavy thump from under the boat sent a shock though his his body.

"Jeez, what was that?" Jack craned his neck to see over the bow.

Henry sat up and looked at the water behind them. "We hit a tree limb, see it?"

Jack turned in his seat. Bobbing in the water a

few feet behind the motor was a log.

"Sorry, Jack," Sheila said, "we should have been watching but I got too sleepy. It doesn't sound like it hurt anything, do you think?"

"Naw, everything's OK," Jack said, anxious to absolve Sheila of any blame.

"Sheila, you really have to do better. Fall asleep on your watch again and you walk the plank," Henry said.

Sheila leaned over the side of the boat reaching into the river and threw a handful of water at Henry.

"You're really asking for it now," he said as he reached over the side and started splashing handfuls of water at Sheila moving his arm like a windmill.

She covered her face, then leaned over the side and began splashing at Henry, wetting Jack in the process. Jack tucked his head down by his knees, enjoying the feel of the cool water as the drops landed on the back of his neck and in his hair. They stopped the splashing when the boat began to rock dangerously.

"You started it, Sheila. You bail." Henry pointed to water sloshing in the bottom.

"I've got it." Jack said. "There's not much."

"No, make her do it."

But Jack already had a can in his hand, scooping up water in one hand and holding the throttle in the other.

"Look! That's the cemetery up there." Sheila was looking toward the top of the bluff they were passing. "We're almost to Grandma and Grandpa's farm."

"Then that must be Big Tow Island." Jack pointed to the head of an island in the distance.

Henry shielded his eyes and gazed across the shimmering water. "That's it, all right."

To reach Big Tow they would have to cross the channel. Jack's palms grew sweaty. He told himself the channel here was narrower than at the marina, that they would make it across in just a few minutes. Gripping the throttle tightly, he twisted. The engine growled and he turned the boat toward the island. He wanted to get this over quickly.

Jack was tense for the time they were out of

reach of either shore, but they crossed the open water without a hitch. When the boat approached the southern tip of the island, Jack began to relax. He throttled the motor back and turned north again, along the island's shore. Henry and Sheila stared intently into the trees at the water's edge. A blanket of wild grape vines hung from the branches like a sheets of green chain mail, making the island look impenetrable.

"Look for a place to put in," Henry called out.

"Oh sure, and how are we going to get through all that stuff hanging from the trees?" Sheila answered.

They continued on without talking for several hundred yards, all eyes on the shore.

"How long is this island anyway?" Jack asked.

"Miles," Sheila answered. "It goes way past Grandma and Grandpa's farm."

"Look! There's some kind of opening there." Henry pointed to an inlet under the vines. "Maybe we can get in there."

"C'mon, Jack. Let's try!" Sheila said eagerly.

Jack worried whether the water would be deep enough. He knew the boat drew little water, but if they got stuck . . . well, they could probably push themselves off with the oars. He turned the boat toward the island.

They entered the inlet, gliding under a canopy of vine-covered trees. The bright sunlight was replaced by shade and the air became cooler. A pungent odor of river water and sunbaked vegetation surrounded them. Jack stared into the trees trying to see what was ahead, but their low branches blocked his view. "I can't see any place to get through."

"Look straight ahead. It looks like the water keeps going," Sheila told him.

"Where?" Henry asked, leaning forward to look.

"Right there," she answered, pointing. "Under those trees."

Sighting down Sheila's arm, Jack saw an opening through the trees that looked like the mouth of a cave with a watery floor.

"I don't know if the water's deep enough."

"We can at least try," Sheila retorted. "We can always push the boat out again."

"Sure, we can try. Watch those branches that're hangin' down." Jack felt a stab of embarrassment. He should never have even hesitated. Now she'll think I'm chicken. He opened the throttle slightly, steering the boat toward the narrow space of dark water.

In the bow Sheila readied herself to push the branches out of the way.

Henry picked up an oar and pushed it into the water. " We've got plenty of water." He pulled the dripping oar back out. "I couldn't touch bottom."

As they entered the opening, Sheila lifted the branches over her head. "Watch out!" she called, "I can't hold them."

Sheila and the front half of the boat disappeared into the leaves. Henry ducked down in his seat to let the branches pass over his head. Jack crouched low as they came toward him, then he was engulfed in leaves as branches scraped across his back. It occurred to him that instead of being stuck on the bottom they could become tangled in tree limbs. But he didn't dare stop now.

Sheila suddenly shouted: "Hey, we're clear!"

A moment later Jack felt the sun on his back again. He sat up. They were in a narrow waterway with tall reeds, marsh grasses and cattails on both sides. A breeze caused the boat to sway slightly.

"Hey, we made it!" Henry exclaimed. "We're in here. We're actually in Big Tow Island."

"Right, but where do we go now?" Sheila slumped in her seat. "We can't just get out and go walking around. There's water everywhere."

"We just have to find some solid ground," Henry answered. "Let's keep going."

"We can if there's enough water," Jack said. "You better check again."

Henry picked up the wet oar and thrust it down into the water. This time it stopped two-thirds of the way up the handle. When he pulled it out, mud slithered off the end. "I'd say it's nearly four feet. That's enough, isn't it?"

Jack heard but was slow to answer. He was remembering a boat trip with his father and how the motor died when the propeller got tangled in weeds. There were weeds all around them, but he wasn't going to sound like a chicken again. "I guess it's enough."

"Let's go on then and I'll keep checking."

Jack twisted the throttle and the boat began to move forward. He sat as tall as he could on the seat and craned his neck, following the band of water that wound randomly through the reeds and marsh grass. Mosquitoes soon found them and buzzed near his ear. He swatted at them with his free hand. Sheila and Henry were doing the same. A chorus of frogs serenaded them from deep in the reeds. The sun was now directly overhead, scorching his shoulders and back through his shirt. He debated whether to take it off.

Suddenly Sheila yelled: "There's an alligator! Look!"

Henry and Jack both jumped up, causing the boat to rock. Ahead to the right Jack saw what Sheila was looking at. It *did* look like an alligator..

"Sheila, what are you yelling about? There aren't any alligators around here." Henry shielded his eyes. "That's just a log."

"Made you look, didn't I. Anyway, it looks like an alligator. You can go back to sleep now."

When they were close to the partly submerged log, two bumps on top moved, then plopped into the water. "Back to sleep?" Jack said. "The only ones sleeping were those turtles. And we had to come along and wake them up."

Sheila's giggle gave Jack confidence, realizing he could say things to make her laugh.

After several more minutes, the waterway narrowed. As the grass and reeds closed in around them, Jack began to worry about the propeller. The last thing he wanted to do was sound chicken, but Henry and Sheila had no idea what could happen. "Hey, do you think we should turn around?. These reeds are gettin' thick. If they get in the prop, we could get stuck here."

"C'mon, Jack, just a little farther." Henry raised out of his seat. "I see some trees up ahead so we *have* to be coming to dry ground."

Sheila stood to look. "I see them, but they all look dead."

Jack stood up to look as well, shifting his weight from foot to foot to keep the boat steady. In the distance he could see the tops of bare trees, their gray branches woven together like giant brambles.

"See them, Jack?" Henry asked.

"Yeah. Sheila's right, though. They all look dead."

"Let's just go that far and see if there's dry ground."

"What do you say, Sheila? Do you want to?"

"It's all right with me, but I don't want to get stuck. You turn around whenever you think we need to, no matter what Henry says."

"All right, as far as those trees. Then we're turnin' around."

Jack sat back down and twisted the throttle. It took longer than he expected to reach their target. As they approached the trees, the high grass and reeds closed in on them. Sheila pushed them aside but they became thicker, nearly obliterating their watery trail. Henry moved forward to help her. Then Jack was struck with another worry—once they got to those dead trees, could they find their way back?

"Don't worry, Jack," Henry called out as if he read his mind. "We're almost there."

"I'm not worried about getting there as much as I am getting back. This stuff is getting so thick I don't know whether we'll be able to find the way we came."

"Like Indians. We'll just follow the broken reeds."

Jack wasn't convinced, but the sea of grass and reeds suddenly ended and the boat glided into a forest of dead trees. Over the years since their death, the sun had bleached the trees to a light gray, while the wind and weather had twisted their trunks and limbs into grotesque shapes. Jack's imagination likened them to some kind of creatures ready to pounce on any intruders, as they might have done to those men last week.

The sunlight dimmed, filtered by the lifeless branches overhead. Jack began to feel uneasy. He shifted into neutral, letting the motor idle as he stared at the naked trees, making sure they didn't turn into something else. Over the sound of the idling motor came the melancholy call of a lone gull, its cry echoing among the brittle branches. The frog chorus had vanished, left behind in the reeds. Around the tree trunks stood pools of stagnant water brimming with rotting branches and vegetation that filled the air with an odor of decay. Between the pools he saw nothing but mud that looked as if it could swallow anyone who stepped in it. Jack stared at the scene, picturing countless squirming creatures living in dark brown slime just beneath the surface.

A tree trunk with no upper limbs caught his eye. It had somehow become twisted, its surface blemished with craggy holes and protrusions. The more he stared, the more its features seemed to form an elongated face with deep set eyes that frowned at him wickedly. He almost cried out before he forced himself to look away. It's only a tree, he told himself.

They were all quiet, taking in the eerie landscape. Henry broke the silence. "I wonder where those guys were when they were attacked?"

"What are you talking about? What guys?" Sheila asked.

"The guys that got attacked out here," Henry answered.

"You mean here on this island? When?"

"A couple days ago. Didn't you hear about it?"

A water snake slithered from an exposed tree root into the water. Jack saw it but said nothing, listening.

"No, I didn't. Maybe you ought to tell me, Henry."

"Heck, it's been in the newspaper and everyone's talking about it."

"I guess I'm the only one who doesn't know, so tell me."

Henry told her what he remembered from the newspaper story.

"Did they catch whatever did it?"

"I don't think so."

"Henry Starker. Would you tell me what we're doing here then?" Sheila leaned toward him, anger blazing in her eyes. "Why do you have to bring me to places like this? You watch! This will turn out just like the time we went into that tunnel in Grandma and Grandpa's cellar. And the thing that attacked those doctors is probably the same thing that killed Lloyd."

"How could that be, way out here? Besides, isn't this exciting? We could be exploring a place nobody's ever been before. Hardly anyone ever comes here because of the stories."

"I know. And it sounds like they're true."

Jack listened to them argue, goosebumps rising on his skin in spite of the warm sun. "Wh-what do you think attacked them?"

"It probably was those old guys you hear about." Sheila picked up the can Jack had used to bail as if she was about to throw it at Henry. "They probably exist, you know. Stories like that aren't made-up out of thin air."

"I'll bet there *is* something to those stories," Jack said, eager to agree with Sheila.

Henry glared at him, a look of betrayal on his face. "Why did you want to come out here then?" he asked sharply.

The sting in Henry's voice caught Jack by surprise. "Because you and Sheila said out at the farm that we should explore Big Tow Island sometime."

"Right. We *all* wanted to. But that was before those three men were attacked, which changes everything as far as I'm concerned." She threw the can at the bottom of the boat.

"OK, OK. I'm sorry I didn't tell you. I thought everyone knew about it. Look, we're safe enough in the boat, but we can turn around and go back right now if you want."

Without the slightest hesitation, Sheila said: "I say we go back now."

"Let's at least be democratic. What do you say, Jack? Do you want to turn back or look around first?"

Jack had been thinking about the men who had been attacked while he kept his eye on the barren trees to be sure nothing was lurking behind them. He was slow to grasp Henry's question. "Wha-? Um, go back now? Well, if Sheila wants . . ."

"OK, OK, you're going to do whatever Sheila wants. Let's go ahead and turn around." Disappointment showed on his face.

Jack felt he couldn't win. He had sided with a girl, a girl that made him feel things he had never felt before, and betrayed his oldest and best friend as a result. His arm was heavy as he shifted the boat into forward. The space was tight. He would need some help turning the boat around.

"Sheila, can you take the oar and push us back around when we get close to the bank?" he called. He was embarrassed asking Sheila.

"Sure, I'll get it."

Sheila picked up the oar by her feet. As the bow approached the bank, she set the oar against a log and pushed. Jack shifted into reverse and backed toward the opposite bank, going as close as he dared. When black mud started churning at the stern, he quickly shifted into forward and headed back the way they came.

"Way to go." Sheila gave him a beaming smile. A warm glow spread through his entire body. Now all they had to do was to find their way out.

As the boat left the old trees, Jack sat straight in his seat looking for mashed and broken reeds that would tell him the way they came, but the reeds were tall and untouched everywhere he looked.

"Do you see where we came out?" he asked.

"I'm looking," Henry answered.

"What about there?" Sheila pointed to a spot.

"Yeah, that could be it," Henry answered. "Let's try it."

Jack steered the boat toward the place he thought she meant. He increased the speed, thinking they might have to force their way. When the boat reached the line of reeds, its blunt bow rode over them and they began to slow.

"Dammit!" Jack shouted, twisting the throttle. The motor responded with a high-pitched growl, but they continued to go slower. He opened the throttle wide. The motor raced momentarily, then began to sputter, gave a wheezing cough and died.

"Oh, swell." Sheila turned toward them and folded her arms. "Now what do we do?"

"Shit! I *knew* those weeds would get all tangled up in the prop." Jack struck the throttle with his palm.

"Can't we get them out?" Henry asked.

"I guess we can try." Jack was mortified. He had failed to get them through the reeds and had fouled the propeller trying, maybe ruining the motor. All in front of Sheila!

"You guess? Look, we *have* to get it untangled unless we want to spend the night here waiting for someone to find us." Sheila turned to Henry, then to Jack. "You both remember who we told where we were going, don't you?"

Henry looked up at the sky. Jack was perplexed.

"*No one*, that's who. No one knows where we are, so if we aren't back by dark, our parents will go crazy and have everyone under the sun out looking for us. But they'll have no idea where to look."

Jack's face felt like it was on fire. Why did he always have to do such dumb things? Especially around people he wanted to like him the most. Was there any way he could ever redeem himself to Sheila? He *had* to get them out of there.

"Don't worry, I'll get it untangled." Jack spoke as confidently as he could.

"How?" Henry asked. "Do you have to get in the water?"

"I don't think so. Somehow the motor lifts up. Let me see if I can get it." Jack got on his knees, stuck his head out over the water and peered down at the mechanism that attached the motor to the boat. He had watched his father tilt the motor and remembered a latch somewhere he had pulled. He spied a handle that looked like a possibility and pulled on it. There was a metallic click, but nothing happened.

"Hey, Henry," he called, bent over the stern. "Pull up on the back of the motor when I say. OK, now."

Henry pulled and the motor slowly tilted forward. The propeller emerged from the water in a snarl of reeds and grass.

"We got it up!" Jack shouted.

"Good work, you guys," Sheila said. Jack felt her hand on his back as she leaned over to look, her face next to his ear. His skin started to tingle. "Want me to help get those weeds off?"

"I'll do it," he answered and began tearing at the tangle with both hands. The strands were tough and wiry. After working for several minutes, he stood up to stretch.

"Here, I'll do the rest." Henry bent over the back of the boat.

"They're all out," Henry shouted moments later. He straightened up and shook a long string of mud-coated grass from his hand. "The prop's free. Give the motor a try. Want me to pull?"

"No, that's OK. I'll do it," Jack answered, eager to do something that might impress Sheila. He first twisted the throttle slightly, then braced himself. With a firm hold on the handle of the starter rope, he pulled hard. The motor coughed twice. He pulled again, and again the motor coughed. After several fruitless tries, he squatted down on his haunches, out of breath.

"Maybe it's just flooded," Henry suggested. "Doesn't that happen with motors?"

"Yeah," Sheila agreed. "I remember when Grandpa's tractor gets flooded. He waits a few minutes, then tries again. Usually it works, I think. Just give it a minute."

"Same thing on cars," Henry offered, "except Dad sometimes pumps the gas pedal. That helps it start."

Jack remembered what *his* father did when their old Dodge wouldn't start. Usually he was drunk when it happened. First he would grind the starter until the battery wore down. Then he would open the door and lift himself out of the front seat shouting every foul swear word Jack had ever heard. He prayed the neighbors couldn't hear, but he knew they did. Next his father would stand in front of the car and kick the bumper and front fenders. With each kick the whole car rattled. When his father got tired of kicking, he would climb back in the driver's seat and punch the starter hard with his foot. This time the old Dodge would start, mostly to avoid more punishment, Jack believed. He could relate to that.

"All right, let me try it again now." He hit the top of the motor with the palm of his hand as he braced himself. "For luck," he announced. He gave a hard yank on the starter rope. The motor coughed, started to run roughly then smoothed out.

"Good going," Sheila cried out over the sound of the motor. "Let's get out of here."

Jack backed the boat out of the tall grass. When they were clear, he shifted to neutral and let the motor idle. "What do we do now," he wondered out loud, "try another place?"

"I say we go the other way," Henry said, looking earnestly at Sheila. "Look, we tried going back through that grass and it didn't work. We must be almost halfway across the island already and I'll bet this stream or creek or whatever it is goes all the way through. We'll come out on the other side, then we can head back."

"OK," Sheila answered, "I guess that's the thing to do, but I sure hope you're right. What about you, Jack? You want to try going across?"

"Yeah, I guess. It's the only other way to go." He shifted into forward and turned the boat toward the island's interior.

When they reached the place where they had turned around moments earlier, Jack felt them passing a point of no return. His uneasiness returned and his eyes darted from tree to tree, making sure nothing was watching. It was well past noon and the sun bore down heavily through the bare branches. The air was hot and damp. Jack drove the boat slowly, following the winding waterway through the dead trees, wary of logs or branches that could foul the propeller. Twice they came to trees which had fallen across the water but managed to get under the large trunks. Sweat ran down his face and chest, soaking his shirt. He wiped his face with the back of his hand, wishing he dared go faster so there would be a breeze. He remembered the apple in his pocket but the sour smell of decay and stagnant water had taken away his appetite. Henry and Sheila were quiet, staring at the dark brown water in front of them.

The fun was gone.

"Look up ahead!" Henry called out. The sudden sound of a voice made Jack jump in his seat. "We're coming out of these old trees."

Jack stood slightly to see over Henry's head. It was true, the dead trees ended just ahead. A welcome sense of relief swept over him.

"At last. Do you think we're across?" Sheila asked, sounding hopeful.

"Maybe . . . I sure hope so," Henry answered, "but it seems awfully soon."

Jack could now see open water and a shoreline in the distance.

"Look beyond that water," Sheila cried. "Do you think that's Illinois?"

"Can't tell," Henry said as he stared ahead.

A moment later the boat passed beneath the last of the bare trees, and Jack saw that the open water was only a large pond. With no wind, its glassy surface reflected the trees and reeds that lined its shore. The only sound was their idling motor. Jack's spirits sank again.

Henry pointed to the shore across the water. "That sure isn't Illinois."

"So tell us, where do we go now?" Sheila stood and waved her arms, gesturing at the shore around them as she talked. "Do you see any way out of here?" She sat down again, crossing her arms, an exasperated pout on her face.

"No, but just because we can't see one from here doesn't mean there isn't one. Maybe if we cruise around the edge we'll find one."

Jack saw no sign of a way out of the pond except for the way they came. "Yeah, that's what we'll have to do."

"How's the gas?" Sheila asked. "It seems like we must've used a lot."

Jack checked the gauge on top of the fuel tank apprehensively. He hadn't looked at it since they left the marina. The gauge read between a quarter and a half a tank. "There's enough to get back," he answered without knowing for sure.

"Good, if only we knew *how* to get back. And what about the things that attacked those men? The longer we're here, the more time they'll have to find us."

Jack was quick to reassure her. "We should be safe as long as we're out here in the water."

He looked over to Henry expecting him to nod in agreement, but Henry was sitting unusually still, staring vacantly toward the opposite shore. He looked strange, Jack thought, as if he had fallen asleep with his eyes open. Then Henry's mouth opened slowly as if he was about to speak. Instead of speaking, his mouth gradually closed, and he continued to sit stiffly, staring into the distance.

A moment later Sheila also not!ced that Henry was acting strangely. "Henry! Henry!", she called out, trying to get his attention. Still he remained rigid, nothing moving except his mouth which slowly began to open again.

"C'mon, Henry, what are you doing?" she asked in a loud voice. Henry gave no sign he heard her, but his mouth continued to open and close as if he was talking in slow motion.

"Hey, Henry," Jack shouted. "Wake up! We gotta get going!" Henry's eyes remained vacant. Only his mouth moved. Jack started to worry that Henry wasn't acting.

Sheila shifted next to Henry and pushed his shoulder. "Hey you! Come on back here." Henry's upper body moved with her push then returned to its former position like a plastic clown with a weight in its base. She looked quizzically at Jack. "What do you think's wrong with him?"

"I don't have a clue. I've never seen him act like this before. Do you think he's sick?"

"Oh, he's probably just acting. Henry, cut it out now!" she shouted in his ear. "We've had enough."

Jack watched the expression on Henry's face start to change. His mouth remained open but his eyes began to focus, as if he had decided to look at some distant object over the water. His eyes began to widen, changing the vacant expression on his face to one of wonder or disbelief.

"C'mon, Henry, quit it. You're scaring us," Sheila pleaded. When he still didn't respond, she put her face directly in front of his, blocking his view. "Henry, if you don't stop, I'm going to throw water on you."

Henry leaned slowly to one side to avoid her face and continued to stare across the water. Sheila again put her face in front of his and he returned to his upright position, still staring into the distance. "C'mon, Henry, quit playing games. We've got to get out of here," she begged. His face remained blank.

With an exasperated look, Sheila reached over the side, filled her cupped hand with water and threw it in his face. "See!" she said. "I told you."

Water dripped down his nose and chin. Henry hadn't even flinched.

"I'm warning you, Henry, if you don't quit I'll do it again." And she did. Still he stayed rigidly in place, but his mouth began to open again and his eyes narrowed. Sheila returned to her seat in the bow and looked away huffily.

"Jeez, it's like he's in some kind of trance."

"Whatever he's in, he's going in the water next if he doesn't quit it."

"It looks like he's staring at something, maybe that's what's making him act like that." Jack shielded his eyes and looked at the opposite shore. The bright sun made brilliant sparkles on the water. Jack squinted. He could see nothing but the reeds and trees. He strained to get a clearer view. This time he saw something different—an old tree trunk with a pointed top out among the reeds. He blinked and stared again. It looked even more like a figure, like a person. He looked away for a moment to rest his eyes, then he stared again. Yes, it *must* be a person, standing out in the water. It looked like it was wearing dark clothing and held a long stick or spear. A chill ran across his skin like a cold wind, making all the hair on his body stand upright.

"Look at that!" he called anxiously to Sheila. "Look over there along the shore. Do you see it?"

"Where?"

"There. Where Henry's staring." Jack pointed.

"It's probably a broken tree trunk, but it could be a person."

"I don't . . . wait, I think I see it. Yeah, I see it! It looks like it *is* a person."

Jack was getting frightened. "What if it's one of those . . . things."

"You said we'll be safe in the boat. Let's go closer."

Jack reluctantly pushed the shift lever forward and twisted the throttle slightly. Henry's head turned slowly with the boat, continuing to stare at the object.

They had gone barely ten yards when Sheila yelled. "Jack! Stop! I can see him."

Jack twisted the throttle to idle and steered left. As the boat came around, he looked intensely at the shore, searching again for the figure. Then he saw it. In the sunlight. It *was* a person, someone in a long dark robe or gown wearing a tall, pointed hat. An old man with a white beard and long straight hair that flowed onto his shoulders, standing so straight and stiff Jack thought it might be a carving. Where his feet should be, Jack could see nothing. The old man appeared to be floating. But Jack could see his eyes—two bright spots that gleamed as if they were reflecting the sun.

Suddenly Henry spoke. "They're here. The Keepers." His voice sounded breathless.

Startled, Jack jerked, hitting the gunwale with his back making the boat rock.

"Whoa, easy there." Henry gripped his seat to steady himself.

Sheila yelled at him. "Henry! It's about time. What were you doing?"

"Listening to the Keepers," he said, somewhat dazed.

"The Keepers? Who're the Keepers?"

"They live here on the island, just like Mrs. Koske said."

Words leaped out of Jack's mouth. "Old Lady Koske? When did she tell you that?"

"Yesterday. At her house."

"You were at her house?" Sheila sounded as surprised as Jack.

353

"Sure. She was nice."

"What? You mean she told you about those Keepers?"

"Yeah."

"For pete's sake, Henry, you knew all this before and you still got me to come out here?"

"Yeah, I wanted to see if we could find them."

"Did you know, too?" she demanded, turning to Jack.

Jack shrunk down in his seat. "No, I didn't. Honest. This is the first time I heard it."

"Darn it, Henry. That really makes me mad. You should have told us."

"Well, maybe I should have. I wanted to, but I was afraid you wouldn't come."

"You're probably right. I don't believe this. You were always afraid of that old woman. What all did she say?" Sheila asked.

"I can't tell you. She made me promise."

"Well, heck with you."

"Was that one of them?" Jack nodded toward the shore. But when he looked again, the figure was gone. "There was someone standing right there a minute ago, someone tall in dark clothes. It looked like an old wizard."

"That was one. They all look like that, I think."

Jack was puzzled. "You looked as if you were in a trance or something. How did you hear them? We didn't hear anything."

"I don't know, really. All of a sudden this old book popped up in my head, like some kind of dream. It opened to pages with strange writing, then I could understand somebody talking, but not really talking, like the words were just there in my head somehow."

Jack was relieved to see Henry back to his old self but wasn't sure whether he was excited or terrified by what Henry was telling them. "We were yelling at you but you didn't move."

"You were yelling? Jeez, I couldn't hear anything but those words in my head."

"What did he say to you?" Sheila leaned toward Henry, looking eager to hear more.

"I'm trying to remember. I think there was more than one, but only one talked to me. Sometimes it was like some of them were talking to each other."

"We only saw one."

"The others were back in those trees. Anyway, he wanted to know if I could hear. He asked over and over until I answered."

"We saw your mouth moving, but we didn't hear you say anything."

"Really? I thought I did. Anyway, that Keeper heard me. He said we shouldn't be here but they wouldn't do anything to us because they wanted me to deliver a message to the people that lived in the village by the river. I guess he meant Bruders Landing."

"Do you think we're safe then? That they won't do anything to us?" Jack interrupted.

"Oh, yeah, at least I think we are."

"Go on, Henry, what else did he say?" Sheila asked.

"They said the Gathering are awake and hungry, but there isn't enough food again." Henry's answers were beginning to make Jack frightened.

"Again? Who are the Gathering? What do they eat?"

"They didn't tell me all that."

"Well, then, what's the message you're supposed to deliver?" Sheila's voice had begun to quiver.

"That the Gathering can't find enough food and are starving, so people in the town have to give them food like they did last time."

"Last time?" Sheila asked. "What does that mean?"

"That's all they said. That people need to provide food like last time. Then they told me how to get back to the river."

"Great!" Jack exclaimed. "How?"

"Back the way we came. They said we'd find the way this time."

"Then I say we get started before it gets too late."

"Wait a minute. Why am I all wet?" Henry asked, feeling his hair and shirt.

"Because you wouldn't talk to us," Sheila

answered. "Now let's go. We'll see if those Keepers really know how we can get out of here."

Jack turned the boat and headed back through the trees, glancing at both banks as they went, afraid he would see the figure at any moment. When they were in sight of the reeds, he began looking for the opening. He saw it immediately, a space where sparse reeds had been bent and broken. "There's the place right there. Why didn't we see it before?"

"Are you sure that's not the last place we tried?" Sheila asked.

"No, the reeds were a lot thicker. This must be the place. Let's head for it," Henry exclaimed.

As the boat neared the spot, Jack could see the waterway they had followed to the island's interior. "Hey, we got it!"

"See! Just like the Keepers told me."

As Jack guided the boat carefully through the reeds, he again heard the frog chorus. The sound was comforting.

"Since it looks like we won't have to spend the night here after all, are you really going to give someone that message, Henry?" Sheila asked. "You know if you do, our parents will find out we've been here and we'll be in big trouble."

Jack began to sweat as he thought about what would be in store for him when his father found out. Running away would be the only answer.

"Maybe not if I tell the sheriff. Mrs. Koske told me some of the same things I heard from the Keeper. She told me I should tell the sheriff."

"Did you?"

"Um, no . . . not yet. I was afraid he wouldn't believe me. You've both talked to him. I'm not sure he believes *anything* we've told him. He probably thinks we're just making this stuff up."

"Well, *are* you going to tell him?"

"Yeah, I'll tell him, but you guys have to be my witnesses."

Chapter Thirty-One

The Embalmer

July 21, 1956

Herbert stood by his office window watching the three kids mount their bicycles and pedal off, his mind replaying the incredible two hours he had just spent with them, listening to things he didn't want to believe. They had sounded sincere, especially Henry who knew the most and seemed to be at the center of things. Still, what the boy knew, or thought he knew, came from some pretty strange sources. The frightening thing was that it might all be true. Certainly it would explain what had been going on for the last few months. A feeling of helplessness rose inside him and he suddenly felt homesick for the mean streets of Chicago. At least there he faced dangers he could understand. But he hadn't coped with those very well either, he reminded himself. His skin grew clammy as the bloody scene in the liquor store flashed into his mind all too vividly. He had come to Bruders Landing to leave all that behind, only to be set upon by different things. Things he didn't understand. Things that could harm his family. Maybe his first obligation was to them. To keep his wife and child safe, which would mean leaving the home he had made with Norma. Leaving Bruders Landing, a place that had seemed so placid and serene on the surface, but deep down harbored danger, a danger he couldn't identify. But hadn't he cut and run once before? Maybe there was no safe place for him, for someone who had done what he had.

But right now he needed to cut out all this soul-searching and self-pity. He *was* the Sheriff after all, and he *had* accepted responsibility to protect the people of Eagle County from dangers, whether he understood them or not. And wouldn't he be protecting his family if he protected the town? This was his second chance, a chance to find out whether he was up to dealing with something mysterious and threatening or just another body with a badge. He left the window and reached for his hat.

It was a three block walk uphill on a humid day in the high 80s. Herbert was perspiring through his shirt when he reached Bruhl's Mortuary. He had been in the old mansion dozens of times, but each time he felt apprehensive, as if some morbid surprise awaited him. Without bothering to knock, he opened one of the heavy oak doors and stepped from the hot sun into the darkened foyer, closing the door noisily to announce his arrival. He waited a moment in the wood-paneled room as his eyes grew accustomed to the dark. The air inside was thick with the saccharine-sweet odor of moldering flowers.

After standing for several minutes, neither seeing nor hearing anyone, he called out: "Hilder? Hilder Bruhl? Anyone? It's Herb Siefken. Anybody here?"

When there was no response, he walked through the foyer toward the chapel. The hall was eerily quiet, the only sound coming from the heels of his boots striking the polished wood floor. The doors to the visitation rooms were on his left. He wondered which ones held a body. When he reached the door to the chapel, he called Hilder's name again.

From somewhere below he heard a muffled sound. That would explain it. The embalming was done in the cellar. He walked past the chapel to the rear of the house. The stairway door was at the end of a narrow hall which was even darker than the rest of the house. A dim light and the sound of voices came from somewhere below. The syrupy sweet odor of old funerals was replaced by a smell of damp mold and formaldehyde. Maybe he would be lucky and find both Hilder and Boris.

Herbert started down the steep stairs, feeling the deep grooves worn into the wooden steps under his feet. With little light to guide his progress, he kept a firm hand on the railing which had been rubbed smooth by many hands before his. Each time he used these stairs he had warned Hilder to install an overhead light before someone fell, all with little effect. Herbert swore at him under his breath.

With a sense of relief, Herbert reached the stone floor of the cavernous room at the bottom, a space that always felt damp and oppressive. Except for the workroom where the embalming took place, the cellar remained exactly as it had been constructed a hundred years earlier. The foundation walls were built with massive sandstone blocks cut so precisely they stood without mortar. Overhead, the stone walls curved toward each other for support, forming high, arched ceilings. Shadowy entrances to smaller rooms and passageways lined the walls.

Moisture seeping between the stones made them glisten like the wet skin of an amphibian. Patches of dark green mold and lichens flourished in the cracks. The floor consisted of large slabs of the same sandstone, grooved with shallow pathways running in several directions created by years of footsteps.

At the far end of the room, Herbert saw light streaming from the open door of the workroom, accentuating the rough stone of the walls and creating shadows with grotesque shapes. He began to feel uneasy.

"Hilder! You down here? It's Herb Siefken."

A hollow voice replied from a distance. "Yes. In here. Come on back."

Herbert walked toward the light, careful not to trip on the uneven stone. Now another odor was added, the strong scent of bleach masking a hint of human decay. He recognized it as the smell of death. Hilder Bruhl was diligent about cleaning his embalming room, but some of his predecessors hadn't been so meticulous. Once the stench of decomposing bodies penetrated the stone, it seemed impossible to get it out.

When he reached the doorway, he stopped. He had been in the embalming room often, but it never failed to make him feel a weakness in his knees. The room had a surreal atmosphere compounded by Wagnerian music Hilder insisted on playing through the hi-fi system he had installed. Except for the floor which had been covered with pale green linoleum, the entire room was white—the arched ceiling, the walls, the cabinets, the linens, even most of the equipment.

Halfway to the peak of the ceiling, fluorescent light fixtures had been attached to the stones. The light from the long bulbs, several more than necessary, lit the room so brightly it made Herbert's eyes sting. Or was it that damn formaldehyde, he wondered? White cabinets with glass windows lined the walls. Visible through the dusty glass were shelves lined with bottles and jars of various sizes and a jumble of equipment and instruments. Between the cabinets were tables with porcelain tops holding various containers set against the wall. Beneath the tables were large metal tubs, each prominently displaying the label of a chemical supply company. At the opposite end of the room were wide stone stairs leading to the carriage house which housed Bruhl's two gleaming black Cadillacs—one a hearse for the coffins and one a limousine to transport grieving family members. It was the entrance Herbert was most familiar with, the one used to bring bodies to the workroom.

At the center of the room, Hilder Bruhl and Boris Brinter stood beside tables, each bent over a corpse, concentrating on their work. Herbert had never seen an embalming. The tables that held the two naked bodies were like long, shallow sinks, raised at one end with shallow channels running their entire length that drained discharges from the corpses into a catch basin at the end. Above each body were tall metal posts that held large jars of embalming fluid. A soft rubber tube ran from the bottom of the jar to the neck of the corpse Hilder Bruhl was working on. The scene reminded Herbert of a Frankenstein movie.

It occurred to him that the bodies might be people he knew. Hilder Bruhl had his back to him, working intently at the neck, blocking Herbert's view of the face. Brinter, however, stood on the opposite side of his table, giving Herbert a clear view. The old man wore a white apron with several dark smears. Herbert noticed it was the same kind of apron Tiny wore in his butcher shop. The corpse looked like that of an old man, thin to the point of emaciation but with an abdomen slightly distended. Skin lay like a soft leather blanket over the hard edges of his bones. Herbert shifted his gaze to the face. In contrast to the rest of the body, the face seemed puffy and soft like dough. Herbert was relieved that it was no one he recognized.

Brinter was using a trocar, a hollow metal tube-like device with changeable points used to release gases from internal organs and to inject embalming fluid. The old man was running his left hand over the the corpse's abdomen, pressing with his fingers. His hand stopped when he found the place he was seeking. He raised the trocar with his right hand, carefully placed the point between his fingers, then plunged the instrument through the skin. Herbert winced. There was a barely detectable sound of escaping air as Brinter stepped back, the trocar still protruding from the corpse's chest. Grasping the rubber hose with his hand, he attached it to the end of the trocar and opened a clamp to let the embalming fluid enter the body.

As he stood staring at the scene in the embalming room, Herbert recalled Lloyd Wischmeier's autopsy in this same room a few days earlier. He had watched as Reuben Blustein went through the gruesome dissection of what was left of the boy. There had been no face to look at. Only a skull stripped of features. Under the bright fluorescent lights the bone had looked gray, while the teeth, which appeared enormous, were shiny white. Hilder's voice interrupted the scene, letting it fade from his mind.

"I'll be with you in a minute, Sheriff,' Hilder Bruhl

called out without turning around. "Boris, I don't care whether you use it or not, but I'm going to get a pump. Putting this fluid in by gravity is a pain. Then you get someone like this with clogged arteries and it takes bloody forever."

"Do vot effer you like." Brinter's tone was noncommittal, his voice heavily laden with a German accent. He spoke without stopping his work.

"There, got it. It's flowing again." Hilder Bruhl stepped back from the table and turned to Herbert, beginning to strip off his surgical gloves. He also wore a white apron covered with stains.

"Sorry to keep you waiting, Herb, but I needed to get that fluid flowing. This guy's been trouble from the start and I've got to have him ready to show tomorrow."

Herbert checked his stomach which seemed to be coming through the sights and smells of the Bruhl workroom fairly well so far. "That's OK. There wasn't anyone around upstairs when I got here so I came on down."

"Hmm, that won't do. I thought Jenny was there. Let me just see if she's there now. I'll be right back."

Hilder Bruhl left the workroom walking ramrod straight as if he was marching in a military parade, a habit he had formed to compensate for his diminutive size. His salt and pepper hair was slicked back, held down by some gelatinous preparation with the consistency of glue. He kept his shirt and tie protected under his apron, needing only to slip on a dark jacket in order go from embalming a corpse to conducting a funeral or greeting mourners on a moment's notice.

Brinter remained bent over the body working steadily, his scruffy, white hair hanging down around his face. Herbert was eager to start asking the questions he had formulated walking from his office, but hesitated when he saw Brinter tilt the dead man's head back and insert his fingers into the mouth, opening it wide. When he removed his fingers, the head and mouth remained in their unnatural position, as if the body was about to scream in protest. With a motion that looked as if he had done it a thousand times, Brinter picked up a beaker filled with fluid with his right hand, at the same time pressing down hard on the man's chest with his left. He held the beaker over the face and tilted it slightly, pouring fluid into the mouth while relaxing his pressure on the chest. There was a gurgling sound as the fluid was sucked into the trachea. Fearing he was putting his stomach to too great a test, he looked away. His questions could wait.

A moment later Hilder Bruhl returned. "I hope you haven't found another chewed-up body somewhere. That poor Wischmeier boy. What a mess. In all my years in this business, I've never seen such a thing. Do you have any idea yet what did that to him?"

"Maybe. That's why I'm here. I need some information that I think Boris has."

"By all means, we want to help all we can. The Wischmeier boy's death isn't the way I like to get my business. Boris, stop for a minute and let the Sheriff ask you some questions."

"I haf much to do here."

"It can wait a while."

Boris continued to work.

"Boris, you can talk to me here or we can take a walk to my office right now. Your choice," Herbert said sternly.

Brinter raised his head, then straightened up to a slight stoop. "Very vell, I vill stop." He came slowly around the tables where the bodies lay. He wasn't wearing gloves.

"All right, then, I have several questions. Do you want to go somewhere we can sit?" Herbert asked.

"We can sit here," Hilder Bruhl answered. "I'll get some work stools." He pulled out three tall stools on casters from behind a door. Brinter sat on one slumped over, stone-faced.

Herbert began: "I've just listened to a very strange story told to me by three kids. The ones at the Gerdes house when Lloyd Wischmeier was killed."

Herbert watched the expressions on their faces as he told about their experience on the island. Hilder Bruhl's eyes grew wide while his mouth twisted skeptically. Brinter frowned, his eyes cast to the floor.

"Those kids must still be in shock over the

Wischmeier boy. I don't think you can put much stock in what they say," Hilder Bruhl said, shaking his head. "Their imaginations may have gone haywire."

Brinter was shifting his weight constantly, his eyes never leaving the floor.

"I know what you're saying, Hilder. But I need to check everything out. When you look at what's happened around here lately, there just might be something to it."

"OK, there might be. But what does it have to do with us?"

"It's this," Herbert said slowly, looking at Boris. "Before they took that trip to Big Tow, someone talked to the boy. And that someone told him what did the killing at the Gerdes place. Told the boy to tell me all about it, and if I wanted proof, I should go to Bruhl's and look at some records Boris Brinter has hidden away."

Boris stiffened, making a motion as if to rise.

Hilder turned to face him. "Records? What records? Do you have some records that have something to do with this?"

"I know nutting about such records." Boris stood, scooting the stool noisily across the floor, and started for his work table.

Herbert stopped him. "Hold on, Boris. Tell me, how long have you worked here?"

"Long time."

"Tell him. Herb, you won't believe this."

"Over sixty years I haf vorked here for Bruhl's. Since I came from Prussia."

"Isn't that amazing? He was working here before I was born. Grandpa Bruhl, Heinrich, hired you in 1890, right?"

"Yah, Heinrich Bruhl hired me ven I vas young." Brinter spoke slowly, avoiding Herbert's eyes.

"How old were you?" he asked.

"Fourteen or fifteen, I tink."

"Grandpa Bruhl taught him embalming, and so far Boris has hardly slowed down a bit, although I do have to nudge him to update his ways sometimes." Hilder smiled slightly. "Boris still does most all the embalming for us. He seems to like it and there's plenty other work for Jenny and me. I was just doing this person today because we're backed up."

"And records? Do you keep records of funerals and bodies you've worked on?" Herbert looked at both Hilder Bruhl and Brinter for an answer.

"We sure do," Hilder Bruhl answered quickly. "In fact, our records go all the way back to 1859 when my great grandfather, Raston Bruhl, took over the business. There are records of each body prepared, whether Bruhl's did the funeral or not, and a record of each funeral. Boris keeps all the preparation records and I keep the funeral records."

"Tell me then, Boris, is there anything in the records that has a connection to the mutilations we've seen in the last couple of months?" Herbert stared directly into his eyes.

Brinter wiped his hands repeatedly on the apron he wore and lowered his head. "There is nutting."

"Hilder?"

"Not that I know of, but I haven't been through all of them. I don't like to handle the old ones too much. Some of them are pretty fragile."

"What about you, Boris? Have you looked at the old records?"

"Long time ago."

"Then what I'd like to do is look through them. That all right with you, Hilder?"

"Those are *my* records. I say who looks through them." Brinter raised his head and glared at Herbert.

Hilder Bruhl was indignant. "What do you mean *your* records?"

Herbert stepped in quickly. "You may have made most of them, Boris, but those records belong to Bruhl's Mortuary and I believe Bruhl's Mortuary belongs to Hilder here."

Brinter continued to glare, his lips pressed tightly together.

Hilder Bruhl turned to Herbert. "Of course you can examine my records, Sheriff. When do you want to do it?"

"Right now."

"All right. All the embalming records are down

here. The ones for the last few years are in those cabinets in the corner and the others are in a room back there. Where would you like to start."

"Where they begin."

"Fine. Come with me, then. I'll show you. Boris, you better come, too. You're a lot more familiar with the old ones than I am."

Hilder started for the doorway. Herbert waited until Brinter moved then followed. As he went through the door, Hilder Bruhl pushed a switch and a bare bulb came on high overhead.

"They're in that room over here." Hilder Bruhl motioned toward a wooden door set low in the stone wall. The wood of the door's surface was mottled with patches of mold and moss. An iron ring hung from its center. Hilder Bruhl took hold of the ring and pulled. The door opened easily.

"Watch your head. Low bridge." Hilder Bruhl walked through standing upright but Brinter and Herbert had to bend to avoid hitting their heads. All the Bruhl's must have been short, Herbert thought.

Inside he found himself in a room dimly lit by an ancient-looking clear light bulb dangling on a cord that hung from a steel rod set in the wall. Overhead was an arched ceiling like the room they had just left, but lower. Its walls were of the same stone as the rest of the cellar. Moisture glistened on the rough surfaces. Strands of cobwebs draped from ceiling arches like tattered lace curtains. The smell was old, as if the room had been sealed for decades.

Several wood file cabinets sat side by side along two of the walls, their tops coated with a thick layer of dust and crumbled stone. Dust-coated cobwebs hung between the drawer handles. A small desk and chair sat against a third wall. Yellowing papers were scattered across the desktop with hardened remains of wax candles along one side.

"Light's not too good in here," Hilder Bruhl said. "I can get you a flashlight from upstairs unless you want to carry papers up there to read. How on earth do you see in here, Boris?"

"Candles."

"That should be good enough for me, too, if you've got some."

"Get some for him, will you, Boris?"

Brinter opened a drawer in the desk and removed two partially burned candles. Taking a kitchen match from his pocket, he lit it with his thumbnail, then lit one of the candles and offered it to Herbert. "The earliest files are there." Brinter pointed. "Each drawer iss marked by year on front."

Brushing away a cobweb, Herbert stooped to peer at the top drawer of the first file cabinet. Printed in faded ink on a small card in front was: *1859-63 R. Bruhl* The file drawer was warped, its face coated with dust and grit. Herbert pulled on the drawer's wood handle with his free hand. It was stuck. He pulled again, harder. This time it came open with a groan. The drawer was filled with large cards packed closely together. Dirt covered their top edges. Herbert handed the candle to Hilder Bruhl and pulled out one of the cards from the middle of the drawer. Notes handwritten in faded ink with old world flourish covered half the page. At the top left-hand corner, he was able to make out a name: *Beulah L. Buescher.* Next to the name was a date: *March 12, 1860.*

"I haven't looked at these in years." Hilder Bruhl brought the card close to the his face. "See? That's the way Raston did it. Name and date at the top and then he noted everything he did to prepare the body. He was a careful man. In fact, we pretty much keep them the same way. Boris still writes them by hand. It's hard to read Raston's notes, though, the ink's faded so bad. In his later ones, the ones you can read better, you'll see notes about the condition of the body and what he did cosmetically to make it presentable. He also describes the clothes he dressed the person in and what kind of casket was used for the burial. Later, when he started embalming, the notes get longer."

"There's no mention of embalming on these cards. When did he start?"

"We can check his records, but I think it would have been in the late 1860s. Embalming only began to catch on after the Civil War. The Army started it by embalming soldiers killed in the war, shipping them home for burial rather than burying them on the battlefields. It was the first time it was ever done like that in a war. I mean bodies have been embalmed in various ways for thousands of years, like the Egyptian mummies, but it had never been done in such numbers until that war. But probably Raston never did it much. Too expensive for most people then. Embalming does make the deceased look better, you know. Some people with money began to want it. Or if the funeral was delayed for some reason, like close relatives coming from a long distance, then he'd embalm if the family was willing to pay. Or if the body was being shipped out of town for burial. That kind of thing."

"So it was optional."

"Yes. It still is, legally, although now it's routine, in America anyway, but hardly anywhere else. In Raston's time it caught on slowly. Usually no one would pay for it unless they had to for some reason. Raston would put the bodies in an ice house out back to keep them from spoiling, then bury them as quick as he could."

"So, even though it's not required, you embalm everyone you get now."

"Pretty much, but there are some exceptions, like when the person is cremated or if the funeral takes place within, say, twenty-four hours after the person dies which some religions require. Then we just keep the body cool."

"When would you say it began to be common?"

"I'd say by the turn of the century the majority of people buried were embalmed."

Herbert turned back to the files. "Boris, where do the records start that you've made?"

"There, in that cabinet." Brinter pointed to a file cabinet a few feet from where Herbert was standing.

"Look, I want to help you all I can, Herb, but we have to get those two people finished out there. Why don't you stay and look through these records all you want while we finish up, all right?"

"I don't vant . . ." Brinter hesitated.

"What was that?" Herbert asked.

"Nutting."

"Come on, Boris, let's go back to work. Yell if you need anything, Sheriff. You know where we'll be."

Candle in hand, Herbert walked along the file cabinets, wondering where to start. All the records since the turn of the century had been made by Brinter, and he certainly wouldn't record anything he wanted to hide. Even if he did, he had plenty of opportunity to destroy the record or change it. If there were anything useful to be found, it would be in the records kept before Boris came on the scene.

Unsure what he was looking for, Herbert headed for the file drawer he had first opened, casually examining the others as he walked by. One caught his attention, a cabinet free of cobwebs. He held the candle close to the yellow label on the top drawer: *1869—73 R. Bruhl.*

He tried the drawer with his free hand. It opened with difficulty, revealing another solid row of yellow cards. He pushed it closed and pulled on the second drawer which opened easily. Inside were large yellow cards like the others, but not nearly as many. Pushing the second drawer closed, he pulled on the third. Balky like the first one, it was also filled by a solid row of the yellow cards. Herbert pushed it closed and read the label on the second drawer: *1874   Town Cemetery   R. Bruhl.*

Herbert set the candle in a holder on top of the cabinet and pulled the drawer out wide. It was half filled. One by one he began to examine the cards. They all seemed to contain normal records of body preparation: time received, condition, cleaning, embalming occasionally, cosmetic work, dressing. The writing was longhand, all in the same neat style, the ink faded but legible. Reaching the last card in the pile, he made a mental note of the date at the top: *September 11, 1874.* He found no cards which made reference to the town cemetery. Why was that label on the drawer, he asked himself? And why was the drawer only partially filled?

He stood up and stretched to relieve a growing ache in his back. While he was concentrating on the records in the file drawer, the muffled sound of scraping had been slow to register. Now he thought he had heard it in the background. He stood and listened for a full minute. The sound was gone. I'm getting paranoid, he told himself. It's time to ask Hilder Bruhl and Brinter a question or two.

As he started for the door, he thought he heard the scraping start again. Again he stood and listened. Again he heard nothing. This is going to drive me crazy, he said out loud. Stooping low, he walked through the doorway.

The sudden bright light of the embalming room made him squint. Hilder Bruhl was covering the body he had been working on with a white sheet. Brinter bent over the other body extracting the trocar from the body's abdomen. Herbert felt a twinge below his sternum.

"Hilder, I need to ask you a question about one of the files."

"Good timing. I'm just finishing up. Ask away."

"You'll understand better back in the file room."

Brinter glanced up briefly, then looked back down at his work.

"OK, but Boris knows those files much better than I do."

"I know, you told me before, but you can probably answer this."

"All right, here I come."

Herbert led the way to the file room and picked up the candle that still burned.

"Look at this label." He lowered the candle to the drawer that concerned him. "It says something different. See it? The words *Town Cemetery.*"

"Sure, I see."

"Do you know why they're on the label?"

"Let's see, 1874. I think that's the year Raston Bruhl relocated bodies from the original town cemetery to Walnut Grove."

"Interesting. I looked through the cards in the drawer and didn't see any mention of a town cemetery. There's nothing in there but regular body preparation records. And unlike the other drawers, this one's only half full.'

"Really?" Hilder Bruhl looked in the drawer, then picked up several cards and began thumbing through them. When he reached the end he stood up. "I think there must be records missing."

"There's another thing. From the looks of this cabinet, someone's opened it a lot more recently than the others."

"How do you know that?"

"The cobwebs were brushed away. That's what got my attention in the first place."

"Let me get Boris so we can get to the bottom of this."

As Herbert waited for them to return, he listened for the scraping sound. Again he heard nothing.

Hilder Bruhl returned with Brinter in tow. The tall old man remained partly crouched even after he came through the low doorway.

"Right there, Boris." Hilder Bruhl pointed to the open file drawer. "The records Raston Bruhl kept when he was relocating the old town cemetery were in there, weren't they?"

Brinter stared silently at the drawer, his head down, hands folded.

"Well, do you know where they are?" Hilder Bruhl asked impatiently.

"Boris, I need your cooperation here," Herbert said. "Those records could be important. You know as well as anyone that the Wischmeier boy was brutally killed. You saw his body. We've got to find out what it was that did it so we can keep the same thing from happening to someone else."

"It von't do no good," Brinter answered, raising his head to look at Herbert with his deep set eyes. His voice was deep and deliberate.

"What won't do any good?" Herbert asked.

"I don't haf any records."

"Look here, Boris," Hilder Bruhl said firmly, "you're the only person that deals with these records and it's been that way since long before I started working here. You must have known they were missing. Now where are they?"

"You could be in some deep trouble here, Boris." Herbert spoke in his official voice. "Since you're the one who looks after the records in this room, I have to think you'd know if a whole section like that was missing. That means either you took them or you know who did."

"All right, Boris, what's going on?" Hilder Bruhl asked angrily. "I've had enough of this. Someone's opened that cabinet recently and you're the only one who's been in this room in months. Those records belong to me. Now where are they?"

Brinter straightened up to his full height which brought him eye-to-eye with Herbert. "It vas my duty to keep them safe, away from prying eyes." He clenched his fists, looking Herbert in the eye.

"It seems to me they were safe right here, at least they had been for nearly a hundred years. I think you hid them," Herbert said, still using his official voice.

"Yes, hid them from *me*." Hilder Bruhl spit out his words.

"I don't think it was just from you, Hilder. He didn't want *anyone* to see them, isn't that right, Boris?"

"Very vell. I vill get them, but you must vait here."

As Brinter went through the doorway still crouched over, Herbert motioned for Hilder Bruhl to stay put then followed as quietly as he could. He saw Brinter's profile in the far corner moving like a shadow against the wall. The shadowy figure climbed onto a crate, then stretched to reach into a crevice over an arched doorway. Using both hands, he retrieved a small chest and stepped gingerly off the crate, placing the chest on the floor.

Herbert quietly took the few steps that separated him from Brinter. "Mind if I see what's in the chest?"

Brinter jerked upright and whirled toward Herbert with an angry look in his eyes. Slowly he reached inside his shirt and exposed a leather cord around his neck. The cord held a single key which he inserted into a padlock fastened on the latch. Even more slowly, he lifted the lid. Inside was a stack of cards like the ones in the file cabinets. Brinter quickly grasped the entire stack in one hand and thrust it at

Herbert.

"These are vhat you are looking for."

"I'm sure they are, Boris, but what else have you got in there?"

"It iss none uf your business."

As Brinter began to close the lid, Herbert leaned over and seized his wrist in a grip tight enough to make him wince. "How about we *all* decide whose business it is." When the tension drained from Brinter's arm, Herbert released his grip and looked into the chest. At the bottom was a journal bound in leather. Herbert lifted it out.

"I think we'll show this to Hilder as well."

Sullenly Brinter pulled the journal from the chest.

Back inside the file room, Herbert laid the stack of cards and journal on the desk. Hilder Bruhl picked up the candle from on top the file cabinet and used it to light another. Brinter stood stiffly to the side.

Hilder Bruhl examined the first card in the stack, then leafed through the ones beneath it. "These are the missing records, all right. They're a day-to-day account of exhuming bodies from the original town cemetery."

"Good. Maybe they'll tell us something. Now what's this?" Herbert picked up the journal and opened it, careful not to damage the fragile leather binding. The first entry had been handwritten with a flourish:

Journal of Thaddeus P. Bump
June 15 to June 25
In the year of Our Lord, 1846
May God Have Mercy On Our Souls

Gently turning the pages, Herbert found lengthy entries starting with the date of June 15, 1846. "Hilder, this is a journal written in 1846, it says, by someone named Thaddeus Bump. You have any idea who that was?"

"Bump? Thaddeus Bump? No. Can't say that I've heard that name before. It's sort of unusual. The kind of name I'd remember if I heard it.'

'What about you, Boris. I'll bet you know who Thaddeus Bump was since you were keeping his journal in such a safe place.'

They both waited, but Brinter didn't reply.

"Boris, you're really trying my patience," Hilder Bruhl said in a near shout,. "This is about to be the last day of your sixty years here if you don't start cooperating."

"If you read it, you vill know."

"You better be right about that."

"Tell us this much, Boris, did Thaddeus Bump live here?" Herbert asked as he browsed through the pages.

"I cannot tell you more."

"Well, you're going to have to or you'll have more trouble than losing your job. Have you heard of obstruction of justice? It's a felony charge when someone withholds material evidence of a murder. And I think that's what you're doing here. So I need an explanation and it better be good."

"I took an oath. That iss all I can tell you. Even if you put me in jail."

"An oath? What kind of oath? In 1846?" Hilder Bruhl cried out in disbelief. "For God's sake, Boris, not even *you* were born then. What's so secret about these records anyway. The sheriff *should* put you in jail. Hiding records that belong to me is the same as stealing."

Brinter clenched his fists tightly at his sides. "Those records aren't yours. They belong to your great-grandfather, Raston Bruhl. And the oath I took vas vith your grandfather, Heinrich. He vas a great man, your grandfather. I vill not break my oath for you or for anyone."

"All right. Enough for now, Boris," Herbert said, looking directly into his deep set eyes. "I'm taking these back to my office to read, then I'm coming back to see you. Make sure you're here."

Chapter Thirty-Two

The Journal

July 21, 1956

Herbert turned the fragile note cards gently as he read Raston Bruhl's record of the exhumations at the old town cemetery. His reaction was amazement bordering on disbelief. Abruptly, six days into the grisly work, Raston's notes ended. He knew the cemetery relocation couldn't have been complete. Where were the remaining notes? Does Brinter have more? Or did something happen to Raston Bruhl?

But six days of notes said more than enough. Raston Bruhl had stuck to the facts, no embellishments or suppositions, and the facts were incredible. If he hadn't seen what he did at Walnut Grove Cemetery, Herbert was sure he would think Raston Bruhl was either delusional or smoking opium. Or the old rumor about his ghoulish side was true. Herbert refused to consider that possibility. He had seen bodies in the same condition as Raston Bruhl described seventy-five years earlier—stripped of flesh, skeletons dismembered, bones in a jumble inside the coffins. Raston Bruhl had found no sign the coffins had been opened, but mentioned a small hole in each one. Just like Walnut

Grove. Maybe Raston Bruhl was lucky, Herbert thought. He might have had the good fortune to die before he had to confront whatever was doing this.

He knew where Raston Bruhl had been digging. The old cemetery was in the heart of town—the site now occupied by Bruders Landing High School. Herbert tensed. Which meant that whatever had mutilated the bodies a century ago had come that far from the bluffs. And if they had done that a hundred years ago, what says they wouldn't do it again?

With a heavy sigh, Herbert laid the cards back on his desk and picked up the leather-bound journal. Inside the front leaf was a letter addressed to Harman Hanzfig and Raston Bruhl. As he picked it up to read, the letter fell apart at its creases.

Carefully he pieced the letter together on his desk like a jigsaw puzzle, then studied the faded writing. When he had finished reading what he could make out, beads of sweat covered his forehead. Gentler this time, he opened the journal to the first page. The paper was heavier and in better condition than the letter, but the ink had faded. Holding his desk lamp close, he attempted to decipher the writing. Try as he might, he could make out few words. The next page was in the same condition. But on the third page the writing stood out clearly.

June 20, 1845

. . . . Then I saw more of those things, tall figures that looked like skinny old men. They stood stock still, saying nothing. I shouted again, trying to get them to answer, but still they said nothing, standing like they weren't even breathing. I could see them staring at me with eyes that looked like there was fire in them. Suddenly I started to get this vision, a book emerging from a fog bank, opening in my mind. It was like looking through mist, but I could see words on the page. What is even stranger, I didn't need to read the words to know what they said. In fact the words didn't even look like they were in English. Voices started getting into in my head somehow. I knew it must be those old men from the way they looked at me. They said not to

go any further into the island. It sounded like they meant it. They may have looked old but they were big and carried long staffs. I don't mind saying they scared the bejesus out of me. I told them I wouldn't move. They seemed amazed and delighted that I answered.

The voices asked me about the explosion on the river. They wanted to know what caused it. Whether I had done it. I answered that it wasn't me, that it was a steamboat that blew up and I was just a passenger. They were very concerned about smoke and fire and wanted to know if an explosion would happen again. I said I could not guarantee that it wouldn't.

Then I started hearing all manner of voices at once and I realized those old men were no longer talking to me; they were talking to each other. All I did was stand and listen. It was as if they had opened a window in my head and forgot to close it. I don't remember their exact words, but they were worried about the explosions and fire hurting something hibernating in the bluffs. Then a voice started talking to me again, wanting to tell me things. It goes against everything in my soul to believe all that the voice told me, but I feel it is my duty as a Christian to set it down as I understood it and let others judge for themselves. And as God as my witness, everything I set down here is what I heard.

Those old men, or whatever they are, have lived on that island for centuries tending a flock of some kind of creatures. They call themselves Keepers and their flock the Gathering. While these Keepers are like shepherds, the Gathering sure don't sound anything like sheep. The truth is the Gathering don't sound like anything I ever heard of. They cannot tolerate light so they stay in caves and tunnels in the bluffs above Bruders Landing. They hibernate like bears, but not just for the winter. They hibernate for years, maybe as long as a half century. There's an entrance to those tunnels on that island, the portal they call it. The Keepers won't let anyone near it. I didn't see it or learn where it is, but I must have been getting close to it when they stopped me.

The Keepers were accustomed to only brown people living near them until white people came. They are worried about the white people, about how we live and what we do, whether we are a threat to the Gathering. They began to ask questions that puzzled me at first. They wanted to know whether we live longer than brown people. And why white people don't bury their dead under mounds of earth like the brown people did? I answered as best I could.

The scariest part came when the Keepers talked about making sure the Gathering had food. It seems like when they come out of hibernation, they have a hellish appetite and the Keepers must make sure they have enough to eat. In the past they said there was plenty of food, but with white people coming the Keepers are worried there might not be enough any longer. It sounded like they have trouble keeping the Gathering under control when they're hungry.

The Keepers never said right out what the Gathering eat, but I heard enough to know. Just the thought is an abomination and I would be cursed forever if I put it down on paper, but I will faithfully write what I heard.

The Keepers said the brown people put food for the Gathering into the mounds they built at the top of the bluffs, but white people bury it in individual holes. When I realized what they were talking about, I was so shocked I couldn't move. As soon as I got my wits back, I took off running as fast as I could back the way I came. Thank the Lord, that was the last I saw of the Keepers.

Why they told me all this I do not know, but it made me want to get far from that island as quickly as I could. I thank the Good Lord to still be alive and want to improve my chances of staying that way.

Thaddeus Bump   A.D. 1846

The sun was about to set when Herbert finished reading. He leaned over the journal, resting his face in his hands. If what Thaddeus Bump had written was true, the town had more of a problem than he ever imagined. Bump wrote that the creatures hibernate for a half-century. If the Gathering have come out of hibernation, the last time they were awake must have been around 1890. It was time to have a talk with Sonia Koske.

Chapter Thirty-Three

The Revelation

July 23, 1956

Herbert stepped loudly as he walked across Sonia Koske's front porch, signaling his arrival. He had never met the woman but he had heard stories that she was reclusive, unkept, even frightening according to the neighborhood kids who thought she was a witch. But her yard looked neat enough, and Henry said she had been kind to him when she persuaded him to come inside. There must be several sides to the woman. Which one will be here today, he wondered? One of the porch boards felt spongy and he stepped off it quickly. All the shades and curtains in the front windows were drawn. He pushed the button to the doorbell and waited. Several seconds went by. He pushed the button again, holding it down longer. As he was about to knock, there was the sound of movement inside. Seconds later the door opened a crack.

"Are you the sheriff?" a soft voice asked.

"Yes, ma'am. I'm Herbert Siefken."

"Come on in, then, Sheriff Siefken. I've been expecting you."

Sonia Koske wore an old-fashioned black dress with a ruffled skirt. An oval brooch was pinned at the neck. Her gray hair was neatly brushed and pulled back into a bun. With her hands gracefully folded in front of her, Herbert thought she looked more like a librarian than a witch.

"There are some things I need to talk to you about, Mrs. Koske," Herbert said, stepping inside.

"Yes, I should think so. And it's *Miss* Koske." She led him through the small foyer into a living room comfortably furnished with pieces Herbert thought would serve a fashionable Chicago antique store well. The chairs and couch had dark wood frames, artfully carved, and were upholstered with deep purple or blue fabric in remarkably good condition. Two lamps with exquisite Tiffany shades sat on matching side tables by the couch, glowing in a display of rich colors. Another Tiffany shade hung from the light in the center of the ceiling. The room had a pleasant aroma of potpourri.

"We can sit in here, Sheriff, if that suits you." There was a tightness in her voice.

"That suits me fine." Herbert selected a chair with its back to the wall out of habit.

"Would you like a cup of coffee? It's already made."

"Yes, yes, I would."

"I'll be right back." Sonia Koske disappeared into the next room.

As Herbert waited, a framed photograph on the table next to the couch caught his eye—a group of six men and two women standing on the steps of a building that he recognized as the old City Hall. Since the building was torn down in the 1920s, Herbert thought the picture had to be over thirty years old. Five of the men wore dark suits with narrow lapels and white shirts with starched collars, looking as if they had stepped out of the last century. The sixth was a boy in his late teens or early twenties dressed in work clothes. The two women were dressed in long skirts with white blouses as if they worked in a shop or office. One looked about the same age as the men and one about the age of the boy. There was not a smile among them.

"An interesting picture, don't you think?" Sonia Koske walked back into the room carrying a tray with coffee service and a plate of cookies which she placed on a gleaming wood coffee table in front of the couch. "Do you see anyone you know?"

As Herbert stared more closely at the picture, Sonia Koske busied herself pouring coffee. "Do you take cream or sugar, Sheriff?"

"Uh, yes. Both."

"One lump or two?"

"Three, actually."

"Since we just met, Sheriff," she said, handing him a cup of coffee, "I'm not surprised you don't recognize me. I was just eighteen when that picture was taken."

"When was that?"

"In the late 90s . . . 1898, I think."

"Who are the others?"

"The woman next to me is the town's first woman mayor, Harriet Stadtlander. I was her secretary," she said proudly. "The man on her left was a member of the town council, Bernard Heitmeier. Next to him is another councilman, a doctor, Dr. Hentzel, Kurt Hentzel. He was also the coroner. Next to me is the sheriff, Wilhelm Unterhoff, and next to him is Heinrich Bruhl, Hilder's grandfather."

Herbert squinted at the young woman. There was a resemblance, but he never could have identified her.

"And the young man, Sheriff, do you recognize him?"

There was something vaguely familiar about the face. "Not Boris Brinter?"

"Very good, Sheriff. Yes, that's Boris. About eighteen, I think he was. Not very pleasant looking even then, do you think?"

Brinter had been a large, well-built young man, taller by half-a-head than Heinrich Bruhl who stood next to him, While the others looked solemn or deadpan, Brinter's expression bordered on hostile, sinister even.

"No, not exactly a friendly looking fellow."

"He's a bad man, Sheriff. Real bad. A killer!"

"What? Do you mean that?"

"Oh, I mean it all right. He killed more people

than I could guess." Sonia put her cup down on the tray. "And he'll kill *me* if he finds out that I told you anything about what they did."

"What *they* did? Who's they?"

"Them, the ones in that picture."

"Miss Koske, you can tell me whatever you know, and you'll be safe. I won't let anyone hurt you, not Boris Brinter, not anyone." Herbert tried to sound as reassuring as he could, although he was no longer sure he could keep anyone safe. "I'll make sure of that."

"Maybe you can. Boris is an old man now. But I'm old, too. And I've lived a lot longer than I ever expected to, that's for sure."

Herbert dropped three lumps of sugar into his coffee, staring at the cup thoughtfully. "Henry Starker gave me your message. Quite a story he had to tell. It takes some doing to believe it, so I talked to Boris, if you can call it talking. It took a little persuasion but he gave me some interesting things. The notes Raston Bruhl made when he moved the bodies from the old town cemetery to Walnut Grove, and a journal written by a man named Thaddeus Bump."

"That's good, Sheriff. I'm glad you got those things. I was afraid Boris might have destroyed them. If you've read them, you know what's down in those bluffs north of town and out on Big Tow." Herbert noticed a tremor in her arm as Sonia Koske lifted her cup.

"Yes, I've read them."

"Good, then you know the danger. I want to help, but it's very dangerous for me." Sonia's voice had begun to quiver slightly and Herbert could sense her fear.

"You mean Boris Brinter."

"Yes, Boris Brinter. And he doesn't kill gently. When he realizes I talked to you, he'll come for me. You can be sure of it." Sonia Koske put down her cup which rattled against the saucer.

"Don't you worry about Boris. I'll keep my eye on him for you, but you have to tell me what you know." Herbert stared directly into her gray eyes.

"Very well," she replied, sounding resigned. "I'm an old woman anyway, but I'm sure you'll do what you can. My first contact with those things on Big Tow

Island, the Keepers, was when I was eight years old. My pa was a big drinker, especially on holidays. On that Fourth of July, Pa and Mum took me and my two brothers for a picnic in our boat to the beach across from Big Tow. The beach below the Gerdes place." Sonia gave Herbert a knowing look as she said the name.

"Pa started drinking from a jar of whiskey he brought as soon we got there, before noon it was. We all fished awhile, then we had the lunch that Mum had packed. It was a hot, sunny day so my brothers and I went for a swim while Mum cleaned things up. Pa went back to fishing . . . and kept on drinking. After a while my brothers got tired of the water so they laid down on the sand and went to sleep. I decided to go see if Pa was catching anything. He seemed glad to see me, although he wasn't seeing anything too clearly at that point."

"*Sonie*, he said to me, that's what he always called me, *I ain't caught a gol'darned thing here. See that ol' rowboat tied to the tree over there? Let's you 'n me head over to Big Tow there and see if the fishin's any better.*

"Now that made me kind of scared. I heard stories about that place. Everybody in town had. It was hard not to. Kids told them to each other at night, around campfires and the like. So I told Pa I was afraid, but he wouldn't listen. "*C'mon, Sonie, ain't nothin' to be afeared of*, he said. *Ya can't believe all those crazy stories.*

"So he took me by the hand and led me over to the boat. He fumbled with the rope for a while. I was hoping he couldn't get it untied, but he did. *Jump in*, he said. And I did like I was told. He started rowing out from shore, not rowing very well, the oars kept popping out of the water for him, but he kept going. The current was pretty strong and it kept pushing us to the south. It seemed like a long time until we got close to the island. I sat in the back and kept looking at the shore, getting more and more scared, thinking I'd see something awful come out of the trees.

"When we were maybe ten yards from shore, he quit rowing, out of breath. *I'm agonna try 'er here*, he said. So he started casting toward shore and reeling in, catching nothing and getting more and more disgusted. And he kept taking pulls from his jar. Me, I just sat there, staring at the trees along the shore, sure something terrible was going to pop out any minute. Then he started rowing along the shore again. When we came to this little inlet, he rowed us into it. I was terrified. The shore was closing in on both sides of us and pretty soon I couldn't see the river any more at all. Finally he stopped rowing.

"*Sonie,* he said, *watch me now. I'm gonna cast over in those snags there.* Then he stood up, real shaky. The boat rocked, almost going over. I screamed, and he got it steady again.

"*I got it, Sonie; don't worry,* he said. Then he reared back to cast, and he just kept leaning backwards. When he saw he was going over, he yelled and tried to catch the side of the boat. Everything seemed in slow motion, his hand letting go of the rod and grabbing the side, then he went in, still holding on, pulling the boat over as he went down. I was screaming and trying to grab onto something, but the boat was turning over. All of a sudden I was in the water and I couldn't touch bottom. I yelled for Pa to help me, but he . . ." Sonia Koske stopped, a catch in her throat.

"Sorry, Sheriff," she said, doing her best to recover. "Even after all these years, it's still hard for me. He wasn't much of a man, but I did love him. I remember it all like it was yesterday."

"That's OK. Take your time. You're doing great." Herbert still held the coffee cup near his mouth but had yet to take a sip.

"I never saw him after that. When they found his body the next week, he wasn't fit for anyone to see. The boat had righted itself when he let go. I grabbed onto the side and kicked and kicked, crying and screaming, until it wouldn't move any further. Somehow I had managed to push it against the bank where I could touch bottom. I dragged myself up that mud bank and started looking into that water for Pa, all the time yelling for him. When I couldn't find him, I figured I had to get help. But I was pretty turned around and there were weeds higher than my head all around me. So I headed through them in the direction I thought was the river, but I was wrong. After a while I came through all these dead trees to a big pond. I remember it was spooky. By this time I knew I was lost and started to get real scared, so I just sat down on the ground and started to bawl. And that's when I heard them."

"Heard *them*?" Realizing the cup was still in his hand, Herbert set it back on the tray.

"Yes, well, not really *heard*, I saw these images of books opening and words just popped in my head."

"Words?"

"Yes, words."

"What were they?"

"They said that I had to go back to the river. I was so surprised, I stopped crying and looked up. Three old men were out in the water. Standing there, just like the stories." Sonia Koske leaned forward. "*It was the Keepers*," she whispered.

Herbert tried not to look incredulous. "What did they look like?"

"Tall, thin, old like the tree trunks. Taller than anyone I'd ever seen. With pointed hats, and beards, and they wore long robes that reached to the water. I was too far away to see their faces clearly, but I remember their eyes." Sonia's own eyes began to widen. "They were bright, gleaming, like light was coming out of them."

"Did they say anything else to you?"

"No, just to stop and go back to the river, which was scary enough. Luckily I had enough sense to know I had been going the wrong direction. So I got up fast and ran back into the weeds and didn't stop until I came to the riverbank. There I sat, crying and sniffling, until two men out fishing came by and saw me. I told them what happened and we went back to where the boat was to look, but there was no trace of Pa, so they took me back to town with them."

"I'm really sorry, Miss Koske. That's a terrible thing to happen to someone at any age. Did you tell the two men, the fishermen, about the Keepers?"

"No, I didn't think they'd believe me. I didn't tell

anyone, not then. But that was just the beginning. There were things that happened later with the Keepers and their Gathering, horrible things. It all started about ten years later in the 90s . . ." Sonia Koske's voice trailed off and her eyes took on a faraway look. Whatever thoughts had come into her mind began affecting her physically. Her face, which had been soft and vulnerable as she talked about her father, became pinched. Even the way she sat seemed to change, more hunched over with a slight hump on her back.

Herbert felt himself become tense. "All right, the 90s. Tell me what happened then."

Sonia Koske raised her head and focused on his eyes. "The Gathering came out of hibernation, but there wasn't enough food for them. Embalming has poisoned it. They were starving and went hunting for food. Sheriff, they were hunting for *people*."

Herbert sat speechless.

"It was so awful here. People started finding mutilated bodies and the whole town was in a panic. And now it's starting again!" Sonia Koske's face became so pale, Herbert was afraid she might faint. He rose to help her, but she steadied herself.

"OK, take it easy. Where were you when this was all happening?" Herbert's mind was racing. The mutilations had happened before. What had the town done then? How did it end? There was much he wanted to know.

Sonia Koske took several deep breaths. "I was working for the mayor, Miss Stadtlander. I heard everything that went on. They would have meetings about it, about the deaths and the missing people. The sheriff, the councilmen, the local veterinarian and a couple others. They were baffled about what was doing it."

"After those meetings, what did they do?"

"Miss Stadtlander talked about abandoning the town, getting everyone out. But the others wouldn't hear of giving up their homes and businesses. They said they would lose everything. They argued about it hot and heavy with Miss Stadtlander. At least a dozen people had been killed by this time, including a five-year-old boy who fell into an old cistern one night while he was playing. His father heard him screaming and came running with a torch, but he was too late. There wasn't much left of any of them. Then Heinrich Bruhl came to one of the meetings. He told them that he knew what was doing the killing. Everyone was skeptical until Mr. Bruhl showed them Thaddeus Bump's journal and the notes his father, Raston Bruhl, made when he dug up the old cemetery. *Read that*, he says as he laid them on the table. I remember it was deathly quiet in the room while they all took their turn."

"I can imagine." Herbert pictured the scene, fearing he could be part of a similar one.

"I knew that the notes and journal must say something horrible. After Miss Stadtlander finished reading, she just sat there. She looked so helpless, so depressed. Finally she told everybody she had no choice but to order everyone out of the town. Then everybody started talking at once. One man, I'm not sure who, refused to believe any of it. A few men started walking around the room cursing and shouting, saying they would never agree to abandon the town, no matter what. They all finally left without agreeing on anything."

"I understand their confusion, believe me."

"The mayor locked the notes and the journal in her desk, but I had a key so I took them out and read them. That was when I decided I had to tell her."

Herbert raised his eyebrows.

"I was waiting for Miss Stadtlander when she got to her office the next morning. As soon as she sat down at her desk, I came in and told her about what happened to me on Big Tow. Part of the time I was crying, but I managed to get it all out. She didn't say a thing until I finished. Then she just said two words: *My God.*"

"What did she do after that?" Herbert's chair creaked as he shifted his weight.

"When all the others arrived later, she asked me to wait outside and closed the door. After almost an hour, the door opened and she came out by herself. She said she had told the people in the room what I had told her and asked me real nice to come into the room with her. I was *so* scared going in there, let me tell you. My legs were shaking when I sat down, all these grim-faced men in their dark suits sitting around that table staring at me. And right across the table from where I sat was Mr. Bruhl."

"Heinrich Bruhl, Hilder Bruhl's grandfather?"

"Yes. He did most of the talking. He said Miss Stadtlander told them what I said, then he warned me about lying and making up stories, saying it was a sin and I could go to hell for doing it. Then he asked real angry-like whether the things I told Miss Stadtlander were true. I simply nodded my head, knowing they all thought I was crazy. Then he demanded I tell everything to them as well. So I told them as best I could about hearing the Keepers. I thought they would all break out laughing, but they just sat there staring at me. Then Miss Stadtlander thanked me and said I could go."

"Do you know what they did?"

"Oh, yes, I know. That night Mr. Heitmeier, one of the councilmen, was killed. His wife found him missing from their bed in the middle of the night. They searched and searched for him. Finally they found his bones and the nightshirt he was wearing in the pit under their outhouse. They figured he got up sometime in the night to relieve himself and, well, you know."

Herbert tried not to picture it. "Yeah, I think I know."

"When the news got around about Mr. Heitmeier, a lot of people in town, whole families, began to pack up and leave. Miss Stadtlander was gone most of the day. When she got back, she called me into her office. She said she understood what an awful experience I had on Big Tow Island with my father dying and how scared I must have been. But now she said that my family and everybody else in town was in danger of ending up like Mr. Heitmeier. That we'd all have to leave Bruders Landing unless they could find out some way to stop the killing. Finally she asked me if I'd be willing to go back to Big Tow and try to contact the Keepers. The very idea nearly scared me to death, but she was very persuasive."

"You went back there?" Herbert was astonished.

"Yes. I think there had been a lot of discussion,

but finally they all decided I should go. The Sheriff took me, Mr. Unterhoff, and Mr. Bruhl. Dr. Hentzel went, too."

"Did you find them, the Keepers? Or should I ask, did they find you?"

"Not the first day. Those men had never been on Big Tow Island before and it was getting dark before we found an inlet that led to the interior. So we went back early the next morning. I remember it looked as if it were going to start raining any minute. We entered that inlet and they kept asking me whether they should go this way or that, but I didn't know. Nothing looked familiar. Those men were nervous, let me tell you. They kept looking all around and fingering the triggers on their shotguns. I was so afraid one would go off. Around noon it got darker and thunder was rumbling in the distance. Then it started to rain. We came to some open place like a big pond, and the rain was coming down like cats and dogs. It was hard to see anything. They had decided to turn back, one of them saying I probably dreamt the whole thing anyway, when I heard them."

"The Keepers?"

"Yes. Well, you don't really hear them. They said to stop the boat, or something like that. When I looked through the rain, I could make out two of them, standing over the water like wooden statues, not more than twenty yards ahead of us. The sheriff saw them, too, and started pointing so the others would look. He looked scared. They all did. I was pretty scared, too, but the sheriff said I had to try to talk to them, so I did."

"How did you do that?"

"I didn't know what else to do so I just shouted what the sheriff told me to. I said something like the Gathering were killing nice people in our town. We wanted to know why they were doing it. Why the Keepers were letting them?"

"Did they answer?"

"Yes, the words came in my head but all they said was we had to go back. So I shouted again. Then they started talking. They said the food the Gathering gets from the ground is making them sick and many are dying. To keep from starving, the Gathering now have to kill their food. When I told this to the men in the boat, Dr. Hentzel and Mr. Bruhl guessed right away what had happened. They said to tell the Keepers that we didn't intend to poison the Gathering's food, that it was an accident and that it would stop."

"Did you tell them?"

"Sure, I yelled it at them as best I could."

"Did they answer?" Herbert asked before she could finish.

"Right away. They said they needed food now for the Gathering's young. They were very insistent. And the Keepers had come closer. It got very scary. When I told the men, they were afraid the Keepers were coming after *us*. The Sheriff wheeled the boat around so fast we almost tipped over and we got out of there."

"They didn't come after you, did they?"

"No. At least I don't think they did. The boat was going pretty fast and I never saw them any more."

"What did they do after that?"

Sonia Koske didn't answer immediately and seemed to struggle with what she was about to say.

"It's taken me this long to speak up. I should've told someone long ago. I've never been very brave."

"Going back to Big Tow Island seems pretty brave to me."

"Maybe, but I really didn't have much choice. That night after we got back there was another big meeting in the Mayor's office. This time they had me come in and stay. The same people were there plus one more, Heinrich Bruhl's helper."

"Boris?"

"Yes, Boris Brinter. When I came in, he was sitting there stone-faced, his eyes cold as ice, a mean smirk that never went away. He was a big, strong kid and his hair was long and scruffy even then. Of course it was blonde in those days. It gave me a chill just to look at him. I never did find out where he came from or where Heinrich Bruhl found him. When the meeting started, Sheriff Unterhoff told about finding the Keepers and what they had told me, that the Gathering had young and needed more food. Dr. Hentzel explained the problem with embalming and said they would either have to take unprepared bodies to the island or abandon the town. Mr. Bruhl said when there are family members around, it would be difficult to fake the embalming even if they could fake a burial. The body would start to smell and family members would get suspicious. Besides, he said, business was slow and he didn't have any bodies. The last person who died in town was Bernard Heitmeier and the Gathering had already seen to him. Miss Stadtlander thought dealing with the Keepers was hopeless. That they should go ahead and get everyone out of the town to save their lives."

"But that's not what happened."

"No, that isn't what happened. God knows that's what they should have done. Mr. Bruhl said there was no way he was going to abandon everything he and his father had worked for. That there *was* a way they could get food for the Gathering and he intended to do it."

Herbert's skin began to crawl as he felt some terrible revelation coming.

"The others wanted to know how, of course. Mr. Bruhl never came right out and told, but he said there were people around town without families, people that wouldn't be missed like drifters, ne'er-do-wells and the like. He said these people would finally be doing the town a service by saving it from the Gathering. Well, the room got deathly quiet. Mr. Bruhl told them not to worry, that they wouldn't have to get their hands dirty. He and Boris would take care of that. But they would have to help them deliver."

"Deliver? Deliver what?"

"Dead bodies. To deliver corpses to Big Tow."

Herbert shivered. "Did the mayor, Miss Stadtlander, go along with this?"

"Not at first. She and the coroner were against it, but Mr. Bruhl said something to them quietly that I couldn't hear. They both got these terrified looks on their faces. After that they went along."

"Did you ever learn what Bruhl said to them?"

"It must have been a threat."

"What kind of threat?"

"I'm not sure, but I've always thought he told them they would end up feeding the Gathering one way or another. By then it was nearly midnight. As they were about to leave, Mr. Bruhl said there was one more thing. Something in the tone of his voice made the room go very still again. He told us we all had to take a solemn oath, *on our graves* were the words he used, that we were never to tell a living soul anything about what had been talked about in that room or what they were about to do. And he looked right at me after he said it. I knew exactly what he meant."

"Which was what?"

"That our lives depended on keeping our mouths shut. He said Boris Brinter would make sure we all kept our word. I took a quick glance at Boris. He had this murderous smirk on his face that as much as said he was looking forward to his assignment. I'll *never* forget that look. It still scares me just to think about it."

"Remember now, I told you I would take care of Boris," Herbert said firmly.

"Thanks, Sheriff, I know you'll try. Heinrich made him pledge to kill anyone who said a word about what they were doing. You can be sure no one there that night ever doubted for a minute that he'd do it. And if there was any doubt that night, it was over very quickly."

"How do you know?"

"Because right after that Boris began his work."

A tremor ran through Herbert's body. "How can you . . . are you sure?"

Oh, I'm sure all right. I never actually saw him, but I heard about it. Miss Stadtlander knew about most of them. It made her so upset. She would talk about them in her office. Sometimes to me, and sometimes to the coroner, and sometimes to no one at all. Finally it drove her mad. She killed herself, you know."

"No, I didn't know."

"It was up north along the bluffs. About a year after the killing started."

"You mean to say the killing went on for over a year?"

"Longer, more like three or four. After a few

months, Miss Stadtlander was just looking awful. She could hardly do any work, and I don't think she was sleeping at all. One evening she left the office in her buggy and drove north to Walnut Grove Cemetery. They found her horse and buggy in the cemetery the next morning. Her body was at the bottom of the bluff, right across from Big Tow Island. I guess she couldn't live with it any more. They buried her two days later. At least they buried a coffin."

"Jesus!" was all Herbert could manage to say.

"One of the councilmen, Mr. Schuler, took over as mayor and made it clear I was to stay on as his secretary. He wasn't bothered at all by the killing. In fact, I think he sort of relished it and I heard more than ever about what they were doing."

"So by this time it had been going on for over a year?"

"Yes. I didn't know how it was done, or what they did with the bodies before Mr. Schuler was mayor. After that, I learned more than I ever wanted." Sonia Koske paused, looking as if she was gathering her thoughts.

"Can you tell me what they did?"

"Yes, I'll tell you, but I need some water, Sheriff. Just let me get a glass. Would you like one?"

"No, no thanks."

Sonia Koske rose unsteadily from the sofa and went to the kitchen. For a moment Herbert feared she might not come back, somehow disappear. But he heard the water run and then she reappeared. She sat back down heavily on the sofa and sipped from a lavender water glass.

"Mr. Bruhl and a couple of the others would hunt for someone they thought could disappear without much fuss. Usually a bum or a drifter, maybe even a traveling salesman. A lot of new people were coming into Bruders Landing in those days. Many of them never made it out. But they weren't the only ones. Boris also did a few townsfolk Mr. Bruhl had it in for. They'd lure them to Bruhl's Mortuary or out to the country. Then Boris would kill them, strangle them with a rope so they wouldn't bleed all over, a garrote they called it."

"Do you know where they took the bodies?"

"At first they took them by boat to Big Tow Island, somewhere in the interior, but they were real nervous about somebody seeing them on the river. So they started taking them to a house north of town where the Gathering had burrowed out of their tunnels."

Herbert shifted to the front of his chair. "Do you know where?"

"The Gerdes farm."

Herbert felt another piece fall into place. "How did they know to do that?"

"Old Man Gerdes found some strange holes with a bad odor, one in the cellar of his house and one out in his root cellar. When he told the sheriff about them, he put two and two together."

"So Old Man Gerdes was in on it."

"Yes, after he talked to the sheriff."

"Does Lyle Gerdes know about this?"

"I don't think so. Lyle was too young to know what was going on and I doubt his father ever told him."

"How long did this go on?"

"'Til they were sure the Gathering had gone back into hibernation, in 1903, I think. I almost got used to it, it went on so long. At first I had nightmares all the time, then only once in a while. Frankly, I was sure they'd get caught, but they never did. You'd think someone would have figured out that something was happening in Bruders Landing with all those people disappearing."

"And the Gathering didn't kill *anyone* during that time?"

"No, not that I know of. So I guess it worked to feed them, but it was just exchanging one set of killers for another."

Herbert was numb, not knowing whether to console her or thank her. Neither felt right.

"I'll never forgive myself for waiting so long to tell someone. At least I finally got the courage. I've had a long life, longer than I ever expected. Now Boris can go to hell where he belongs."

"With Heinrich Bruhl and the others dead, you think Boris will still try to hurt you after all these years?"

"Think? Sheriff, I *know* he will, as long as he's still breathing. He swore to Mr. Bruhl that he'd do it, that he'd kill anyone of us in that room that said anything about what they were doing. And he will, I know it. He's killed so many already what's one more old lady? Frankly, it's a wonder they got him to stop killing after the Gathering went back to hibernating. Boris went mad for it, for the killing. I guess anyone would after a time, especially someone like him who's belfry is full of bats in the first place. He got too eager, wanted to kill more and more people, I heard. And I think he did, too. Killed some people on his own. Even Mr. Schuler was worried about it. I heard him tell Mr. Bruhl more than once he had to get Boris under control."

"Did he do it? Get Boris under control?"

"Yes, Mr. Bruhl sent him somewhere for a while. When he came back, he had calmed down a little. But Mr. Schuler said Boris was only biding his time until the Gathering came out again so he could get back to feeding them."

"Well, we're sure not going to give him that opportunity. But do you think he might try?"

"He might. It's the killing he likes."

Silence hung in the room for a moment as if the spectre of Boris Brinter had entered. Herbert was deep in thought.

"Miss Koske . . . Sonia," he said tentatively, breaking their silence. "Would you be willing to go to Big Tow Island one last time . . . with me?"

There was no sound in the room until Sonia Koske uttered a deep sigh. "Why do you want to go?" A great weariness had crept into her face.

"If I can . . . if you can contact them again, the Keepers, there's something I could tell them. Something that might get them to leave. If not, well . . . "

"Then, I'll go, Sheriff. When?"

"Soon, I think. Tomorrow."

"Yes, it had best be soon."

Chapter Thirty-Four

The Last Night

July 23, 1956

As soon as he left Sonia Koske, Herbert walked quickly to his office and called Norma. In a voice as firm and calm as he could muster, he told her to turn on the cellar light and leave it burning, then to close the cellar door and lock it so Albie couldn't go down accidentally. Norma asked the obvious question—did this mean they were now in danger? He told her he didn't think so right then, that he'd explain when he got home. To his relief she stayed calm.

He hadn't forgotten his promise to Sonia Koske. As soon as he had hung up the phone, he called Hilder Bruhl to make sure Brinter was there. The mortician assured him that Brinter was still working; that when he finished, he always went straight to his tiny apartment at the rear of the old mansion's third floor. Herbert told him to call his office if he should hear Brinter leave. Next he wrote out an order for the night deputy on patrol to check Sonia Koske's house every half hour. Then he forced himself to attack the mound of paper and mail on his desk that he had neglected since Lloyd Wischmeier was killed.

Herbert left his office at 6:30 intending to drive home, only a half hour later than he had promised Norma, but a nagging concern drew him to Sonia Koske's house. He drove by slowly, looking for anything moving, anything out of the ordinary. There was nothing unusual in front. Turning at the corner, he crept down her alley. When he could see her back door, he stopped the car and sat with the motor idling, watching. Nothing unusual there either, but a concern gnawed at him like an itch he couldn't scratch. Driving back to the street in front of her house, he pulled to the curb a few doors away and waited. When the night deputy approached in the cruiser for his check, Herbert eyed him closely. The cruiser slowed to a crawl, the deputy peering at the house through the passenger window. When the cruiser came abreast of Herbert's car, the deputy saw him and waved, giving the OK sign. Herbert waved back. If only he had more people, he could station a deputy at Sonia Koske's house. But that was impossible without double shifts for himself and two deputies, and taking on that expense based only on some vague concern would be hard to justify. Now it was nearly 7:30. He would be late getting home again. Another broken promise to Norma that needed mending. He started his car's engine, trying to persuade himself that the measures he had in place were enough to keep Sonia Koske safe.

Herbert closed his front door loud enough to be heard. He was still worried about Sonia Koske. Her vulnerability had revived memories of Chicago, of his father, of Selma, of the clerk in the liquor store, memories he once thought had been put to rest. He didn't want Sonia Koske added to the list. Norma's voice carried from the kitchen, scolding Albie for not picking up his toys. He lingered for a few moments at the door savoring the sounds of normalcy.

"Norma, hello, I'm home," he called out.

"We're in the kitchen. Be out in a minute."

"To hell with it, I've done all I can tonight," he muttered and walked to his favorite chair, settling in wearily. It was the time of day for a cold beer. He certainly could use one, but thought better of it.

Something told him he would need to go back out tonight. Should he call Sonia Koske now, to make sure she was all right? That wouldn't work. She doesn't have a phone. Besides, he needed time with Norma and his son, time that might take his mind off those things in the bluffs for a while.

Minutes later Norma appeared through the kitchen door carrying Albie dressed in his pajamas. At the sight of his father, the boy broke into a large grin and held out his arms. Norma sat him in Herbert's lap.

"Here, he's all yours. You might ask him why he was such a stinker eating his supper. It took me quite a while to get it off his face."

Herbert gave him a hug, then held him at arm's length looking sternly into his eyes. "Well, sport, what do you have to say for yourself? Mom says you gave her trouble eating the good supper she spent all that time making for you."

Albie squirmed and looked down at the floor.

"No defense, eh sport? Well, then, guilty as charged. Now you behave for your mom, you hear?"

"Yes, Dada," Albie mumbled sheepishly, as if he understood.

"Good," Norma commented, "there's nothing like a little guilt to influence behavior. It's way past this child's bedtime. How about you doing the honors now that you're finally home?"

With Albie tucked in bed, Herbert and Norma sat at their kitchen table. Herbert ate his warmed-over dinner slowly without much appetite. Norma sipped a glass of beer.

"What was it tonight, Herb?" Norma asked, looking sympathetic. "More about that gruesome murder?"

"Yeah, a lot more." Herbert laid down his fork and told her about Raston Bruhl's notes and the journal, then about his meeting with Sonia Koske. Norma listened without speaking, an incredulous look on her face.

When Herbert finished, Norma looked into his eyes. "I'm asking you again, Herb, are we in danger? Should I take Albie somewhere he'll be safe?"

398

"No, not yet any way. There's no sign those things have come as far as town."

"Then why did you call this afternoon and tell us to stay out of the cellar?"

"Just a precaution. It made me feel better. Besides, there's no way to be sure they won't come this far again."

"Again? What do you mean again?"

"Remember, according to Raston Bruhl's notes, those things had gotten into the old cemetery."

"Good lord, Herb. That's where the high school is."

Herbert lay in bed staring at the ceiling. Norma was breathing heavily next to him, the sounds of peaceful sleep. He was envious. He desperately needed some rest, to be fresh for what might be in store on Big Tow. But like so many nights before, sleep wouldn't come. His foreboding about Sonia Koske continued to eat at him. It had been there all evening, always in the back of his mind.

The glowing hands on the clock read 12:30, barely thirty minutes from the last time he checked, and he wasn't getting any sleepier. He gave a heavy sigh and sat up. Might as well get up and do something. Maybe a call to the office. He pushed back the sheet and climbed out. Norma stirred but didn't wake. He crossed the bedroom in his bare feet and stepped into the hall, closing the door softly.

Once downstairs he turned on the light and went to the phone in the kitchen. Lester Hammond was on duty and answered on the second ring.

"Lester, this is Herb. Anything going on?"

"Seems quiet enough. Got a call an hour ago about a fight at GiGi's. I sent Howard over in the cruiser, but things had died down by the time he got there. He chewed out the bartender and left. Then I just hung up with Mrs. Hausknecht. Said she can't find Fred."

"Well, that's nothing new. Have you started calling the bars?"

"No, said she'd already called 'em. No one's seen

him all night. That's when she called here."

"That is strange. Better tell Howard to keep his eyes peeled. In fact you better tell him to check the bars himself to make sure. I don't know where else Fred would go, unless he got drunk before he left home and is wandering around the streets somewhere."

"Right, Herb."

"Tell me, what's Howard's report on Sonia Koske's place?"

"All quiet. He was there, oh, twenty minutes ago I guess it was. Said nothin' was movin'."

"Hmm, I think I'll run by pretty soon myself. Maybe I'll have a look for old Fred at the same time. I'm slow in going to sleep anyway."

"Suit yourself, Herb."

It took Herbert less that ten minutes to reach the street in front of Sonia Koske's house. He had driven normally, resisting the urge to turn on the flashing lights. He slowed to a crawl as he approached. The moon had risen, its glow leaving a shadow behind every object it touched, moon shadows that could conceal someone who didn't want to be seen. He forced himself to look at each one, watching for movement, anything at all that didn't fit. Seeing nothing suspicious, he drove past the house and turned the corner.

As he entered the alley, he saw a light in one of Sonia Koske's second floor windows. What the hell was she doing up at this hour? He stopped the car by her rear walk. For a moment he hesitated, then picked up his flashlight and got out. When he reached the small stoop by the back door, he climbed the two wooden steps carefully to avoid making any noise that might alarm her. He pulled on the handle to her screen door. It was unfastened. He opened it and turned the knob on her back door to test the lock. The door opened at his touch setting off an alarm in his head.

He quickly switched on his flashlight and looked around the doorjamb. There were no signs the door had been forced, but that was no guarantee someone hadn't broken in. It was an old lock that could be opened with a skeleton key. He had to contact the old woman, to make sure she was all right, which meant waking her up.

He pushed the door open wide and called into the house: "Miss Koske. Sonia Koske. Can you hear me? It's Sheriff Siefken."

He listened for a moment. No response.

"Miss Koske. Wake up. I have to talk to you. It's me, Sheriff Siefken."

He knocked loudly against the back door with his flashlight. A light came on in the house next door and a neighborhood dog started to bark, but there was no sound from inside. He stepped through the doorway and ran his hand over the wall, feeling for a light switch. His hand touched it and he pushed on the button. An overhead light in the kitchen came on. Before him was an overturned chair. Red smears on the floor formed a trail that led under his feet. Behind him the trail continued out the back door.

"God dammit!" he said as anguish built inside him. Moving quickly he followed the trail of blood with the beam of his flashlight through the kitchen into the darkened hallway. The trail led to the foot of the stairs, then up the steps. He took them two at a time. A light came from one of the bedrooms. He sprinted the short distance to the doorway.

The bedroom was in shambles. His heart was pounding. A table lamp lying on the floor lit the room, its shade torn and bent. The bedclothes had been partly ripped from the mattress and hung down over the side of the bed. A pool of crimson had formed in the center of the mattress which was dotted with red speckles. One pillow had been ripped, its feathers covering the bed like snow, many of them soaked with the blood. The red trail he had been following led to the bed. Herbert stood nearly paralyzed in the doorway, imagining with horror the terrible struggle that had taken place. He had failed her. Jesus, I can't even protect an old lady, he heard himself say. He felt as if he was starting to melt and his legs began to sag. He caught himself as he was about to collapse.

A quick look around the room revealed no telephone. He retraced his steps downstairs. There was no phone in the kitchen either and he didn't remember seeing one in her living room that afternoon.

"Shit!" he muttered and hurried out the back door to his car. Just as he reached the vehicle, a car sped toward him down the alley, stopping a foot from his rear bumper. The red light on the roof started to flash.

"Howard! Where the hell have you been?" he shouted.

Howard Fincher, a short, rotund man in his early thirties, exited the cruiser awkwardly, adjusting the hat on top of his prematurely bald pate.

"Sheriff, I was just here twenty minutes ago."

"Did you see that light on up there?"

Fincher looked up at the window. "Uh, no. I don't think so."

"Was it on ? Yes or no."

"Maybe it was on. I figured she must be up going to the john or something."

"Well, her bedroom looks like a slaughterhouse and she's missing. It looks like she was attacked, then dragged out of the house. There's a trail of blood leading out back door. Take your flashlight and see where it goes. Quick now, in case she's alive. If you see Boris Brinter lurking around, hold him. But be careful. He's dangerous."

Herbert raised Lester Hammond at the office on his car radio. "Lester, pay attention now. We might have another murder. Sonia Koske. I'm in the alley back of her house, but this time there may be a killer we recognize. Howard's here. Call in Gus and the other guys and get the other two cars rolling. Tell them we're looking for Boris Brinter, but to get on over here pronto. Then call Hilder Bruhl. He didn't call, did he?"

"Not tonight."

"OK. Ask him if Boris is there. If he isn't, ask him where he might be. Also, ask him why he didn't call and tell you Boris had left. Get back to me right away after you talk to him. Got all that?"

"Got it, Sheriff."

"Oh, and call Norma. Tell her Sonia Koske's missing and I won't make it back home tonight."

Fincher was nowhere in sight as Herbert returned

to the house. Flashlight in hand, he began to search the interior. He turned on every light he could find as he went. As he was about to climb the stairs to the second floor, there was a knock at the front door.

"Everything all right in there?" a muffled voice called out from the porch. The neighbors had arrived. Herbert walked into the living room and opened the door. A startled man in robe and pajamas stood in the doorway. A woman huddled on the sidewalk behind him. Herbert recognized the man's face but couldn't think of his name.

"Oh, Sheriff, I'm sorry. My wife heard our dog barking and made me come out and . . ."

"Fine, I understand. We're looking for Miss Koske. How long have you been awake?"

"Um, just a few minutes."

Herbert called to the woman on the sidewalk. She walked forward tentatively.

"We've just discovered that your neighbor, Miss Koske, is missing and may have been attacked. Did you see anything unusual around her house in the last hour, any kind of activity at all?"

The woman answered in a gravelly voice: "No, I was up but I didn't look out the window until the dog started to bark a few minutes ago. That's when I saw a light on in the house."

"You didn't see anything at all?"

"There was one thing. About an hour ago I got up to go to the bathroom. I go a lot during the night, you know, and I usually look out the window when I'm in there. And right there in the Doppelmeyer's driveway was this big hearse. Now that struck me as odd, since I couldn't figure what a hearse would be doing there at that hour."

"The Doppelmeyer's live on the other side of us," the man explained.

"Anyway, before we came over here after the dog was barking, I looked to see if it was still there and it was gone."

"Is their driveway in the back of the house, off the alley?"

"Yeah, all of them are in this block," the man

answered.

"Thank you. That's a great help. We'll contact you if there's anything else we need. Now please tell anyone you see to stay away from the house."

Herbert hurried out the back door to his car. Hammond answered his radio call promptly.

"Lester, did you reach Hilder?"

"Yeah. He thought Boris was still in his room but went to check. He said he'd call right back."

"When he does, tell him Boris left with his hearse if he doesn't already know. Did you raise the others?"

"Yeah. Norma says she understands and our guys are on their way."

"Good. Tell them we'll be looking for Bruhl's hearse with Boris Brinter driving, but to get on over here. I'll wait with Howard until they come."

Herbert walked back toward the house. Fincher was nowhere in sight. "Howard!" he shouted, not caring that he might wake-up more of the neighbors. "Where the . . where *are* you?"

"Here, Sheriff," said a voice some distance away. "I'm on my way."

Herbert drummed his fingers on the screen door. A mosquito buzzed by his ear. He swatted at it without thinking. Seconds later Fincher appeared through an opening in the tall hedge at the side of Sonia Koske's house. He was stepping carefully.

"What's the matter?"

"I don't want to disturb the trail. It leads through the hedge here." Howard pointed his flashlight at the ground. There were smears of blood on the grass and hedge. "I followed these traces of blood through here and across the neighbor's yard. As far as I can tell, they end at the driveway next door. I think someone put her in a car."

"Good work. It was probably Boris Brinter in Bruhl's hearse. Now we just have to find him. You go on and search the house. See if you find anything, and keep the neighbors away. I've got an idea where he might have gone. When Gus and Bill get here, tell them to start looking for that hearse. And tell Gus to stay by his radio. I may want him quick."

He drove out of the alley too fast and the cruiser's front end hit the dip at the street. The car was still rocking as he turned sharply, its tires groaning for traction. If the things Sonia Koske told him were true, there were two places Boris was likely to take Sonia Koske. Where should he look first? She said they had taken the bodies to Big Tow. After they got nervous about being caught, they took them to the Gerdes farm. Where would Boris go for a boat? And where would he go on Big Tow? The island could wait for daylight. He would go to the farm.

"Sheriff to base. Lester, listen up." Herbert spoke rapidly into the radio as he drove. "Did Hilder call back?"

"Yeah. You were right. He said he couldn't figure how Boris took the hearse out without him hearing, but it's gone."

"No surprise there. I'm headed for the Gerdes farm now. Raise Gus and tell him to meet me there pronto. And have Bill relieve you."

"It's OK, Sheriff. I'm not that tired."

"Going to bed's not what I had in mind. I want you to get down to the marina. We may be making a trip to Big Tow."

There was silence for a moment. "Got it," Hammond finally answered.

Herbert checked his watch as he approached Walnut Grove Cemetery. It was 3:20. The moon was low on the horizon, the night darker.

As he turned into the lane to the Gerdes farm, the canopy of tree limbs blotted out what little light the moon still cast. At the end of the dark canopy he could see the profile of the old house looming like a giant shadow. It had an ominous look. The Gerdes's should have left on some lights, he thought. He stopped at the front steps, and turned on the cruiser's spotlight, shining the beam around the house and the farmyard. There was no sign of the hearse. He picked up his flashlight and got out. Cautiously he circled the house, then the barn and outbuildings. Nothing. Brinter wasn't there . . . or was he? He could have parked the hearse somewhere else, or put her body in the cellar and left. He had to check.

Herbert climbed the few stairs to the front porch and tried the door. It was locked. No sign of forced entry. He checked the windows on either side of the door. Also locked. He walked around the house to the back door, checking windows as he went. Tight as a drum. The back door was locked as well. He started around the other side checking windows, moving fast until he came to the storm door that led to the cellar. He took hold of the iron ring that served as a handle and pulled. The door rose reluctantly with a scraping noise. He opened it as far as it would go and rested it on its hinges. The hook that would have locked it dangled free. He pointed his light down the stone stairs, searching for a sign that Boris had been there. The steps were clean, no bloodstains, but he would have to go down and check. It would be risky without someone to watch his back, but there wasn't time to wait for Gus. He returned to his car at a trot.

"Sheriff to base. Lester, I'm at the Gerdes house. There's no sign of Brinter yet. Did you reach Gus?"

"Yep, just a couple minutes ago. He's on his way."

"Call him again and tell him I'm going to search the cellar. I'll go in through the storm door on the west side. Got it?"

"Got it. You should wait for him."

"I'll think about it."

He stood over the open storm door, thinking briefly of what might be waiting below, then went down the stairs. The beam from his flashlight swept the dirt floor. No blood. He walked toward the octopus-like furnace and his head brushed a beaded chain. He pulled it and a dim bulb lit the space around him. Cautiously, he rounded the large furnace, checking the floor. Several feet ahead he saw the stairs from the kitchen. Beyond the stairs, the beam disappeared into darkness. He approached the stairs, playing the beam across the floor. Near the bottom step was the bloodstain left by Lloyd Wischmeier.

He pointed his flashlight toward the old cellar and for a split second thought about waiting for Gus. In the distance he could make out a large door. He began walking toward it, shining his flashlight from side to side. The piles of boxes and discarded furniture cast shadows that seemed to follow him. Then the beam landed on the door again. It was even more massive than he remembered. The door stood slightly ajar. Shifting the flashlight to his left hand, he patted his revolver. Now he had to move fast. His muscles tensed.

He seized the door's handle in his free hand and yanked. The rusty hinges resisted, but the door moved grudgingly. He opened it wide enough to enter and pointed the flashlight into the black room. The putrid stench inside was all too familiar. Two figures were on the floor, next to the pile of rocks under the opening in the wall. Clothing covered their faces.

He unholstered his revolver and aimed at the closest figure, wondering which was Sonia Koske. "Boris! Put your hands behind your head!"

Neither figure moved.

"Do it now, Boris! Put your hands behind your head. I'm not fooling around here."

There was still no movement by either figure. He approached the first one and nudged it with the toe of his shoe. Still no movement. He shoved it with his foot until the figure rolled part way onto its side, a shirt falling away from its head. Herbert stifled a cry. The figure was never going to respond. Its head was bare bone—a skull resting on a pile of hair and a ragged shirt—its jaw open wide, as if it had been screaming. The eye sockets were vacant. Herbert stepped around the body and shined his light on the second figure. He pushed away the clothing with his foot. The face was stripped away.

"Jesus!" he muttered. Instinctively he shined his light at the opening. There was nothing but a black hole.

He played his light back over the bodies. They were lying in a pool of blood, both fully clothed, bony hands protruding from their shirtsleeves. From their clothing it was obvious he was not looking at Sonia Koske and Boris Brinter.

"Sheriff, you down here?" A voice came from

outside the room.

"Yeah, Gus. Back here in the old cellar," he shouted. "Keep coming if you've got a flashlight."

"Are you kidding? I brought two."

Herbert was kneeling on a newspaper next to the bodies going through pockets as Mecklenberg entered the old room. "Oh, my God!"

"They each have a little money on them but no ID. They could be looters, or just a couple of drifters who picked the wrong cellar to hole up in, or . . ." Herbert paused, thinking.

"Or what?"

"Or Boris made a delivery earlier to slow us up."

Herbert pushed open the shredded shirt on one of the bodies with the end of his flashlight. The flesh was gone entirely from the rib cage and shoulders. The bones were still moist, dotted with small, pinkish remnants of flesh. He could see through the chest cavity to the bloody shirt beneath. "Looks like everything's gone but the bones."

Stepping around the pool of blood, Herbert went to the next body which was on its side. He pushed on the shoulder with his flashlight, rolling the body onto its back. The front of the shirt was shredded and blood soaked. The skin on the chest was missing from the chin to his belt, exposing the chest cavity. Under the ribcage Herbert recognized parts of the lungs, esophagus, stomach and liver, partially chewed and steeped in blood. His stomach began to revolt.

"Jesus Christ!" Mecklenberg turned his head and vomited. Herbert kept swallowing to avoid doing the same.

"I must've interrupted them feeding on this guy when I came with the light." Herbert gestured toward the opening. "You can bet they're in there, waiting."

Mecklenberg stared at the opening. "What should we do?"

"Get out of here, that's what. I'll call Lester and have him tell Reuben to come out here with plenty of lights. Then we'll go find Boris."

"But this guy, the body, when we leave those things'll . . ." Mecklenberg choked, stopping in mid-sentence.

"I know. But in the condition he's in, it's not going to matter much. And maybe it'll satisfy their appetite for a while."

Chapter Thirty-Five

The Confrontation

July 24, 1956

Fatigue began to overtake him as Herbert drove out of the Gerdes driveway. It was getting hard to think clearly and the thought of a few hours sleep was seductive. But sleeping would have to wait until he had found Sonia Koske, or what was left of her. He had hoped the sunrise would rejuvenate him but a drizzly fog had risen from the river, settling over the valley and concealing the sky. His headlights reflected off the waves of mist rolling from the bluffs. Navigating the river would be treacherous. He reached for the radio mike.

"Sheriff to base. Is that you, Bill?"

"Right, Sheriff."

"Good. Where're Lester and Howard?"

"Lester left for the Marina a few minutes ago. Howard's still at the scene."

"All right. Gus and I just left the Gerdes farm. We didn't find Brinter but we did find two bodies in the cellar where the Wischmeier boy was killed. They're a mess. No ID. Call Reuben and tell him. He'll need to get out there, but he needs someone with him. Tell him to take Hilder. And to take plenty of lights. Since Boris wasn't at the Gerdes farm, he might have headed for Big Tow. He'd have to steal a boat to get there, so Gus is going to check the roads along the river to see if he spots the hearse. I'm on my way to the marina, but I've got to make a stop first."

It was 5:10. The first glimmers of light over the horizon began to make the fog opaque. His knock on the front door of the Starker house was tentative and produced nothing. His second knock was strong enough to wake up the household. A few minutes later he heard shuffling inside. The door opened and a disheveled Roy Starker appeared, a robe hastily wrapped around his pajamas.

"Morning, Roy. I'm awful sorry to wake you up this early, but it's kind of important."

"Uh, it's all right, Sheriff, we're about, uh, I'm usually up soon," Roy Starker managed to say as he struggled to open his eyes fully. "What time is it anyway?"

"It's going on 5:30. Much too early for me to be knocking on your door, I know."

"Well, it doesn't happen often. Want to come in?"

"For a minute."

As Herbert stepped into the hallway, a voice called down from the second floor. "Roy, who on earth was at the door?"

"It's the Sheriff, dear."

"Oh, my. I'll be down in a minute."

"There's no coffee made, Sheriff, but I can make some quick. You look like you could use it."

"Yes, I could, but . . ."

"No buts. Come on in the kitchen and sit."

Herbert followed him through the hall as Delores Starker came down the stairs, entering the kitchen behind them. From the look of her hair and make-up, Herbert never would have guessed she had been asleep ten minutes earlier.

"Good morning, Sheriff. This is a surprise. Is there trouble? Is it Henry? Has he done something? Let me make you some decent coffee." She took the coffee scoop from her husband's hand as she talked.

"I'm sure it's a surprise, Mrs. Starker. This *is*

411

about Henry, but he's done nothing wrong. Frankly, I need his help."

"Help you? Henry?" Roy Starker looked mystified.

"Now, Roy, don't be so shocked. Henry's a very capable young man," she said proudly as she took three coffee cups from the cupboard.

"He certainly is. Still, I wouldn't do this if we didn't have kind of an emergency on our hands. You see, last night someone attacked and kidnapped one of your neighbors, Sonia Koske."

"There, you see, Roy? I told you I heard a commotion over there last night. That's terrible. Right here on our block. Do you know who did it?"

"We have a suspect and we think he took her to Big Tow. Now that it's getting light, we'll start a search."

"Big Tow? Nobody goes to Big Tow. What has that island got to do with Henry?" Roy Starker asked.

"Henry can help us with our search. I shouldn't be telling on him like this, but he's been there before. Just a few days ago. And something happened to him on the island that can help."

Delores Starker nearly dropped the coffee cups. "Henry? On Big Tow? Oh, he couldn't have. How would he even get there?"

"On a friend's boat. I'd like him to go with us as soon as possible, as soon as he can be ready."

"You mean he went there after those men were attacked, maybe killed?"

"Yes, it was after that."

"It doesn't surprise me," Roy Starker said. "That boy is usually up to something, always fancied himself as some kind of explorer, even as a little kid. I don't want to even think about the other places he's been."

"But he's still asleep," Delores Starker said, starting to balk. The coffee cups rattled in her hand.

"We can wake him, if that's the only problem," Roy Starker responded. "Will he be in any danger, Sheriff?"

Herbert took the cups from Delores Starker's hands, afraid she was about to drop them. "A deputy and I are going. You can be sure we won't let anything happen to him."

"Aren't you taking a big search party?" Roy Starker asked.

"We'll call for more people if we need to. Right now we're not absolutely sure that's where Miss Koske is. I've got deputies looking other places as well." A search party is exactly what I *should* be taking, Herbert thought. But if there's any hope of contacting the Keepers, I can't take a crowd.

"Well, if you need him, we'll get him up, won't we?" Roy Starker gave his wife a look that discouraged her objection. "But I'd sure like to know how you think he can help."

"Hopefully he can introduce us to some people he met."

Fog billowed over the dock changing the light to shades of dark gray as Herbert, a full gas tank in each hand, led Henry to the boat slip. The air was cool and wet on his face, unusual weather for July.

Lester Hammond waited behind the steering wheel, a cigarette burning in his mouth, the motor idling.

"Henry, meet my deputy, Lester Hammond." Herbert stepped into the stern of the boat then loaded the extra gas tanks from the dock. "Lester, this is Henry Starker. He's here to help us when we find Miss Koske."

"Welcome aboard, Henry. Glad to meet you." Hammond held out his hand which Henry took.

"I know what you're wondering, Lester. Henry here was on Big Tow with some friends three days ago and saw the Keepers. He says the Keepers contacted him. I'm hoping they'll do it again."

"Well, you've seen a whole lot more than me, that's for sure. I've lived here all my life and never seen 'em." Hammond flicked the cigarette butt into the water.

"Henry. Put this on." Herbert handed him a life jacket.

"But it'll be too hot."

"Just put it on and sit in the bow. OK, Lester.

Let's go."

Hammond pulled the shift lever to reverse and backed the boat out of the slip. Shifting to forward, he headed for the gap in the marina's levee that led to the river.

Herbert shifted in his seat and leaned close to Hammond. "Gus radioed me right before I got to the Starker's." He spoke softly so Henry wouldn't hear. "Mel Schwartz is missing and his boat's gone."

Hammond stiffened, tightening his grip on the throttle. "I used to go fishin' with the guy. What happened?"

"My guess is he caught Boris stealing his boat."

As they glided into the river channel, the fog engulfed them and the world seemed to disappear.

Herbert called out: "Better stay close to shore so we can keep our bearings. We don't want to overshoot it."

The drone of the motor lowered and the boat slowed, turning slightly. A moment later Herbert could make out the faint outline of the riverbank through the mist.

Henry was twirling the ties on his life jacket between his fingers. "Sheriff, do you mind if I ask you something?"

"No, go ahead."

"Are you going to shoot them?"

"Who, you mean the Keepers?"

"The Keepers and those things . . . the Gathering."

Herbert scowled. "We don't shoot people except to save lives. We talk first whenever we can." The scene in the liquor store flashed through his mind as soon as he spoke. This time he *would* talk first. Besides, he wasn't at all sure shooting would do much good.

The boat moved steadily through the water near the shore. Muffled by the fog, the motor sounded as if it was running in a padded room. Herbert stared ahead blankly.

"We're coming to Walnut Grove up there on the bluff, Sheriff," Hammond announced. "Big Tow should be coming up off to our right. I'm going to head across the channel."

"All right, Lester. Take us across. You know where we're going."

"I should. I've spent my whole life avoiding that durned place and now this will be the second time I've been there in a week."

"Henry, when we get to the island, I want you to point out where you went. We'll go the same way."

"I'll try. It's so hard to see anything."

"You'll be able to see well enough before long."

Hammond turned the boat in a wide arc to the east. Almost immediately they were swallowed by the swirling fog. As the boat moved steadily through the water, the fog seemed to lighten like it was about to lift, then closed in again, dimming the light as if the day was already drawing to a close. For several minutes Herbert felt utterly alone, that they had somehow left the world behind. The only thing visible were his companions in the boat who looked like apparitions in the shadowy mist.

Suddenly a tree line loomed in front of them. "For Christ's sake, Lester, slow down! We're headed right into those trees!"

"Don't worry. I see 'em. That's it. The Big Tow herself." Lester eased back on the throttle and the boat settled in the water, nearly coming to a stop.

"OK, now. Take it slow and head north again. Stay as close as you can to shore. We want Henry to be able to spot the place they turned into the island."

Lester nudged the boat in close to the bank, moving at trolling speed. The shoreline looked surreal with wisps of fog mingling among the trees and brush. Suddenly a dull thump sounded from under the hull. The boat lurched to one side and the motor revved momentarily, then settled back to its low drone.

"Jeez, what was that?" Henry yelled. A muffled echo answered from the shore.

"We must have hit a log," Lester called out. "I think we're all right."

"We've got to keep a sharper eye out. See anything yet, Henry?"

"No. Wait, maybe there." Henry pointed. "Look in

those trees."

Herbert saw an indentation in the bank at water level. "Take us in closer, Lester. We'll have a look."

"I remember we went under some branches."

The bow of the boat slid under the overhanging limbs, then came to a stop with a soft bump.

"I think we're on the bank, Herb."

"I guess this isn't it," Henry said.

"OK, back it out."

Lester shifted into reverse quickly and pushed the throttle forward, backing the boat out from under the limbs.

"Keep going north," Herbert told him. "Henry, you tell us when you see something. We'll try anywhere you think might be the place. I'd rather bump into the bank again than miss it."

Henry stared diligently as they went. They all stayed very quiet, as if somehow they could hear the inlet when they were close.

Moments later Henry leaned toward the island squinting his eyes. "That might be it there."

The fog lifted a little. Herbert looked where Henry was pointing, a small inlet almost hidden by overhanging tree limbs. "We may have something this time. Let's have a look."

As the boat reached the low branches, Herbert ducked. Wet leaves brushed over his back as they went under. In a moment they were clear, the line of trees behind them. Herbert raised his head. They were in a narrow waterway hemmed in by tall reeds and grasses.

"Do you think this is the way you came?" Herbert asked.

"I think so. That tall grass looks familiar."

"Where did you go from here?"

"We stayed in the boat and followed the water until we came to a bunch of dead trees and a pond. That's where they were. At that pond."

"All right, we'll do the same. Lester, follow this waterway. Take it slow." Herbert touched his revolver out of habit. Should he have brought the shotguns, he wondered?

As they went deeper into the island's misty

interior, the waterway gradually narrowed. Reeds and grass brushed the sides of the boat. Herbert stood up carefully, but still couldn't see over the tall vegetation. When he sat back down, he noticed that Henry looked tense.

"Does this still seem right to you?" Herbert asked softly.

"I . . . I think so."

Ahead through the fog Herbert suddenly saw a row of tall figures with tentacles that seemed to be reaching toward the sky. He leaned away, startled.

"This is right. There're the dead trees," Henry said.

"Good. Did you get through them OK?"

"Yeah, we got through. The pond should be just a little ways further."

A limb scraped along the port side of the boat with a mournful screech as they entered the barren trees. "Careful here, Lester. There'll be a lot of snags."

"You're tellin' me." Hammond was hunched forward in his seat, straining to see what might await them in the water ahead.

They were surrounded by thick, gray tree trunks that stood stiffly in the mist like a silent army of specters. Herbert gripped the sides of the boat tightly. An occasional drop fell on his head and shoulders from the bare limbs.

At the speed they were moving, it seemed like hours until they were clear of the trees and reached the open water of a large pond. Fog undulated over it in waves.

"Do you think this is the place?" Herbert asked.

Henry was slow to answer. "I think so, but I can't see enough to be sure. When we were here before, we could see the other side."

"And that's where you saw the Keepers?"

"Yeah. They were standing out in the water, but not like they were standing in it. I mean they weren't wet or anything."

A wave of soft mist rolled over them leaving tiny droplets of water on Herbert's face. When the mist passed, the light grew brighter. Suddenly the entire pond became visible. Across the water he could see the shore lined with craggy trees like those they had passed through.

"Do you see anything now?"

"No. I mean I see the trees on the other side but nothing that looks like the Keepers."

"OK. Lester, take us along the shore to the other side."

"Right, but I don't like this place. It gives me a bad feelin'."

"Good. Maybe that means we're getting close to something." Herbert was getting the same feeling.

Hammond drove the boat slowly along the edge of the pond. Waves from their small wake lapped among the exposed tree roots. Herbert kept his eyes moving, first to the front, then to the shore. Wispy strands of fog meandered through the bare trunks. Suddenly something caught his eye, something deep among the tree trunks. Then the mist closed in and it disappeared.

"Hold it, Lester. Back up a ways."

Hammond shifted to reverse. The boat halted, then backed slowly.

"There. In there." Herbert said, as the cloud of fog drifted away. "Do you see it?"

"I see something," Hammond answered.

"Take us in there. It looks like a boat."

Hammond headed the boat toward the narrow space between tree trunks. As they approached, a water-soaked limb reared out of the water in front of them like a giant eel, threatening to scrape over the top of the boat.

"Watch it!" Herbert called out. Henry remained sitting stiffly upright, not moving. As the limb was about to hit him, Herbert leaped forward and shoved it to the side. The wood was slippery, covered with wet scum. He picked up a rag from the bottom of the boat and wiped his hands. "Cut the motor and lift it out of the water. We don't want to lose the prop. We'll pole it in." Henry didn't move.

When the motor stopped, they were suddenly in complete silence. Herbert felt disoriented, as if they had passed into another world. He picked up an oar from the bottom of the boat and shoved it into the soft mud under the dark water. The boat kept moving, but when he pulled the oar free it from the mud, the boat nearly came to a stop. Two steps forward and one step back, he thought. "Lester, take the other oar and pole on that side."

As Herbert prepared to shove his oar into the water again, he noticed that Henry still hadn't moved. "Henry, you all right?"

There was no response.

"Henry!" he called again.

Henry remained utterly still.

Herbert laid down the oar and moved to the bow next to Henry. He looked into his face. Henry was glassy-eyed, staring straight ahead.

"Damn, Henry! What's wrong?"

Henry's eyes began to focus, but not at Herbert, at something in the distance. Then his mouth started to move, forming words but making no sound. Herbert turned his head in the direction Henry seemed to be looking. Fog wafted through the barren trees, bending and shifting as if it were alive. He stared hard, trying to force his gaze through it, to see what had Henry so mesmerized. Then the fog lifted momentarily, and he thought he saw a figure before it closed in again. He leaned toward Hammond. "Don't say anything," he whispered. "We might have a contact here." His skin was tingling.

For several minutes Herbert watched Henry intently, then began to worry that he might have gone into some kind of trance, one that could be harmful. As he was about to shake him, Henry turned his head and looked at him calmly. "The Keepers are here," he said simply.

"Where?" Herbert managed to ask.

"There, in the fog."

Herbert stared into the shadowy grayness with eagerness and apprehension. "I can't see them, Henry, can you?"

He nodded. "They talked to me, in my head."

"You mean like before?"

"Yeah, like before."

419

"What did they say?"

"They thanked me for delivering the message."

"What message?" Herbert was perplexed.

"The one I told you, that the Gathering are starving, that they need people to bring food like last time."

"How did they know you gave me the message?"

"They said the same man who came last time brought them food."

It took only a second for Herbert to realize what that could mean. Sonia Koske must be dead and Brinter had delivered her body to the Keepers. If so, he had failed her completely. A dark feeling of depression and helplessness began to press on him. "Did they say where he took her?"

"To the portal."

"The portal? That's the entrance to where the Gathering hibernate." He remembered it from Thaddeus Bump's journal.

"I think so. They also asked whether we brought more food."

"What did you tell them?"

"That I didn't think we had food. So they wanted to know why we came."

"And?" Herbert getting anxious.

"I said you were the sheriff and had something you wanted to tell them."

"Did they say they would listen?"

"They said they couldn't hear you, then everything faded."

"You mean they left?"

"I don't know, but their voices are gone."

"Dammit! So close. We've got to find that portal."

"Isn't that a little dangerous?" Hammond asked sheepishly. "People disappear out here, you know."

"Probably. But maybe it'll get the Keepers to talk to us."

"Sheriff, I don't think they'll let us go there without bringing food," Henry said.

"Then they'll *have* to talk to us." Herbert answered more confidently than he felt.

They began poling again through the dark,

muddy water. The object Hammond spotted indeed was a boat. It had been pulled onto a mudbank. As they drew alongside, Herbert saw blood smears on the seat—and the body of Mel Schwartz in the bottom.

"Damn. I guess I was right about Mel catching Brinter stealing his boat. He must have taken Miss Koske with him. Lester, radio the office and tell them we found Mel Schwartz's boat with Mel's body in it and that it looks like Brinter took Miss Koske into Big Tow somewhere. Tell them we're going to follow, and to have Bill get here with some help. You better also try to tell them where we are."

"Got it."

Herbert climbed over the bow onto the bank. Footprints in the slippery mud and the mark of something being dragged showed the direction Boris had gone. He didn't want to risk taking Henry any farther but he needed him. "OK, Henry, you're next."

Henry hesitated for a moment, then jumped from the bow onto a mossy spot. Hammond finished the radio message and stood ready to follow.

"Lester, hand me that extra gas tank."

Lester lifted the red tank and handed it to Herbert before stepping onto the bank. "You got plans for this, Sheriff?"

"Not yet, my plan is to talk. I'll carry it for a while then you can spell me."

They followed Boris' trail single file, Herbert leading, then Henry, then Lester.

"He sure didn't try to cover his tracks," Hammond called from behind.

"He must not have thought we'd would find him this fast," Herbert answered in a loud whisper. "Hold it down now. He might be close." He turned to look at Henry, staring at his eyes. Henry looked back. No contact yet, Herbert thought to himself. "Stay behind Lester," he said. Henry stepped to the side and Hammond moved past.

Both the mud and the footprints ended as the trail led to higher ground which had been spared the high water. Here the trees still flourished, their limbs in full summer leaf. Even the fog had a different texture, feeling more dense and wet. Moisture collected on Herbert's face which he wiped away with his sleeve. With no footprints to follow, their attention turned to a trail of trampled leaves and broken branches. Herbert's uniform was soon soaked through from brushing against the wet leaves. After several more minutes of walking, the fog lifted slightly Herbert saw they were approaching a low hill. The undergrowth thinned as the ground became rocky. Loose stones clattered underfoot as they walked. There's no way Brinter won't hear us coming, Herbert thought.

In the hard, rock-strewn ground, the trail soon disappeared. Herbert set the gas can on the ground, took off his hat and wiped his face. He signaled for the others to remain still. Everything seemed unnaturally quiet, no sounds of anything alive, no birds, frogs, nothing.

"Which way do you want to go, Sheriff?" Lester whispered.

"I'm not sure. Let me think a minute."

"I think the portal's over that way." Henry pointed to the left.

Herbert was skeptical. "What makes you think so?"

"It's just a feeling I got, like that's where the Keepers are."

"We'll have a look, then. Lester, you lead and carry this gas tank for a while. Henry, stay close behind me."

Hammond walked warily into the fog. Herbert followed, glancing frequently back at Henry.

A pounding of feet on the rocks in front of them brought Herbert to a standstill. Suddenly a figure emerged from the mist several yards in front of Hammond, racing toward them, white hair flying as it ran. It seemed like something out of the wild, more like a crazed beast than anything human. Its hand was raised high over its head holding an object that looked like a short spear. Instinctively Herbert grabbed Henry, pulling him into his body. Moving with uncanny speed, the figure quickly covered the distance to Hammond who held out his arms to protect himself. In an instant the figure was on him and its upraised hand came down sharply. Hammond cried out as he was hit, making an effort to wrap his arms around the figure, but his limbs had lost their strength. The figure slipped away as the deputy crumpled slowly to his knees.

Herbert released his right arm from around Henry's waist and reached for his revolver, but the figure had seized the gasoline tank Hammond was carrying and disappeared into the fog as abruptly as it had emerged. Herbert shoved his revolver back into its holster and turned his attention to Lester. He was kneeling with his arms at his side, his head bowed, staring at blood spurting from the thin object protruding from his chest.

"Oh, sweet Jesus," Lester cried. "Look at that. The bastard's killed me."

"No, he hasn't," Herbert answered quickly. "We're going to get you back. You'll be all right." His words had little conviction. Lester's blood was spurting steadily, a tell-tale sign the object was embedded in his heart. As Herbert tried to support him, Lester grew limp. Herbert held him under his arms, letting him collapse gently to the ground. Lester stretched out on his back, his eyes wide in terror. His mouth moved but no sound came out. Herbert knelt next to him. He seized the object protruding from Lester's chest in his right hand and pulled. There was a slight sucking sound as it came out. He bent over and opened Lester's blood-soaked shirt. The puncture wound gushed blood with every heartbeat. Herbert pressed his hand over it to stem the flow. Gradually he felt the spurts grow weaker under his palm. Lester's eyes lost any focus, then his head slowly rolled to one side. Blood stopped flowing from his chest.

"Dammit," Herbert swore softly. "Just goddammit." He looked in the direction the figure had gone, seeing only fog. "Henry, keep a sharp eye out while I tend to him."

He pressed at the base of Hammond's neck, checking for a pulse. There was none. He tried at his wrist, then again at his neck, feeling nothing. Lester Hammond was dead, murdered a few feet in front of him

423

as he had stood watching. A great tiredness washed through him. He sat down limply, his hand on his deputy's forehead. Questions raced through his mind. Could he have reacted faster? Was he unable to use his revolver? No answers came. He remained sitting, the strength drained from his body

"Is he dead?" Henry looked stunned, his eyes watery. Herbert knew he had to put his own feelings aside, somehow pull himself together. Henry needed comforting and Lester Hammond's killer had to be dealt with. A craving for vengeance stirred him, beginning to restore his energy. It was an old feeling. This time he welcomed it.

"Yes, he's dead. I'm sorry you had to see this, Henry. You've been a strong young man and I need you to be strong a little longer. I have to go after the man who did this. Can you do it with me?"

"Yeah, I . . . I can do it."

"Good boy." Herbert still held the weapon he had pulled from Hammond's chest. He opened his fist and stared at it. He had seen it before, in Bruhl's workroom. A trocar. Boris Brinter had used it to puncture the body he was embalming. He was good at it, too good.

"It looked like an old man that did it," Henry said, "like the guy who works at Bruhl's."

"You're right, Henry. It was Boris Brinter. We got careless. I never guessed he'd ambush us like that. Didn't think he was capable of it, actually. I should never have underestimated him. You can be sure it won't happen again."

"Are we going to take him back now?"

Herbert's head was spinning. The shock of the sudden, violent death was mind-numbing, yet an idea had begun to form, one that made him disgusted with himself, but one that might be necessary. He stood silently for several moments, thinking hard, then he made his decision.

"No, not yet, Henry. Lester can still help us, maybe even more than before."

Herbert hoisted the body onto his shoulders in a fireman's carry and set off at a determined pace in the direction Boris Brinter had come. Determined to prevent another ambush, he carried his revolver in his free hand. So the Keepers wouldn't talk when we had no food, he thought to himself. Well, now we do. He was sure Hammond would forgive him for what he was doing, no matter what the result, but it was repulsive all the same. As his imagination portrayed all the unspeakable things that could happen to his deputy's remains, he plunged on into the mist, straining his eyes to see as far into it as possible.

Suddenly he was no longer aware of Henry's footsteps behind him. "Henry?" He swung the body around windmill fashion and looked to the rear. Henry was there, twenty steps behind, walking fast. "Henry, you've got to stay close."

"I know. I was until just a minute ago when the Keepers talked to me."

"When, just now?"

"Yeah. They saw we were bringing food. They said we should take it to the portal."

The weight of the body on Herbert's shoulder suddenly felt heavier. He wasn't sure he could go on. Was this worth the desecration of Hammond's body? He would prevent that if he could, but he couldn't back out now. There was too much at stake. "Then that's what we'll do. Just stay close."

Herbert set off again, following a slight depression in the rocky ground that seemed to be a path. At times he thought he lost it, then the semblance of a path would appear again, keeping them on course, drawing them to the portal. Occasionally he saw scrape marks in the dirt, a sign of something heavy being dragged.

The path circled the hill that had been in front of them. He glanced at it as they passed. Was this the place they had found the doctor? He wasn't sure. Suddenly movement caught his eye, a flash of white from a tree on his left.

"Henry, run back!" Herbert yelled as a figure flew at him from behind a tree barely ten yards from where he stood. This time there was no hesitation. In one swift motion he raised the revolver and fired. The shot resounded through the trees, and the figure vanished as quickly as it appeared. A sharp echo bounced off the hillside, then faded into the fog and foliage. He had fired hurriedly and had undoubtedly missed. He laid the deputy on the ground and walked cautiously to where the figure had disappeared, his revolver pointed to the spot. There was no sign of anyone.

Henry came rushing back up the path. "Did you get him?"

"I don't think so, no time to aim. But he'll think twice before he tries to surprise us again."

Herbert returned to the path and was about to hoist the body onto his shoulders again when he saw Henry standing strangely silent, his mouth slowly opening and closing. "Henry?"

When he didn't answer, Herbert tried again. "Henry, are they here?" This time he knew what was happening. Squinting, he peered into the mist in all directions. By the hillside on the right was a tall object. At another time he wouldn't have given it a second glance, just another dead tree trunk. But this one was staring with two glittering eyes. It was a stare that seemed to touch his mind, trying to bore its way in. He looked again at Henry. Suddenly Henry's blank eyes focused.

"They're here, one of them anyway."

"I think I see him," Herbert said, looking again at the figure at the hillside. "What did he say?"

"He asked why you made the big noise."

Herbert nodded.

"He said they can't have that noise here. They would have to stop us if we did it again."

Stop us? That's an understatement, Herbert thought as he holstered his revolver. "Tell him there will be no more noise if they make sure the man with long, white hair doesn't do anything to keep us from delivering this . . . food."

"OK, I'll try." Henry's eyes went blank and a moment later focused again. "The Keeper said no one will stop us from taking food to the portal."

"You're getting good at this, Henry. Tell him we'll take the food, but I need to talk to them first."

"OK." Henry's eyes glazed over momentarily, then he spoke: "He said they'll talk but only at the portal. It sounded like he meant it."

"All right, let's go." Herbert hoisted Hammond's body onto his shoulders. He was tempted to take his revolver out again but decided against it. Certainly the Keepers were capable of keeping Brinter at bay.

The path led between two trees with massive trunks closely together—an opening through the brush and brambles that grew thickly on both sides. Was this the portal? Surely not, he told himself, unless it leads underground. When he reached the opening, he paused.

"We must be getting close to the portal," Henry said in a low voice. "I can sense the Keepers close by. The air has a different feel somehow when they're around."

Herbert focused on his skin for a moment. The only sensation he noticed was the weight of his deputy's body making his shoulders ache.

"Let's find out if you're right. Stay close, now." Tightening his grip on the body, he stepped between the two trees scraping the body against the bark. Henry followed.

On the other side was a dark clearing. The canopy of tree limbs overhead and the thick brush in all sides made it appear like a large hall. Immediately Herbert smelled the foul odor. Henry started to cough. "Don't breathe too deeply and it won't be so bad," he told him.

Little light penetrated the leaves. Herbert paused to let his eyes adjust. Straight ahead at a distance Herbert could make out the hillside. Under foot the ground was packed as hard as stone. He could see no way out other than the way they came.

The space felt so full of danger he could almost taste it. He knew Henry should go no further, that he should tell him to run back the way they came. But he didn't. There was still enough light to see, which meant the Gathering wouldn't be around. Then, too, the Keepers believed they were delivering food, which should mean they'd be protected.

Henry came closer and spoke in a voice near a whisper. "That awful smell. It's the Gathering, isn't it?

Do you think they'll come after us?"

"No. Not while there's light. Besides, the Keepers think we're bringing food."

"Yeah, and they're waiting for us." Henry pointed toward the hillside.

Through the gloomy light, Herbert made out a row of figures standing straight and stiff in the distance. The palace guard awaits, he thought to himself. He started to walk in their direction, then thought better of it and laid the body gently on the ground. "See if you can contact them. Ask them where the white-haired man is."

Henry stood silently. Moments later he spoke: "They said the man is taking food to the Gathering. They want us to take our food to the portal."

"I need to talk to them first. Tell them that."

"OK," he answered. Then: "They said to leave the food in the portal, then they would talk."

Herbert wasn't about to surrender the body of his deputy. "Stay close now and be ready to run out of here the minute I tell you."

"Don't worry, I'm ready."

Herbert knelt, pulled the body over his shoulders, then stood slowly. It was getting harder to do. He began walking toward the Keepers, his senses on high alert. The putrid odor became stronger. As he drew closer, the row of figures became more distinct, standing like carefully spaced trees that had died and lost their limbs. There were six tall figures, taller than any man. Each was draped in a gray robe that reached to the ground, holding what looked like a long staff. On top of each figure was a pointed hat. Closer still, he could see white hair hanging from beneath their hats, and long white beards. But it was the eyes that mesmerized him—it was as if they somehow were penetrating his body. He began to feel giddy as if he was becoming entranced and forced himself to look away.

The figures began to move, seeming to float rather than walk, the row separating at the center. Through the gap Herbert saw a large black hole in the hillside. It was tall and narrow, taller than the Keepers, and surrounded by massive gray stones set into the hill. He paused. They had reached the portal.

"They said to put the food inside," Henry whispered.

Herbert thought hard. Was Boris in there? No matter, he didn't intend to go in there. And he wasn't about to relinquish his bargaining power before there was a chance to talk. He walked slowly toward the black opening. As he approached, the stench became so strong he desperately wanted to cover his nose. Behind him Henry began to gag. Herbert reached for the handkerchief in his pocket then thought better of it. He might need that hand for something else.

The stones around the opening were even larger than they had appeared from a distance. At the top was the largest, embedded like a capstone. All were worn smooth as if they had once spent a long time submerged in the waters of the Mississippi.

Herbert stopped walking and stared into the opening. He could see nothing but darkness. Slowly he leaned over and let the body slide from his shoulders.

"Don't put him down there," Henry hissed, his voice shaking. "They said they want you to put him inside the portal."

There was fear in Henry's voice, but Herbert didn't intend to let his deputy become some creature's meal. Gently he laid Hammond's body on the ground.

When he straightened up, he saw that the Keepers had come closer. "Henry, tell them I can help them find food for the Gathering."

When Henry didn't respond, Herbert turned to look at him. Henry looked as if he had turned to stone, terror lining his face as he stared high over Herbert's head.

"Look out!" Henry screamed, pointing to the top of the portal.

Herbert turned instantly. Brinter had somehow climbed to the top of the portal, hunched on the large stone like a vulture waiting to feed, his face contorted with the look of a caged wild animal. Even before Herbert had time to react, Brinter sprang at him, another trocar in his upraised hand.

Herbert steeled himself, concentrating on the

point of the weapon which Brinter swung as he fell. At the last second, Herbert struck the old man's wrist with his forearm, blocking the blow, still the force of the fall knocked him off his feet. He landed on his back, momentarily stunned. As quickly as he could gather his breath, Herbert struggled to rise, expecting Brinter to strike again, but he had scuttled away.

Henry was yelling to get his attention. Brinter had picked up Hammond's body, carrying it under one arm and the gasoline tank under the other. An instant later he disappeared into the black hole of the portal. Herbert leaped to his feet, scarcely able to believe the old man's strength. The Keepers stood on each side of the opening. The old embalmer was going to feed his deputy to the Gathering and he had to stop him, which meant entering the portal. But would the Keepers let him? Hell, he thought, they probably *want* me to go in there. To them I'm just another course for dinner.

Clutching his shirt pocket, he found the penlight he always carried; then he felt his belt where his flashlight remained in place. They both had good batteries, he had checked. But should Henry come or stay? Since he was the Keepers only communication link, they surely wouldn't harm him. The Gathering, on the other hand, were hungry.

"Henry, I'm going in. You stay here. Tell the Keepers I'm after the man with white hair, that I won't harm the Gathering. Take this penlight just in case."

"All right." Henry grasped the penlight with a hand that was trembling.

Herbert unhooked the flashlight from his belt and undid the strap that secured his revolver.

"They sound worried," Henry said.

"Good. So am I."

The Keepers hadn't moved, but the glare from their eyes seemed stronger and more threatening. Herbert steeled himself for whatever might happen and bolted for the opening. In a flash he was past them, inside, untouched.

He entered a darkness so dense and complete it was as if he had gone blind. At the same time he was assaulted by a stench so intense he felt faint. He stopped to get his bearings. There was no sign yet of the Keepers following.

When he felt something brush his cheek, he quickly turned on his flashlight. The narrow beam cut a swath of light into the blackness, illuminating what appeared to be the interior of a cave eroded out of the limestone hill. He played the beam over the walls. The Gathering were near, he was sure, waiting just beyond his light.

The passageway ahead was wide, the roof several feet higher than his head, high enough for the Keepers. Unusual rock formations protruded from the walls, casting grotesque shadows in the light. At each slight move of his hand, the shadows swayed as if they were alive. He shined the beam over the clay floor. It was littered with bones, piles of them. They were human, he was sure of it. When he touched one with his foot, it disintegrated. He gasped in surprise. It was a feeding room of the Gathering—and had been for a very long time.

The flashlight was his lifeline, but the light would warn Brinter. He would have to be careful where he pointed it and keep watching for Brinter's flashlight ahead, hoping he saw Brinter's light before Brinter saw his. Surely Brinter was using one. Without a light, he would have no protection from the Gathering, or would he? He was carrying Hammond's body. Maybe it gave him some kind of immunity.

Herbert decided to memorize a path through the cave as far as his flashlight would penetrate, then follow it with the light off until he had a brush with the Gathering. He stared at a path through the bones, then switched off the light and began to make his way.

He walked as if stepping on broken glass. With each passing second, his tension grew, sensing the Gathering's presence, anticipating an attack like in the mausoleum. Something soft and velvety brushed the back of his neck. Instinctively, he batted at it with his hand. At the same time he stumbled on a pile of bones which rattled across the floor. Instantly he turned on his flashlight. A skull with a splintered hole in its forehead stared up at him. He saw two holes in his pants leg.

He pointed the flashlight down the passageway again. Several yards ahead at the point where the beam faded into the dense blackness, he saw a mound of clothing. He walked to it without turning off his flashlight. It was a woman's dressing gown. He pulled it away with his foot. Beneath were the remains of a body. The person had been torn into pieces, the bones still pink and moist. The skull, which was face down, rested in a pile of matted gray hair. The long hair was unmistakable. It was Sonia Koske. Brinter had made his delivery.

"Dammit!" Herbert cried, slapping his holster. The echo carried down the passageway.

How could he have let this happen? Another death because of him. His shoulders sagged as a heaviness formed in his chest. A tear slid down his cheek and he stood for several minutes, unable to move.

Then a faint sound from deep in the tunnel put his senses back on alert. This isn't the time to stand around feeling sorry for myself, he thought. He had to find Brinter and retrieve his deputy's body. Judging from the condition of Sonia Koske, there was precious little time to do it.

"I'm sorry," he said as he gave Sonia Koske's remains a last look and headed down the passageway, walking swiftly, his flashlight pointed ahead. He had gone nearly fifty yards when he detected a new smell. Something was burning. He continued walking and soon a glow appeared ahead, yellow and flickering. A fire! As he moved closer, the glow grew brighter and the cave began filling with an acrid smoke. The air became thick and oily and his eyes began to burn. He started to cough and had to crouch low to breathe. What was Brinter trying to do, stop him or drive the Gathering away? Damn that guy, he muttered.

The light grew brighter as he approached and he began to feel heat. Rounding a curve, he saw flames on the bare rock in the center of the passageway. Boris was using the gasoline.

Herbert tried to look beyond the fire, wondering whether it was possible to jump beyond it, when he heard shouts echoing down the cave walls behind him.

"Sheriff! Sheriff! Wait!" The shouts were muffled but Herbert recognized Henry's voice immediately.

The shouting was followed by the clatter of someone running blindly, scattering bones across the rock. Herbert was alarmed. The boy had only a penlight and the Gathering were probably all around him. He started running back toward the entrance, shining his light into the passageway.

"Ow! Jeez! What are those things!" came the shouts.

"Henry! Hurry!" Herbert yelled. He could see a tiny light bobbing in the distance.

"I am, but it's hard. There's stuff all over the floor! OK, I see your light."

Henry materialized out of the darkness at a run, stopping only when Herbert grabbed his arm and pulled him close. He was shaking.

"You all right there, fella?"

"I . . . I think so. But it's scary in here. Like when me and Sheila were in the tunnel at Grandma and Grandpa's house," Henry answered, still catching his breath.

Herbert ran the beam of his light over Henry's skin and clothes. There were several small holes in his shirt and pants and red marks on the back of his arms and neck as if he had measles. He hoped the creatures weren't carrying some disease.

"I thought I told you to stay put. What on earth made you come in here?"

"The Keepers. They'd been standing still, not saying anything after you went in. Then all of a sudden they bunched together and I heard them talking about a fire inside the portal. Whether you or the white-haired person set it, they weren't sure. They said the fire and smoke would hurt the Gathering so they had to put it out. They also said they'd come after the people in the tunnel. That's when I knew I had to warn you, so I ran around them as fast as I could through the portal and just kept running until I found you."

Herbert looked over Henry's head back toward the entrance. There was no sign of the Keepers. But they

433

seem to be able to turn up anywhere they choose, he thought, so they must have somehow gone past us to put out the fire since they were afraid it would harm the Gathering. He turned his head and looked back into the cave. The glow had disappeared.

"Thanks for warning me, Henry, but I don't want you risking your neck like that again, you hear?."

"Aw, Sheriff. I had your penlight. Besides, I wasn't getting along that well with the Keepers."

"From the looks of your skin and clothes, that penlight was barely enough. Those things were about to get a piece of you."

"I know. I could feel them brushing against me when I was running. Soft, but sometimes like little needles sticking my skin."

Herbert was in a quandary. Should he take Henry back outside? The Gathering were all around them, he was sure of it. He could almost feel them beyond the light, but the Keepers had apparently come into the cave and he had to talk to them. Henry was his only way to do it.

"The fire's out. Maybe now the Keepers won't come after us," Henry said softly.

"Maybe not. The problem is they don't know the bad guys from the good guys. There's only those who bring food to the Gathering and those who don't. And right now we aren't bringing the food. Let's hope they figured out it was Boris who set the fire and go looking for him. Can you contact them?"

Henry was silent for a moment. "No, I'm not getting anything. Either they're mad and cut me off or the rock interferes somehow."

"OK, but we shouldn't be the only ones concerned. Let's see if we can worry Brinter a little."

"Boris! Boris! This is the Sheriff. I know you can hear me. That fire you set riled the Keepers. They're coming after the person who did it, which means you. They think you meant to harm the Gathering. You bring Lester's body back, and I'll help you get out of here."

Herbert's voice echoed down the passageway. Brinter would have to be deaf not to hear.

"I don't think he's going to answer," Henry

whispered after a few moments.

Henry sounded normal again after running the gauntlet through the Gathering.

"You're right. We have to go after him. Stay close behind me now. If I stop, you stop, and stay absolutely still. I'm going to walk fast. Shine that penlight behind you. And shout if you feel anything. Anything at all."

"Don't worry."

Smoke still lingered in the air when they reached the place in the cave where Brinter had set the fire. As they walked over the blackened rock, Herbert could still feel the heat. He shined the flashlight from side to side as they continued on, aware that it would signal Brinter that they were coming. But with Henry along and the Gathering all around, he couldn't risk turning it off. There were few bones on the floor now, letting them walk faster. He pictured the Gathering scattering in front of them as they came with their light, then regrouping behind as soon as they past. How deep into the cave would the Keepers let them go? Was there a place ahead where the Gathering came to hibernate for all those years, a place where they breed, some sort of nest where they keep their young? It would seem likely. If that's the case, the Keepers surely would never let them get that far. Boris was ahead of them somewhere. The Keepers would stop him first. But where were they?

The passageway began to narrow and and rock formations no longer lined the walls. The air had become heavy and damp and breathing took more effort. Herbert guessed they had come beyond the original cave to a tunnel carved by something other than water, maybe the Gathering. If so, why was it so much larger than the tunnels in the bluffs? Maybe those tunnels were only for hunting.

When the tunnel began to slope downhill, the rock felt slippery under his feet. He pointed the beam of his light at the tunnel floor. Water glistened on the rock which was dotted with lime deposits.

"Careful, Henry. It's getting slippery. Hold onto my belt."

Henry did as he was told.

Gradually the descent grew steeper. They must

be coming to the river. How far did Boris intend to go? Abruptly, Herbert stopped to listen. Henry bumped into his back. They both stood silently for a moment. From somewhere ahead came a scraping sound. A chill ran over his skin. Would it be the Keepers? No, it had to be Brinter, not far ahead. He signaled Henry not to talk. The passageway continued to narrow causing his shoulders to scrape on the sides. After descending a few more minutes, the floor began to level out. Water now dripped steadily from overhead, gathering into pools among the rock and seeping into his leather boots.

They must be under the river. This was the connection between the bluffs and Big Tow Island. He thought of the incredible weight the rock overhead must be bearing.

"Henry, you OK?" Herbert asked even though he could feel Henry's hand grasping his belt.

"Yeah, I'm OK, but my shoes feel like I'm walking in buckets of water."

"Mine are soaked, too. I figure we're under the river."

"That's what I thought. How far do you think this goes?"

"Maybe as far as the bluffs. I don't think Boris can go much further than that. Those tunnels are too small."

They had made their way through the water-lined tunnel for several minutes when the floor sloped upwards. Soon water was no longer dripping from overhead. They must have reached the bluffs and Boris still had Lester's body. Did he drag it all this way for protection from the Gathering? Or was it to make sure they would follow, to lure them into an ambush? Or maybe the old man was just crazy and didn't have a plan at all.

Herbert didn't have long to wait for his answer. The stench he had grown all too familiar with suddenly became much stronger. He began swallowing rapidly to keep from vomiting. He had to stay focused for whatever was ahead.

"Sheriff, that smell!" Henry said. "It's so bad I think I'm going to throw up."

"Go ahead if you need to. It's OK." Herbert slowed their pace. Seconds later he felt Henry's hand tug on his belt and heard him vomit. When it was quiet, he said: "Feel better?"

"I guess, but I still smell it."

"Cover your nose with a handkerchief."

"I don't have one."

Herbert reached into his pocket and pulled his out. "Here, use this. It'll help."

"Thanks. That's a little better."

"Good, then let's keep going."

They had not walked many yards farther when the walls and ceiling seemed to disappear into some black void. Herbert's first thought was that they had come to a huge chasm or drop-off. Quickly, he shined the light down at the floor in front of his feet. The beam fell on an arm. It was another body. The face was gone but there was no mistaking the uniform. He stifled a gasp. He hadn't been able to save his deputy's life and now he had lost his body as well. There was a sudden weakness in his legs, but Henry was pressed against his back and he managed to stay upright.

He shined his light beyond Hammond's body. They were standing at the entrance to a large cavernous room. On the high ceiling, rows of stalactites hung down like giant icicles. For as far as he could see on both sides, the walls were honey-combed with holes, reminding him of the the walls in Walnut Grove's mausoleums, except the openings were smaller and far more numerous.

Slowly he became aware of a low buzzing sound reverberating through the cavern. The sound was powerful, as if it were an accumulation of thousands of smaller sounds, causing a slight tremor in the rock floor.

"What's that sound?" he heard Henry ask.

Herbert thought he knew. It had to be the Gathering, their young nestled in the darkness, deep in the holes around the walls, wanting to be fed.

They had reached it—the Gathering's nest, the place where they hibernate all those years, where they reproduce, nurture their young. The Keepers would be here, watching, making sure no harm came to their flock.

Suddenly he heard the sound of running feet.

"Henry, watch out! He's here!"

Out of the darkness came the sound of liquid jostling inside a container. Herbert leaped backward, pushing them both into the tunnel as gasoline flew out of the darkness. His instinct had saved them from being completely doused with fluid, but some of the gasoline had splashed onto his shirt and sleeves. Before he could regain his balance, a flaming match flew toward him, landing at his feet. The gasoline coating the cavern floor erupted with a brilliance that was blinding. As he pushed Henry farther from the flames, one of his sleeves caught fire, spreading across his shirt. He knew he had to roll to put out the flames, but he couldn't leave Henry unprotected. Quickly he wrapped both arms around the boy and pulled him to the floor, rolling over and over through the tunnel. Pain radiated across his arm and chest from the burn, but the fire on his shirt was out. He raised his head and reached for his revolver, expecting Brinter to charge through the flames. The tunnel was filling with smoke and the buzzing had grown much louder, vibrating through the rock. Herbert's eyes burned and tears ran down his cheeks. He could scarcely breathe without choking. When Brinter didn't appear, he pressed his face against the floor and told Henry to do the same.

After taking several breaths, he rubbed his eyes and forced himself to look up again. Through the billowing smoke, he saw a grotesque silhouette engaged in some macabre dance, laughing and gyrating behind the flames. Then there was a whoosh of sound and the flames leaped high again.

"Sheriff," Brinter cackled. "Are you burning? Answer me! Are you dying?"

Herbert said nothing.

"If you're not, you vill be. Just like old Raston Bruhl. All burnt up." Brinter's cackling continued.

Herbert grabbed Henry around his shoulders to shield him from the sight.

"Burning iss such a slow vay to die. So painful.

And it makes such a mess of the body. Tell me, Sheriff. Are you burning?"

The flames shrank but the smoke remained thick, choking the passageway. Herbert stayed low to the floor with his hand on Henry's back. With his free hand he brushed the handle of his revolver to assure himself it was still there. He considered shooting Brinter in the middle of his dance, then charging through the dying flames and tackling the old man. The thought of having Brinter in his grasp was exhilarating. Then Brinter began to cough and his gyrations slowed. The old man was getting tired.

"Sheriff, I heard them talking!" Henry said excitedly in a low voice. "The Keepers think the fire and smoke will kill the Gathering's young. They've been telling Brinter to get rid of it, but he can't hear them."

Through the smoke Herbert saw three tall figures hovering behind Brinter. Suddenly the old man somehow rose to the top of the cavern, an incredulous look on his face. Then he flew, shrieking and flailing, into the flames. His body hit the cavern floor with a crunching sound, bounced slightly, then rolled down the tunnel through the fire, scattering the flames. He came to a stop a few feet in front of Herbert. Soaked in gasoline from the floor, Brinter's clothes and long hair erupted in flames. He writhed and screamed for help, then struggled to a sitting position beating madly at the fire burning his scalp and chest.

Herbert was tempted to go to him, to try to smother the flames, but told himself it was useless. The old man could never survive the burns even if he could put out the flames. He circled his arm tighter around Henry's head and ears and covered his eyes with his hand while Brinter's cries echoed through the cavern. It seemed much too long before they stopped.

The Keeper's solution had been effective. The fire was scattered and lost much of its vigor after they hurled Brinter through it. Only now the odor of burned flesh was added to the oily smoke that filled the passageway. Herbert had to get them out of that narrow space quickly. The cavern was their closest hope. He waited until the only flames were down to a flicker, then turned on his flashlight.

"Henry, turn on your penlight. I'm going to crawl forward. Follow me but stay as low as you can. Stay close to the floor. When we go past the bodies, don't look." It was hard to talk without coughing.

"I'll be right behind you, Sheriff."

Head low, Herbert crawled to Brinter's body which still smoldered, the skin blackened and crusty. Wisps of smoke rose from fissures in his chest and neck. His hair was burned away, his face no longer recognizable. Herbert pushed the body to the side of the tunnel.

"You're about to be a well-cooked meal for the Gathering, old man," Herbert whispered. "I can't think of anyone who deserves it more."

Beyond Brinter's body the floor was blackened. Herbert pressed his hand against it. The rock was hot. Was it too hot for them to make it across? He crawled forward and put most of his weight on his knees. Not too bad. They could do it.

"The floor's hot, Henry. Put your weight on your elbows if it gets too hot for your hands. And keep low."

"Ouch! It *is* hot!" Henry exclaimed.

Herbert kept crawling. Small flames still flickered on each side, dancing against the rock walls. A few feet farther, the floor was cool. Herbert raised his head and took a breath. Smoke filled his lungs and he began to cough. Quickly he sank back to the floor. It was a moment before he could speak.

"Henry, be sure to keep your head down. There's still a lot of smoke. If anything happens to me, take my flashlight and get out fast."

"OK, but you be careful. I don't want to leave here by myself."

Herbert started crawling again. When he reached Hammond's body, he shined his light over his arms and face. Except for his face, Hammond looked intact. The fire had kept the Gathering away. Gently, he rolled the body to one side and crawled into the cavernous room.

As he had hoped, the smoke was not as dense, but the buzzing noise was nearly overpowering as it reverberated around the rock walls. He rose to his knees and shined his light around the room. Directly in front of him was the gas tank, its cap missing. He moved it slightly and heard a sloshing sound. Then through the thinning smoke he saw they were not alone. Two of the Keepers stood five yards in front of him, their eyes burning like live coals.

"Sheriff, I'm scared," Henry whispered loudly. "The Keepers are still frantic about the fire. They're saying they should have kept Brinter from entering the portal. Now those two might be after *us*."

Herbert knew this was his last chance to talk. Somehow he had to make them listen. He grabbed the gas can by the handle and picked it up.

"Henry, come over by me, quick."

Henry did as he was told, staring up at the two Keepers who had come a step closer.

"You have to contact them."

"What do I say."

"Tell them I'll use the gas in this can to light the fire again unless they listen to what we have to say." Herbert trembled slightly. He hoped it wasn't evident in his voice. It was important to sound confident and in control.

Henry went rigid, staring at Herbert with wide eyes. Clearly he didn't want to make the threat.

"Do it now!" Herbert ordered.

Henry turned toward the two Keepers. As his lips moved, their eyes glowed more intently. Then Henry was still.

"Well, what did they say?" Herbert asked firmly, trying to conceal his anxiety.

"Nothing, they didn't say anything. They're making a sound like a growl. It's scary."

Herbert needed to do something more to get their attention and do it fast. He drew his revolver and aimed straight into the face of the Keeper on the left. At the last second, he aimed higher and fired. In the darkness of the cavern the flash was blinding, the sound crashing against the rock walls like a cannon shot. The bullet whined into the distance.

Herbert again leveled the revolver at the Keeper's face. He held his breath, watching them intensely. As the echo faded, neither of the Keepers had moved in the slightest.

"Henry, tell them I'll use this again unless they stay where they are and listen."

It wasn't long before Henry spoke. "They said they'll listen to what we say but they seem antsy."

Herbert spoke firmly: "Tell them we know how their food was poisoned. But it'll remain poisoned and there's nothing we or anyone else can do about it. There's more so don't wait for an answer."

Henry spoke a moment later: "OK, what's next, but hurry."

"Tell them it's dangerous for the Gathering to keep killing food themselves. If they do, people will find a way to kill them. Go ahead, now."

While Henry was quiet, Herbert watched for a sign that the Keepers were communicating but they continued to stand perfectly still.

After a pause, Henry said: "They said there's no other way. Their duty is to protect the Gathering and they have to kill their food unless people bring it like before."

"Tell them there *is* another way. They can *move* the Gathering. They can go to a place where their food isn't poisoned. There are places like that, in other countries. Then the Gathering would have food and wouldn't have to kill, and no one would try to kill them. Go on."

The smoke had gradually thinned and Herbert rose to a crouch as he waited for the Keepers' response. He wanted to tell them about embalming, and about places where embalming wasn't routine, places where there would be food for the Gathering. Once the Keepers knew this, he hoped they would move the Gathering. He was convinced the Gathering were scavengers not killers. And there were plenty of other scavengers that fed on human remains—beetles, worms, even tree roots. It wasn't evil, just a process of nature. If the Gathering could find bodies that weren't filled with embalming fluid, he was sure they wouldn't kill. If the Keepers would listen, he could tell them places to go. But it would mean moving the Gathering a long way, to

Canada or Mexico. Would they go that far? *Could* they go that far? What if he could convince them to move to another town? That still might be all right. He could live with that. They would find more Indian burial mounds and cemeteries filled with bodies buried long before embalming. No one would be harmed and there should be enough food for the Gathering to last centuries. After that, well, he wouldn't dwell on anything after that.

Henry interrupted his thoughts when he turned with a dreadful look of fear on his face. He spoke with his voice quivering: "They said they won't move the Gathering, that they don't know anything about other places. They've always been here, long before the white people and the poisoned food, and they have to stay. It sounds like they mean it. They think the Gathering are safe where they are and that they can teach the Gathering more ways to get food if they have to. But they need food for the young right now and want to know when we'll bring more. Sheriff, it sounds like they'll do anything to feed those things. Maybe even do something to us." Henry sounded close to panic.

The buzzing in the cavern was growing louder. Herbert knew it had to be the Gathering's young calling for the food that somehow they knew was nearby. As the sound increased, the fire in the Keeper's eyes became a brilliant red. His plan to persuade the Keepers to move wasn't working. They were determined to stay. And they wanted food for the Gathering right away. He sensed their lives hanging in the balance. What should he tell them? If he told the truth, that no one would bring food any more, they probably wouldn't get out alive. If he lied and but no food came, what would be the consequences? The thought of the Keepers then teaching the Gathering even more ways to kill was too horrible to contemplate. He had to make a decision fast.

First and foremost, he needed to save the boy. The Keepers had been unfazed by his pistol shot over their heads, but he wasn't certain that he could do any serious harm by shooting them. Looking back into the tunnel, he saw the smoke had cleared. A few flames still flickered near the walls but were close to dying out. Soon there would be no firelight to keep the Gathering at bay.

"Henry, listen to me. Take my flashlight and start back through the tunnel."

Henry took the flashlight but didn't move.

"Do it. Now!"

Henry turned and started walking unsteadily toward the tunnel.

"Good boy. Keep walking and shine the light around as you go. I'll catch up."

Herbert set the gasoline tank back down on the rock floor, knowing his every movement was watched. That should satisfy them for a minute, he thought. With the revolver still pointed at the Keeper's face, he slowly backed toward the tunnel. When he reached Hammond's body, he paused. The Gathering would converge on the corpse as soon the fire was out. The thought hurt, but he had to leave him behind if he was to get Henry out alive. Several more steps back, he reached Brinter's body, nearly tripping on his arm. The corpse still reeked of burned flesh. As he passed the charred body, the two Keepers seemed to move toward him. Through the dim glow of the flames, he saw others behind them.

"Henry, stop right there."

Herbert backed quickly and caught up to him.

"Lie down, quick now, and shine your light into the cavern. Right, good. When I fire, put your head down right away and cover up with your arms."

Henry dropped to floor. Herbert knelt beside him, held his breath and took aim, using both hands to steady the weapon. As soon as he fired, he threw himself onto his stomach. The bullet hit where he had aimed, penetrating the side of the gasoline tank.

The explosion roared over them like a passing locomotive, instantly followed by a blast of heat and fire. Herbert raised his head slightly and looked toward the cavern. It was like staring into a roaring furnace. The interior was filled with fire, but he knew there wouldn't be enough oxygen for it to burn long.

"Let's go, Henry. You lead. Go fast, but watch

your step. I don't want you to fall. And keep shining that flashlight around."

He had no idea what damage the explosion and fire had done to the Keepers or the Gathering. Even if the Keepers inside were dead, there still might be others, somewhere. Had they all been inside the cavern, or were some up ahead, waiting? And there must be more of the Gathering in the tunnel, probably all around. They had a long way to go.

Henry went through the tunnel at a run, the beam from the flashlight bouncing wildly over the floor and walls. Herbert followed closely, watching his footing as best he could. A fall at this point could be fatal. Every few steps he felt a soft brush against his skin making him cringe. He knew what it was. Then Henry's feet splashed into a puddle. They had reached the river.

"Careful now, Henry. You don't want to slip."

Henry slowed his pace slightly. It seemed much too long before they started uphill, away from the water. Then Henry was running again. Herbert stayed with him, his revolver ready, hoping a bullet would have some effect on the Keepers if they were caught. He glanced repeatedly over his shoulder.

Herbert felt his feet kicking things littering the floor and heard the rattle of bones bouncing over the rock. Then he saw a gray light ahead, and suddenly they were through the portal. A welcome feeling of relief swept over him. Henry slowed, breathing heavily.

"Once we get out through those trees, we should be OK. C'mon, Henry, you can do it."

Henry took off at a sprint. Moments later, as they squeezed through the narrow opening between the trees, Herbert heard voices in the distance calling their names.

Epilogue

After they escaped the Gathering's lair, the mutilation and killing stopped, but Herbert never learned what became of the Keepers or their Gathering. They could have all died in the explosion and fire. Or they could have survived and moved on after all. Or they could still be deep in the river bluffs with the Keepers ever watchful, serving the purpose for which they were somehow created, waiting for the Gathering to wake again. He didn't go back through the portal to find out.

Regardless of what had become of them, as time passed with no more mutilations, Herbert came to believe that he had seen the last of the creatures in his lifetime. He could live his life with Norma and Albie as a small-town sheriff. Then, when it was time to hang it up, he could do as Jack Schoof had done—turn the town's protection over to an outsider who wanted a serene and peaceful place like Bruders Landing. Then, perhaps, the cycle would continue.